The Jesuit Letter

Dean Hamilton

TyburnTree Publishing
Toronto, Canada
MMXIV

While some of the events and characters are based on historical incidents and persons, this novel is entirely a work of fiction.

www.tyburntree.blogspot.com

ISBN: 978-0-9939174-0-0

Cover Design by M. Vecera
Photography by M. Vecera
Interior Design by D. Hamilton

For Mom & Dad,
who pushed me to dream and persevere;

For Deborah,
my bright particular star;

and for Zachery,
who brought me energy & inspiration
in equal measure.

THE JESUIT LETTER

Acknowledgements

No book is ever written in a vacuum. There is a very long list of people who have provided support, advice, encouragement and hope in helping bring this project to fruition.

Special thanks go to my wife Deborah and my son Zach, my parents Rae & Glenora Hamilton, and all my extended family for their support and relentless patience with my sometimes boring obsession with the Elizabethan era.

Special thanks to my editor Karen Conlin, who managed to call me out on all my various grammatical missteps, and Marie Vecera for her hard work in pulling together a superlative cover design. Thanks also goes out to Gary Slye and Heather West for providing my first set of independent "reader's" eyes on the book, giving me much feedback and encouragement to continue on this journey.

Lastly I would like to thank all the wonderful people who stepped up and supported this writing endeavor through contributing to my publishing Kickstarter. Your support helped make this happen, and I hope you enjoy the read!

Thanks,

Dean

Kickstarter Patrons

This page is small attempt to acknowledge the impact and assistance that everyone listed below provided through their kind donations and support for my publishing Kickstarter. They truly helped to bring *The Jesuit Letter* to life.

For that, they have my profound thanks.

Andrea Cameron
Dave Martin
Deborah Kyrzakos
Devon Hamilton
Duke of Wolves
Erin Spink
Freda Colbourne
Gail Kryzakos
Gary Slye
Greg Hood
Heather West
Ivan Szlapetis
James Hamilton
Josh Ricci
Karen S. Conlin
Kim Litchfield
Linda Sukk
Linda Thompson
M Davies

Maria F. Martinez
Melissa Morin
Monica Monroy Estrada
Paisley Family
Rae & Glenora Hamilton
Robert Crosby
Robin Masters
Ron Blondeau
Sameer Masood
Sandro Perruzza
Scott
Scott Fitzgerald Gray
Scott Lininger
Sharon McGaughey
Siobhan Doherty
Steve Dale
Sup3rDave
Superstar Sandy
Susanology

"Since that guilty woman of England rules over two such noble Kingdoms of Christendom and is the cause of so much injury to the Catholic Faith, and the loss of so many million souls, there is no doubt that whosoever sends her out of the world with the pious intention of doing services, not only does not sin but gains merit."

– Cardinal of Como, Secretary to Pope Gregory

Prologue

Spring, 1575

H E HOPED IT had been a clean death. Hugh Hall placed his feet with exaggerated care on the mud-caked slope and gripped the shoulder of his young guide as he slid down the embankment.

The thought of dealing with blood or a wound made Hall's stomach churn. He preferred his dead to be clean and laid out in the proper form, ready to pass on to their eternal rest with dignity and respect, not curled up in a twisted heap or blue and stiff with their limbs askew and eyes staring. Hall shivered in the damp spring air. Death before breakfast was tiresome.

"Where did you say Coburn passed?" Hall asked. The white-haired woodcutter's death was no surprise. His hacking cough rasped off the garden croft's walls each time he rolled his cart past the old stone building on his way to the manor.

"Not far now, Father." Thomas Clopton tugged his woolen cap lower over greasy blond hair, inwardly cursing the slow pace of the priest.

A cock crowed, the sound raucous even at a distance. The pair passed the laneway that marked the edge of the manor. The estate spread much wider, encompassing fallow fields and woodland. The manor's owner and Hall's patron was one of the largest landholders in Warwickshire, holding claim over a significant part of the gentle rolling slopes of the Midlands, the farms, pastures and the broken patchwork forest that was once the primeval Forest of Arden. It was under his protection and influence Hall was able to maintain his secretive profession as a Catholic priest.

"Thomas, I thought Master Coburn's place was east of the road? Are we astray?" Hall could see a thin trickle of smoke rising over the copse.

Thomas glanced back. "He isn't at home, Father. Not far now, just ahead," he said in an encouraging tone. The second son of one of the manor's tenant farmers, he was a thin and reedy youth with a consumptive pallor and nervous hands. Even after two years of attending clandestine services at the manor, Thomas remained ill-at-ease speaking with the priest.

Hall carried a small leather bag containing the necessities of his profession. He avoided the traditional priest's garb. To be found with Catholic vestments was tantamount to a death sentence.

Thomas led Hall down the rutted dirt road, deftly avoiding the soft glutinous mud patches that were all that remained of the previous day's rain. The verge was covered with a scattering of thin grass stalks and sedge, mixed with flowering sorrel and stitchwort. The air smelled wet and cool and green in the morning, redolent with the early blooming plants. From the meadow a rabbit regarded the two passing men with wary eyes before resuming his breakfast of clover.

Thomas veered off the roadway onto a narrow sloping footpath that wound precipitously around the edge of a low hill, passing through a thick tangled hedgerow and into a straggling oak wood. The tumbled stone ruins of a small Benedictine monastery, abandoned for the last two hundred-odd years, stood hard on the forest edge. Only a handful of the larger stones remained marking the broken walls, the rest having been appropriated by locals for building materials and fireplaces. The priest was huffing by the time they reached the oaks and paused to catch his breath.

Hall straightened and silently cursed what was becoming an irritating cross-country odyssey. *The next time,* he vowed to himself, *they can bring the body to the road, where the man can be shriven with some degree of decency and ease instead of having to slog through the spring mud.* A late-hunting owl hooted in the distance, returning home from a long nocturnal stalk. The noise made him uneasy. Owls were notoriously bad luck, and although Hall despised the foolishness of the ignorant, he could not escape the slight shiver of foreboding the sound awoke in him.

Within a few minutes he could see through the thick trees to a grassy clearing within which a small fire was visible. Thomas shuffled through the slimy accrual of leaves littering the copse floor, moving towards the fire. Hall hesitated.

A man sat in front of the fire on a mossy fallen log, his back to them as they approached, tending the fire with a long branch. Thomas stepped closer and said something in a low voice. The man straightened, set the branch aside and stood, brushing his hands fastidiously on his thighs. Hall stopped, looking about in sudden suspicion. No wrapped body awaiting its final journey was in sight. His stomach tightened.

"Well?" Hall said. "You've dragged me from my bed on what is obviously a fool's errand. What do you want?" he snapped, finding some momentary solace in his anger.

The man turned, smiling. One look at that gravestone smile was enough to silence Hall. The man was young, but tall and whip-lean, with dark hair and a short well-trimmed beard framing a cold mouth. A long rapier hung on his left-hip, topped by an elaborate, silvered decorative guard. One gloved hand rested easily on the hilt. The man wore a long traveler's cloak over a dark and richly embroidered doublet.

"Father Hall." The man gestured expansively. "How kind of you to join us on this most auspicious of morns." His smile faded like a winter's sun. "I can see we are going to be marvelous friends."

"Marvelous friends call on me at the manor house. They don't make me march all over God's creation. Why did you have poor Thomas drag me out to meet you, and through a subterfuge no less?" Hall shot a glance at Thomas, who looked away. "Thomas, we shall be discussing this at length."

"Come, Father, sit with me by the fire. Share our commons." The fellow gestured at a small sausage-laden pan balanced on the edge of the fire.

Hall regarded him with a stiff expression. "I think that I had best be going." He turned to follow the sodden path out of the clearing but stopped. Two men were leaning with casual insolence against the moss-encrusted oak beside the path. Both men held long wooden staves.

The man spoke without turning. "Best sit, Father, we have matters to discuss, not the least of which is your bloody Papist profession." He pointed at the damp ground by the fire. "Sit."

Hall looked at him for a long uncertain moment, and sat on the fallen log as far away as possible.

"I am a gardener, not a priest."

"Truly?" asked the man sardonically, "and you tend your hedges with this?" He plucked the small leather bag from Hall's belt. He drew out the small silver crucifix and rosary and gave them a cursory survey before tossing them to the ground with contempt. "We went some considerable trouble to get you here, so don't treat me like a fool."

He began to pace between Hall and the fire. "You know," he said in a conversational tone, "they burned Protestants under that bitch Mary not twenty miles from here? Tossed them on the fire like so much kindling." The man turned towards the priest. "You lack a good scorching, Father." He spat the honorific like an insult. "Don't try me or we'll have you baking like a trussed roast."

"In God's name," Hall asked, keeping tight control of his tone, "what do you want of me?"

4

"What does any man want of a priest? Knowledge."

The priest's face showed his confusion. "You wish instruction in the True Faith?"

The man burst into laughter. The comment drew grins from the man's stave-wielding servants.

"By God, no one can claim you haven't a wit about you. You may keep your tepid, arse-kissing faith for that Italian catamite you call the Pope. Instruction in your faith? No, I want something else."

The man faced Hall. The priest's tongue seemed to catch in his throat at the look on that razor face.

He leaned close to Hall, his breath sour and hot and intense. "I want your master. I want his correspondence. I want to know who he corresponds with, when they correspond, I want to know the content of his every letter, I want to know his codes, his couriers, I want to know every back-alley whore he's covered in all England if necessary but most of all I want to know all his Catholic fellows, and you," he paused for a moment and dropped his voice so low the priest had to strain to hear him, "are going to give it to me."

For a moment Hall felt suspended, the heart fluttering in his chest his only sensation. He forced himself to look into the man's level gaze. There was something deep and feral and unsettling in the man's dark eyes: crow's eyes, sharp, predatory and hungry. He shuddered.

"In the name of Christ, I will give you nothing. I know nothing!"

The man reached up with his right hand and closed it around the priest's throat.

The iron hand tightened. Hall gagged. He pulled at the man's wrist and fingers.

"I could give you that martyrdom you crave, Father. All I need do is close my fist."

Tears formed in the corners of Hall's eyes and his peripheral vision blurred into formless grey and red shadows. The lack of air was overwhelming, shattering, immersing. He could feel nothing but crushing pain in his throat and hear nothing but the frantic cacophony of his pulse. Hall tried to pray but found his panic rising. He felt slow and stupid, buried in a sluggish fog that seemed to reach for him with hungry malevolence.

An instant later he was kneeling on the damp ground, the tang of moss and woodsmoke in his nostrils, his body shuddering with each deep racking breath. The pounding in his chest and ears subsided. He lifted one muddied hand from the dirt and gently grasped his own throat. *Still alive, praise God.*

Two fine leather boots stood in front of Hall's face. Hall looked up. Expressionless, the man looked down at him.

"No martyrdom, Father. Sorry. It would give me immense pleasure to send you footing it to the bowels of Hell, but not today."

Thomas watched the events unfold with growing apprehension. He pushed his lank hair out of his eyes and glanced about, wiping his face with a nervous hand. This was more than he had reckoned with when he had agreed to bring the priest to the glen. He took a wary step backwards only to find himself shoved hard back to his position by the stave-wielding servant who now stood behind him. Thomas shivered and by reflex crossed himself.

Hall massaged his throat, mumbling a prayer. He knew he was down among the fallen. He glanced up. He was afraid. Hall tried to remind himself that what Christ endured on the cross was far beyond his own suffering.

But he was afraid. Deeply afraid. He felt it like a chill ember embedded in his chest.

Hall was no martyr. Living in a comfortable lodging, with food, wine, clothes and the protection of patronage, he felt ill-equipped to endure the rigors of any martyrdom. Comfortably ensconced in the heart of the Catholic supporters of Warwickshire for years and grown comfortable in his hidden practice, the priest had little to fear of pursuivants. The worst fate he would face, he had thought, would be an exile to France, where he would join the growing community of exiled Englishmen in Rheims and live out his remaining years teaching a new generation of exiled priests.

But not death. Not martyrdom. Not like this. To die for Christ should be easy for a man of faith. But Hall did not wish to die.

The man smiled down at him. "Now that we know where we stand, let's have breakfast." He gestured at the log and the small tin plate of links hissing in grease by the fire's edge. Hall levered himself up and sat on the mossy log, massaging his battered throat, a cold, sick feeling growing within in him.

"May I have the kindness of borrowing your knife?"

Startled by the polite request, the priest glanced up in surprise. The man held out his hand. Without thinking Hall handed over the short blade he carried on his belt. The man smiled his thanks and proceeded to spear a sausage.

"Father," the man said around a mouthful, "I am concerned that you not be too angry with poor Thomas here." He gestured at the boy who stood rooted like a tree beside one of the grinning stave-wielders. Thomas edged forward, a wary look on his long face. He licked his lips.

"I know the boy tricked you into coming to our little breakfast but he did so under the best intentions–mine." The man laughed. "He's a good lad, honest and attentive. He earned his money bringing you here." The man stood and placed one arm around Thomas's shoulders, then handed Thomas two small coins with his free hand. Thomas stared at the silver in his palm and grinned, relieved and pleased. "So Father, I want you to forgive this poor boy his trespasses."

Hall stared forward with a stoic expression. He was not a man inclined to forgive at the best of times, and the pain and fear of the last hour was fresh in his mind. "Thomas," he said flatly, "is a betrayer and a liar. I am not inclined to forgive that on the word of the man that paid him his thirty silver coins."

"It was only tuppence, no' thirty." Thomas interrupted with a sullen tone.

The man looked down at the seated priest, a curious expression on his face. "No forgiveness in your soul?" he mocked.

7

"I know you think the boy lied to get you here but he was quite truthful."

Hall looked up, puzzled. The man smiled and with no change in his expression, thrust the short knife hard into Thomas's throat.

For a second, Hall didn't believe his eyes. Thomas gagged, both hands clutching at the small hilt. The blade was rammed up deep under his chin. Thomas staggered, grabbing at the hilt with frantic hands. He pulled the blade out. Red blood pulsed and sheeted down the front of his smock and he stared in horror at his bloodied hands. He dropped the dripping blade in the dirt, turned and took several faltering steps towards the path from the glen, as if the vain and fleeting thought of returning home was running through his mind. One of the stave-men stepped forward and gave Thomas a gentle push back in the direction of the fire. At the pressure, Thomas spun, sliding down to one knee. His eyes, wide and astonished, gazed imploringly at Hall. One eye rolled slowly back, trembling. Hall sat unmoving on the log, frozen in shock and horror. With both hands Thomas grasped at his torn throat. Choking on blood, he slumped into the mud in a forlorn pile. One leg twitched spasmodically, as if still trying to run.

The priest could hear Thomas's wet, laboured breathing gradually slow and mute into silence. The stillness seemed to echo in his ears. The morning breeze died down; even the birds seemed to fall quiet. Hall turned and vomited the acid contents of his empty belly onto the damp ground. His stomach twisted. Death before breakfast.

"Didn't I tell you he spoke the truth?" The man's voice was soft and reasonable. He picked up the blade from the blood-spattered grass. "Best give him his rites, Father, for what it's worth."

Hall looked up at the man as though seeing him for the first time. The man sat, casually flicked the blood from Hall's knife and leaned over to spear another sausage.

Hall shivered and looked away, but all he could see was those bleak, chill crow's eyes, harrowing into his own.

"And now, Father, I want you to tell me everything you know about your master, Edward Arden. Everything."

Chapter the First

Summer, 1575

THE NUDGE IN the ribs was short of a kick, but not by much. Christopher Tyburn came awake abruptly, his right hand reaching for his absent sword even before his grey eyes snapped open, sweeping his dim surroundings. Four years of mornings in Flanders had bred that habit into his very bones.

Tyburn was wrapped in a frayed woolen blanket, secure under the leafy vault of a large shadowy oak tree that was barely palpable in the pre-dawn gloom. A heavy wooden wagon stood hard by the spreading tree. From the stable in the innyard drifted a quiet nicker. The air smelled damp and thick, heavy with the scent of the inn's waste pile. Except for a faint yellow flicker in the kitchen window, the inn was dark. Dawn was a slender promise beginning to eclipse the stars still manifest in the eastern sky.

"Up, you base player, rouse yourself from the muck." The voice drifted down to Tyburn who sat up, cocked his head and glanced up at the shadow standing beside him. Tyburn couldn't see it, but he sensed Alec was laughing at him in the dark.

"I am up, you poxed bastard." Tyburn rubbed his neck. "Not even dawn, you know Oldcastle hasn't even rolled off his whore yet."

"He wants an early start." Alec commented

"God's bones . . ." Tyburn grimaced. He shrugged his shoulders and rolled his neck to loosen the kinks left by the tree roots. Throwing off the blanket he got to his feet. Much the Elder was already busying himself shifting the trunks that weighed down the troupe's well-traveled wagon while his son, Much the Younger, was feeding thin strips of bark and twigs into the embers, building the hot coals he had snatched from the inn's fire into a steady and welcoming yellow flame.

"Too early even for the bloody rooster," Tyburn muttered.

Alec grinned, gleaming teeth masked by the gloom. "Don't fool yourself, that old'un's rooster has been risen all night with that mort."

"It might shock an Oxford man like yourself, but I was speaking of the actual cock's crow," Tyburn commented, his voice sour.

"So was I." Alec laughed and made an abrupt gesture at one of the troupe walking past. "Robbie!" he called, handing a penny to the boy, "go filch us some breakfast like a half-decent servant should."

Robbie took the coin with deft hands and gave the two players a sardonic grin in reply. "And hen's eggs this time, Robbie, none of your goose eggs, you drigger, the bloody things give me the flux."

Robbie waved a quick acknowledgement and vanished into the pre-dawn darkness.

Tyburn sat, pulled on his worn boots, yawned and ran one hand through his dark hair. "Where away today?" he asked Alec.

"North-east, along Evesham road, heading up towards Warwick. Just four days from here to London, but I expect we'll slip over to Coventry, loop north-east and back down through your old

11

steading in Cambridge first. Today, we're for Stratford, up on the Avon."

"So why the early rise?" said Tyburn. The sun was a low lambent glow pinking the eastern horizon.

Alec grinned. "Oldcastle likes his nuncheon." He chuckled at Tyburn's puzzlement. "He's a cheap bastard, but likes to eat well, Kit. He arrives mid-morning in a nice market-town, befuddles the alderman with his charms and sophistication and gets"--he paused dramatically--"an invitation to dine." Alec finished with a gaudy flourish of gestures, a flawless mimicry of Oldcastle's flamboyant and overwrought mannerisms.

Tyburn grinned, unable to prevent himself in the face of Alec's cheery demeanor.

A loud bellow rose from the innyard. Alec winced. "Speaking of roosters..."

"Up, you poxed coxcombs, you coves, we've a road ahead of us!" It was a familiar deep voice, long practiced at projecting to the deepest recesses of an innyard or manor hall. "By God's Mother you are a lazy one, Alleyn, roll out of that blanket you worthless jackanapes, we've a road to be on."

The sun was cresting over the eastern horizon before the troupe was moving down the rutted road, the wagon creaking a weary rhythm behind them, drawn by a sway-backed mottled dun horse that had seen better days.

Tyburn was chewing on a cold chicken leg as they walked, a breakfast courtesy of Alec's largesse and his canny servant Robbie Hobson. "So where did Robbie learn to filch chicken so well?" he asked distracted, trying and failing to contain a cavernous yawn.

"Robbie?" Alec chuckled. "Our Robbie's no common draw-latch[1]. He was an angler in London, until he caught the wrong fish."

"An angler?"

"You know, a hookman. He lifts your goods with a hook on a pole. Sneaky little buggers, every one of them." Alec shook his head in admiration. "Robbie here got caught lifting some fellow's bung[2] and had the catchpoles[3] on him right quick. Ducked into the Boar's Head yard in the middle of performance and stepped right onto the boards, pretending to be a player. That tickled Oldcastle and he sent the bailiffs on their way."

Alec gestured back at Oldcastle, who had perched his oversized bulk with delicate care on the narrow bench beside the drover for the long slog between towns.

"By Jesu, he might be a cheap bastard but if he likes you, he looks after you." Alec concluded.

Behind Oldcastle, the livery flag of the troupe flapped disconsolately in the capricious morning breeze, announcing to the world that the Earl of Worcester's Men were on the road. Tyburn knew that the flag and its livery, along with the paper writ and vellum letters in Oldcastle's trunk, were the only tangible protection the troupe had against town bailiffs and Puritan officials.

The Poor Laws had outlawed the chronic vagrancy and poor endemic to many towns, pushing the indigent into workhouses or prisons or more often into an uncertain wayward lifestyle of begging, haunting the highways and local parishes until either imprisoned or pushed on to a new locale by the bailiffs or sheriff. In the eyes of many Puritan officials, players ranked considerably lower in status than even vagrants, despite the nominal patronage of the queen and the nobility. Only a troupe with influence,

---

[1] Petty thief
[2] Purse
[3] Arresting officer

protection and patronage could safely tour the countryside and remain free of official interference.

The Earl of Worcester's Men were one such troupe. They had been touring since mid-May, following the great roads that threaded south and west, looping up through Bristol and Warwick, before swinging around and heading back into London at summer's end. Death and Worcester's mercurial personality had been the instigators of this season's tour. A brief outbreak of plague in London had provided all the excuse the city officials needed to summarily call a halt to innyard performances within its confines. By itself, Tyburn thought amused, that would have not been enough to rouse Oldcastle into considering a tour. Oldcastle preferred to set up in Southwark, outside of London's jurisdiction, and wait out the closure in comfort but a letter from the earl had "requested, by their kindness" to perform in Winchester for a friend. Oldcastle had acquiesced and so Worcester's Men set forth.

Tyburn was aware he was fortunate just to be accompanying the troupe. He had been performing with them for just under a year, since his return from the Low Countries. To Oldcastle, Tyburn was yet another irritant foisted on him by his unpredictable patron. Christopher Tyburn, late of Her Majesty's service in Holland, was a mere untried performer at a time when apprentice actors were starving in the London streets. If not for the intervention of the Earl of Worcester, who had deigned to assist an ex-soldier for his own particular purposes, Tyburn would be one more ruffian scuffling for an existence in the London back-alleys.

As a paid performer rather than a "sharer" Tyburn also was under no illusions–Oldcastle would keep Tyburn in the troupe only so long as Tyburn could perform to his satisfaction. Oldcastle was an old hand at balancing his patron's whimsies with cold, hard practicalities and "losing" a player foisted on him against his will would have been an easy task after the first few months passed. Oldcastle's largesse could end at any time. Surprisingly thus far, it had not done so and Tyburn now trudged the dusty roads of

Warwickshire enjoying the early morning sunshine and a well roasted chicken leg for his breakfast.

The two walking men were a study in contrasts. Alec Masterson was tall, elegant with fine, aquiline features topped by a shaggy mass of thick blond hair that bespoke his Norse ancestry. Well dressed and cheery, he was the son of a wealthy London guild master, a man whose varied interests in properties and merchantry had purchased him rich lands in Surrey and Hampshire, a fine house in London on a fashionable street and a fat sinecure at court.

Alec's chosen profession upon leaving Oxford had earned him his father's lasting wrath, tempered only by the recognition that it could well have been much worse. A steady stream of Oxford students were abandoning their education in England altogether and voluntarily taking the road to exile in Rheims and Douai to pursue their studies at schools established by exiled Catholic priests. For the exiles, returning to England was a dangerous and difficult undertaking, in particular since the Pope had condemned the queen as a heretic only a few years previous. Even a public renunciation of the Catholic faith couldn't guarantee protection for recusants; many who had departed on a whim or in a fit of rebellious student angst found themselves adrift on the continent in lonesome exile or imprisoned with alacrity upon their return.

Alec's father provided his son a generous staple income, hoping for the day that Alec would come to his senses and abandon his wayward life as a player.

Tyburn was slightly shorter than Alec, but was Alec's converse in both dress and appearance. The dark-haired, saturnine Tyburn was lean and well-muscled. A thin scar edged along his left jawline and curled, tapering up onto his lower cheek like an off-set frown. The scar gave Tyburn's face a sinister cast tempered only by his steady grey eyes.

Tyburn, like Alec, had also walked away from his studies. Ensconced at Cambridge, Tyburn had abandoned his charge five years previous to cast his fate in with Thomas Morgan and Sir Humphrey Gilbert's expedition to Holland and Flanders.

Unlike Alec, Tyburn had no family largesse to fall back on, just the thin credit and the reluctant miser's wage extended to him by Oldcastle. Tyburn's clothing was worn, his boots thin-soled and his doublet threadbare and torn. To an outside observer the difference between vagabond and player was a narrow one at best.

The road the players traveled was rutted, uneven and poorly maintained, following a much older Roman road that had once traced a similar path through the low, rolling English countryside. The landscape was dotted with small farming hamlets nestling together in quiet green hollows and crossroads. The patchwork of old stone walls that had separated the landscape into small mixed plots and parcels had given way to larger allotments and grazing. Sheep foraged in placid flocks across a far hillside and the distant lowing of cattle drifted through the air.

It was mid-summer and the air was redolent with the smell of fresh-cut hay. A small group of men were scything away in the early morning sunlight, slicing through the tall grass and piling it into neat stacks, distance belying the intensity of the labour.

The road itself was a well-trafficked one. A heavy laden cart was trundling slow ahead of the troupe, carrying tight bundled tods of wool. The fine dust swirled behind the cart, drifting back and catching in the players' throats. The winding path of the River Avon to the south, paralleling the road, was bordered by a thick curtain of woods and revealed by the occasional gleam of cool water that shone through the distant trees like a promise.

A kite circled slow overhead and then arced away across the cloudless blue to the east. Tyburn followed it with his eyes, envying its easy grace. In the far distance, a church spire rose above a thin line of trees.

Will gazed wistfully out the narrow shuttered window and shifted his weight on the hard wooden bench. The blue sky hung cloudless and beckoning, just beyond the rooftops. The clatter of a passing cart trundling through Church Street echoed off the stones while the indistinct voices of people passing floated up from beyond the window. In the distance, a dog barked, barely heard over the din of the street and the endless cooing of the pigeons nestling under the wooden eaves.

Will sighed to himself and forced his gaze downwards to his hornbook. The neatly copied Latin passage was still there, waiting for his attention. He felt a nudge on his foot. To his right sat his friend Richard, who. grinned and pointed across the room at the teacher's assistant, trying in vain to sort through a heavy bound Latin volume while balancing another and pointing out a passage to a smaller group of very young boys. The group included Will's tow-headed brother Gilbert, who was gazing with vacant boredom into the empty space of the rafters.

Dust motes danced in the sunshine, spiraling upwards while a small dog lay sleeping in the far corner. The heavy-beamed room was long and felt murky and dark, even with the shutters wide and the sunshine flooding in. Lined with a series of long, dark wooden benches and tables, the room was occupied by some thirty-odd children of various ages from six to fourteen. Another man sat at the end of the room, laboriously writing on an old piece of vellum with measured care. The continual sound and soft bustle of small bodies in constant motion rose throughout the space. Legs kicked, fingers poked and whenever the occasional muffled giggle or mumbled sound was heard, the man in the long gown would glance up, his eyes sharp under his brow, glowering at his charges in unspoken reproach. Moments after his head would drop back to the page, the soft noises would resume.

"Hsst. Will, how's this?" queried Will's immediate neighbour, shoving a tattered piece of script in front of him. Will peered down at it. The paper was tracked with several ink blotches and thin scratchy, elongated letters.

"God's bowels, I can't even read that, Edward--is it Latin or a drawing of a pig?" Will whispered back.

17

Someone snickered quietly. Edward'sround face was pained when Will glanced up from the sheet. Will sighed in exasperation.

"First, it's *collis*, not *coleus*," began Will, speaking in a low urgent tone. Edward looked puzzled and leaned over to look at the tattered paper.

"Are you sure?" Edward asked, his voice rising with his querulous tone. Will and the others winced at the volume of Edward's reply.

"Shut it, you ninny," one hissed angrily, "you're going to get us all in trouble."

"*Collis*," whispered Will. "Hill, right?"

"So what's *coleus*?" Edward was quite puzzled. The other boys shrugged. Will drew a deep annoyed breath.

"It's . . . well. It's . . . um . . . your sack."

"My what?"

"Your sack, your stones . . . you know." Will pointed down. The other boys tried and failed to stifle a quiet burst of laughter as Edward nodded, blushing furiously.

"*Coleus*--what's that?" whispered Richard in a mocking imitation of Edward. "Will, can you tell me the difference between *culum* and *cunnus*?[4] I really need to know."

The other boys tittered, even the ones whose Latin was so indifferent that they didn't know the meaning of the joke. "*Horum, harum* whore![5]" one chirped.

Richard snickered. Will grinned and said "Pedagogue, *peticatum*.[6]" Several boys stifled their laughter by stuffing the ends of their sleeves in their mouths. Emboldened Will ventured, "*Scortum*[7] sup."

---

[4] Culum = buttocks, cunnus = female genitalia
[5] Latin demonstrative pronouns – "his" in the genitive tense
[6] Peticatum = slang for anal intercourse
[7] Scortum = whore

The whip-crack of the long, flat wooden paddle against the table brought the quiet sniggering laughter to an abrupt and startling halt. Ashen, Will looked up and saw the teacher standing beside their table, looking down on the collection of boys. The long stick was poised like a promise over the dark scarred wood surface.

"Verbaarum delectus orige est e lequentrai," the man intoned. He pointed the stick at Will. "Translate."

"Delight in the words and the origin of eloquence," Will replied, watching the stick with wary eyes. The man ventured a thin humorless smile behind his long beard.

The remainder of the class had turned and was watching the scene soundlessly. The assistant teacher had set down his tome and started over, halted by an abrupt dismissive wave of the man's hand. Even the dozing yellow dog had deigned to lift its head, yawned and then settled back down in its sunlight patch.

"The rest of you begone--it is nuncheon." The teacher gestured to the door. The boys scrambled off the bench, Gilbert hesitating for a moment before turning and joining the group as they tumbled out the door and down the exterior staircase, their voices fading. "Not you." The teacher barred Will from leaving. "Sit," he commanded, pointing with the wide, flattened end of the stick.

"Whatever am I to do with you, young Will?" The stern look in his eyes faded and amusement stole across his face. He stroked his long beard pensively. "I don't think I want to hear you complete that Latin you were practicing, do I?"

"No, Master Hunt. I should think not," replied Will.

"You are a hell-wean, make no mistake, Master Shakespeare. Cleverer than any student I have ever seen but a hell-wean nonetheless." He paused. *"Abeunt studia in mores* [8]– do you agree?"

Will nodded.

---

[8] "Studies go to form character"

"By the love of Christ but you do deserve a beating for abusing the Latin, but I am impressed with your vocabulary." The schoolmaster arched a sardonic brow. "And beating you doesn't seem to have much effect. I sense I am plowing in the river, trying to restrain your fancies." Hunt stood and smacked the long, flattened stick against his palm several times with ominous intent.

"Off you go, Master Shakespeare, and try to be back in time for the afternoon lessons."

Will slid off the bench and turned towards the door.

"Will?"

"Sir?"

"There is more found here than your word games. We school you for more than just rote recitation and parroting the Catechism. Sin is all around us in this quiet land, and God. . . well, God is oftentimes not seen or manifested in men's hearts. The world is a place of avarice and pain. Only in God's grace can we walk"--he paused, hesitated, and then continued with greater assurance. "Knowledge can be a path to salvation and understanding of God's great mercies. Remember that, when the time comes."

Will paused, looking at the schoolmaster for a moment, then turned and clattered down the outside stairs.

"Well," Hunt muttered to himself, "you could at least pretend you'd suffered a whipping for my reputation's sake."

Will turned right towards the stony confines of Chapel Street. He hadn't gone four paces when Richard popped out of the doorway he'd been leaning in and grasped Will's upper arm. A full head shorter, Gilbert hovered beside him, an uncertain grin on his face.

"Did you get another whipping?" Richard was grinning.

"Not this time," Will responded, "but I do think I've galled him enough today."

"God's Mercy on you, Will, but your father won't spare you the beating Master Hunt should have laid on you, if he finds out." Richard laughed.

Will winced inwardly. His father had little patience for what he termed "foolish flightings" and games and even less with Will's continuing intransigence at the restrictions and rules of the King Edward Grammar School. Will glared at Gilbert.

"You better keep that trap of yours shut," Will growled, "or anything lands on me, you'll be the worse for it."

Richard nodded in sage agreement as the affronted Gilbert chirped, "Will! I wouldn't blow on you."

"I find you cracking off, I'll whip you good." Will gave Gilbert another hard look, one that failed to make an impression as Gilbert grinned in response.

A cart trundled past, its ungreased wheels squeaking. It was stacked high with heavy yellowing tods of wool and followed by a great buzzing mass of flies. Will regarded it with a jaundiced eye, realizing it was probably bound for Henley Street and his father's small barn.

"Hey, what's that?" Richard paused, listening.

A low brassy bellow rose faint from the southwest.

"Will, it's a troupe!" Richard pulled hard on Will's arm. Another booming trumpet sounded and the rattle of a drum drifted down, tatting light and rhythmic in the distance.

"Come on!" Will shouted at his friend and the two, leaving Gilbert gawping, shot past the heavily-laden carter, dodged a rooting pig and a squat woman carrying a bundle of clothes and headed up Tinker's Lane to where the Evesham Road met Stratford proper. "Last one there is Jack o' Lent.[9]" The boys' excited shouts bounced off the timber-framed buildings, blending with the ragged sound of a trumpet.

Worcester's Men had arrived.

---

[9] Fool figure

Chapter the Second

"**B**Y GOD'S TEETH! Much, you pestilent capon, where's my ruff?" shouted Oldcastle, flinging open one of the traveling chests, almost knocking his servant to the ground in the process.

"Sorr, if'n you kindly wait but a--"

"Stop banting about and find my ruff box. By Heaven, is it too much to ask for a servant who can remember where he left things? I should have you whipped, no--scourged, by God."

Oldcastle's empty tirade came to an abrupt halt when Much's son, standing atop the wagon, pulled out the flat box from one of the chests and passed it down to his father.

Tyburn ignored Oldcastle's endless bickering with his servants and concentrated on poking the loose threads on his embroidered doublet out of immediate view. The doublet's stitching was parting down one side. Tyburn fingered it, doubting it would last much longer.

It was past mid-morning and the troupe had halted by a clutch of tall elms short of the town to prepare for their entrance.

The sun was high and the skies warm, blue and cloudless. Several small farmhouses were scattered about, an easy distance from the road, and to the north a smaller hamlet was visible in the distance. The Stratford church spire stood stolid in the southeast, a yellow-gray mass of stone and wood that sat apart from the main avenues of the market-town, marking where the domain of heaven touched the realm of the mortal.

The road was steady with foot traffic as carts laden with local produce passed, plying their wares in the town. Several mounted riders passed by, including a small band of liveried retainers who trotted past without even turning their heads to glance at the troupe. A man herded a lone cow along the roadway, turning north to the smaller hamlet visible beyond the trees. A small group of children who had been playing on the hillside had gathered by a low stone wall, eyeing the troupe with fascination. As he bustled about with the troupes various accoutrements, Robbie kept a sharp jaundiced eye on their small filching hands.

The wagon had made slower progress than expected on the uneven and heavily rutted road, the jouncing and bumping doing little to mend Oldcastle's sour temperament. At one point Oldcastle had begun calling out lines from the troupe's play list. It was an old traveling memory game, allowing the players to work on recalling their character's lines. The proper response was the next line of the play; however, Alec, irritated that Oldcastle was pressing them on a hot day, refused to cooperate and had insisted on bellowing bawdy lines from the many tavern songs in his repertoire in reply. After Alec worked his way through most of "The Three Drunken Maidens," Oldcastle had given up and concentrated on the remaining players, leaving Alec free to whistle and contemplate the cheerful green hillsides.

Tyburn sighed and, his doublet problems having been rendered at least marginally acceptable, pulled out a long cylindrical object wrapped in some rough cloth from the bottom of a long chest. He undid the ties and unrolled the cloth to reveal. several long swords. Tyburn picked up two and turning to Alec,

23

gave a low whistle. Alec turned and Tyburn tossed him one of the rapiers. Alec nodded his distracted thanks and went back to reshaping a large lavish hat that had been flattened in its travels.

Tyburn examined his own long blade. The pommel was worn with use and the silver damascened guard, although once ornate, was now nicked and dull to the eye, no longer the showpiece it had been in the hands of a young Spanish bravo. The blade however was well kept, a long, razor-edged piece of elegant Toledo steel, thirty-four inches of fatal grace.

It was one of the only blades the troupe carried that was kept sharp. The majority of the troupe's weapons were intended for use in performances and were dulled and corked to prevent accidents. Tyburn insisted on keeping his own sword and had refused point-blank when Oldcastle suggested he dull the blade. Tyburn used a troupe weapon for the staged swordfights, although even Oldcastle acknowledged that Tyburn's ability was such that he was the least likely to inflict any accidental damage on his opponents. One of the few ways that Tyburn had been able to pad his meager income had been to work with the other troupe members, chiefly Alleyn and Alec, on their swordplay. The result was that Worcester's Men were now recognized by even jaded London audiences as being the best at on-stage mayhem.

Satisfied, Tyburn sheathed the weapon and strapped on the belt, settling the sword on his left. Alec grinned and pointed. Tyburn glanced down to see his colorful doublet split down one side. "Christ," he muttered.

Alec laughed and tossed him an ornate yellow half-cloak, edged with delicate silvered needlework. "Here. That'll help hide it from Oldcastle until you can get some innkeeper's wife to mend it for you."

Tyburn nodded his thanks and slung the half-cloak so it hung over the side with the split, donned his wide-brimmed hat, adjusted the feather and straightened. "How's that?" He struck a particularly jaunty pose.

"The maidens of Stratford are quickening as we speak." Alec swept his arm back and bowed grandly. "Although with you I fear their expectations will founder."

The two apprentices were pulling a long brass trumpet and a small set of timbrels out of a cloth sack while Oldcastle and the three other sharers in the company arranged their appearances with care. Jacob Willens, the oldest player after Oldcastle, wore an outlandish selection of clothes, including an enormous oversized codpiece, a peasecod belly and a long trimmed gown with paneled breeches in white and red. He topped the outfit with a small round hat surmounted with a ridiculous oversized feather.

Willens role was Folly, the Jester, the Lord of Misrule, a master of jigs, buffoonery and morris dancing, activities many of the younger players derided as provincial but that were popular with audiences nonetheless. Tyburn rather liked the lively acrobatics of the morris dances, although he was dragged into them rather infrequently in his role as Vice. Oldcastle was a firm believer in using the fundamental stock characters and Tyburn, with his grim visage, was a perfect foil for Alec's Virtuous Youth.

"Daniel and Mundy, bring up the rear with the wagon. I lead, Jacob follows me. Then Jack and Motely sounding the march and Robbie with the banner high. Alec--you, Alleyn and Tyburn provide some flash as we go, but don't lag. No banter and no gammoning off with some doxy making sheep eyes at you," Oldcastle instructed.

"Heads high now, by Christ's bones, you're the Earl of Worcester's Men, so act it, you villains." With that Oldcastle signaled the apprentices. Jack gave the timbrels a rattle and Motely blew hard on the old trumpet, sounding a discordant brassy note that floated across the summer air. The watching children on the hillside leaped up, calling and waving. Oldcastle stepped grandly out onto the road, held both arms skyward and shouted, "God's Grace is upon our endeavors!" He turned, bowed to the company and resumed the march into the town, Worcester's silver, blue and red blazon held high behind him, dangling from its cross-bar.

Alec slipped Tyburn a surreptitious wink and a grin as they set out after Robbie and the apprentices, Alleyn muttering to himself behind them.

The road the troupe marched along was cobblestoned along the sides, sufficient for the wagon wheels, with the uncobbled centre providing a soft, muddy trap for the unwary on rainy days. Today, with the midsummer sun overhead, the center of the road was dry, hard and dusty, trampled flat by the constant flow of commerce.

Jack thumped and rattled the timbrels in rhythm to their pace. As they passed through the line of elms bordering the road, a small flock of crows burst from the trees shading the road, circled twice at dizzying speed and vanished from sight.

Stratford-upon-Avon was an unremarkable Warwickshire market-town, bordered by the river Avon on the south and the edge of denuded remnants of the Forest of Arden to the north. The players could smell the town long before they reached the first set of buildings. The scent was a heavy mélange of woodsmoke, manure and slop heaps, urine, the acrid scent of tanning hides, sawdust, malt, cooking, animals and unwashed humanity.

Tall, timber-framed buildings rose on both sides of the road, interspersed like a set of uneven mottled white teeth. Topped with thick brown thatch and the occasional tile, the buildings varied in size and height, with a handful rising to up three storeys. As the troupe moved further along the street, the buildings' cantilevered upper floors hung out over the lower storeys like a deep jutting brow. Most were plaster-covered, even to the thick timber beams themselves, and their windows were narrow with heavy shutters open to allow a thin wash of summer daylight to stream inside. The players kept a wary eye on the upper windows, watching for household slops and refuse being emptied onto passersby.

The road was busy with foot travelers, most of whom stopped to gawp at the vividly dressed marching troupe. Alec grinned as Oldcastle gestured and bowed grandly to various bystanders, his practiced eye judging by the cut and style of their clothing whether they merited a mere passing nod, an expansive wave or a deep bow.

The Evesham Road that the troupe had followed since before dawn gave way to Rother Street, the street that led to Stratford's cattle market[10], the presence of which was apparent both underfoot and through the nostrils. The players threaded their careful way through patches of thick oozing cattle dung that caked the cobbles, with Willens exaggeratedly tiptoeing around a large repulsive deposit and then pretending to slip, catching himself at the last moment before breaking out in a quick and jaunty jig that made spectators laugh.

"Let's wait till we clear the dung street, then we give them a little taste." Tyburn murmured in an aside to Alec, who nodded in reply.

Alleyn broke out into a quick and lively song. "Sir Eglamore was a valiant knight
Fa la lanky down dilly, He put on his sword and he went to fight, *Fa la lanky down dilly . . .*"

Several women carrying baskets stopped to listen, whispering to one another. A cooper scowled at the troupe as it passed. His pinched face suffused with distaste as he regarded the players. He spat once on the cobbles. Alec rewarded him with a beatific smile that in turn made Tyburn grin.

"And as he rid o'er hill and dale, All armed in his coat of mail, *Fa la la la la la la lanky down dilly,* There starts a huge dragon out of his den, *fa la . . .* Which had kill'd I know not how many men, *Fa la . . .*"

Motely blew hard on his trumpet, his round face pink and glowing. For once the sound blasted forth from the instrument rather than the usual muffled blare, to echo off the yellowing walls of the street.

---

[10] *Rother* is Anglo-Saxon for cattle

Oldcastle paused amidst the small crowd and raised his arms grandly. "God Bless this noble town Stratford-Upon-Avon! We are the Earl of Worcester's Men, players of the best and kindest patron, who has commanded us to pay visit to you and yours. May God's Mercies be upon you!" At that, Oldcastle bowed with exaggerated courtesy to a hawk-nosed woman in a severe black dress and starched white cap. She sniffed and turned away to resume her market duties, her dark eyes harsh as she regarded the passing troupe. Oldcastle merely gave his performer's smile and strode onward.

"Bloody Precisions…[11]" Robbie mumbled as he passed with the banner. Tyburn frowned. The Puritans regularly denounced what they called the bawdy nature of plays and other staged entertainments, one of the reasons that the London Court of Aldermen systematically harassed and restricted such entertainments in the city proper. The Puritans didn't limit their venom to mere players, but reserved the majority of their spite for English Catholic recusants and, surprisingly for the queen herself and her ministers, who they felt were far too lenient in treating what they termed "Popish pomp and rags."

The low sound of metal scraping on metal pulled Tyburn out of his pensive state. He turned, stepping rapidly backwards with his left foot, hand reaching for his rapier. Alec grinned, a quick flash of gleaming white teeth, as he lunged at Tyburn.

Tyburn's blade slid from its sheath and flicked up, deflecting Alec's sword neatly to one side. The two paused, and then Alec began to declaim.

"Foul spawn of strife and discord, face the blade of a true Christian gentleman!"

"Are you a swordsman or an antic[12]?" replied Tyburn, twisting his face into a vicious scowl.

---

[11] Antagonistic term for Puritans
[12] Clown

"Your doom unless you yield, for mine is the righteous cause."

"Methinks you are half-a-pack short[13]. Can you do more than mere sparrow-blasting[14]?"

"I speak with steel," Alec intoned, his voice heavy with portentous emphasis. Stepping in smooth, he lunged the silvered blade towards Tyburn, moving for the opening Kit had left on the inside. Tyburn turned his blade, parrying Alec's attack, and stepped in with a slow counter which Alec in turn deflected with a scraping clash that rang off the buildings.

Alec flung his arm forward again, thrusting the blade at his opponent, making Tyburn wince inwardly. Despite much coaching, Alec still had a tendency to throw his arm when making a thrust, a move that announced his intended line of attack in advance of the action. It didn't matter when you were working the boards[15] but on the street or in a duel, it was a painful and potentially fatal mistake. Tyburn took the blow easily on the forte of his sword and stepped in close, grabbing Alec's sword arm and hissing malevolence. The two stood *en tableau* for a moment before leaping back with a quick bow to the gaping market audience.

"I thank you gentlefolk, for your indulgence. If you are intrigued to know if Virtue bests Vice, please attend on the morrow!" exhorted Tyburn. He and Alec sheathed their swords with a flourish and rejoined Alleyn and a grinning Robbie.

"Did you see that?" breathed Richard. "He handles that stick like a Dunkirker[16]."

"That's no veney stick[17], by Faith," agreed Will. "Think we can see the performance?"

---

[13] Measure of dry goods, in this case, not a full measure....
[14] Cursing
[15] Performing
[16] Reference to Dunkirk, a notorious pirate haven
[17] Heavy stick used for practicing sword-play

"Doubt it. My mother thinks plays are Devil's work," replied Richard in sullen tones, his face tight.

"Will's seen a play!" piped Gilbert.

"Truly?" asked Richard, intrigued.

"In Coventry, we saw the Cycles, and the Mayor's Play three years ago, when Warwick's Men came through." admitted Will.

"Well, your father's an alderman. I expect you'll get to spy this 'un," Richard observed, his voice envious.

"I won't get to spy anything if Gilbert and I don't get to home right quick," Will said, shrugging. He felt bad that Richard's staunch Protestant parents refused to permit him to see the troupes that passed through Stratford during the warm summer months. Will's own father dubbed plays frivolous nonsense and considered them an unwelcome distraction but, due to his position on the town council, John Shakespeare was at least obligated to make an appearance with the other aldermen.

Will himself had vivid memories of the Coventry players marching in colorful procession along the narrow laneways. He remembered the elaborate embroidery of their costumes, the feathered hats and stylized horned masks that hid their faces. He recalled the glorious decorations on the oversized pageant wagons and how they gleamed with gold and red decorative motifs, the jostle of the excited crowds, the raucous cries of the hawkers, and the choking sulphurous stench of the Hell-mouth specially built in the Coventry marketplace[18]. More than anything he remembered the players themselves, drawing in the breathless attention of the audience, grasping it, building upon it and weaving an evocative tale from words and phrases, giving life to all the familiar stories that Will had learned by rote over the years at Stratford's stony

---

[18] The Coventry Mystery Cycles generally incorporated at least one stage location that represented the entrance to Hell, presided over by an elaborately costumed Devil and his demonic minions.

church and on the hard benches and within the airy recesses of the King Edward Grammar School.

It had been so utterly different from anything he had experienced before. The players' measured oration tore away the pallid façade of recitation and drove the deeper meaning of the stories home with astonishing clarity. Will had been swept up, his thoughts caught like a leaf in the wind, soaring upwards and then eclipsed in turn by shadow as the story plunged in a new direction.

Gilbert tugged on Will's arm to clear his head of the reminiscences. Richard grinned askance at Will's distracted look and the three hurried down towards Rother Market to cut over to Henley Street and home.

The Earl of Worcester's Men drew up their procession when they arrived at the Stratford guild hall. They had proceeded down dung-strewn Rother past the stone cross standing in Stratford's main marketplace, down Wood Street and back across High Street. It was a leisurely route but one designed to maximum effect. By the time they had arrived at the guild hall, a small and expectant crowd had gathered and a collection of the Stratford aldermen had congregated on the steps of the building to greet the players.

The guild hall was an impressive structure for a small market town. A large stone chapel dominated one end, with a lengthy, two-floored, timber-framed building stretching the length of the street behind. The building had been plastered and lime-washed to a gleaming white and was roofed with tile rather than the usual thatch. A small recessed stone courtyard led to a second smaller, cantilevered structure. A number of laden wagons and carts with several oxen stood by the doors while men in loose smocks carried bundled goods into the building.

Two men waited on the stone steps leading into the chapel. Neither wore any badge of office but Oldcastle immediately recognized the impatient demeanor of authority. The Earl of Worcester's Men drew up in a ragged line behind him as he stepped forward.

31

One of the men standing by the carts dusted his hands together and walked over to join the two on the steps.

"Master Oldcastle? I daresay you are looking well. It has been, what? Five years?" The man was tall, dusty from his labors, but under his grime he wore a deep blue jerkin and an ornate agate ring.

"My lord, I trust in God that you and yours are well?" returned Oldcastle, bowing deeply, an affable smile on his lips. The man nodded cordially. "My lords aldermen, gentlefolk of Stratford, may I present the Earl of Worcester's Men, a troupe of players who gently request your kind permission to perform." Oldcastle bowed again, then turned and gestured at Motely who stepped forward with stiff self-consciousness, holding a roll of vellum tied with an ornate silk ribbon. The tall man accepted the roll and without deigning to open it, passed it to one of the other men on the steps. He unrolled the document, gave the document with its ornate seals a cursory glance and passed it to the third man. He squinted at it, rolled it back up and handed it to Oldcastle.

"As you can see, we are fully licensed to perform and we beg your kind indulgence to permit our performances within your precincts," Oldcastle intoned solemnly.

The men glanced at each other. One shrugged with indifference. "Very well Master Oldcastle, you may perform but first you must provide a play with no bar or cost on admission–The Mayor's Play–on the morrow at the guild hall. You may enjoy the pleasure of the guild hall for an additional two performances, after which you may use an innyard if they will have you." The speaker looked from Oldcastle to the troupe and then continued. "There will be no undue rowdiness, no Papist nonsense performed and no wild moriscos[19] in the streets. I'll have no woodwoses[20] on my hands."

---

[19] Morris dancing
[20] Wildmen

Oldcastle bowed in acquiescence. "Indeed my lords, we are at your service."

"Anything else needed? No?"

"Your pardon my lord, we have come a long way on the hard hoof with naught but old cheese and bread, mayhaps . . ." Oldcastle ventured.

The alderman glanced at Oldcastle from under his dark brows, and paused theatrically. "I recommend the Bear--good ale." He gave the master player a sardonic grin and gestured to the other aldermen. "Gentlemen, let us sup." The three passed into the small courtyard, disappearing through the open doors.

"Bastard merchants." Oldcastle muttered balefully under his breath. Alec suppressed a grin at Oldcastle's sour expression and the troupe turned back down stony High Street to find the Bear Tavern and some much needed drink.

"Bastards." Oldcastle repeated. "Nothing but bloody curst bastards."

Chapter the Third

JOHN SHAKESPEARE KNELT over the wide, sunken puering vat and lifted out the soaked hides, draping them untidily over a long wooden pole he had propped against the log pile. The stench was vile, hanging like a thick blanket in the air, although it seemed not to trouble the buzzing mass of flies occluding the sunshine. Shakespeare studied the level of the putrid liquid within the container for a moment, gauging if it required additional supply. Not quite, he thought, but by the end of the week, he would again have to empty out the waste buckets into it[21].

With that, he stood and hefted the sodden, dripping mass of treated hides draped over the pole. Grunting with the weight, he maneuvered them over to a large barrel filled with milky-colored water and slid them in. With the pole, he pushed the hides to the bottom of the barrel, giving them a few quick stirs to release any

---

[21] Vat used for tanning hides, generally filled with a mixture of dung and urine.

trapped air bubbles. Satisfied, he leaned the pole against the back of the house.

He glanced at the small wooden drying barn behind the house. Two hired men were unloading a large cart laden with bundles of greasy sheepskins and thick bundles of shorn wool. Not officially licensed as a wool merchant, John Shakespeare knew he was violating the law in dealing with the fleeces but he was less than sanguine about the ability of the Merchants of the Staples to enforce their empty statutes. He had been trading in wool for more than ten years and had only one court appearance to show for it.

Shakespeare was a glover by trade, a profession he had apprenticed in almost twenty years before, laboring long hours cutting forms and patterns, mastering the delicate tracery of the glover's stitchwork, assessing and selecting leather, learning the intricacies of tanning, the taste, texture and feel of hides. The rank, earthy tang of leather seemed to cling to him everywhere he went, permeating him, crowding about like a second skin.

A loud clatter from within the house drew his attention. Will and Gilbert never arrived anywhere quietly, even church, he thought, no matter how often their mother scolded them. He gave the yard a cursory survey, wiped his damp hands on his smock and ducked into the house. The boys' arrival reminded him that it was time for the midday meal.

The sound of his wife remonstrating Will and Gilbert in the house's sturdy kitchen brought a brief smile to his face, cracking the stern façade he maintained for the world at large. Shakespeare's round, often jovial face masked a sharp and ambitious mien and a quick intelligence that made him a careful and cautious negotiator, an acumen that helped him navigate the often treacherous rural Stratford politics. Stratford had managed to avoid much of the sectarian turmoil that had unsettled other areas within Warwickshire, due to the collective determination of the Stratford aldermen and leading property owners to assiduously avoid any form of confrontation with the oft-shifting vagaries of the nobility and the throne. Stratford minded its business first and foremost, and protected its own.

He ducked under the low lintel into his small workroom. The narrow window shutters were flung wide, allowing natural sunlight to ribbon across the space, striping a battered worktable festooned with pale lengths of leather and hide, several battered wooden hand forms, scrapers, cutters and the distinctive fanned and hooked blades of the glover. Several tanned hides hung from the beamed ceiling, swaying minutely in the air currents.

Shakespeare hung his smock on a wooden peg. An abrupt knock at the door startled him, and he leaned past the dangling leathers to peer out the open window. A worried frown creased his face. Hugh Hall stood on his doorstep, impatiently staring at the portal.

John Shakespeare hesitated and then strode to the front door, waving a quick dismissal at the serving girl as she entered from the kitchen in response to the knock.

"Master gardener . . . may I be of service?"

Hugh Hall glanced past him, and then shifted his weight. "Good day, Master Shakespeare. I must speak with you with alacrity."

John Shakespeare looked Hall in the eyes, not liking the pallid colour permeating his face or the tiny shift in his expression. Hall wasn't supposed to come here. "I'm afraid the gloves are not ready yet, perhaps in a few weeks. . ." Shakespeare trailed off, hoping Hall might take his hint.

"No, this concerns, um . . . another task for you, master glover, some fitted gloves." Hall glanced behind him, like a rabbit in expectation of a stooping hawk. "May we discuss this in your workroom?" Hall looked at Shakespeare, his eyes expressing the emphasis his voice dared not.

Shakespeare sighed and moved aside, gesturing to Hall to enter. After Hall ducked into the workroom Shakespeare pulled the door closed behind him.

"You're not to call--" Shakespeare began in a low voice.

"I know, I know, my friend, but it could not be helped," interrupted Hall, lowering his voice. "I have . . . a package, a letter, from our mutual acquaintance that must be sent on this instant. I cannot pass this message, it must go direct."

Shakespeare stared. *Damn the man anyway.* It was unusual to have correspondence coming direct from Hall. The messages were supposed to come only through Jemmy Thomas, on his regular monthly journey to London. Jemmy plied his trade through the Midlands, carrying wool goods, fine cloth and specialities from the London markets to the Midlands of Warwickshire and Sussex.

"Jemmy won't be through for another two weeks at least. If you want to wai--" Shakespeare began.

"No!" Hall said, his voice sharp. He continued in a quieter tone, "I'm sorry, my friend, but it cannot wait. My master is bound for Kenilworth but this reply must be sent anon. It is critical that our acquaintance receive it and . . ." Hall lowered his voice even further. "I fear it is not safe."

Shakespeare's eyes narrowed under his dark brows. "You fear pursuivants and yet you come here--to my home? Directly? Why not just hire a beadle[22]? Sir, you are a fool."

Hall stared hard at Shakespeare, meeting his eyes with a level gaze. "I am on errand for Master Arden. I will be calling on several other tradesmen over the course of the day. There is no possible connection that can be made to this business."

Shakespeare stared with bleak eyes at the disguised priest, his mind racing. "I cannot deliver it." He spoke in soft emphatic tones. "There can be no connection between the priest and myself. My wife is a known recusant--I pay the fines. I am a man of status, of office. You know this. I walk a sharp path in my position."

---

[22] Herald or crier, a proclamation

"Time is short. I would not ask except in dire necessity. The letter must be delivered. It is in the service of God and the Church." Hall continued to stare in expectation.

Shakespeare glanced around the room. All of this, all he had built--the properties on Greenhill and Henley, the land in Snitterfield, his position in the community, his very life--all hung on a slender and tenuous thread.

"Consider it a penance for your past sins." Hall's voice was ice.

Shakespeare laughed, the sound hollow, refusing Hall's eyes, remembering his role in presiding as the Stratford chamberlain over the destruction of the guild chapel's rood loft[23], hearing the pointed snapping crackle of the broken gilded wood in the bonfire, and smelling the thick pungent lime wash shrouding the pious saints on the defaced frescos. *Burning the symbols of the True Faithwas enough of a sin to stain any man.*

"I had little choice, as you well know." He glared back at Hall then looked down, resigned. "Very well, leave the letter. I will pass it along with all due haste."

Hall eyed Shakespeare with cold satisfaction, and then nodded. The disguised priest left the glover's residence without a backward glance, proceeding down Henley Street before turning into the market. Hall did not deign to notice the hunched form of a shambling farm laborer trailing behind, carrying a non-descript bundle on one shoulder. The laborer pushed back his limp hair from his face, noting the building that Hall had departed with its small wooden glover's sign hanging beside the doorway. The man inclined his head, nodded to a shorter man in a greasy apron seated on a bench on the corner by a small alehouse and continued down Henley Street, following Hall.

---

[23] The rood loft & screen were common features in medieval churches, separating the nave from the choir or chancel of the church. They were often intricately decorated, gilded and lavishly constructed, often incorporating a gallery and an elaborate crucifix.

John Shakespeare sat on his bench staring at the neat oil-skin-wrapped letter. With Jemmy not due for two more weeks, Shakespeare would have to pass the letter on himself. He grimaced. He was well known enough that trekking out to Shottery to deliver the letter would be noted. Like as not, someone would ask what the alderman was doing traipsing through the elms and hayfields. The letter needed to be delivered, but he pondered how to do it with circumspection and care, and without garnering notice.

He stood and rummaged on his workbench. Retrieving a pair of delicate lady's gloves, he laid them beside the letter.

"Will," he called. "Will!"

Will ducked his tousled head around the corner. "Sir?"

"I need a note." Shakespeare's voice was gruff.

"Yessir," replied Will, stepping into the room. He retrieved a single sheet of parchment, a wooden board, quill and ink from the sideboard and knelt on the floor.

John thought for a moment, and then quickly dictated:

"Honored Sir, I deliver to you this pair of gloves and a correspondence from our learned friend. Please pass the gloves as a gift onto your goodwife. The correspondence must be sent on forthwith to our visitor. This must be circumspect, yet swift. I remain your loyal servant, under God,"

Will paused and then wrote the note without pausing, the quill stroking in careful curlicues, dipping like a bird on the wind.

"How's that, sir?" Will held up the thin parchment to his father. "Would you need any verse for the package?"

John squinted at the paper, then taking the quill from Will made a ragged and careful initial on the page. In truth, John Shakespeare had few letters, but for the sake of pride and position, both the father and the son tacitly never acknowledged that fact.

"That'll do." He patted the boy on the shoulder. "No verse needed today, but after you finish supping, I have a task for you. I need you to run this over to Sturley's place in Shottery."

Will stared at his father, curious, noting the oilskin-wrapped letter on the table, sealed with red wax. "And school?"

"Not today. If they have any humours about it, tell Master Hunt to speak with me. You can help with the wool afterwards." He gestured towards the barn behind the house.

Will grimaced but the expression vanished just as fast as it materialized. His father did not appear to have noticed, lost in thought.

"Let's not keep your mother waiting." John Shakespeare laid one hand on Will's shoulder and guided him out of the workshop. Will glanced back at the letter and gloves on the table, his curiosity piqued.

A short, wide man with a shabby hat, long, lank, greasy hair and granite eyes sat on the narrow wooden bench of the ordinary[24], sipping sour, hop-rich ale from a leather tankard, ignored amidst the morning bustle of the street. He eyed the glover's tall house from under his hat. The man's name was Cuttle.

Cuttle took a long draught from the tankard. He had been seated at the ordinary, unnoticed, for more than an hour. The presence of a day labourer drinking away his wages was neither extraordinary nor unusual and Cuttle had sat on this same bench during Hall's last two visits to Stratford-on-Avon, watching the glover's comings and goings with needled eyes.

The priest, Cuttle thought, was a purblind, arrogant fool. The glover was not. Hall seemed to think he could scuttle safe along a middle path, serving a dollop of treason here, a waft of gossip there and still continue to control his circumstances. The priest tried to sidle his way out of promises like a Bankside whore, speaking assurances and then prevaricating on others, as though treason could be a part-time occupation.

---

[24] Eating & drinking establishment

Cuttle hawked and spat into a puddle of urine at the edge of the road. He had followed the glover twice but the man was far more circumspect than the priest.

The spy felt the weight of his heavy, bone-hafted knife hanging from his belt. It would have been a pleasure to slit the priest's throat and dump his body to rot in a ditch but his instructions were to grant him enough rope to hand himself and follow where the fool led them. Cuttle was disappointed. Myriad days of shadowing the bastard had given him a healthy dislike for the Papist scum. Immersed beneath that thought, in a very small measure, he was secretly relieved. Killing a man of God, no matter if he was a damned Catholic or not, was chancy business.

He had been born in London. Raised by his uncle in a desultory fashion, Cuttle had embraced the vicious underbelly of London life, disdaining efforts to apprentice him to a local farrier in favour of more sordid activities. He had begun as a petty thief, one of London's roaring boys, before moving up to assume a role as the right-hand of one of Southwark's leading filch-men[25]. Even by London standards, Cuttle's ambitions made him a marked man. When he stabbed one of the Upright Men in a tavern brawl, he found himself with the choice of a bitter death in a squalid rookery or a hurried flight to the countryside.

The choice was made easier by the opportunity for well-paid employment. The London street lords would not live forever, and Cuttle knew his exile was always only a knife's edge away from ending. In the meantime, his current employer provided coin and some measure of vicious amusement.

Cuttle gulped warm ale and recalled his instructions. His employer had leaned back on his ornate carved chair. "Let Hall believe he has led us astray. Follow the letter. It will lead us to the Jesuit. Don't lose the letter. It will be critical to the success of our

---

[25] Criminals or thieves, generally referring to an organized gang rather than an independent petty thief.

endeavor. Once we know its destination, you may need to restore it to our possession." Cuttle had nodded. As he turned to leave the man commented with off-hand diffidence. "Kill whom you need to but try not to make it too"--the man paused--"dramatic."

That instruction had made Cuttle smile.

Kill whom you need, he thought. *Kill whom you need.*

He sipped his ale, humming to himself, content for now to watch the glover's house.

Chapter the Fourth

TYBURN CURSED, PULLING his hand back. Peering closely at the edge of his palm, he spotted the thin, dark sliver of wood embedded deep in the skin. He bit the protruding end and slowly pulled it out, spat the offending wood onto the floor and shoved the stubborn timber hard into place. He regarded the almost complete staging ruefully.

The hired players had the task of readying the stage area for the next day's performance, a job made much easier in Stratford by the not infrequent traffic of traveling troupes. The guild hall kept a set of worn wooden scaffolding in storage behind their barn which served as both an occasional construction platform for roof repairs and a makeshift stage for performances. The scaffold provided a raised stage and, when blocked off by a hanging canvas, a shallow tiering area for the players.

Tyburn surveyed the scaffold stage. It was almost time to raise the thin scenery curtain the troupe carried rolled up in their wagon. Once that task was completed, the day's work was done, except for the minor task of securing the wagon and costumes for the night. Robbie and the Muches would sleep in the barn to guard the troupe's costumes. The costumes, owned by Oldcastle and the other sharers, were the troupe's biggest single investment. They were worn and stained but rich and elaborate, gilded and heavy with intricate threadwork. Tyburn had been vehemently instructed in the importance of the costumes by Oldcastle when he first joined the troupe. "I can replace a player, but don't bloody well tear a single thread on these pieces, you whoresons, or I'll have you beaten raw," Oldcastle had growled.

Willens, always more helpful than Oldcastle, had explained to Tyburn that while mannerisms, stance and speech spoke to the nature of the character, costumes were the fastest way to establish the role an actor was performing, in particular to an unsophisticated audience. Most of the costumes of Worcester's Men were old cast-offs donated from monied patrons including the Earl of Worcester himself, who had turned over several out-of-style court outfits which Oldcastle had re-sized to fit his ample frame[26].

Alec swung himself up onto the boards and thumped down beside Tyburn, legs dangling. He grinned. "Time, I think, for some refreshment. Even Oldcastle wouldn't begrudge us that after this work."

Tyburn glanced at his friend, reflecting on Alec's unerring ability to disappear when the heavy labor began.

---

[26] Sumptuary laws in England at the time were quite specific on what fabric, style, and color of clothes were permitted. Clothing directly reflected one's position in society. In 1574 Queen Elizabeth passed the Statutes of Apparel stating *"The excess of apparel and the superfluity of unnecessary foreign wares thereto belonging now of late years is grown by sufferance to such an extremity that the manifest decay of the whole realm generally is like to follow."* The Sumptuary Laws existed for a number of reasons, not the least of which was to support the English textile and cloth industry at a time when exports were being severely curtailed by Spain. Players were, for all practical purposes, the only members of society exempted from the restrictions of the sumptuary laws and as such, were provided with far more social mobility than was common in most professions.

"Unless they're selling ale for alms, I'm out." He grunted, shoving a wooden pin into place to secure the stage boards.

'What?" exclaimed Alec in mock horror. "Reduced to begging for your pots? We can't have a player from Worcester's Men all amort[27]."

Tyburn stiffened and Alec spread his hands in innocence. "Don't get your stiff-necked pride out of place. You can earn your drink with this." Alec jingled his closed fist before turning over Tyburn's right hand and pouring several coins into it.

"And this is?"

"Oldcastle's latest errand, naturally given to me as he knows I'm the only one in this blessed troupe that can be trusted with money, by God's bones. We need some new bladders for the performance tomorrow as Much sat on the last one yesterday." He paused, grinning. "Can't think how that could have happened."

Alec's eyes twinkled as he continued. "Oldcastle gives money to me. I give it to you. You negotiate a stiff price for the wares and pocket the difference. Then you can join me in drunken revelry and we will sing wanton songs, gamble and curse the Precision bastards that inhabit this horrid little place!" He gazed at Tyburn, cocking one eyebrow.

Tyburn weighed the coins. Knowing Alec, he had probably dropped several extra into the allotment as his way of alleviating his friend's penury. A slow smile broke across Tyburn's face. "Bene booze awaits[28]," he said with a dry chuckle. "Just don't pull me into your dice game this time."

Alec laughed. "Drink, dice and women! The vices of soldiers and players alike. I would have thought you conversant with all three." Behind him Alleyn and Daniel began hoisting the thin scenery curtain over the crossbar.

---

[27] All amort = out of spirits
[28] Bene booze = literally "good drink" or strong liquor

"Oh, I'm conversant, believe me. I've been fleeced by so many Scots in Flanders, being fleeced by Englishmen is a pleasant change. I'll stick to Primero, being that you can't chop a card without getting caught.[29]"

"Coads!" interrupted Alleyn from his perch on the ladder, "you two want to stop cracking and help us get this bugger hoisted?"

"Coming, darling," cackled Alec. Tyburn laughed and both men climbed onto the staging to pull the curtain along the crossbeam.

Clair pushed the stray curls of her hair securely back under the starched white cap. She glanced down the long, dim, windowless kitchen where the potboy was feeding small nuggets of wood into the oven fire one after the other. The air smelled of woodsmoke, bread and spice. Looking back to the table she returned to kneading the heavy bread dough, turning it with practiced hands.

Her mother, she thought with wry memories, would not have approved. Beatrice deBrage had rarely set foot in the manor's extensive kitchen except to scold and upbraid the servants and cast a suspicious eye on the buttery and the larder for pilferage. Clair's mother had passed away several years before but throughout these ten months she had been back in the manor house, Clair still caught herself hesitating in guilty anticipation of a scolding.

Beatrice would have been scandalized that her daughter thought so little of her birthright as to work as a common scullery maid. Clair, however, enjoyed the kitchen, not the least because in winter it was the warmest part of the house, but also for the

---

[29] Primero = card game, "chop a card" = secretly change a card's location in the deck

comfortable companionship she found in cooking and preparing the day's food. It reminded her of her own kitchen for the brief few months her independence had lasted.

She paused; working the thick dense dough made her forearms ache. The kitchen servants were chatting while they worked, laughing in low tones and with an ease that Clair envied. Her role as the mistress of the household excluded her from much of the conversation, so she contented herself with listening to the cooks and the scullions delving into the latest gossip.

The house had been busy. Her father had hosted a number of court visitors over the past week, all of them traveling to Kenilworth in advance of the queen's annual summer progress. The queen and her multifarious household with all of its assorted servants, followers and hangers-on had inched its deliberate way through Warwickshire in a long, slow and heady pageant. The Earl of Leicester had decorated several miles of road with long silk banners hung from poles to help guide the queen's train to its destination. According to her father's guests, the earl's largesse had decorated only a small section of road. After the queen's retinue had passed, the earl's servants frantically removed the flags and raced ahead to adorn the next crossing.

Clair found this quite amusing and somewhat touching. It was said that this was the earl's decisive effort to pay court to the queen, a woman who routinely baulked at marriage and was notorious for keeping her many suitors in a state of perpetual uncertainty. Clair rather envied the queen's ability to forgo what was for most women a difficult and often insurmountable problem.

For herself, it was an ongoing pain. Time had dulled the ragged edge it had once possessed, whetting it down to a fine, keen sense of loss that clung like an unwelcome shade. Clair had married the son of an Oxfordshire landowner, a match her mother had arranged through her cousin, but one that despite its nature had blossomed into an honest and loving relationship. She found an endearing openness and an acceptance with James that had been lacking in the close confines of her own household. She had thrown herself into her married life with relish, anticipation and excitement.

It had lasted four months.

Her eyes stinging, Clair wiped her hands clean on her apron. *I will not cry,* she thought vehemently, *I will not.* Her thoughts were bleak, remembering the long slow weeks of wasting sickness; the hot, stifling room; her husband shivering with perpetual chills under four blankets, one soaked through with fever sweat; the bland assurances of the chirurgeon[30] claiming that bleeding would reduce the sanguine humours of the fever; the endless, foul-smelling poultices and possets[31] that failed to help; and the bitter realization that Fate's capricious wheel had turned, and no one could save him.

She wiped her eyes unobtrusively. *I will not cry.* She grew angry with herself for slipping back into self-pity. Clair found herself restored to her parents' house--unwilling, hurt and aching with a loss unlike any she had ever known.

Her father had not evinced such pain when her mother had passed. *Was it only women who felt such broken hurt?* She took note of the hard tinge of anger underlying the pain.

Under her father's roof it was no better. She felt like an exile within her own family home, the situation made all the worse by her having experienced a life beyond the confines of the manor.

She took a steadying breath. She had overheard one bright piece of news. According to one of the local cartmen, a troupe of players had arrived in Stratford and were going to be performing the Mayor's Play at the guild hall on the morrow.

She resumed kneading the dough. Stratford received troupes intermittently through the summer months, although so far

---

[30] Chirurgeon – A doctor or surgeon. It should be noted that this was quite different than a barber-surgeon who actually performed operations and was typically regarded as marginally above a butcher.
[31] Medicinal drinks

none had come since early May when Warwick's Men had performed in the guild hall. The few indulgences Clair allowed herself as a widow were reading poetry, riding, and, on those rare occasions when circumstance permitted, attending a play or musical performance. These last were few and far between and often dependent on her father's whims.

Clair set the completed bread dough on the flat wooden paddle, alongside three other loaves ready for the oven. She was making manchet, a fine, white bread that was much higher quality than the typical coarse, brown fare. Most households didn't have the ovens to bake their own bread and instead relied on local bakers either for their supplies or for access to the ovens to bake them in. The estate kitchen was well equipped. She looked up as a dark-haired, long-faced maid entered the kitchen, the girl's eyes darting about as she wrung her hands.

"Is there a problem?" Clair asked.

"My lady, your brother is here," the woman replied, "speaking with Henrietta. Outside."

Clair wiped her hands clean on the apron and headed at a brisk pace through the kitchen door, past the vestibule and out the arched heavy wooden doors that led into the back garden court. Clair's brother was leaning against the corner beam, bending down to talk to a young girl in her early teens. One gloved hand was reaching out to take the rim of the heavy wooden bucket she was hugging to her chest.

"Albert!"

The man's eyes flickered in Clair's direction, annoyance narrowing them imperceptibly. The hand released the edge of the wooden bucket. Albert kept his eyes locked on the girl's and cast a mere hint of a smile down at her. He straightened and looked towards Clair, the faintest color suffusing his face.

"Henrietta, you are needed in the kitchen. Now." Her flat tone brooked no disagreement. Henrietta headed inside, pausing to look back at Albert, who smiled a slow, languorous grin as the girl turned away.

Clair regarded her brother. Albert deBrage met her gaze with studied indifference, but Clair shivered despite the banked expression in his dark eyes. He was unruffled but she always felt a restless energy about him, a palpable and edgy vigor that made her nervous and wary. His expression broke into an abrupt and insincere smile at her discomfiture. One hand rested on the hilt of his ornate silver-hilted rapier.

"Cooking again, Clair? Why do we have servants, anyway?"

She wasted no time on niceties. "Albert, stay away from Henrietta. She does not require your attentions."

Albert laughed and lolled his head back, eyes glancing skyward. "That kitchen mort? Please, Clair, at least bear me the credit I'm due. I have no interest in the stewed prunes[32] from your kitchen, although she is younger than most of the rancid ones in your employ." He cocked his head as if contemplating other differences.

"I am sure you can find plenty of women outside of my kitchen maids." She said. Seeing his empty expression, she dropped her voice low and tight, barely audible. "If you touch any of my servants again, I will geld you with your own blade in your sleep."

Albert laughed. "What a shrew you are now in your sorrows, baiting about like a sparrow in an attic. You may keep your maids with their 'honor' intact," he commented off-hand. "Not because you threaten, but because I have other matters that demand my attentions. While you"--he noted the spatters of bread dough on her apron--"labour like a common scullion, I am planning a placement within court that will see our family ensconced as a leading party in Warwickshire, with all the emoluments that such a position accrues." He weighed her reaction, then added, "However, despite my own interests, I will not neglect my duties on your

---

[32] Brothel whores

behalf. Not the least of which is finding you a suitable match. Mull on that for a time, bereaved sister."

He disappeared through the court archway, whistling idly and scuffing his booted feet along the path.

Clair watched with a stoic gaze until he disappeared from sight and then let out a shaky breath. He was unpredictable, intemperate and dangerous at the best of times. Six years before Albert had killed his own man-servant in a supposed fencing accident at the London house. The man had inadvertently fallen onto the blade during a practice duel, a fact duly sworn to by the other servants present. The legal trial provoked a minor embarrassment for her father, as he was temporarily banished from court. Once the verdict was passed the stigma clouding the deBrage presence at court and in Warwickshire society vanished. Even the usual bravos who heckled and mocked most opportune scandals with unrelenting malice were warily silent on Albert's offence.

Clair turned back towards the kitchen. Henrietta would have to be sent away. She would have thought the girl too young to warrant her brother's attentions but obviously that was a mistake. Five maids, she thought bleakly, over four years. Two had vanished outright, their personal belongings packed and gone overnight, disappearing swiftly and completely--no hue and cry, the families silent and resentful when Clair had pried. "Gone away," they had claimed.

Another two, tight and silent, wrapped in their own thoughts, departed and disappeared into the London throngs. And the last one, Clair remembered, sent down as a thief, desolate, haunted and crying, gone to the Woodstreet Counter[33] and never heard from again.

---

[33] One of fourteen City of London prisons, the Woodstreet Counter primarily served debtors, misdemeanor offenders and petty thieves. It burned down in 1666 in the Great Fire of London.

She shivered.

Her brother. By Christ. What manner of man was he, she wondered.

Christopher Tyburn stepped to one side, deftly avoiding a thick, oozing dung heap that had been deposited on the verge of Henley Street. The offal pile was almost thigh-deep, thick with flies. A crooked bald man leaning askew on a small barrow leered a toothless grin at his discomfiture. "Tha's Watly's," he said gesturing off-hand at the waste. "He's a wort'less cullion, can't be bither'd ta cart his dung." He spat at the pile, just missing Tyburn's foot. "Alderma' be having his head soon n'off."

Tyburn grinned back. "You should see London. That's just a cobblestone." The crippled man waved off-hand as the player proceeded down the street. Kit paused at the small hanging sign with a painted glove that decorated the front of a substantial house. The timber-framed door bespoke a fair level of affluence. According to the proprietor of the Bear, the resident glover was a former mayor and current alderman.

Before Tyburn could knock, the door flew open and a young dark-haired boy holding a canvas-wrapped packet in one hand darted through the opening, wobbling sideways to avoid the player. The boy paused fleetingly to gape, open-mouthed, at Tyburn before turning down the roadway and heading towards the market. The boy kept angling his head back to scrutinize the player, almost stumbling into the noisome dung pile Tyburn had so carefully skirted.

A man with a thin beard and a well-rounded face stood in the door. He regarded Tyburn up and down with an appraising eye, noting the rich yellow half-cloak that Tyburn had appropriated from the costume store and the embroidered doublet beneath. "One of Worcester's Men, I daresay?" he asked. "What can I do for you? I am John Shakespeare, master glover."

"Master glover, we have need of your services." Tyburn pulled a sample bladder from his belt and the two men were soon deep in conversation.

Unnoticed by either man in the doorway, Cuttle set his worn leather tankard aside and slid to his feet from the bench. His narrow eyes followed Will from under his wide laborer's hat, noting the canvas packet Will clutched in one hand.

Lead on, boy, Cuttle thought darkly, *lead on.*

Chapter the Fifth

KIT TYBURN LEANED on the bench, his back pressing against the canted timbered wall, critically surveying the four pasteboard cards in his hands. A worn cyclopean knave of hearts gazed back, accompanied by two clubs, four hearts and a wistful diamond queen.

"Vie." Tyburn muttered, tossing several pennies into the pile on the table. "Bid primero thirty-two."

Willens, who when outside of his florid costume and offstage had the pale and cautious air of a destitute banker, regarded Tyburn with a judicious gaze. He tossed a handful of pence into the pot, laid his cards face-down on the table and drank a deep draught from his leather mug. "You sir, are an accomplished liar, a rogue and a vagabond." He considered his bid. "Primero forty-four. I'll see your vie."

Tyburn grinned and sipped his ale. Alec, sitting across from him on a low stool, gave his cards a bare glance before tossing his coins into the pile with studied indifference.

The negotiation with the glover had been stiff. Shakespeare had left Tyburn with just enough from the transaction to pay for his evening ale and stake his play in the game. He had played with caution, winning two minor hands early and skating past several others with minimal losses. A few more hands, he speculated, and he might have enough coin in his pocket to pay off his weekly allotment to Oldcastle.

"So, Warwick next for you fellows?" asked the fourth at the table, a long-nosed local Stratford merchant named Robert Deege. Deege dealt in the wool trade and in the course of three hands had subjected the players to a litany of bitter laments on wool prices, the state of the roads, government levies, wayward shipments, underweight tods, the poor quality of wool from Essex and the lamentable behavior of the Scots.

"Oh no," tutted Willens, "Warwick is right out for us I'm afraid."

"How so?" Deege's voice boomed . "It's a splendid town, much taken with plays and what-nots."

Alec chuckled. "Oldcastle doesn't get on with the Leicester's Men. A few years back we rolled through Lincoln when they were performing. They were doing . . . what's it called? That one with the devils?"

"Feist or some such nonsense," responded Willens, gulping his ale.

Alec nodded. "So, Oldcastle is very out of sorts over Leicester's boys eating our meats[34]. He dons the rags and makes himself a cacodaemon[35] and sneaks into the innyard when the performance is on."

Willens smiled. Tyburn rolled his eyes askance, having heard the tale before.

---

[34] Variant on an "eater of broken meats" as in eating the scraps from another's meal, or filching.
[35] Evil spirit

"So the scene has all Leicester's men dancing around, dressed as demons, tempting the King towards endangering his immortal soul." He paused for sip. One of the Stratford locals, sitting on the bench listening, surreptitiously crossed himself. "And suddenly they stop and they start looking around. Why? 'Cause there's one too many devils on stage." He laughed. "Leicester's Men start to get nervous and Cleve–playing the King–is pale as a spring moon and starts to panic. They got this extra . . . son of Cain, who's just standing there, smoking and reeking of sulphur, and they don't have a clue," he whooped, slapping one thigh.

"They called off the performance," Willens said. "Had to, Cleve shat himself." The audience laughed in appreciation. "They figured it out when they found out we had passed through. Sent Oldcastle a letter threatening to geld him, if he ever dared Warwick again."

"Probably an empty threat, "Alec said, "But our noble troupe leader values his pillicock[36] too much to darken Warwick again." Deege gave a sage nod, his jowly cheeks bobbing in accompaniment.

Tyburn gestured with impatience at the limp pasteboards in Deege's hand. "Your vie."

"By God's arms, so it is." Deege regarded his cards with deep suspicion, tapping his long nose absently. "Revie." He tossed a small silver coin onto the pile. "Bid primero forty-eight."

Tyburn looked at his cards. At best he had numerus[37] and the groat[38] irked him. It would take most of his remaining stake to cover Deege's vie. He could swigg[39], which would be the sensible course, given that Deege probably had at least numerus as well.

---

[36] Penis
[37] Two or three cards of the same suit
[38] Small silver coin
[39] Fold

Tyburn looked narrowly across the table at the corpulent merchant's face.

"Pass." Tyburn tossed two cards onto the table. Willens promptly dealt him another two. Tyburn picked up the pasteboards and glanced at them. He felt a low quiver of excitement. An ace and a court card, both hearts. Four hearts. A fluxus[40].

"I'll see your vie . . and revie." Tyburn tossed his remaining pennies onto the pile. "Bid supremus fifty-five."

Willens burst out laughing. "By God's bowels, you must have a low opinion of your friends, Kit! You weave some performance at the card table at least. I'll swigg as my hand is emptier than my tankard."

Alec glared at Tyburn. "I'll see your vie, Kit. By the sweat on your brow, you are carrying nothing more than a primero[41], and lucky to have that is my guess."

Deege glanced from one to another, and then looked down at his own cards. "Pass for one." He tossed a card onto the table. Willens dealt another pasteboard. Alec watched with interest as Deege pulled out another silver groat and flipped it onto the pile. "Revie." His drawl was cold as he glared at Tyburn across the table.

Tyburn looked at the coins. His stomach clenched in anger. The bastard was trying to buy the pot. He could hear the blood rushing in his ears and feel a faint lightness in his head. The world narrowed to a tight, cohesive focus. His face betrayed nothing. He raised his eyes, meeting Deege's. "Unfortunately, Master Deege, I have no further coin."

The clink of several coins interrupted him. "I'll stand for Kit's vie," said Alec. "I'll swigg and then we'll see how the cards fall."

Tyburn looked expressionless at Alec and shrugged.

---

[40] Flush, four cards of a suit
[41] One card of each suit

"Well Master Deege, you have a hand to show?" Alex suggested.

"Supremus sixty-seven," Deege said in triumph, laying the ace, six and seven of clubs and a two of diamonds on the table.

Alec made a show of goggling in amazement before turning to Willens. "Ha! Told you he was in Fate's graces."

Tyburn flipped his cards onto the table. "Fluxus fifty."

It was Deege's turn to goggle in astonishment at the painted cards. His corpulent face flushed dark.

"Well, you're a better performer than I credited, Kit," Willens said into the momentary silence.

Deege flushed darker and reached for the coins. Alec caught the man's hand before it could touch the pile. "I really wouldn't." Alec leaned down and whispered something quiet into Deege's ear. Tyburn couldn't hear what he said but the wool merchant paled and slowly pulled back his hand as if extricating it from a trap. He shoved back his stool and stood, glowered at Tyburn with accusatory eyes, turned and walked out the door.

"What did you say to the poor fellow?" Tyburn asked, raking his small pile of copper and silver into his purse.

"I told him where you got your name." Alec said with a chuckle, "There are advantages to being named after a place of execution, you know. Now you can kindly split a portion of your winnings with Jacob and me for throwing you that sheep in the first place."

"Be a long time before he chances his hand at cards with a playing company again," noted Willens. "That was a nice bit of conveyance[42], by Heaven."

"Don't tell Oldcastle we're fleecing locals or he'll lift a cut and thump us for good measure," grunted Tyburn.

---

[42] Trickery

Alec smiled lasciviously. "I don't expect we'll see him or the Bear's maid until tomorrow."

"I can't think where he gets the strength. Radishes?" Tyburn quipped in response.

Willens laughed, running one hand ostentatiously through his thin grey hair. "Oldcastle and I might be grey on top but it still stands to when it's needed."

Tyburn counted out a handful of coins for his compatriots and handed them over. "Here," he said, "I've got to go pluck a rose.[43]" Both men turned and, still trading barbs, pushed across the common room to join Alleyn and Motely.

Tyburn stepped out through the open door. The Bear didn't have a proper innyard like its larger cousin across the street, the Swan. The common room opened out onto Butt Lane, paralleling the drifting waters of the Avon. The sun was pushing long shadowy fingers towards the river. Two swans glided along the near bank, a mated pair pursued with ardent attention by a short procession of cygnets.

Tyburn walked into the adjacent alleyway to relieve himself against the side of the inn. From the foul stench that permeated the alley, this was the common practice among visitors.

"Ha, you cursed little flick[44]. Hold still!" The shout drifted down the laneway where Tyburn stood. Curious, he moved down the lane to where it opened up into a small intersection. A small collection of rough benches littered with leather tankards outside of a low house marked the location as a cheap ordinary. A woodpile stood alongside one wall, extending several feet from the adjacent lane.

"Come here, you poxed bastard!" A low, wide man in a broad-brimmed hat and farm laborer's clothes yanked hard, pulling

---

[43] Urinate
[44] thief

a boy out from behind the woodpile. A second man stood, arms akimbo, glowering down at the thief.

"I'm going to bleed you boy, for trying to take what's mine." The standing man's voice was chill and dry.

From the shadowy recesses of the laneway Tyburn glanced at the youngster, recognizing the dark-haired boy with the high forehead and clever eyes. The glover's son.

Will was terrified. His stomach knotted with tension and hot tears blurred his vision. The man's hand was rough and tight and holding his arm in a vise-like grip. The man yanked again, holding Will high, so his feet barely touched the ground.

Will thought bitterly, *How could you have been so stupid?*

Will had set out through the yellow afternoon, pleased to have evaded his afternoon lessons and the tedious task of sorting wool in his father's barn. He was positive he could spin a convincing enough tale for his father to account for why the short walk to Shottery had taken most of the afternoon. He set off at a fast pace, ducking through the winding laneways and back alleys, cutting across Back Lane and through the line of lofty elms that marked the road. He cut across the fields and picked up the walking path west.

After delivering the letter and the package to Master Sturley's small farm on the outskirts of Shottery, Will had meandered down to a quiet tree-shielded stretch of the Avon and hunted for frogs in the marshy bend of the riverbank before returning late to Stratford and the toil of the wool barn. His father had pounced and enquired if the package had been delivered. Once he had heard Will's assurances, John Shakespeare had thanked Will and walked back to his worksop, a distracted look on his face.

The disconnect had continued through dinner, with his father forgetting the blessing and saying little beyond grunts at the table. Will had taken advantage of his father's seeming deep thinking and contrived to slide out of the house once the meal was complete. Will had met up with Richard and both boys had determined to slip over to the Bear to listen in on the stories of the visiting players.

While ducking through the noisome alley that abutted Sheep Street, Will froze at the sight of a stout, lank-haired man in a worn farming smock. He was carrying a small buff-colored letter in one hand. Will stopped so suddenly that Richard plowed into him from behind, almost toppling Will into the greenish muck that coated the lane.

"Od rat it, Will! Why'd you stop?"

Will made a violent shushing gesture. "Shut it!" He stared after the man and his companion. They pulled back a couple of benches at the ordinary and called to the server for tankards. The letter had been tossed on the bench but Will could see the irregular red dab of wax sealing the letter and his own neat, curling penmanship just below.

His father's letter, he thought.

Will looked at the two men. Neither man was familiar to him but that was not unusual. Stratford had more than its share of itinerant day laborers passing through, heading to Warwick and Coventry, and the usual slovenly cursitors[45] that traipsed in on the road seeking work. Most were only around for a short period until the haymaking was finished, and then, lacking any permanent status, were pushed onto the next parish by the bailie[46].

Will chewed the inside of his lip. His father had been quite concerned about the delivery of the package, and Will knew enough about gloves and the Sturleys to recognize that his father's concerns had to have been about the letter. Sturley valued his cows well above his wife; he would never deign to spend coin on gloves for her.

"C'mon, Will," Richard hissed with impatience. "Let's go!"

---

[45] Wanderer, vagabond or tramp
[46] Bailiff or Constable's Officer

Will shook his head. "No. That's my father's letter. I don't know how they ended up with it, but I need to get it back."

"Will, you're daft! They'll thump you raw, or turn you over to your father and he'll thump you raw! Let's go."

"No. Meet me over at the woodyard. I'm going to get that letter back." Will began to sidle up the alleyway, using the dark shadow of the woodpile for cover. With luck, he could just reach out from the end of the pile and pluck the letter off the bench before either man could notice it was gone.

Richard watched with nervous eyes for a moment and then ducked back down the lane, shaking his head in disbelief. *Will was a polestar for trouble*, he thought. *Best to put some distance between him and his foolishness.* He would meet Will at the woodyard and hoped, for once, Shakespeare's reckless confidence wouldn't be misplaced.

Stupid, Will thought through the pain, as his arm was yanked even higher. He stood as high as he could on his tiptoes, trying to relieve the grating tension on his arm. Abruptly the man pulled his head back by his hair.

"Hullo. It's the glover's son," the other man said. "I'm not sure a beating will suffice. This one'd caulk on us quick."

"That's my father's letter," Will hissed through clenched teeth.

"Is that so? Well, it's my letter now, ain't it, little flick?" the first man replied, breathing sour ale into Will's face.

Cuttle regarded Will with a face carved from flint. "Bust up that jaw nice and he won't say a word." He pushed his ill-fitting hat back, stepped forward to where Will dangled impotently and drew back one hand.

"I think," a voice intoned, "it might be best for you to let go of the boy."

Cuttle turned. Tyburn was leaning against side of the tavern, inspecting one hand casually.

Cuttle looked the player up and down, weighing the finely cut yellow cloak, the broad feathered hat and the foppish doublet.

"Best for you to go back to your jakes[47], Cully, and stay out of our business."

Kit wasn't sure why he had decided to intervene. Petty thieves and draw-latches were a penny a pound in London and beatings were the common currency of punishment. He had walked past far worse without turning his head or breaking his stride and, God knows, he thought, the horrors he had seen in the streets of Haarlem and the little Dutch towns of the Lowlands made almost any punishment these men were preparing to mete out pale by comparison. But something about the boy's fine features and his dark, almost hooded eyes caught his eye. Kit sighed to himself. *Damn me for tilting at vapors.*

Cuttle turned away from the player with a final disdainful glance but froze at the slow rasping sound of a sword being drawn. He turned back.

Tyburn reached out with his blade and speared the fallen letter, lifting it up to his left hand. "What do we have here?" he asked diffidently, peering at the envelope and its embossed wax seal.

"That's mine, Cully!" grated Cuttle.

"Really?" Tyburn drawled the word with deliberate laziness. "You didn't strike me as the literary type." He pulled the letter off the tip of his rapier. Cuttle watched the sword until Tyburn clumsily sheathed it.

"Give over," Cuttle growled as he reached for it with his left hand, "or I'll plant that play-actor face of yours in the dungheap." He took a cautious step forward, wary of the sheathed sword but feeling emboldened by the man's obvious lack of skill with the blade.

"Certainly," Tyburn began, "a fellow of your obvious force utterly effaces one's vigor to resist." He extended the letter.

---

[47] Privy or toilet

Satisfied, Cuttle strode forward and reached for the folded parchment.

Tyburn stepped in with a quick, lithe motion and slammed his right foot into Cuttle's groin with sickening force. Caught by surprise, Cuttle staggered. Two hands grasped his jerkin and the alleyway spun as Kit cut the legs out from under him and ground him into the fetid soil of the laneway.

Dazed, Cuttle tried to haul himself upright as a booted foot crushed into the back of his neck, pressing his face into the dirt.

"You whoreson, you'll bleed out for that 'un!" The other man threw the boy to one side and came towards him with a hissing oath.

Tyburn moved back two paces and waited. The air of languid indifference he had carried was gone. To an outside observer the transformation was startling. Tyburn had transmuted from indolent bystander to something much more predatory and refined. He had the keen look of a hunting hawk, just loosed from a gauntlet, arcing high before a stoop.

It was all about waiting.

Flanders had been damp and cold and dull and dangerous. The motley collection of soldiers in the Lowlands that made up the small English expedition under Morgan and Gilbert had been a mélange of ex-Sea Beggars[48], Prussian mercenaries, English soldiers-of-fortune and rake-hell adventurers, leavened with a healthy mix of brutal Scottish Highlanders and amoral Dutchmen. They were hard, cruel and unscrupulous men, men who prized loot, fighting, drink and women. They were routinely drunk, undisciplined, licentious and lice-ridden. They fought among themselves almost as much as they fought the Spaniards but fight they did. They had honed their belligerent skills in the dank and stony streets of

---

[48] Sea Beggars – the name assumed by the Calvinist opposition to the Spanish rule of the Netherlands. They mostly operated as coastal pirates, raiding the Spanish, until they captured the port of Brill in 1572.

Edinburgh and Haarlem, in the hard arenas of clan warfare and on the chill decks of the Dutch brigand fleet.

In their ranks, Tyburn had been well-schooled.

The man stepped forward, looking to close fast and pull the interloper off balance, to reach out with his massive calloused hands and break this bastard player.

Waiting was over.

Tyburn sidestepped and slammed his open hand into the lunging man's throat. The man gagged and choked, both hands inadvertently pulling away from their intended target. Tyburn's booted foot raked down his instep causing him to lurch forward, his advance turning into a painful stumble, Tyburn arced a hard closed left fist into the man's right ear and followed it with another into his stomach. As his opponent bent over, Tyburn levered his arm and slammed him headfirst into the cornerpost with a sickening crack.

The man fell like a brick.

Cuttle glared up at the player and rose, head swimming. One hand dropped to his belt, grasping the bone hilt of his dagger.

Tyburn regarded Cuttle with a chary stare and flipped back his yellow cloak, tapping the hilt of his rapier. "That's a path you don't want to tread, friend," he said in a mild tone, shaking his head.

Cuttle spat red-tinged spittle into the dirt and measured the distance between them with a cautious eye. Recognizing the futility of facing a rapier with the short blade, he relaxed his hand and stepped back.

Behind Tyburn a chorus of voices within the tavern began to sing an uneven medley. "A cup of wine, that's brisk and fine, Come drink and join our song-a..."

Cuttle reached down and pulled his compatriot to his feet. The man swayed unsteadily and Cuttle pushed him to the wall. He reached for the letter, but a booted foot slid forward and stood on it.

"Leave it." The words were flat. Deadly and flat.

"It's mine," Cuttle said through gritted teeth.

"Really?" Tyburn asked, a mocking smile on his face. "What does it say? You can read it, can't you?"

The song from the tavern continued. "And drink until the Leman mine; And a merry heart lives long-a..." Tyburn could pick out the thin, wavering voice of Motely deep in his cups.

Cuttle flushed, his face dark with anger. Tyburn caught the man's eye for an instant. Something sparked red in the depths like a glint of slivered glass, a promise from the Furies.

"Bing a waste[49]," Tyburn said coldly, "Back to your pots, or by God's Mercies, I'll leave you feeding the crows."

"This isn't ended, Play-actor." Cuttle said turning away and shoving his companion ahead of him down the alleyway. "Not by half, it isn't. Another time."

"Fill the cup and let it come, I'll pledge you a mile to th' bottom." The sound drifted with lazy tones through the warm evening air.

The two men disappeared and Tyburn let out a long breath. He picked up the letter from the dirt. Aside from some smudges and a neat tear where his sword had speared it, it was unharmed. Tyburn glanced around. The boy was long gone, vanished into the growing twilight during Tyburn's brief altercation.

Kit shrugged and slid the letter inside his doublet. He would return the letter to the glover later, after tomorrow's performance. He turned back to the Bear, grinning at the roaring bellow of Alec's voice cutting through the others.

"Let's drink until the cup is done; Who joins us not; God rot him!"

The last line was roared out in a dubious chorus a second time by the players as Tyburn rejoined the throng in the common room.

---

[49] Bugger off, to leave.

66

Chapter the Sixth

"I F YOU WILL learn to condemn God and all his laws, to care neither for heaven nor hell, and to commit all kind of sin and mischief . . ." The shout echoed off of the light stony face of the Stratford guild hall, causing heads to turn and necks to crane up and down the street. "You need go to no other school, for all these good examples you may see painted before your eyes in *plays*." The white-haired, black-frocked man spat the last word with vehemence at the passersby.

"Will not a filthy play, with the blast of a trumpet, sooner call thither a thousand, more than an hour's tolling of a bell bring to a sermon a hundred? It is a tool of Hell's foul master. It pulls servants from their masters, apprentices from their labors and parts maids from their virtues."

"He's good," Alec remarked, watching the dark-frocked Puritan hector the crowd. "Watch how he pauses to catch their eye. Good projection, powerful intonation . . . by Jesu the man's a natural!"

Tyburn chuckled. The two men were sitting on a low wall watching the townsfolk gathering for the Mayor's play. "Best we recruit him before Warwick's Men do."

A lock of long white hair had pulled loose and hung down across the Puritan's forehead and eyes. He flicked it back contemptuously and flung his hand skyward, as if by sheer force of will he could pull the heavenly spheres themselves down to earth. "Is it not true that of sloth comes pleasure, of pleasure comes spending, of spending comes whoring, of whoring comes lack, of lack comes theft, of theft comes hanging, and there is an end of this world?" He shouted the last at a pair of apprentices who were mounting the guild hall steps. The two young men hastened inside to escape the harangue.

"This is good stuff," continued Alec, "You really ought to be paying attention."

"He's cribbed it from the *Arte of Rhetorique* and one of Stockwood's sermons," Tyburn noted absently. His observation met with a dense silence from Alec until he raised his head and looked at the blond man. Alec was shaking his head in slow, mocking scorn.

"How in Heaven's name do you remember that?" Alec asked. "And more important, why?"

"You mean you don't? What exactly did you study at Oxford, anyway?"

Alec gazed skyward thoughtfully, as though seeking whatever the Puritan had been grasping for in the vast cerulean blue. "Drinking." He paused. "Whoring." He waited another beat. "Gambling. That pretty much covers the essentials, I should think."

"As long as you've mastered the essentials . . .".

Alec gave him a sidelong look of pity. "Christopher Tyburn, clinging to his sense of reason and rationality like a priest on a whore's bare tit."

Tyburn shook his head. "We'd best get inside before Oldcastle has a fit." The two men stood. Alec ducked through the low side-doorway into the dark timbered guild hall.

Tyburn paused, his movement arrested.

A woman was gliding through the milling crowd on the street, parting it with a natural ease, trailed by her maid. She was tall and graceful, wearing a simple patterned dress but the cut and the material was expensive. She wore a French hood over her hair, which although pinned, spilled out over her neck in artful auburn-red curls. She turned her head and gazed steadily in Tyburn's direction for a moment. He glimpsed pale eyes, assessing, observing and weighing the world. Pale they might be but he sensed they disguised a warmth and depth that was unshared with the casual observer. He watched as she threaded past the white-haired demagogue on the steps who paused in his railing long enough to warrant a swift nod and smile from the woman. She glided past, up the steps and into the guild hall.

The white-haired man resumed his Puritan harangue but Tyburn didn't listen. He stared at the guild hall doorway and exhaled long and slow, aware from the tightness in his chest that he had been holding his breath. Stratford was full of surprises.

Will's eyes felt hot and gritty and filled with sand. He had not slept. After slipping out of the altercation the previous night without retrieving his father's letter, he had crept home filled with trepidation and still shaking from his narrow escape. He knew his father was involved with recusants in and around Stratford. On rare occasions they would meet in the Shakespeares' commodious kitchen, discussing the various pronouncements that trickled down from London and the church and how to best manage the tricky knife's edge that lay between obedience to the Crown and the eternal damnation of one's own immortal soul.

Will would betimes sit quiet in the corner, listening to their deliberations, perched high on the edge of the heavy wooden sidetable like a bird limed on a branch until his father invariably noticed him and ushered him from the room, whereupon he would loiter in the hall outside the door, listening with one ear cupped to the thin wall. The immediacy of the Crown's proclamations tended to win out and the recusants dealt with their hidden faith through a practical and expedient outlook that, to outside eyes, bordered on hypocrisy.

A significant number of Stratford families remained quiet practicing Catholics, while overtly manifesting a Protestant façade. They hid their Catholicism behind a silent and impassive mask. Most of the locals, with a handful of Puritan exceptions, accepted the façade without question or query, recognizing it was better to bow to the inevitable and not enquire too stringently as to the depth of any one person's faith. Given the turbulence of the last few years, the rise and fall of the nobility and the Crown seemed malevolently shackled to the Wheel of Fate. It seemed only inevitable that the Wheel would turn and England would return to the True Faith. The queen herself often chose a middle path, disdaining the Puritan calls for stronger measures against the Catholics.

At least until the pope made his pronouncements on the heresy of the queen.

Pius V's *Regnans in Excelsis* bull had declared Elizabeth a heretic. The inevitable fruit of the Pope's declaration was that allegiance to the Catholic faith was now seen as a definitive act of betrayal of the Crown, and manifested in rebellion against the queen herself. Recusancy, once merely problematic and expensive, was now treasonous and subversive. The very act of having a child baptized or the dying shriven became a hushed, secretive ceremony, fraught with peril. Fines were the least of the worries. Treason hung like a cloud over all of the minor crimes of recusancy, a shrouded path that ended at the rack, the noose, and the dull rust-flecked pikes abutting London Bridge.

Will shivered at the thought. He had to find that letter. The only one who knew what may have happened was Sturley.

He slid out of his bed in the grey light and dressed hurriedly, careful not to wake Gilbert. He crept on silent feet down the stairs and out the back, skirting past his father's noisome tanning vat. Will could hear the faint trundle of a cart along Henley Street but otherwise Stratford was just beginning to stir. The short burbles of song thrushes welcoming the thin dawn threaded through the trees as Will slid past the barn, scrambled over the low stone wall and cut across the fields for Shottery. The light was low, flat and unyielding.

Will was nervous. He knew the proper thing to do, the sensible thing to do, would be to tell his father about the letter. Will's face grew hot at the thought of explaining the loss to his father and how he had failed to retrieve it. And now it was in the hands of a player! Will knew as well as anyone that players, however entertaining they might be, were base and wretched individuals given to excess, appetite and vanity. They were, he had been informed, lower than the lowest beggar, purveyors of a ruinous profession.

And now one of them had his father's letter.

Will angled off the road, heading towards Sturley's small farm, located about half a boggy mile from the Shottery village. He clambered over a weed-covered wall, and pushed through Sturley's small grazing plot across to the barn. The sun, burning through the low clouds, was pushing shadows westward across the chalky rutted roadway.

He was never sure afterwards what made him stop. It was the faintest of noises, a mere suggestion of rhythm and timbre in the far-off voice that made him pause. A shiver ran up his spine as he recognized the man from the alleyway. Will froze and then looked around. He ducked into the open stable and slid into a darkened and empty stall piled with dusty hay. The foul aroma suggested that Sturley hadn't been cleaning the stall out properly but Will paid it no heed, ducking low and pulling straw from the pile behind him to bury himself from view.

The voices grew in volume.

"...can't just leave 'im," a man's muffled voice concluded. Will lay breathless in the dry straw, the light granules of dust making his eyes water and his throat catch. Motes danced in the

71

sunbeams now angling through the slats of the barn, spinning and circling in a slow whirl. He listened, hearing Cuttle's sharp reply.

"Some nosy bastard will find 'em. By Christ," Cuttle swore. "Why'd you have to work him so hard? We needed him to talk. He doesn't do us any good caulked off."

The other man became defensive. "I warned 'im. I tol' 'im to tell us where 'twere bound. Could jus' leave 'im up?"

"No. We don't want the magistrates poking about. What about the woman?"

"She's a dead 'un."

"Bene. We'll toss the place, get him in there and torch the lot."

"What about the letter?"

"Bastard player has it. We'll tickle him and get it back." Cuttle brooded momentarily. "Where's that cozening Jesuit nesting--that's the question. We need that 'un, he's the key . . and you, stupid bastard, took off the only 'un that can steer us to him." Cuttle glared daggers at his compatriot.

The man wilted visibly. "I tol' you it weren't my fault. deBrage tol' me to work 'im . . .." The man's voice trailed off in the face of Cuttle's wrathful glance.

"Well now you know the drift[50], so keep to it or I'll serve you like you served him."

The voices faded as they moved towards the house.

Will tentatively raised his head from the hay pile. He slowly clambered out, feeling the brittle stalks snapping beneath his weight. . Limbs stiff and nearly numb, he felt spent, his hands cold with sweat and shaking. He took in a deep shuddering breath. And then another. His heart had slowed to almost normal as he made to leave the stable.

The creak of the rope gave him a start.

---

[50] Scheme or plan

Will turned.

The body hung free, secured by a rope tightly crimped and knotted under its arms. It swung slow, pivoting in the early morning light. It was Sturley.

His toes brushing the ground drew a faint tracery in the dirt, a morbid pendulum swinging in the subdued light that filtered through the stable. Dried blood coated one side of his head, matting the shock of hair. His eyes were bare slits, the whites swollen and egg-like beneath their lids. His mouth was slack and loose.

Will took a step back and then hesitated. He gathered himself and edged forward, leaning down to peer up at Sturley's battered face.

"Master Sturley?" Will stammered. "Master Sturley? Can you hear me?" The coppery scent of blood hung in the air.

Sturley's head twitched and rolled. Sturley mumbled something too low for Will to hear.

"What's that?" Will whispered, leaning in.

". . . r . . . r . . . run." Sturley said in a faltering gravel-filled voice. "Run, boy."

Will turned and ran back to the stable stall, scrambling through the wooden beams and slipping deep into hiding. Seconds later Cuttle and his accomplice entered the stable again and crossed to where Sturley hung insensate.

Cuttle paused, took one judicious glance around and then gestured at the other man to lay hold of Sturley's dangling body.

"Got 'em?" Cuttle asked. The man grunted an affirmative and Cuttle sliced the taut hemp with his knife. Sturley slumped boneless over the other man's shoulder and moaned.

"Shut it, you purblind wretch," the man grumbled under Sturley's considerable bulk.

Cuttle pulled Sturley's head back with a yank and glared into his battered face. "Should have told me what I needed to know, cullion, and you be dying a sight easier. What's that God-cursed Jesuit to you anyway? Just another Papist bastard who gets you to die for him. You'll be toasting 'cause of him." Sturley was beyond making any reply. His eyes had rolled back and stared sightless to one side. Will shuddered and closed his eyes tight lest Cuttle feel their scrutiny.

The two men moved out of the stable, hefting the dead weight of the body. Cuttle kept wary watch for any visitors. The moment they disappeared from view, Will slid back out of the stall and dashed in the opposite direction, heading for the pasture. He threw himself over the low stone wall, his back pressing hard against the mossy grey stone. The rough surface scraped his back through his thin shirt but he paid it no heed. He jammed one hand into his mouth to muffle any wayward sound as tears streamed down his face. Behind him, dense black smoke began to billow out of the farm cottage windows while flames rose to lick at the dry thatched roof. Within minutes, the structure was a mass of red flame. Faint shouts of alarm arose from Shottery and a distant bell began to peal.

By that time, Will was well across the flat sheep pasture, running as fast as his eleven-year-old legs could manage.

He did not look back.

Chapter the Seventh

TYBURN SLIPPED OFF the boards, dropping neatly into the narrow tiering space the troupe had set up behind the makeshift stage and the curtain.

Oldcastle was still resolutely declaiming the play's finale on the makeshift platform to an attentive Alec while Willens, dressed as Tom Bedlam, scurried about in a last capering and mocking jig around the pair. Tyburn pulled the stylized half-mask off and mopped the beads of sweat from his forehead with a damp sleeve. The room was hot and the air moist and heavy but Tyburn felt the usual rush of exhilaration after a successful performance. He always felt lofty and elevated, as if a great weight had slipped, Atlas-like, off of his shoulders. Vice had been agreeably seen off, the Virtuous Youth restored to the path of Righteousness, Bedlam banished from the stage and order restored. All that remained was for the beauteous maiden to sidle onstage to be joined in betrothal to Virtue.

The youngest and most fresh-faced of the apprentices, was pushed up onto the boards behind the curtain by Daniel and Alleyn. Motely, whose innocent and beardless face masked a lecherous soul that would have given pause to a Southwark punkaterro[51], had his voluminous skirt bundled in his arms to ensure it did not catch on the stage boards. Once secure in his footing, he dropped the material, smoothed it out so it fell properly and stepped with delicate grace through the curtain to take Alec's hand.

Oldcastle as Mercury, resplendent in his gold half-mask, ornate trim and a silvery cloak, gave a final rhetorical flourish and the four principles bowed deep to the audience. Shouts of approval, cheers and several lewd asides directed at Motely arose along with a genial burst of laughter at the unfortunate Bedlam, who, blinded by his oversize hat, wandered the small stage in confusion instead of departing with the others. Willens pulled the hat off, cut a vigorous stomping jig that rattled the stage boards, and evinced a hearty wave before dropping behind the stage. Robbie darted forward and gathered up several small coins that had been tossed onto the boards in appreciation.

The tiering area was crowded. Tyburn gave his friend Alec a quick slap on the arm and slid along the wall until he was clear of the stage. Much the Younger scrambled around the edge of the stage, fetching both lanterns used to help light the stage area. In truth, the guild hall offered only marginally better facilities than most innyards. On a fine summer day, protection from the elements was unnecessary and the guild hall windows, even flung wide, allowed less light than the performers preferred. The elevated staging was beneficial, giving the standing audience a better view of the performance, but the makeshift stage was too narrow for more than a handful of the company at one time. The most useful aspect

---

[51] Pimp or purveyor of "punks" - prostitutes

of performing at this venue was the lack of a ready supply of drink for the players, Tyburn thought with amusement. Oldcastle was quick to dock pay from anyone that performed poorly due to drunkenness. More than one performance had gone disastrously awry due to some cheap nappy ale[52] or bastard lire.[53]

The room was emptying, as most of the audience except the well-off had been standing for the performance. Three rows of benches had been set up for sitting customers, and they had been full. Tyburn found his gaze drifting back to the cool-eyed woman with the auburn hair who had sat, rapt, throughout the performance in the second row. Early on he realized that she must have been familiar with the play. His sharp eyes caught her mouthing several lines silently to herself. Granted, the play was a performance staple, so it would have been unsurprising if she had not seen it or a version of it, but it was still rare to find anyone who knew the lines by heart.

Through the thinning crowd Tyburn caught sight of Oldcastle pushing his way past the dregs of the audience in pursuit of one of the Stratford aldermen who was beating a swift retreat to the door. The alderman's exit was somewhat problematic due to Jack and Mundy obstructing his path. Tyburn slid along the far wall and leaned against the doorway, effectively stoppering up the only alternate escape. The alderman, turning away from Jack and Mundy, froze momentarily at the sight of Tyburn, still costumed in his darkly ominous role as Vice, idling sliding his rapier up and down in its sheath while whistling tunelessly.

Oldcastle, his round face effecting an affable and genial aspect, approached the town official with an ambling and deceptively casual walk and bowed.

---

[52] Strong ale
[53] Sweet Spanish wine

"My dear sir, I trust you found some enjoyment in our performance?"

The man paused before replying in measured words. "Master Oldcastle, you and Worcester's Men were"--he halted, as if searching for the appropriate phrasing--". . . adequate. It was . . . satisfactory. As we indicated, you are free to hold two more performances, at charge, within the precincts of the hall. I wish you a fine day."

The alderman turned as if to leave but Jack stood in his path. He was staring past the alderman, eyes fixed on some distant space high above the alderman's left shoulder. He looked like an insensate mountain. The alderman paused, deflated, and Oldcastle spoke again.

"Kind sir, does your town have no largesse to spare for a troupe such as ourselves?" Oldcastle pitched his voice louder, drawing the attention of the departing audience with his next words. "It is common tradition and courtesy to offer a remittance to performers." He dropped his voice with ominous emphasis. "Even adequate ones."

The alderman paused and looked nervously about the room.. Tyburn grinned. The other aldermen had disappeared in haste, leaving their compatriot alone on the field. The remnants of the audience were watching with evident curiosity, including the tall woman and her rather horse-faced maid, who whispered to each other. The alderman nodded a slow and painful acquiescence. He pulled a small purse from under his ornate belt and counted a handful of coins.

"For your performance. Nine shillings." he muttered and upended the cupped hand over Oldcastle's outstretched palm. He turned to leave.

Oldcastle glanced down at his hand and without a pause called "Sir!"

The alderman stopped and turned. Oldcastle stepped forward, raising one hand to silence the chattering crowd. "Sir," he spoke again, but turned as he did to indicate that he was speaking to all of those present. "I was unaware that so rich a town as Stratford-Upon-Avon, famed for the quality of its wool and its malt and the acuity of its merchants, was so full of sorrow, poverty and woe." Oldcastle's voice was deep and sonorous, projecting even into the street outside. Curious faces peered through the doorway.

With a touch of aggrieved asperity, the alderman replied, "What are you blathering about?"

Oldcastle paused and then raised the hand holding the coins. "To think that your town is so poor as to be unable to properly recompense a wayward band of players . . nay, I can but think of your pain, of the children suffering for their bread." The alderman's lips thinned. Oldcastle continued, gesturing to the watchers, "The kind alderman has proffered us nine shillings, but given the obvious lack you suffer, particularly the aldermen"-- Oldcastle rubbed a hand over his stout belly--"I am loathe to take it. I understand that your poverty before God has made you, shall I say, lacking in pride . . and other manly roles." Oldcastle made a lewd gesture, hidden from the alderman. The audience, now laughing openly, began to jeer the man. The woman hid her smile behind her hand.

Oldcastle raised his hands palms out, to quiet the watchers. "Nay. Such generosity cannot be countenanced. Please, sir, do take back your *nine* shillings, until such time as you can suffice to reward visitors with generosity more suitable to one's pride and station."

The alderman stood still, anger playing across his face. His lips were thin and tight. He reached down and pulled out his purse, pouring out another handful of coins. "No sir, I see that I have miscounted. Allow me to correct the arrears with another five." Oldcastle cocked one eyebrow. ". . . Six," the man continued in a tight voice, correcting himself, "shillings."

"Such munificence! Surely you are blessed by Christ our Savior himself." Oldcastle jingled the coins in his closed fist, bent his head and bowed low, with an elaborate flourish of the white and gold feathered mask he still held in one hand. The alderman, his eyes glacial, stepped past and with short, clipped steps hastened through the door and moved down the street.

"Fifteen. Not bad," observed Jack.

Tyburn grunted agreement. "He'll charge it back to the town corporation as eighteen shillings and pocket three as well as his expense. Bastard merchants." He turned back to the stage only to be stopped by a slight tug on his cloak.

"Your pardon, captain, a word?" Tyburn turned. The man was short with a round and genial face perched atop a wide colored ruff that was the size of small dinner platter. He wore a dark hat adorned with a russet band and a worn curling feather. Small beads of sweat speckled his brow.

"I am so very pleased to make your acquaintance! I understand from Master Oldcastle's introduction that you recently served in the Low Countries."

"Yes." Tyburn conceded with reluctance. Oldcastle routinely exaggerated his troupe's background when introducing them to audiences and Tyburn's soldiering in the Lowlands was often embroidered with descriptions of him as the "bane of the perfidious Spanish," a "Captain of the Companies" and, once, to Tyburn's intense chagrin, "the Bastion of God." Tyburn himself preferred not to dwell on that campaign. There were too many restless nights where the memory of the sodden cold of the Dutch countryside, the tench of burning bodies, the shouts of the steel-clad Spanish *tercios*[54] and the thick blood-soaked mud of Goes and Walcheren flitted through his mind's eye, stealing sleep.

There is nothing like Flanders, he thought, echoing the biting, sarcastic fury that the phrase exemplified for the English contingent, who would call it out when wading the inevitable water-filed ditches that surrounded every mile of Dutch countryside. He felt a shiver ripple up his spine and for the briefest of instants he could

---

[54] Companies

80

smell the coppery scent of the spilled blood that Alba's force had left like a carmine trail across the Lowlands. He could taste the cold in his mouth and see the brilliant scarlet sprayed vivid across the clean white snow. He remembered the girl's blonde hair spilled loose from her scarf. *Annika.*

Despite the warm summer day, he shivered.

No, there is nothing quite like Flanders.

". . . would be wonderful! Are you acquainted with him?" The portly man was still speaking.

Tyburn shook his head to clear it and focused his attention on the gentleman, noting from his clothes that he was in the service of some wealthier household. A secretary of some type, Tyburn guessed.

"I was saying, how very gratifying to make the acquaintance of one of the Queen's Men's, the Chosen Disciples who have bearded the godless Spanish in Holland. Might I assume you served under Sir Thomas Morgan?" The man continued without a pause. "The sinful wickedness of the Papists is, I fear, without measure. The very stench of Hell's own fires clings to them and no matter how they might perfume themselves, their sins will see them out. The Spanish will drown in their own blood and feel the wrath of their Master, the Horned One, for their failures." He paused for a breath. "But, your pardon, sir, I speak of these matters in my own ignorance, forgetting I stand before a man who has engaged in God's own war against the Papacy, a holy warrior defending the innocence of our poor Dutch cousins . . ."

Tyburn held up a hand to halt the man's speech before it could erupt into another unfettered discourse. The man stopped in expectation. "For your praise, sir, I thank you. As for my actions, they were few, so I cannot lay claim to the praise you pass my way. I will, however, ask what might you wish from me?"

"Oh, yes," the man resumed cheerily, "I am William Bromley, the principal secretary for Sir Thomas Lucy. Sir Thomas is planning a small dinner gathering at his estate and, by happy coincidence; you and your illustrious troupe are gracing our community with your thespian presence. Sir Thomas requests the honor of your attendance upon his gathering the afternoon after tomorrow at Charlecote."

Oldcastle, who had been hovering just behind the perspiring secretary like a fat silvered blowfly, cocked his head and slid forward. "Of course, my dear sir, we would be delighted to perform for your master Sir Thomas. Does he have a preference? A comedy perhaps? Or a tragedy? We have a new one, of cunning power and waspish disposition, sure to stir the tears of his Lady." Oldcastle's eyes gleamed lupine.

'Something diverting I think--a comedy. Not too rustic, though." The secretary continued, his voice pensive. "And nothing--offputting--I mean, offensive to the eyes of God. Sir Thomas would prefer nothing that scandalizes. He is not, er, inclined to forgiveness towards those that do not express the proper devotional practices."

In short, thought Tyburn, nothing that smacked of Catholicism.

"Sir Thomas is known for his ardent pursuit of Catholic heresy, and I know," the man continued, "that some troupes of your profession lean towards such performances. They are not acceptable."

"But of course. By God's grace we would never incline to perform any Papist rubbish." Oldcastle glanced at Tyburn, who bobbed his head up and down obediently, like a puppet on a string. "Pure, moral, upright and English! Those are our watchwords."

"Marvelous! I admit, we had despaired of having any performance beyond the usual diversions. The queen's summer progress arrives at Kenilworth any day now and has quite monopolized all performers from Warwick." The man burbled, "But at least you are available." Tyburn struggled to keep his face serene as he watched the frown flit over Oldcastle's face for an instant.

"We will expect you just after the midday, at the Charlecote gatehouse. The performance will be held in the great hall. Now, what recompense would be suitable?"

Tyburn knew that Oldcastle panting like a hound at this open-ended query.

"Well, Master Bromley, between gentlemen I do not think we need spend too much time bandying about accounts. What would you think fair recompense?" queried the rotund thespian with an innocent and innocuous expression.

"Perhaps . . . umm . . . thirty shillings?" Bromley replied with an airy gesture. "Would that be appropriate?"

Oldcastle almost choked. It was easily double what he assumed he could haggle. "Indeed, that should be--adequate for our needs. Shall we say, fifeteen now and the remainder at the performance?"

The man obligingly counted out a handful of coin, depositing it in Oldcastle's open palm. "We shall see you at the Gatehouse the morning after tomorrow."

"Indeed, sir," replied Oldcastle, eyes gleaming with satisfaction.

Bromley beamed and then turned back to Tyburn. "Captain, I have one other favour to request of you."

Tyburn nodded, puzzled.

"We would appreciate you attending upon Sir Thomas after your performance. Not for dining," he added with haste, "but he and several of his acquaintances are, I know, greatly interested in the events of the Lowlands, and the opportunity to converse with a man of skill and experience would be a rare treat for him."

"I am interested in hearing your tales of daring myself." The contralto voice made Tyburn's head swivel sharp around. The tall woman with the auburn hair was standing off to one side, watching and listening to the conversation with interest. "Your pardon, Master Bromley, it was not my intention to interrupt."

The man gave a broad smile and took the woman's extended hand. "Nonsense! You need never apologize for gracing us with your presence, my lady Carey. I trust you and your father will attend at Charlecote?"

"Indeed yes. If only for the opportunity to see the Earl of Worcester's Men perform once again. They were"--she inclined her head in Oldcastle's direction--"rather more than adequate, or so I thought."

Oldcastle smiled winningly at the young woman, a smile that came frightening close to a leer as he gave her a quick, encompassing look. Tyburn felt a twinge of irritation.

"So, master player, do you have some stalwart tales of war to stir your audience? Brave battles won and enemies routed?"

"Probably not," replied Tyburn.

"Ha! Our Captain Tyburn is always far too modest about his service," interrupted Oldcastle, leaning forward, giving Tyburn a quick stage signal with his left hand to follow his lead. "His account of the siege of Haarlem is riveting--a true tale of courageous resistance against an implacable and ruthless foe. Many are the times my friend here has told me of the horrors the Spanish inflict daily upon the innocent Dutch . . .but I cannot speak of it in your company my lady, it would not be appropriate for your ears."

The woman turned her gaze to Tyburn. "No stalwart tales then, Captain?" The gentle mocking tone stung Tyburn's temper to life.

"Unless you consider finding a starving woman and child frozen solid on the doorstep of your billet or being ordered to collect Spanish heads for display over the gates to be stalwart, then the answer would be no." The woman paled at the vehemence in his voice. "Or perhaps you might find it in the time the Spanish forced their prisoners out onto a frozen lake, and took bets on whether they would freeze or drown first once they fell through. The winner," Tyburn continued, "if I recall, was an eight-year old boy, who stayed afloat for near twenty minutes before he sank under the ice."

Tyburn felt Oldcastle's meaty hand pulling on his shoulder and heard the corpulent player's voice, as if from a great distance, spinning excuses and apologies.

The woman's face was pale, and her eyes hooded and distant, yet thoughtful. She gave Tyburn a look that made him burn with a guilty sense of having landed a questionable blow against an innocent party.

"I look forward to your performance on the morrow, gentlemen." She graced Oldcastle with a nod, Secretary Bromley with a bright smile and Tyburn with a measured glance. Maid in tow, she slipped into the sunlit roadway.

Tyburn sighed inwardly, cursing his own foolish temperament.

"So," Bromley continued, ignoring the verbal clash with the aplomb of a seasoned servant, "you will I trust be able to speak, ah, adroitly with Sir Thomas and his guests?"

Tyburn stared at the man for a long heartbeat and then bowed his head in acquiescence. "Certainly, sir, I would be honoured to make his acquaintance."

"Wonderful! Good day gentlemen!" Giving the two men a thin forced smile, the secretary waved his hand in dismissal and turned away, easing his bulk past the last bench before disappearing into the sunlight that dappled through the doorway.

"God be with you, sirrah!" called Oldcastle as the man departed. He turned and gave Tyburn a hard punch to the shoulder. "God's teeth! What is your bloody problem? Just smile mysteriously and make up some blather." He glared at Tyburn through reddened eyes, waving the mask for emphasis. "Spin them some rare tales--just don't yarn any truth in it. We want them happy, content and intrigued for more."

"You don't think they want to know the truth?"

"Truth? What's truth? They want to hear what they want to hear, and you--you need to tell it to them. Tales of sordid evil Spaniards dying by the dozens, piked by stalwart God-fearing Englishmen, that's what they want to hear."He stared at Kit for a long moment. "Truth? By God's holy bowels what kind of a fool are you?" He snorted. "You serve them their drinks well-sauced[55], with no bate[56], and leave the nonny-nonny[57] aside."

He continued, jabbing one finger at Tyburn's chest for emphasis. "We could stand well out of this. More commissions, more manor set-to's and the like, less market-town traipsing." He grimaced. "I hear tell that Burbage is thinking of building a permanent theatre in Shoreditch by Holywell. We get the right sort of influence, there might be some possibilities, so you ingratiate yourself to those high-toned bastards. You tell them some blood-curdling pieces, get them roused, make them see that Worcester's Men are England's." He nodded sternly. "Warwick's have Leicester. He's tight in court with Burghley and his ilk. Bloody courting the queen from what I hear. We need more than just Worcester; we need a voice with pull in court, or we'll be stuck in an innyard, picking coins from the dust and begging for our pots. Clear?"

Tyburn nodded, impressed that Oldcastle was actually looking beyond the summer tour for once. He must be concerned, Tyburn thought. Normally the man's planning didn't extend beyond the next woman within easy reach.

Burbage's plans had been the topic of much taproom discussion but most players didn't think a permanent theatre would be possible. The Puritan aldermen that ran London hated the troupes with a passion and would seize on any convenient excuse to shut down the performances. The Red Lion had made an attempt at a permanent venue a few years prior but it foundered within a season. No one would walk to Mile End in the winter mud to see a play, in particular with innyards in Southwark offering performances just across the bridge. Burbage was a canny

---

[55] Drink, tobacco or food spiked with herbs, often hemp. A vice brought back from the Netherlands by soldiers.
[56] Strife or discord
[57] Nonsense expression often used to allude to or render indelicate terms in Italian songs

businessman, Tyburn knew, and if anyone could make a permanent theatre work, it would be him. God help the troupes that were caught out.

He felt a hand slap down on his shoulder. "Another brilliant performance from Virtue and an adequate stab at acting by Vice." Alec was grinning under his feathered cap. "Why are you looking all pensive and moody again? Oldcastle dock you for more debts?"

"The problem," Tyburn said in a wry voice, "is that I'm bloody parched."

"God's death! We can't have that." Alec reached out and grabbed Mundy, still in his finery as he passed, throwing one arm over his shoulder. "Let's go get this beauty drunk, shall we?"

The rest of the troupe raised a cheer and as he turned Tyburn caught one last sight of the auburn-haired woman and her maid, on the sunlit street. He felt an exquisite tightness in his chest and for an instant thought he felt her eyes on him. Then she stepped away into the street like an autumn leaf falling into a river, sliding smoothly out of sight.

He let his breath trickle out slow, being left with, to his own intense surprise, a sense of powerful anticipation. He knew she would be at the Charlecote performance.

Stratford was full of surprises.

Chapter the Eighth

MUNDY GAVE A satisfied belch and set his now empty tankard down on the table, his movements slow and deliberate, as though he was selecting with particular care the final resting place for the mug. Alec and the others shouted and passed him another full mug.

The ordinary was crowded and dense, despite a smattering of rain that was turning the early evening prematurely dark. The air was thick with the miasma of unwashed bodies, spilled ale and the faintly repulsive scent of burnt meat. . A quiet game of dice was going on in one corner but Tyburn was content just to sit, his worn boots propped up on a bench, a half-full tankard of ale perched on his knee. For once he had coin in his pocket and no urgent need to try his chances in a vain effort to avoid complete penury.

"Right, then, try and answer this one." The speaker was the innkeeper's brother, a horse coper[58] who had been drinking with several apprentices since the mid-afternoon and had been trading

---

[58] Farrier or blacksmith

stories and drinking bets with the players. "Two men are 'erding sheep to market. They get to havin' a bate[59], so one of them murther's t'other. Pray guess what he took him off with and I'll stand the next round." He knocked twice on the table with his grimy hand and grinned, his teeth black and crooked, glinting like wet stones. "An' jus to show me generosity, I let you have three guesses. You don't guess right by the third, you buy me and my fellows the round." The apprentices laughed in appreciation.

Alec scratched his head in thought but before he could say anything in response the drunken Mundy lunged forward and slurred, "His dagger!" Exasperated, Alec shoved Mundy back onto his stool.

"Shut it, you capon!" Alec stared at the coper. Not obvious, he thought, not a dagger or a walking stick, something different . . .

"A big bloody stone!" slurred Mundy. Willens clamped one hand over Mundy's mouth and yanked him backwards off his stool, walking him to the end of the table.

"That's two!" cackled one spotty apprentice in a blue smock. Alec gave the boy a pointed look that made him subside into grinning beery silence.

"You can't count that one," Alleyn complained.

"Oh but I does, by Jesu. One more guess." The man smiled, a confident and contented look on his round face. His friends exchanged loose and foolish grins and one rubbed his hands together mockingly at the players.

Alec was silent and pensive.

"A sheep."

Alec lowered his gaze from the timbered ceiling and turned his head towards Tyburn, who sat off to one side, both eyes closed, hands folded around his half-empty tankard.

---

[59] Argument

"He killed him with a sheep." Tyburn opened one eye and gave a gimlet stare at the horse coper.

The coper was silent.

"A sheep." Tyburn repeated. There was no question in his voice.

The coper sighed heavily in resignation. "Yes, 'twere a damned sheep," he acquiesced to the groans of the apprentices, glaring at Tyburn. "He grabbed the sheep and laid the poor soul right dead wit' it. In Yorkshire it was. Codso[60], never had to pay off on that one before."

The players gave a cheer and waved the barman over to the table for another round of the heavy warm ale.

Alec gave Tyburn's feet a push and slid onto the bench opposite.

"A sheep?" he said, still exasperated.

Tyburn opened his eyes. "Seemed obvious and rational," he drew the latter word out slow, "that he had to hit him with something unexpected."

"Who murders someone with a sheep?"

"My experience is that you kill with what's at hand." Alec saw something glimmer in Tyburn's eyes and arched an eyebrow in an unspoken query. Tyburn noticed the question.

"A cooking spit."

"A cooking spit? When was this?"

"At Walcheren. Lost my pike," Tyburn continued in a laconic tone.

"So you used a cooking spit?"

Tyburn shrugged. "As I said, you use what's at hand. Dead from a cooking spit, dead from a pike, makes no difference."

Unsure of how to reply, Alec took a deep draught. "Kit, you're a bloody strange man." After a moment, he raised his

---

[60] "God's Own" – an oath

tankard in a mock salute and drained his drink. "I'm off to the Bear." He winked lewdly.

"Oldcastle won't thank you for filching his mort," Tyburn cautioned, gesturing to the end of the bar where Oldcastle was deep in conversation with two local tradesmen. They would, he reflected, be lucky to walk away with their boots if Oldcastle was negotiating with them.

Alec shrugged, irritated. "We're men, not monks. He can bellow on as he likes about drunkenness and vice, I don't see him keeping his carrot dry[61]. Which reminds me." He reached over and lifted the folded yellow cloak from the bench beside Tyburn. "You've borrowed this quite long enough and I can't cut a dash even with barmaids if I'm soaked in rain." Alec slung the cloak over one shoulder, fastening it around his collar. He smoothed the expensive fabric and folded it back to reveal the intricate silvered stitchwork. "How's that?"

"You look like a mincing ponce," Tyburn observed. "But somehow you make it work."

"The green of jealousy does not become you," Alec replied loftily. He drained his mug and tossed it into the corner. "Try to keep Mundy from passing out, it'll save you having to carry him back to the inn."

"We'd leave him to sleep it off, but God only knows what trouble he'd get into when he woke up."

Alec laughed and threaded his way through the maze of benches and rough-hewn tables, careful not to catch the cloak on the wood.

Tyburn yawned and shook his head to clear the fuzziness that seeped its way gradually into his mind. The loss of the round of drinks seemed to have quieted the strident horse coper and his cronies, and the talk had turned to the inevitable and bitter tenants'

---

[61] Carrot = penis

THE JESUIT LETTER

diatribe around the enclosure of some common land to the south-east.

"T'ain't right," muttered one pock-marked man. "That pasture be common use. My da' used to till the corner near the oaks."

One of the other men jeered. "Your da' never tilled a furrow unless it was with some rancid doxy. He jus' liked to bleat about deBrage."

"deBrage is rightly a bastard. Enclosing more land up near Wilmcote. Turning out folk that been there for years . . . bloody sheep."

"He's a greedy coxcomb, no doubt," observed the horse coper. "Heard tell that he laid suit on his son-in-law's properties, claiming back the dowry." The man nodded and laughed at himself. "Takes an amount of brazen greed to chase a dead man's leavings-- and not for the widow, but for his own self."

"He's a collier[62], no less," agreed the pock-marked man, slurring his words.

Alleyn and Willens sat down the bench and proffered Tyburn a fresh tankard. "What's the occasion?" Tyburn asked, for Alleyn was habitually absent when the bills came due.

"No occasion. Took it off Mundy. If'n he has another, we'll be dragging him home," said Willens. Alleyn laughed, his face puffy and red, eyes gleaming. Tyburn sat up and took a drink. The men were soon deep in conversation.

"Right, you drunken sots, we've a performance on the morrow and it's full dark." Oldcastle tapped one meaty hand down on Alleyn's shoulder. "Somebody bestir that bully rook[63]!" He aimed a kick at Mundy, sprawled against a chair by the thick beamed wall.

---

[62] Cheat and a trickster
[63] Fine fellow

The three men looked up. Willens drained his mug, and the others followed suit. Jack and one of the other apprentices grabbed Mundy and hoisted him by the belt onto his unsteady feet. Mundy stood like a man adrift in a gale, tilting visibly until Jack grabbed him with a muttered curse and slung one arm over his shoulder.

"You go mewling and puking you do it t'other way," Jack growled askance. The others laughed.

"Loan us a glim, will you?" Oldcastle demanded from the barman. The man reluctantly slid a couple of short rush candles across the table. Oldcastle scowled at the man but took the cheap lights. He lit them on the hanging lamp and passed one to Willens.

"A good night and God's blessing," he called, and Worcester's Men filed out the door.

The rain had ceased but the air was still thick with the heavy taste of it. It felt heady and verdant, and Tyburn breathed in the night, his head swimming from the ale. The town was dark except for a few scattered yellow lights visible in windows along the street. The clouds in the east glowed with a wan and pale luminescence from the moon radiating behind them but the light was so diffuse it failed to push back the enveloping dark. The men followed Oldcastle down the gloom of the street. The rush candle offered a poor light. Oldcastle walked slow at first, mindful of a breeze or fast movement extinguishing it. The flame sputtered and jittered.

"Mind 'im!" a voice called imploring, followed by the sound of deep retching and a splashing sound. Mundy hadn't made it far, thought Tyburn. Alleyn laughed unsympathetically although, in truth, all the men had been in Mundy's position at some point on the summer tour.

"Codso, pick up your bloody feet!" Jack's voice rumbled. The breeze guttered the candles again and the high clouds slid, curtain-like, apart to reveal the waxing gibbous moon. A rushing tide of pale light swept the street, sending shadows fleeing with whirling, stately grace like birds flushed from the trees.

"What's that?" Willens's voice sounded hollow in the night air. Tyburn couldn't see where he was gesturing. Something had caught Oldcastle's eye as well as he turned to the right, lifting the pitiful candle in a vain effort to discern what Willens had spotted.

Tyburn glanced away from the candle to keep his night vision intact and stepped to one side. Out of the corner of one eye he could see a shadowy bundle sprawled across the verge of the road. It looked like a dark bundle of discarded rags, except for the sight of a pale, splayed hand that lay upturned on the road.

"God's blood," muttered someone as the moonlight and the sputtering taper pushed back the darkness. Tyburn stepped forward, feeling a tight sickening lurch in his stomach as he spied a light bundle of cloth carelessly balled up and tossed on the roadside. He knew that cloak.

He knelt beside the body. "Bring the glim," he said, his voice terse. Oldcastle leaned over, the yellow rushlight casting a dancing shadow across the dirt. Tyburn reached out and turned the body by the shoulder. The slight sputtering flame unveiled Alec's pale face, eyes still, open and unblinking. Dirt clung to the side of his face where it had lain in the road. The ground was damp and dark, soaked with blood, the coppery scent tingeing the air like a heavy spectre. The men raised a chorus of angry, stupefied laments. A muffled thump sounded as Jack unceremoniously dropped the drunken Mundy into the roadway. Tyburn was silent, absently reaching out and brushing the dark earth particles from his friend's face, feeling that all-too familiar sickening dread in his chest. And the slow, roiling rage growing within, like a winter's seed.

"Dear Christ . . ." Oldcastle sat back on his heels, brushed one hand over his eyes momentarily, thinking furiously. He reached over, grabbed Alleyn by his doublet and pulled his ear to his mouth. "Go and find the Bailie. And then fetch a cart." Alleyn stood stock-still, gazing at Alec's body in evident shock. "Do it now. Take Jack with you," growled Oldcastle. Alleyn started, eyes wide with shock, and then with one last look headed up the street with Jack in tow. Mundy lay supine in the roadway, asleep.

Oldcastle gripped Tyburn's shoulder hard and pulled. Kit spun on his heels, and glared at Oldcastle who met the stare stonily with his own. "We've things to do. Get his purse. The Bailie will steal him blind when he arrives, so take his coin. Jacob," he said evenly,. "gather up the cloak and anything else we'll need. These thieving bastards will take it all and profit from the death of our friend, and I won't allow it. We'll sell it on and send it on to his father, along with his share of the takings from this damnable town." He stared at Tyburn hard. "Do it now."

Tyburn glared at Oldcastle. His hand flexed by his sword hilt even as he forced himself to push down the red, red rage that had begun to burn bright within him. It was a fierce and abiding anger that he hadn't felt in a very long time. Not since Haarlem, not since Annika. He wanted nothing more than to free that silvered blade and coat it in blood. With an effort he closed his hand into a tight fist and lowered it onto his thigh. Tyburn let out a deliberate, even breath, calming himself, even with the scent of Alec's mortality riming the air.

This wasn't Oldcastle's doing and Kit knew well enough that the old man was correct. The locals would steal everything they found when they arrived. His fellows would be lucky to have an old shift to bury him in.

Oldcastle paused and let the air trickle from his lungs in relief. For the space of a few heartbeats, Tyburn had seemed to radiate violence; it had hung cloaked like a live thing, stilling the sounds of the night and making Oldcastle wary of the nascent intensity of the man beside him.

Tyburn forced himself to nod in acquiescence. Vengeance and answers, he thought, would have to wait. He turned back and, borrowing the taper from Willens, surveyed Alec's body. When they had found him, he had been almost face down in the dirt of the roadway, half-curled into himself, his cloak torn asunder and discarded. One hand lay open and extended but the other was drawn tight to his chest, as if protecting himself. Tyburn reached out and took his friend's lifeless hand. The fingers were closed over something. He reached for the digits, expecting to find resistance. He had noted in Flanders that often, in death, a man's hands would clench around his valuables and weapons, a death-grip, hard to loosen, reluctant even after the spirit had fled to release what it had held dear.

Alec's fingers were loose. Tyburn opened them easily and pulled a small coin-shaped object from his hand. His eyes narrowed in puzzlement. It was no coin but rather a wax disk, embossed on both sides. In the dim light of the cheap rush candle, he could not determine what it said. He slid the wax disk into his pocket.

The cause of Alec's death was plain for all to see. His throat had been neatly and deeply sliced across. and the wound gaped wide in the moonlight. Alec's eyes glittered in the dark. until Tyburn reached out and closed them. Willens's gorge rose at the sight of the wound; he turned away to stare at the cold white stars now visible through the thinning cloud above. Tyburn forced himself to scrutinize the ruinous injury. He had seen death before in all the horrific variants men could devise in wartime. The lucky died in battle. Quick and brutal though their fates might be, it was preferable to the oozing, rank death from a wound, with limbs putrefying and blackening, or the slow retching death from wasting disease or the sweating sickness, which plagued the damp Lowlands. Preferable too, to the slow racking and torturous death as a prisoner. Heretics died by inches in Spanish hands.

His eyes alighted on Alec's doublet and jerkin, both of which had been cut open at multiple points, the stitching ragged, torn and cut, as though a hungry dog had worried at his clothes.

"By Jesu the Savior, what happened to him?" Willens muttered. "Padder[64] or moon-men[65]?"

"No Egyptians[66] in Stratford," scorned Oldcastle. "Belike we'd have heard of them. Maybe some local ruffians thought to roll

---

[64] Highway robber
[65] Gypsies

a player . . . why in God's name was he wandering about without company?"

Tyburn smiled without humour, his tone sour. "He was going to the Bear to cover your barmaid." Tyburn opened Alec's doublet. "His purse is gone."

"No, it's here." Willens pulled a leather purse from under the edge of Alec's belt. Tyburn's brows knit together in puzzlement. "Give over. That can't be his. Alec had the fancy one, cheveril[67], embroidered." He took the rough leather purse in puzzlement and gave it an experimental shake. It was hefty. He poured the contents into his left hand. The clink of heavy coins made Oldcastle lean in close with the taper.

"Silver."

Oldcastle sucked in a deep astonished breath. "Nonsense! The boy didn't carry that much." Oldcastle glanced at Tyburn. Tyburn shrugged, grim-faced. Nothing about this killing made sense. "Later," Oldcastle said, gesturing for Tyburn to put the purse and its contents out of sight. Tyburn tucked the bag into his doublet pocket.

Christopher Tyburn felt a bleak chill winnow down his spine, raising the hairs on the back of his neck. In the momentary illumination from the taper, he had half-glimpsed a familiar design on the silver coins. A shield, divided into four quadrants, replete with castles and lions. He knew the inscription encircling the centre design by heart: *PHILIPUSolloDoHISPA*, Philip II, by the grace of God, King of Spain and the Indies.

The silver was Spanish.

---

[66] An alternative name for gypsies. Gypsies or *Roma* were regarded with great suspicion in Elizabethan England. Seen generally as thieves, vagabonds and vagrants, they were also often welcome in rural areas as travelling entertainers, magicians, fortune-tellers and tinkers. The term "Egyptians" came about from the mistaken belief that the *Roma* came from Egypt.
[67] Soft kidskin

Chapter the Ninth

THE DIRT FLOOR of the barn was damp even through the thin scattering of hay that had been spread out across the floor for a cushion. The building was old but functional, used for storing winter fodder for cattle or sheep. The thick wooden beams climbed cathedral-like into the broken darkness of the loft. An owl nested high in the peak of the rafters, stretching his pinions and rustling, as though disquieted by the unexpected company. Tyburn shifted his own weight on a low wooden form, propped both elbows on his bent knees and looked across the draughty open space at the small farm cart drawn up with its dismal cargo.

Alec's body had been cloaked in a cheap linen winding sheet. It lay across the bed of the trundle cart, visible as a pale ethereal mound in the still dark. Alec was slated for burial in the churchyard in the morning. Oldcastle had stormed violently when the local curate had tried to deny the player's the right to bury Alec in the churchyard. After copious threats, a spate of red-faced bellowing and a small bribe, the pock-faced church warden had agreed to bury Alec, but only on the north side of the small burial yard, in the corner where unbaptized children were commonly interred.

Robbie had been perched on an upended wooden bucket until sleep stole his willpower. He now lay sprawled on the ground beside the cart. He had been furious when he found out about his master's murder and had insisted on keeping watch over the body with Tyburn, as had several other troupe members. The rest had drifted off back to the inn to catch a few scant hours of sleep before preparing for the next day's performance. Oldcastle had stubbornly refused to even consider cancelling the guild hall performance, claiming that Alec would never have wanted Lord Worcester's Men to forfeit a performance on his account.

Tyburn rather doubted that sentiment. Alec was always happy to skulk off from minor performances, given an expedient excuse. Kit suspected that Oldcastle's mercenary instincts realized once word of the murder got out, the performance would be packed and the man had no desire to forego the revenues, despite the loss of a key performer. It would help cover the burial fees.

In the dim quiet, lit only by a small lantern cajoled from the curate, Tyburn pulled out the leather purse that Willens had found on Alec and fished out one of the silver coins. There were fifteen coins in the purse, all identical, all with the crowned shield containing the lions and castles of Castile and León on one side and the Pillars of Hercules on the other. Tyburn fingered the coin ruefully. Once upon a time he would have done almost anything to have his hands on this much silver. *Not this day,* he thought with palpable bitterness.

The coins were Spanish, clean, well-rounded and unclipped[68], an unusual circumstance. Spanish coins were not

---

[68] Coinage was often "clipped" whereby small amounts of the silver were surreptitiously removed or clipped on the edge as it moved through the economy. This often resulted in the debasement of the coinage.

unknown in England. Spanish ducats were often used in the Lowlands, and Hawkins, Drake and other sea raiders brought new supplies of Spanish coinage into Plymouth and London, spending it on malmsey and sack[69] in the bousing kens[70] of Southwark, or losing it in the stews and bear-baiting rings. It was strange to find it in Warwickshire.

Alec had had no Spanish silver. Tyburn had borrowed enough monies from him in recent weeks to know that with certainty. Yet Willens had not found Alec's purse, so it had obviously been snatched. He shook his head, feeling a dull ache that radiated from his temples across his head like a weighted bar. Common thieves would have taken all the money, not left a small fortune in plain sight to be picked up by the next passerby. His assailants had gone to the trouble of slitting the seams of his jerkin and doublet, something only careful searchers would have done. They had been looking for something.

He let his fingers trace the coin inscription *Plus Ultra,* "Beyond the Limits." According to one of the Dutch Sea Beggars he had met in Holland, the inscription was a declaration of Spain's claims to the New World and its riches. A declaration and a threat. *Bastards.* The Spanish seemed obsessed by the gold and wealth of the New World. It fueled feverish ambition and armies and grandiose schemes. He recalled that the Inquisition had declared the population of the Netherlands heretic in '68, condemning them to death, a fact that gave Alva's troops free rein in their depredations. *Plus Ultra* was more than apt, he thought.

The owl shifted again, folding and unfolding its wings, bobbing nervously on its high seat. Its huge yellow eyes warily regarded the man seated below. Its head pivoted, tracking with evident hunger the slight wavering in the straw that marked the passage of a mouse.

---

[69] Sweet Spanish wine & sherry
[70] Ale house

The local watchman had been every bit as foolish and venal as Oldcastle had warned. After having been roused from his sleep by Jack and Alleyn, the man had meandered down the street to where the players stood in a half-circle around the corpse of their friend. He had stood gawping over the body, a bright oil lantern suspended from a pole pushing back the encroaching darkness. After several awkward moments, he had looked up, lifted his lantern pole and with fustian grandeur demanded, "Which'n one of you took thus 'un off?"

The abrupt chorus of abuse and scorn the players heaped on the man silenced that foolish line of questioning, but he had then demanded the return of the dead man's property, pending his inquiry. In the face of his obstinacy the players relented and handed over the torn jerkin, which seemed to satisfy him and would doubtlessly pad his pay for the next month. The swift arrival of the constable and one of the aldermen completed the fiasco as they were far more concerned with the removal of the dead man from the streets than with who might have killed him.

Tyburn felt the banked anger stir. The constable had regarded the players with narrowed eyes, muttering quietly to the alderman in a long, low litany of abuse that carried in the still evening air. Players were, at the best of times, regarded by many as barely a step above vagrants. The baleful glance and supreme indifference to the bloodied corpse at his feet put the constable squarely with the majority. The alderman, to his credit, had ignored the constable's tirade and had made arrangements for a cheap linen shroud and small trundle cart to be fetched from his own barn to transport the body.

Another brief altercation occurred when the players went to wrap the body. The bailie, a short man with a greasy fringe of hair and thick yellowing fingers, insisted on removing Alec's doublet and breeches. After Tyburn reached over and hauled the short man away by the scruff of his neck, the constable had ended the argument by threatening the players with the stocks, a whipping and a suspension of their license to perform. Oldcastle had intervened and the players had reluctantly handed over the remainder of Alec's personal properties to the bailie, who, mustering an air of ruptured dignity, had bundled the bloodied clothes with some twine. The fine yellow cloak had been secretly stowed away by Willens.

The cloak. Tyburn turned the idea over in his mind, despite his weariness. Why strip it and toss it? And why abandon a small fortune in silver, yet steal a purse with a handful of coinage?

The shock of the realization went through him like a heated blade. The attackers had been hunting a player in a yellow cloak, practically the only thing visible on a dark night with the moon occluded by cloud. They weren't looking for Alec at all.

The sensation was visceral. Tyburn felt the blood drain from his face. Horrified, he glanced over to the chalky wrap laying supine on the cart, guilt coursing through his veins. He half-expected the body to rise, a grotesque spectre, and lift a soulless, accusing hand. His eyes felt hot and throbbing and his head spun. *Damn me. .* He wished he could find solace in prayer but that privilege was dead to him.

Tyburn loosed a slow, cautious breath and gripped the hilt of his rapier hard with both hands, holding on to what was tangible. The pounding in his ears faded. The body remained still. The owl above stirred again, restless, sensing the uneasiness of the man below and impatient to stalk the decrepit outbuilding for prey.

They had been hunting him, Tyburn realized.

But why? There were only two possible candidates that sprang to mind--the card-fleeced wool merchant, who was probably not above hiring a couple of boot-halers[71] to take some quick and dirty revenge on a cozening[72] player, and the two alleyway charmers that had been beating the alderman's youngster. He toyed with the idea of the merchant but discarded it. No merchant worth

---

[71] Brigands or freebooters, hired muscle
[72] Cheating

his salt would ever leave a year's worth of wages on a corpse. That left the two men from the alleyway.

Tyburn rubbed his beard thoughtfully. The accent and the quick readiness of the blade called to mind the London rookeries, not the pastoral landscape of Warwickshire. The shorter man, in particular, had moved with the same feral intensity that Tyburn associated with the predators of the London streets. He was, the player reckoned, no mere farm laborer or ditch-digger, which made the incident all the more peculiar.

From long and bitter experience, he knew peculiar spelled trouble.

He reached into the inner pocket of his doublet and pulled out the folded letter he had retrieved the previous day from the altercation. The letter was thick, sealed with a dark, heavy wax blob that had cracked and broken. A neat stab mark from the rapier was the only outstanding blemish. The name written on the exterior was Master Edward Sturley, which meant nothing to Kit.

He tapped the letter against his knee. The boy had claimed the letter was his father's: Shakespeare, the glover and alderman, a former mayor, as he recalled from his previous conversation. He opened the letter. Inside was a short note written on a thin,worn piece of parchment. A second smaller envelope, made of thicker and heavier paper, was tied with a thin string and sealed with scarlet wax. There was no embossed impression on the seal. He read the note, his eyes scanning the tight spidery handwriting.

It was clear that the sealed letter was not the glover's correspondence but one he was passing on to another. The man was a conduit.

"Coads," Kit cursed softly. Secret correspondence, Spanish silver and a dead friend. It was quite astonishing how swiftly one's life could slide remorselessly into Hell.

Tyburn regarded the sealed letter with wariness. Outside, the Plough was sinking into the western horizon. The night was ebbing fast. He had a choice to make.

The body on the cart was utterly still. Tyburn had seen friends die before. Avenged or unavenged, they stayed dead. Revenge would mean nothing to Alec; he was far beyond that mortal appetite, and Tyburn himself had long since abandoned any hope of God's grace.

But he wanted to know. Answers, he thought, seldom presented themselves simply. They had to be wrested from the world, hunted and winnowed out, not for revenge, but to help assuage that deep need to know, to understand, to pull some infinitesimal bit of comprehension and order and judge the purpose behind it. Purpose gave it meaning, and death without meaning was one adjourned of honor or faith.

He had in his hand the end of a long thread. The question was whether or not he deigned to pull it. He could follow it or leave it to lie fallow and untouched. It was a simple choice, albeit one with potentially mortal results.

He nodded to himself, glanced at the cart and grimaced. There hadn't been any choice. Debating his actions in this way was just so much vanity. He knew he couldn't leave this to lie--not for revenge, not for God, not for duty, but simply because he had that burning need to know, a restless hunger that drove him along the path of his fate. He felt it in his bones, in his blood. It was feckless and foolish and insatiable and it rode him like a shadow.

I'm Fortune's Fool, treading the boards blind and tilting at the empty air. A poor wayward knight I'd make.

He wanted to know. He needed to know.

Without glancing down at the letter in his hand, he broke the wax seal between his fingers. It split effortlessly.

The owl, weary of lingering and awaiting the man below to depart or rest, launched itself silently into the dusty air of the barn and with sure, swift, thrumming bass beats of its wings, knifed phantom-like through the dark star-flecked opening in the rafters and out into the night. Its eerie, echoing keen shivered through the still darkness.

Tyburn smiled in grim recognition of that call. A thread had just been pulled.

Chapter the Tenth

THE SOLID ANGLED beams of the attic room where Will and Gilbert slept were barely discernable in the early morning light, hints of dark wood that were felt rather than perceived. The air was stuffy, thick and constricting. Will stared upwards from his thin mattress, the blanket pulled up to his chin, his eyes flicking in vain around the dark layered ceiling, seeing nothing but the faint coruscate of color on the inside of his own lids when he closed them. He listened to Gilbert's slow, steady breathing beside him, feeling his brother's light, thin body shifting on the edge of the bed. Gilbert, for some strange reason, slept perched on the absolute outside edge of the bed, poised like a cantilevered story over the wood floor. Will could, and had in the past, give his brother's sleeping form an occasional tiny push, sending him plummeting onto the cold floor.

On this particular morning such antics were far from his mind.

He reached up into the darkness, stretching outwards, reaching for the nothingness in front of him. .

He had no idea what to do next.

It had seemed so simple. Retrieve the letter for his father and return it to its proper destination. But now, Sturley was dead, the letter recovered by a player. Will shivered. He had no idea what the letter contained but knew that his father was in regular communication with other recusants in Warwickshire. In the past, letters and packets had drifted through the Henley address, passed on with quiet regularity to other families or households, or some to the merchants that passed through every few months winding their way to Coventry, Warwick or London, or sometimes further afield. Will remembered one letter that his father had fussed for days over before forwarding it onwards. It had been destined for York. As to the contents of the letter, Will suspected even his father didn't know. John Shakespeare could read the numerals and common words he needed for his business and properties, albeit in his fashion. He could not write any letters beyond his own signature. Will served as his primary scribe.

His father was not a letter-writer. But someone was.

He shuddered, remembering the leaden weight of Sturley's bound form twisting on the rope end, the heavy creak of the hemp and the tracery of blood speckling the earth.

The house was stirring. A faint tinge of light began to outline the narrow attic window at the end of the room. He could hear faint, light footsteps–his mother's scullery servant–padding about in the area of the hearth downstairs, feeding the banked coals. Several minutes later he detected the faints curls of wayward wood smoke giving the air a sharp bite. A cock crowed outside and Will heard his mother pouring the chamber pot into the vat John Shakespeare used for collecting urine for his tanning. A flock of starlings began a noisy salute to the rising sun from their perch in the elm near the barn.

Will leaned over and gave Gilbert a shake. His brother waved one arm, rolled over and fell back asleep with a grunt. Regretting his earlier charitable inclination not to dump his brother out of the bed, Will pulled the blanket off of him.

"God rot you, get up!" Annoyed, Will gave his younger brother a hard shove. Gilbert sat up, rubbed his eyes and gave him a smile of such surpassing innocence and verve that a surge of instant guilt for his anger washed through him.

The two boys dressed and went down the narrow staircase. Their sisters were bustling about the kitchen with mother. One was helping the scullery maid prepare some vegetables while the youngest was making faces at one-year-old Richard. Will slipped past the commotion with practiced ease and led Gilbert into the barn and their morning chores. They fed the goats, the chickens and the ducks, hauled firewood and water, and checked for eggs in the small wooden coop. They lifted the wooden cover off the puering vat and stirred the noisome liquid, sliding out the reeking and sodden hides, draping them over a long pole and carrying them in a solemn and malodorous procession into the drying barn where they were hung on racks.

Breakfast was blessedly short. Will and Gilbert scrambled upstairs to fetch hornbooks and quills. Will strapped his copy of the *Book of Common Prayer*, his well-thumbed copy of Ovid and his commonplace book[73] into a neat carrying satchel. Gilbert was much less burdened, carrying only his grammar book and his hornbook with loose parchment protruding. Will shook his head in exasperation. Gilbert left a trail of used parchment wherever he went. The younger boy yawned sleepily as they both pushed out the door onto Henley Street. Two younger children raced by, hooting and waving sticks, as they chased a gray cat down the roadway. The cat easily dodged the blows and, hopping up onto a wooden fence post, gave the two children a scathing look through narrow yellow eyes before disappearing into the long grass.

The two boys turned their reluctant feet down Henley Street, angling through Rother to pick up Richard before wending their

---

[73] Notebook

way to High Street. Richard was talking in a voluble constant stream that Will managed to ignore. As they dawdled their way along High Street, Will found his nervous eyes shifting to every darkened doorway and shadowed alleyway. The events in Shottery were never far from his mind.

"It's a question of how much to trust."

The voice spoke almost in his ear. Will started and turned, almost falling.

"Careful." The man reached out a quick balancing hand before pulling it back and regarding Will with a steady gaze.

Will stared. It was the player.

The man before him was tall, even without the wide-brimmed feathered hat. The grey eyes that looked back at him were clear and honest, with a hint of something akin to a banked fire. Will's immediate impression was that the player could see right through him. He had one of those knowing gazes that invited conversation and confession. The man's face was narrow, crowned with cropped dark hair and framed by a tapered beard. A thin white scar traced along the edge of his left jaw and hooked up at the end in a curlicue, not unlike a signature.

Will took two abrupt steps back in sudden fear. The man raised both hands in placation.

"You've naught to fear from me, boy."

Will took another careful step back. Richard and Gilbert had stopped several feet further down the road. Gilbert looked confused until he recognized the tall man.

"Will, it's the player we saw the other day! The Dunkirker!" Gilbert stepped forward excitedly, one arm flailing in imitation of a sword until Richard yanked him back.

"We need to talk," the man said to Will in a low voice. "Somewhere quiet."

Will nodded in reluctant acquiescence and turned to the other boys. "Richard, take Gilbert with you. Tell the schoolmaster I'm helping my father today."

"You certain of this, Will?" Richard asked, giving Tyburn a baleful look that spoke volumes. Will had told him about the incident in the alleyway when he had caught up with him at the timberyard after escaping. It confirmed Richard's sour opinion of all players as wastrels and brawlers.

"Yes, take Gilbert to school and try to get him to keep his trap closed."

"Can I beat him?" Richard suggested.

"With sticks," Will confirmed loud enough for Gilbert to overhear.

Gilbert was quieted by the threat for a moment, his excitement quailing before his brother's wrath. The two boys turned back up the street, both of them glancing back at Tyburn and Will several times before the man led the boy away.

Tyburn took Will into the Crown's dusty innyard. Two carts stood by the kitchen entrance, so they settled on a bench across from it. Will noticed the location had a view of both entrances and the exterior staircase leading to the inn rooms upstairs.

"So they call you Will?" the man asked.

"Yessir."

"My name is Tyburn. My friends call me Kit." This met with silence. "As I said earlier, it's a question of how much to trust."

The boy made no response but glanced at Tyburn with a keen and quizzical eye.

"Some might say it madness to trust a stranger. You should sooner trust in the tameness of a wolf or a whore's oath, as trust a stranger of passing acquaintance." The man paused and removed his hat, giving his head a weary scrub. "Yet you and I have a connection. We are both marked men."

"Marked?" Will asked in a small voice.

"Aye, marked. Your lost letter is a millstone around my neck, a bane that has already sent one innocent man to the graveyard."

"Master Sturley . . ." Will said.

Tyburn cocked his head, regarding the boy with a quick look. "Sturley? The man to whom the letter was addressed? He's dead?"

The boy looked confused. "Wasn't that who you were referring to? His wife is also dead."

Tyburn whistled soundlessly to himself. "No. One of our troupe was murdered last night." His voice, despite its control, had a ragged edge to its inflection. "As far as I can tell they suffered some confusion in the dark and thought they were killing me. " He paused. "These seem to be serious people."

Will watched the player's features cloud in thought and then the mask slid back into place. The man turned to Will and gazed at him with eyes the color of thunderheads. "I'll do you the grace of speaking plainly. I need to know what in God's name is going on. What is in this letter? Why kill for it?"

The boy hesitated. He let his gaze travel across the innyard, staring outward and reaching for his reply. "Your pardon sir, but as you noted, it is a question of trust."

Tyburn made no response, gazing steadily at the boy.

"Fair face may hide a doubling dissembling heart," Will said, turning his head to look directly at the player for the first time, meeting his gaze. "I do not know if you are a man in just assemblage or one in sly disguise, gilding himself for his own purposes."

"You've got a fair piece with words, boy; that was well said. In answer, nothing spoken could verify my *bona fides*, although I'll note I fail miserably on the 'fair face' aspect. I would hope my actions spoke to my character. I could have left you to the Fates the other night." He tilted his head, giving the boy a quizzical look. "You'd still be picking your teeth out of the mud if I had. And my friend might still be alive."

The boy, eyes averted from the player, nodded in tentative agreement.

"These are dangerous days, boy. Whoever is behind these slayings has a bastard's nature, deformed of conscience, seeking only power and fear."

Will shivered but gave another barely perceptible nod.

"So what say you? Do we seek an alliance against these vipers? Or fall singly?"

Will nodded, recognizing the futility of his position. He was, he thought, angling between Scylla and Charybdis. He grimaced to himself. Master Hunt would probably be pleased with the metaphor although the player would not be flattered by the comparison.

"Good." Tyburn regarded the eleven-year-old with a sharp eye. He well recalled his own habit at that age of answering every question with the response best qualified to slide out from under trouble. He had no doubt that young master Shakespeare would be every bit as adroit at avoiding any real promises but, he thought, you take allies where you can. Even when they were short.

"So . . . now what?" Will asked, puzzled by the long silence that had followed his nod.

Tyburn appeared lost in thought, regarding a small group of noisy men across the innyard who were rolling a series of barrels out of the inn storeroom and hefting them into the wagon. Tyburn rubbed the stubble on his face tiredly, observing that the men wore the bear-and-ragged-stick livery of the Earl of Leicester, procuring supplies for the multitude descending on Kenilworth for the queen's summer progress.

Reaching into his doublet, Tyburn pulled out the folded letter. Will reached out with one hand to take it but Tyburn moved it away.

"That is my father's letter . . ." Will began.

"I would hope not, given how this missive tends to carry death in its shadow." Tyburn unfolded it. "I opened it last night."

Will began to interrupt but thought better of it and closed his mouth into a thin, tight line. Tyburn read aloud the note that Will had written for his father.

"That's your father's note, right?"

"Yes. I wrote it for him. I am his quill."

"And this one . . ."--Tyburn pulled the smaller letter out of the packet--"is the one being couriered to your Sturley." Will nodded.

"I opened it as well last night." He turned his head at Will's audible huff. "Your pardon boy, but I'll remind you that my friend is dead and the letter your father passed on appears to be at the centre of these events."

Will, his curiosity overcoming his irritation, leaned in closer. "What does it say?"

"We'll get to that," Tyburn commented off-hand. "Tell me about Sturley."

Will hesitated. "He's a farm holder in Shottery--a small village near here. He has some cows and a small acreage with some apple trees. My father bought some property from him two years ago adjacent to some fields that came from my mother's family. Sometimes he sells us hides for leather."

"Not a man given to correspondence." noted Tyburn.

"No. I don't think he can read."

"Was he Catholic?" Tyburn asked, keeping his voice casual.

Will did not answer. Kit glanced at the boy's face and the closed expression on it.

"Are you Catholic, Will? Your parents?" Will stood and turned to walk away. Cursing his own impatience, Tyburn caught the boy's arm. "Wait."

The boy hesitated and then glared at the player with obvious anger. "My family is a closed book to you—none of your business. I do not care to see my family in ruin from calumnious words."

Tyburn spread his hands wide in a conciliatory gesture. "My apologies."

"I am not a fool, master player."

"Obviously not," said Tyburn, gesturing at the neat bundle of schoolbooks. In an effort to give the conversation some normalcy Tyburn commented offhand, "I see you're reading Ovid. You are well-versed in the classics?"

The boy calmed somewhat. "Master Hunt insists on a mastery of Ovid, Cicero and Caesar."

Tyburn chuckled in a rueful voice. "My father always used to complain 'too much Caesar, not enough scripture.' He was probably right."

Will resumed his seat on the bench and Tyburn sat. "You read Plautus[74]?" the player asked, trying to distance himself from his earlier gaffe.

The boy's face brightened. "We do a play at the end of each year from Plautus. He is my very favorite!"

"He's a standard for us on our tours," Tyburn confessed. "Anytime a troupe lacks a play or needs a staple, out comes Plautus. We always need to rewrite him though. With a limited troupe, some of his work involves too much doubling and too many change-ups,[75] every time you turn about it's a new costume and back on the boards." He tapped the letter on his knee for emphasis and glanced down at it.

"Master Sturley was not the end recipient of the letter?" Tyburn said, moving back onto the focus of his questions.

"No," said Will. "I overheard the man say something about..." He hesitated and then continued. "Something about a Jesuit."

Tyburn felt a slow tingle at the base of his spine. "A Jesuit? You are certain that was the term?"

"Yes," Will replied. "What's a Jesuit?"

The player made no reply, gazing thoughtfully at the letter.

"What's a Jesuit?" Will persisted.

---

[74] Titus Maccius Plautus (254-184 BCE) was a Roman playwright famous for his farcical comedies with their familiar stock characters, 'doubled-up' twins, fathers & sons and confused familial relationships. . English renaissance theatre drew heavily on Plautus as the foundation for many of its comedic plays.

[75] Doubling refers to the common practice of having a single actor play multiple roles in a play. It was particularly prevalent in travelling troupes which had a limited number of players to draw on.

"Trouble," replied Tyburn distantly. "Trouble." Will heard the change in the man's tone, the flat intonation that seemed to hang in the air like a noose. He thought about asking again, but the expression on the man's face made him hesitate. Finally he asked, "So just what is a Jesuit?"

"A priest. *Societas Iesu* is an arm of the Catholic Church, the 'soldiers of God' they call themselves sometimes. They serve the pope. Absolutely. Some of them are teachers, some of them missionaries and some of them . . some of them are more than that."

Tyburn regarded Will with a sharp glance out of the corner of his eye. "How's your Latin?"

Will stiffened in defense, remembering he was supposed to be in school. "Good."

"*Ad Maiorem Dei Gloriam.* That's the Jesuits' motto."

"For the greater glory of God," translated Will.

"Yes. And towards that end, some of them will go to very great lengths." His comments were interrupted by a confused commotion at the cart. A grey-bearded man was heaping abuse on one of the liveried men who had jammed a cask hard into the cart, splitting a strake. Dark liquid was running out of the broken barrel, soaking into the dry ground. "Bodwin, you drunken capering fool!" the man shouted, the sound echoing off the enclosed innyard, masked only by the helpless laughter of the other workers as Bodwin, fumbling with the barrel, managed to drop it onto the carter's foot. Bodwin swayed like a pine in a tempest, drunk despite the early hour.

Tyburn grimaced. "The letter," he continued, "is curious. The wax seal is high quality but with no embossed device. The parchment is new and untracked. Clean-edged, fine-cut--a paper of quality, probably Italian." He glanced at the boy. "Any comments?"

"Why do we care about the paper?"

"We don't, we care about who wrote it. The paper at least tells us it comes from a person of quality, or some such person or household with easy access to fine paper."

"What does it say?" Will tried hard but failed to keep his exasperation out of his voice.

Tyburn grinned at the boy's impatience. "Here, I'll read it to you. . 'Best wool, eighteen tods, two and twenty shillings.'"

The boy looked confused.

Tyburn continued. "'Hops, two barrels, six shillings. Gruit[76], three firkins, fourteen shillings and eight pence.' Shall I continue?" The boy's brows were knitted, giving his face an unseemly scowl. "It goes on–ten lines. Prices and amounts for wool, broadcloth, hops, malt, leather, armonic[77], white meats[78] . . ."

Still scowling, the boy reached out a tentative hand. Tyburn released the letter, watching Will as he scanned the document, eyes flitting.

The player waited.

"This is nonsense!" the boy blustered. "For one thing his prices are wrong, except for the wool. No one would pay two crowns for this type of leather." He paused, thinking. Tyburn, reluctant to interrupt, remained silent. The boy glanced at him with a keen look. "It's a cipher, isn't it? I mean, who writes a merchant list on fine paper?"

Tyburn grinned. The lad was sharp as a blade and quick. He had looked at it for at least an hour in the dim-lit barn before realizing that the values were inconsistent. "I think so. But," he said as he reached over and took the letter, "I can't figure out the cipher itself. It's a puzzle. It's not a Caesar and the numerals don't correspond to any letter patterns I can discern."

The Caesar was a simple letter-substitution cipher, often used by merchants to ensure some degree of privacy in their communications. It was, Tyburn knew, in common usage, but whatever was in this missive was not a common one. He had read

---

[76] Spice mixture used in brewing ale
[77] Armenian clay used for medicinal purposes
[78] Cheese and dairy products

Trithemius's *Stegonographia*[79] on ciphers and his *tabula recta*[80] but was unable to discern any comprehensible pattern in the letter. An hour of pointless scrawling letter patterns and substitutes in the pre-grey dawn light on the back of his line sheets had convinced him of that fact. Whatever the letter writer had ciphered would stay ciphered, as far as Tyburn could tell.

"I don't know very much about ciphers," Will confessed.

"I think our time might be better spent trying to determine the recipient or the sender of the letter, rather than deciphering the message." Tyburn observed. "Would your father be inclined to help?"

Will shuddered. "No."

The player shrugged. "If we can't trace it, might be best to speak with him direct." Will started to interrupt but Tyburn held up his hand, waving down Will's objection. "Given that the men seeking it seem inclined to kill first and ask second, taking it to the authorities probably implies the content of the letter would be as dangerous for your father and your family as keeping it quiet and hidden. That route may be no safer. Your father knows who passed it to him–that's a link we may well need. Someone wants it, but until we know why and for what purpose, we have no clear action we can safely take."

The boy quieted as he realized Tyburn was not suggesting turning the letter over to the local magistrate.

"We can hold off dealing with your father for now, but you need to understand." The player fixed the boy with a sharp eye. "That door may close. We need to know."

---

[79] Johannes Trithemius (1462-1526), a German monk, was widely considered one of the first practical theoretical cryptographers. His work, *Stegonographia*, was placed on the *Index Librorum Prohibitorum*, the list of books prohibited by the Catholic Church, in 1609. At least some of his work was 'at large' in England in 1563, in the library of John Dees.

[80] A Tabula Recta is a square table of repeating alphabets. . Each row is shifted slightly to form a substitution table. The repeating alphabets allow the creation of a polyalphabetic cipher allowing the substitution of letters to shift throughout the message.

Will nodded in slow agreement.

The grating squeal of the ungreased wheels filled the air as the liveried men led the two laden carts through the narrow gate, the drunken Bodwin shambling in the wake. Tyburn glanced at the shortening shadows on the ground. The morning was lengthening. . "I have to go to the churchyard. You'd best keep yourself scarce for the rest of the day. See me after the performance this afternoon and maybe we'll have some things to consider."

The boy nodded in acquiescence.

"And keep a weather eye out for those bastards. You don't want to be repeating last night." Will nodded again, stood, and followed the cart through the gate without a backwards glance. The dark liquid from the stove barrel on the cart still dripped onto the dry ground, leaving a delicate, sticky smear in the roadway delineating the cart's path. It reminded him of the dark spattering beneath Sturley's bound form. The boy shivered despite the early morning sunshine and resolved to spend the day hidden under the oaks by the river, fishing out of sight of any casual passerby.

Tyburn watched the boy's slight form until it vanished around the building, then turned and trudged up the dusty road towards the churchyard. He had a friend to bury.

Chapter the Eleventh

THE SHOVEL CUT hard into the thick clay, slicing the thin tree roots that had wended their furtive path through the soil. With a grunt, Robbie hefted the dark earth out of the new-dug grave onto the grass and surreptitiously wiped his eyes. The mid-morning sun was bright and warm. Alec's linen-shrouded body lay on the trundle cart, patiently awaiting its final resting place. Oldcastle was perched on a nearby flat-topped headstone, shifting his ample buttocks from side to side as the hard stone began to dig into his backside.

"That pit dug yet, Robbie?" he called, his voice tinged with impatience.

"Near enough," the young man replied. "Need to move some of these little 'uns first." Robbie began to toss a small collection of yellowed bones onto the soil pile. By their size, Tyburn judged them to be a child's.

"Leave off that." Oldcastle grimaced. "I've no doubt they won't care that Alec will be joining them. Plenty of room for all of us in that well you're digging."

Robbie ignored him and finished collecting the small bones into a neat pile, wrapping them gently with burlap sacking. Tyburn braced himself and extended a hand to the young man, helping him scramble out of the open grave. Robbie gave his clothes a cursory dusting, an action that was merely for effect given the depth of the grime that coated the boy.

Seeing Robbie had completed his work, the other members of the troupe began to drift back graveside while Willens, Robbie and Tyburn picked up Alec's body and laid it on three long rope lengths resting on the grass. Oldcastle looked around impatiently for the church warden, but not seeing any sign of him signaled for the men to lower the body into the grave.

"Bastard churchmen can't leave us alone when we're performing, but can we find one about when we bury our friend? Not unless coin crosses palm," Alleyn grumbled as the rope slid through his hands. Alec's body descended in a series of short jerks.

After a moment Alec rested at the bottom of his grave. Robbie stooped and lowered the burlap sacking with the loose bones into the end of the grave with surprising gentleness. The men slid the ropes out and lined up at the graveside. The only missing members from the troupe were the two Muches, who were guarding the troupe's wagon. Motely stood at the end of the open grave, holding the long wooden pole with its crosspiece from which the Earl of Worcester's pennon flapped and snapped in the steady morning breeze. Oldcastle stood and cleared his throat vigorously. A handful of curious townsfolk watched from the roadside, including a number of children.

"By the Grace of God, we are gathered here to preside over the burial of our friend and compatriot . . ." intoned Oldcastle.

Tyburn let his thoughts drift as the troupe leader prosed on. *The man hates the expense of the funeral but can never resist an opportunity to parade himself.* The mere presence of the curiosity-seekers was enough to ignite Oldcastle's performing instincts. Had no passersby been present, he would probably have given a quick prayer, tossed in some dirt and moved on to an early meal.

He glanced up at the sun angling high in the cerulean blue. The breeze carried the cool, green smell of cut hayfields as it flickered and twirled the leaves of the trees that lined edge of the churchyard, sending dappling shafts of sunlight over the stone and wooden grave markers. Birds were lilting from deep among the leaves and the quiet buzz of a bee as it rumbled past was conspicuous. It was, he thought, a perversely beautiful day.

". . . by Jesu, the Savior and for God and the Queen, may her magnificence never fade. Amen." Oldcastle finished, with a surprisingly elegant bow in the direction of the roadway and the small crowd that had now gathered. He gestured to Motely, who dipped the troupe's flag to the grave and held it for a minute as the players bowed to their friend in respect for the final time.

The group then turned away as Robbie began the task of filling the grave with the loose soil. A cheap wooden marker with Alec's name on it lay to one side. Oldcastle had promised a stone marker in the near future but few of the players believed he would follow through on it. More characteristically, he would bill Alec's wealthy father for the cost of the funeral and the imaginary stone marker and deliver himself a healthy profit from the circumstances, Tyburn thought with uncharitable malice.

"Tyburn, a moment please."

Oldcastle ambled over to where Kit stood, watching as Robbie and Motely shoveled dirt into the rapidly filling grave. Oldcastle gave the half-filled hole an impatient glance and, grasping Tyburn's arm just above the elbow, led him away from the troupe into the shade of the oaks.

"I'd best have that bung[81] we found with Alec," he began.

---

[81] Purse

Tyburn gave a caustic snort. "Not likely."

Oldcastle stiffened and tightened his grip. "Don't mock me, boy. That clink ain't yours. Give it to me and I'll see it right for Alec's family."

"You wouldn't piss on Alec's family if they were on fire," Tyburn replied, giving the troupe leader a look, ignoring Oldcastle's efforts to make his arm grip more forceful.

"You bastard cony-catcher[82]." Oldcastle hissed into Tyburn's ear, careful to pitch his voice low so he could not be overheard. "If I hadn't taken you into Worcester's Men, you'd be dead in some gutter, or laid to rest in a laystill[83]. You give over that bloody purse and every lour[84] in it or . . ."

"Or what? You're already a player shy. You going to drop two on a single tour? You ready to shelve the job in Charlecote as well, because that's what'll happen. How are you going to cover off both lead roles--with Motely and Alleyn? Maybe you can do that in a week, but not sooner, not well." Tyburn pulled his arm from Oldcastle's iron grip and faced the man, using his greater height to stare him down.

"I'll do the comedy instead and cover it with Willens in the lead. He can out-act you in his sleep," Oldcastle grated.

"You'll sever your troupe and wash out your whole summer tour. With the Boar's Head[85] and the innyards closed to plays in London, you'll be sitting on the bench next to me, begging for drinking coin." The two men glared at each other. Tyburn could see Oldcastle's ham-like fists clenching and unclenching.

"You think Worcester will protect you?" sneered Oldcastle in a scathing voice. "We get back to London and I'll break you. You

---

[82] Tricksters or con-men
[83] Manure heap
[84] Money
[85] Innyard outside Aldgate where Worcester's Men performed

won't be able to be an Abraham-man[86] without my say-so. Roar away, you cullion, much may it profit you."

"What you need to ask yourself, is who's pulling Worcester's strings on my behalf? Cross that bridge if you dare."

Oldcstle stared at Tyburn's cold grey eyes, and felt himself filled with a sudden impotent fury and a sickening suspicion that his patron would indeed back Tyburn.

"You think you can frighten me with some gaster[87]?" He'd take a different tack this time.

"The coins are Spanish."

Oldcastle stopped in mid-rebuke. A puzzled look washed the fury from his expression. The man's round face screwed up in perplexity as he thought through the obvious implications. "The boy had no Spanish silver," he said in a soft tone, as if to himself.

"Exactly. Somebody left it, for the purpose of implicating Alec for some scheme." Tyburn kept his face set and his thought, that the trap had been meant for him and not Alec, to himself.

The burly troupe leader let his breath trickle out. "That's a bloody expensive ambush." Tyburn nodded. "To what purpose? We're a bleeding playing troupe; another three days and we're gone anon. Probably be two years before we'd roll back through Stratford."

"I don't think we were supposed to find him. He was supposed to be found with the Spanish coin. Someone wanted to implicate him in something, for their own purposes. My guess is they selected a player because we're transient--maybe he was supposed to look like a courier carrying a message. Either way, Alec's dead, and the trap, such as it was, has gone awry because no one is trumpeting about finding a purse filled with fresh-minted Spanish silver."

---

[86] A vagrant that feigns madness. Also know as a "Poor Tom"
[87] Spectre

"Fie!" Oldcastle spat into the grass. "All the more reason for you to hand over the bung. I can have that silver hammered down and recast soonest."

"No. You can't do it here without someone noising it about--and more to the point, whoever did this will undoubtedly come looking for their monies."

Oldcastle stroked his beard in thought. "They come looking for you, don't expect us to raise hands for you. Belike I tell them my own self."

Tyburn smiled down at the man. "They come looking for me," he said, one hand tapping his rapier hilt, "they may find more than they bargained for."

The voices were pitched low, but despite the precaution they still resounded through the wood-paneled corridor in a low vibrato. Clair tried to ignore the urge growing within in her to stop and listen whenever she passed through the hall. Her father and her brother, undoubtedly, she thought. The two had held frequent meetings in her father's private chamber in recent weeks, though the content of the discussions had not been shared. Each time she passed, she found herself walking with lighter steps, her head craning to discern the muffled voices.

Her brother's comments on her widowed status had rankled. He used words, she thought, like others used daggers, sliding them in through chinks in armor, past ribs or obstructions, with the intent to inflict a mortal wound. The real difficulty, she knew, was that he was partially correct. She had spent the better part of the last year hiding from the world, burying her grief in the familiar, if corrupted, byplay of family. It had taken her months to recognize that without her mother this place could no longer be considered her home. She cursed her own folly in having returned here from Oxfordshire, angry at herself for listening to her father's relentless wheedling imprecations. She had been wary of his intense interest in her late husband's lands, but her own grief had stilled the whispers in her head. By the time she realized his intent, he had filed suit against her in-laws, laying claim to more than half their estates, far exceeding any reasonable widow's claim.

She shook her head at herself as she realized that her slow promenade down the hall had seen her rooted like a tree for several minutes. She turned down the side-passage and then jumped as the heavy door to her father's study slammed open. Guiltily she sidestepped into the window alcove of the side corridor.

". . . you call this skulking about. For the land to be legally forfeit to the Crown, it must be treason. No less." Her father's voice drifted down the corridor, filled with its usual impatient wrath.

Albert's voice slid into play. "Nonsense! We have more than enough from Hall."

"Not enough for Leicester. The man may be greedy but he is a stickler for the details. He will not pursue the matter without the hard evidence, in Arden's own hand."

Albert snorted derisively. "You trust him to uphold his side of the bargain?"

"Then we sweeten the pot. Throw Topcliffe a bone, get him to manage Leicester. Put him on the Jesuit. You know what a fanatic he can be. If he doesn't find the letter and the Jesuit, then the blame falls from us and onto Leicester's own man."

"We can always throw him Clair," Albert suggested.

There was a thoughtful pause. The calm, smooth reply from her father made her insides clench and twist. "A very apt suggestion, boy. Yes, Topcliffe will chase that possibility like a dog after a hare, and we can use another friend at court. He is landed, I believe?"

"In Yorkshire and Lincolnshire, but the man's hungry for more. He'll jump."

A third voice interrupted. "And the player?"

Her father's voice cut off the third speaker. "Use Topcliffe and Lucy to travail him. Let them retrieve the letter for us, but locating the Jesuit is our priority now. Give Topcliffe the scent. Tell him about the silver. Knowing him, he'll settle the player for us as well as the Jesuit."

"I want him dead." The third voice grated.

"What you want is not at issue." Her father's voice cracked like a whip. "You take your orders. For now, we need the Jesuit and we only have six more days until the summer progress departs. With him, the letter and Hall's testimony, we'll have this wrapped. Arden will be twisting in the wind, Leicester will be ecstatic and we will have Warwickshire in our pocket."

Albert gave a thin laugh. "And Clair will have herself a new husband."

Her father's reply was lost in the closing of the door. The sound of heavy feet moving down the corridor made Clair shrink back into the alcove's reassuring shadow. A short, thick man with calloused hands and a permanent scowl stepped past, heading towards the rear entrance to the hall. His brows were knitted in frustration and he was cursing under his breath.

She waited for a few moments to ensure that no one else was coming down the hallway before moving past the junction, turning down the side corridor and heading for the stairs, her breath coming in short, stifled gasps.

Chapter the Twelfth

WILL AND KIT found seats on a rough wooden bench next door to the Bear Tavern. Most of the remaining members of Worcester's Men had filed inside and were now liberally hoisting tankards of warm ale. The quiet pall that had settled over them in the wake of Alec's death had been lifted somewhat by the success of the afternoon's performance.

Word of the murder had spread among the populace of the small market-town the previous evening, so the curious were out in throngs. With a stoic realism born of hundreds of performances in myriad dusty innyards, the Earl of Worcester's Men threw themselves into their craft. The play had been reworked by Willens, roles doubled up and cut in order to allow for Alec's absence. Mundy was pleased that he was permitted to fill Alec's Virtuous Youth role. In the past he had been relegated to minor female roles, with the occasional opportunity for a more robust part. Oldcastle, who had always insisted the boy was good for nothing beyond women, had abruptly reversed himself and loudly proclaimed for Mundy, a fact that left Tyburn amused as he himself had been selected by Willens for the Virtue role. Instead Tyburn had continued in his now expanded role as Vice, albeit without the choreographed fight scene as Mundy's handling of any blade was questionable. Instead he doubled most of Alec's other roles and, beyond the grief for his friend, reveled in the challenge of the fast-changes, revolving characterizations and the new dialogue.

Tyburn sipped his ale and grimaced. He and Will were examining the letter for what felt like the thousandth time. "There's nothing here." Tyburn said, feeling the coil of frustration that had been growing inside him tighten. "I can't find any commonality in the cipher. I'm not a cryptographer." He looked at the paper and sighed. "Maybe there's a key written into the numbers--you use the fourth letter, then the seventh letter and so on?"

"Maybe." Gloom and doubt scudded across Will's face.

Tyburn glanced at the westerning sun and began to fold the paper away. "I think we've wasted enough energy on this tripe." He took another draught of the ale. Perhaps if he drank enough of it, things might start to make sense, he thought. He ran one finger over some rough crude letters that someone had carved deep into the surface of the bench, now worn smooth and polished by much custom.

"I think I'd like to be a player," the boy commented.

Tyburn snorted, amused. "What brought that on?"

Will looked thoughtful. "The way you bring things to life in your plays--great events, people . . . it's . . . like being able to assume another's place in life, to live in a world that is bright as the sun, to make things come alive." The boy stared up at the western sky. "I guess it's a way to pretend to no longer be just Will, who does his schoolwork, copies his lines, goes home and carries out his chores like a dutiful son." The words burst out in quick succession. "The more I learn, the more I see, this place seems so much less than it was." He looked sidelong at Tyburn. "Why are you a player?"

Tyburn took another long drink and studied the passersby. The street was quiet at this time of day. A cart rumbled past, heading for Clopton Bridge. "I was a student. Then a soldier. Now a player. No one is ever any one thing." Kit turned and looked at the boy. "Everyone is a player, Will, even you. No one ever shows their true face to the world. You have one face for your mother, one for your friends, one face you turn towards enemies, one you reserve for lovers . . . the world is naught but a great playhouse within which we all have our roles, wherever Fortune bears us." He took another deep draught. "Everyone wears a mask, Will. Everyone. Never trust to the surface of things."

"Not even yours?"

"Especially not mine," Tyburn replied, distracted. A small group of six men had rounded the corner of Sheep Street. They conferred for a moment and then two of their number disappeared through the door of the tavern. The others split into two parties, one group staying near the front of the establishment, the rest turning down the dank laneway that bordered the inn.

Tyburn watched the men out of the corner of his eye. They wore rapiers. Tyburn was certain he spotted the heavy sway of a peasecod cuirass under one man's long coat but with only a brief half-glimpse he could not be certain. What was certain was that the men moved with a purpose.

"Here." Tyburn took the folded letter and the heavy leather purse found with Alec and handed it to Will. "Take this purse as well. It's Spanish silver so don't show it about. Don't spend it, don't lose it. Hide it. Make sure it's where it won't be found by anyone."

He stood up from the bench, picked up his tankard and waved aside Will's questions. "Away with you. I'll find you tomorrow morning, before we leave for Charlecote."

As Will turned to leave,. Kit gave him one last reminder. "Remember--hide them well and tell no one." The boy nodded in reply and trotted past Middle Row towards home, the purse and the letter secreted under his shirt. He looked back in time to see the player duck under the low beam of the tavern door and disappear inside. He hesitated, wanting to know what was going on, but conscious of the heavy bag of coins nestled under his shirt he turned and trotted up the street at a rapid pace.

Tyburn ambled over to the door. Several locals were exiting, muttering under their breath. One leaned over and whispered in an aside to Tyburn as he passed. "Wouldn't go in there, lad, shaping up for trouble it is."

When Tyburn entered, Oldcastle was talking animatedly at his usual corner table with Willens and Mundy, discussing the day's takings. The remaining players from Worcester's Men were gathered in a small circle around a table near the hearth, playing dice. The ostler had already disappeared into the back room, although Tyburn could see him watching through the curtain. Even the drab that cleaned tables was gone. The two men had taken up positions near the counter and were watching the players with covert stares. They wore rapiers and although they held tankards in their left hands, they showed no sign they were interested in drinking them.

"A cater and an ace[88] bigod! The man wins!" exclaimed Motely. Jack grinned in response and reached out one massive hand to scoop up the two cubes.

"You sure he's not cogging and foisting[89]?" replied Alleyn.

"You wait and watch him lose his day's takings in a moment." The group laughed, for Jack was perpetually in debt due to his gaming.

Tyburn paused just inside the entranceway. The two newcomers were watching the troupe and had their backs to him. To one side he saw an untidy bundle of horse blankets the tavern keeper had stacked in a bin against the wall. These were used by anyone who elected to sleep in the inn common room where the men were drinking. Tyburn edged along the wall, reached down and tugged out a filthy, frayed blanket. He dropped his hat on the floor near the door and wrapped the blanket around himself like a cloak, covering his head, and let his posture slump, adopting the

---

[88] A cater is a four, an ace a one.
[89] Cheating

crouching, supplicating mien of a street beggar. He limped his way into the room, head down, one leg dragging as if palsied.

The men spared him one brief glance before resuming their watch on the players. One man's hand flexed near his rapier hilt. Tyburn judged that whatever was going to happen would happen soon.

"Ale?" he whispered in a low hoarse voice. "Who'll show their love of Christ by buying a poor cripple some ale?"

The men ignored him. Tyburn sidled closer. "Noble sir, will you spare some alms?" He tugged on the nearer man's sleeve.

"Away you," the man said, his voice harsh. His hair was cropped short and his face scarred with the pox. A narrow beard fringed his jaw.

"'Pon my faith, what manner of man treats his fellows so poor. I am dear tempted to chastise you."

"Look you prat," the man began, turning towards Tyburn who at the same instant rose to his full height and slammed the pewter tankard into the man's face. Tyburn felt a momentary pang of regret for his lost ale as the man's eyes rolled back in his skull and he flew backwards, one flailing arm striking his companion across the shoulder. The other man gave a great shout and dropped his hand for his rapier but it was too late. Tyburn was already inside his guard and he brought his hands back, thrusting forward on the man's chest, feeling the hard steel of the cuirass under the fabric of his doublet, giving him a vicious shove that sent him sprawling off-balance across the counter and onto the floor near Willens and the others. The man was on his hands and knees, scrambling to his feet with one hand drawing his sword when Tyburn stepped forward and kicked him in the face. He went down with a shriek of pain, the rapier rattling across the floor to land at the still-seated Oldcastle's feet. The men at the dice game gaped in amazement.

"What by God's precious blood are you doing!" exclaimed Oldcastle. Willens had leaped to his feet and looked at Tyburn with uncertainty.

"We've got trouble," said Kit.

The door to the tavern burst open and the two men from outside stepped in, swords drawn, eyes darting around the room. Tyburn's rapier slid out like a snake's tongue and the men regarded each other in wary readiness, in a moment of balance and calm. Tyburn tightened his grip, assessing the two swordsmen before him. Still holding the verminous blanket in his left hand, now he spun it around his arm so only a loose fold of cloth hung free. It would help guard his left and, if unwrapped at the right moment, could entangle an adversary's blade. He moved ahead in a quick stamping dart, blade sliding forward.

"Cease!" The command was shouted from the open doorway.

The two men facing Tyburn warily took a step back and lowered the points of their weapons. A well-dressed man in his mid-forties stepped past the swordsmen, gently pushing the blades to one side. The man had a long, lugubrious face made lengthier by a square-cut beard. His head was surmounted by a thick fringe of hair and an expensive felt hat with a high crest of yellow feathers. His shirt was silk, covered with a embroidered checkered doublet surmounted by copious amounts of expensive lace. He wore a wide, heavily starched lace ruff, tinted a faint shade of blue, in a style that had gone out of fashion in recent years. A thick chain of office hung around his neck.

"Feckless ruffians," the man observed as he surveyed the two victims, one unconscious, the other rolling on the floor holding his nose and hissing in pain. "Help Gibbs, will you, there's a good chap," he murmured in an aside to one of the swordsmen. The man nodded and replied, "At once m'lord." He sheathed his sword and bent to haul on his arm.

In the stunned silence that followed Willens doffed his hat and bowed deep, followed in haste by the other players and Oldcastle. Tyburn for his part, one wary eye on the remaining swordsman, dropped the moth-eaten blanket on the floor, sheathed his blade and gave a cursory bow.

The man waved the players back and gestured for them to put their hats back on their heads. "Resume your covers, gentlemen. I would have your master attend me. Back to your matters." With a few muttered comments and some wary glances, the troupe resumed their places at the far table.

Oldcastle stepped forward. "How may I be of assistance, m'lord?"

"You are Master Oldcastle? Then this inflictor of hapless carnage must be Captain Tyburn?" He smiled. It was thin, slightly insipid and uninspiring. "I am your patron, Sir Thomas Lucy."

The troupe leader started. "Sir Thomas, we did not expect..."

Lucy waved one hand in diffident reassurance. "I am here on another matter entirely, which occasioned me to bring my men for assistance, a fact that seems to have precipitated your Captain Tyburn towards violence." He gave Tyburn a sly glance.

"For which he profusely apologizes."Oldcastle stammered in response, seeing his new commission potentially flying away like a startled grouse.

"I profusely apologize, my lord," intoned Tyburn. "I thought they were thieves come to steal our takings on this day. I was mistaken."

Lucy waved off the apology with airy largesse. "No matter. I should have been more circumspect and come myself but given the situation, it was deemed prudent to avail myself of armed men." The man seemed unable to stand still, roaming at will in a short, small circle, peering at the dice game which had resumed in the corner, picking up and inspecting Tyburn's now empty tankard, even glumly examining the dilapidated countertop with a critical eye.

"So this is the formidable Captain Tyburn, yes? Your reputation precedes you sir. My friend Hollington mentioned you in one of his letters--claimed you killed four Spanish officers at Walcheren. If I recall correctly, he called you the deadliest swordsman in the Lowlands." The question was unspoken.

"Master Hollington does me credit, but I fear he may be listening to exaggerated soldier's stories," Tyburn replied. Willens looked at Tyburn in a new light, as he had heard nothing of this side of his friend.

"In any case, we will save that discussion for after the performance tomorrow." Lucy's eyes never seemed to focus on the person in front of him, but roamed with restless abandon, taking in the dark wooden beams of the tavern, the smoky detritus of the fireplace and the irregular splatter of blood from Gibbs that had smeared across the rushes covering the floor. "I am, among other roles, the justice of the peace for Warwick. I am here," he continued, "to examine the circumstances in the death of your man, Alec Masterson."

Oldcastle stiffened and his eyes became wary. "We thank you for your assistance in this weighty matter. Alec's death was a horrendous shock for our company. How may we be of assistance to you in this matter, my lord?"

"Questions. Questions, questions, questions. They are vexing, are they not?"

"Indeed, sir." Oldcastle barely finished the second word.

"I will come directly to the point, Master Oldcastle. Spanish silver." The diffidence was gone, replaced by a vulpine gaze.

"Spanish silver, sir?" Oldcastle echoed back in his most casual voice.

"I have it on good authority–from a trusted source–that your player Masterson was in fact a courier carrying letters, tokens of authority and coin--to be precise, Spanish silver. These monies and accoutrements were intended as a part of a jesuitical conspiracy to assassinate our Sovereign Queen." The room went dead silent. The dice players were frozen, listening. "The infernal machinations of the Papists and their anti-Christ Pius are legion. They would overthrow our Blessed Sovereign and place a reign of terror and devil-worship in her place. They would burn the righteous and lift high the traitors that lurk amongst us. They would," he spat, "place a Spaniard or that bitch-queen Mary on England's throne."

Oldcastle's mouth was agape in a mix of bafflement and terror. It was almost worth it, Tyburn thought, to see him at a loss for words. Tyburn burst into laughter. The unexpected sound cut through the silence like a shot. Lucy's eyes slid to Tyburn. "Alec's no conspirator. Nor a courier. If he ever accepted monies to carry a letter--any letter--chances are great the coin would be taken but the letter would end up at the bottom of his trunk for several years at best."

Lucy turned his head, gazing obliquely over his shoulder to regard Tyburn with hooded eyes. "I assure you my source is impeccable."

"With respect Sir Thomas, your source is mistaken. We found no letters, nor silver or any such." Lucy stepped closer to Tyburn, his eyes examining Tyburn's face. They lingered in speculation on the thin scar highlighting Tyburn's jawline and then darted away.

"Then you will have no objection to my men searching your wagon and belongings?"

Oldcastle gave Tyburn a quick searching glance. "No, of course not, my lord, provided they do no damage to our costumes and accoutrements."

Lucy smiled. His teeth protruded, the lower set blackened like shiny pebbles from drinking sugar water[90]. "Good! I am glad you consented willingly. My men are already at work. I would have been sore disappointed had I needed to revoke your license. It would have been extraordinarily disruptive for my entertainments on the morrow."

"Quite," Oldcastle said. Tyburn caught the tight undercurrent beneath the troupe master's voice.

"And now yourselves?" Lucy continued.

---

[90] Sugar water was a very common drink among the nobility and at court prior to tea and coffee becoming a more established beverage. Queen Elizabeth herself was described as having teeth "like small black pearls" due to regular imbibing.

"Sir?" Oldcastle asked.

"A search," Lucy replied in a patient tone, "of your persons. For the silver."

"Sir, this is an affront." Oldcastle puffed up like a pigeon. "We are the Earl of Worcester's Men, we are not party to any conspiracies, purveyors of information or plots." He drew himself up. "Worcester's Men are England's. We do not bow to Rome."

"Then you have nothing to fear," Lucy soothed, one hand fanning the air in a placatory gesture. He signaled. Two additional men stepped out of the back room, having made their way in through the kitchen entrance. With reluctance Oldcastle consented to the search. Lucy's men, joined by the unfortunate Gibbs, whose nose had been broken by Tyburn's kick, began to search the men, beginning with the dice players.

The search, Tyburn thought, was perfunctory at best. They did not feel the seams of clothes for hidden coins sewn into the fabric, or check the men's hats for secret pockets. They turned out all the men's pockets and emptied their purses and bungs onto the table, sifting them for anything Spanish looking. There was a moment's excitement when one of the men thought he had found a Spanish coin but it was merely a Dutch doit[91]. Aside from a disgusting slab of rotting cheese that Motely had been inexplicably carrying in one pocket, nothing extraordinary came to light.

Gibbs stepped up to Tyburn, a bitter light clear in his eyes. "Pay you back for this 'un, I will," he hissed in undertone as he pulled roughly at Tyburn's pockets. Tyburn's small supply of coinage, most courtesy of his card game from the previous day, was emptied and examined. The search of Tyburn was more assiduous than that of the other players, due to Gibbs's angry thoroughness.

There was a sudden hiss of triumph from the man, marred by his now broken nose. He slid a small round disk out of the inner

---

[91] A small Dutch coin

pocket of Tyburn's doublet. Tyburn felt a sudden stab of disquiet. He had forgotten the small waxen disk that had been found clutched in Alec's nerveless hand. He had tucked it into an inner pocket and the concerns over the Spanish silver and the letter had driven it from his memory. He cursed inwardly as Gibbs held the disk up and gestured to Sir Thomas.

Sir Thomas ambled over to the counter and, taking the wax disc from his man's hand, peered at it with myopic eyes. "My lor—" Tyburn was cut off by Gibbs slamming his fist hard into Tyburn's abdomen. Tyburn folded over gasping in pain. The blow had been precise, hard and well-aimed. He coughed, trying to pull air into his lungs.

"Nobody asked you to speak, cully." Gibbs grated in Tyburn's ear, pulling him up straight, none too gently.

"Now, now, kindly let the gentleman speak." Lucy was flipping the disc over to regard the underside. He smiled. His wet, blackened teeth glistened. "So, Master Tyburn, you were about to explain this item?"

"I . . ." He got no further as Gibbs punched him in the stomach again, harder this time. Tyburn gasped and retched and dropped onto one knee. Willens stepped forward to intervene but Oldcastle held one hand against his chest, giving his head an almost imperceptible shake. Lucy's remaining men, their hands ready on their swords, kept their eyes fixed on the players grouped around the table, who stirred restively.

Kit gagged once more, tasting vomit and bile in the back of his throat. He coughed. His vision was blurred with pain. He spat the detritus onto the rush-covered wooden floor and straightened, one hand holding his stomach. He glanced at Lucy, whose expression hadn't shifted in the slightest. He maintained that look of mild, innocent inquiry and vague, unformed pacific happiness. Tyburn could taste the coppery taste of blood in his mouth. In the back of his mind, he burned. He watched Gibbs out of the corner of his eye, assessing and measuring.

"My lord," he began again. Gibbs's fist didn't have far to travel but this time Tyburn was prepared. He had thought through the event through in his mind, seeing it happen, rehearsing it in his imagination, steeling himself. In a blurring fast movement, the player pivoted, feeling the fist brush past his belly. His right hand shot out and grasping Gibbs's wrist, pulled it hard across the corner of the worn wooden countertop. Tyburn twisted himself around, his back now to the man but his left hand clasped over his right and with brutal, sickening force, he yanked the arm down against the counter, throwing his weight on it, bracing it so it couldn't lever away from the downward pressure.

Gibbs's arm broke with the nauseating snap of a breaking twig.

Without pausing to enjoy any sense of satisfaction, Tyburnwhipped his left arm backward, the elbow cracking into Gibbs' already broken nose with wicked efficiency. The man toppled backwards, the arm flailing loose, his face a mask of blood. The screaming caused Lucy's men to turn and take an involuntary step backwards. Their swords were half-drawn before Lucy waved them back to position. He regarded the bloody, writhing figure on the floor with bemusement.

"Now I see why the Spanish took a dislike to you, Captain."

Tyburn spat on the man now lying twitching and clutching at his shattered arm and raised his eyes to regard the nobleman. "As I was saying, I had forgotten about that thing. We found it in Alec's hand when we found his body. I tucked it into my pocket and thought nothing else about it until your man fished it out."

Sir Thomas held it out to Tyburn. "You know what it is?"

"No idea, my lord."

"It appears to be a Catholic sacramental, an *Agnus Dei*[92]." He tossed the small disk to Tyburn who looked at it with caution. The

---

[92] Literally "Lamb of God", a reference to Jesus Christ.

small round wax disk was embossed on both sides, one with the image of a small lamb bearing a cross, the other side with the crossed keys of the Papacy. He cursed to himself.

"The pope himself blesses these Papist amulets," Lucy said, his voice even but with an undercurrent of triumph. "How do you explain its presence on your 'innocent' friend?"

Tyburn, thinking fast, replied, "I don't, my lord. How it came to him I cannot speak for certain, except that it doubtlessly came to him after death."

Lucy looked affronted by the statement. "Nonsense! How can you make such a claim?"

"Is it not true that in death a man's grasp is exceedingly tight? Does he not grip hard, with all his strength as though to stay his departure from this earth?" Kit turned to the swordsmen and gestured to them. "Have you not found it so?" One man nodded and several players murmured their acquiescence.

Gibbs was on his knees now, shivering, holding his right arm out extended away from his body. His left hand groped in vain at his scabbard, trying to draw his rapier. . Tyburn gave him a look of scathing contempt that left little doubt in the stricken man's mind on what might happen if he succeeded in drawing his blade. The man subsided on his haunches, crooning to himself as blood dripped copiously from his crushed nose to puddle on the floor.

"This Catholic token is wax, my lord. Not so hard that I cannot crumble it with the pressure of my fist. If clutched in the hands of a dying man, especially one that died by violence and not peaceably in his sleep, would it not be crushed or damaged? This is immaculate, my lord, and was held loose in his hand when found. It was placed. After death." Tyburn pointed at the surrounding men in the tavern. "Do you not agree?" The Earl of Worcester's Men nodded in agreement.

The look on Lucy's face would have curdled milk. He pursed his lips. "Perhaps you are correct, Captain Tyburn. It does not matter. It is clear that some diabolical plot is in motion and whether your player was involved or no, I cannot in good conscience permit you to depart this locale until the matter is thoroughly laid to rest."

Oldcastle exploded. "We are bound for Coventry in three days' time. You have no justification for staying us!"

Lucy turned his gaze to Oldcastle. "I have all the justification I require. I have *prima facie* evidence of your involvement in some heinous Papist plot, tangential though you might claim it to be." He stepped forward. "I can seize your goods and your chattels. I can place you in the stocks, Master Oldcastle, for the idlers and the car-men[93] to mock, if I deem it necessary. It is my authority as justice of the peace to rescind your permission to travel beyond the boundaries of this parish. If necessary I shall revoke your letters of performance."

A line of red fury was sliding up Oldcastle's face. "I shall be writing to the Earl of Worcester, my lord, in the strongest possible terms regarding this infamy. . This is an unseemly affront against an innocent party. We are the ones offended against in the wrongful death of our friend and fellow player! Why would you restrain us?"

"You are involved in this, Master Oldcastle." Lucy sighed, as though the conversation was becoming tiresome. "I cannot permit your troupe to depart until the matter of this Jesuitical plot is settled. You may, of course, appeal to Leicester direct but I suspect you will not receive any reply until well after the queen's departure, which is not for some days.

"You are still free to carry out your trade. I will not prevent you from continuing your performances in the town, so you may continue to maintain yourselves according to your custom. Permission to travel outside of the confines of Stratford is, however, strictly forbidden, with the exception of your duty in Charlecote, to which I look forward with immense anticipation." He smiled.

---

[93] Dung cart drivers

The look on the troupe leader's face was a study in anger but there seemed little he could do. Lucy was well within his prerogative to restrain the players. Indeed, Tyburn thought, the comparative laxity of Lucy's restrictions was surprising. He rationalized that the man saw no purpose in physical confinement of the players. It was cheaper and easier to allow them to fend for themselves without having to delve into his purse to provide board for the men.

Oldcastle nodded his reluctant burning acquiescence and, removing his hat, gave his temporary patron a polite, if restrained, bow. The remainder of the troupe hastily doffed their headgear and bowed in response. Sir Thomas Lucy smiled that thin-lipped humourless smile and, as he turned to leave, paused. "Your man Masterson--one of your better actors?"

"Indeed sir, a sore loss for our company."

The man gave a smile that appeared genuine, the first such since entering the tavern. "Then I will be forced to reduce your remuneration for tomorrow. I will, by God's hand, not be experiencing your best performance due to your tragic loss of one of your best players. I think some reduction in the cost would be equitable, don't you agree?" He nodded at the speechless Oldcastle and signaling his men, stepped out past the Bear's heavy doorframe into the sunlit street. His men gathered up the unfortunate Gibbs and the other supine man and left.

The troupe was frozen, regarding Oldcastle with wary eyes, waiting for the inevitable cannonade of obscenities, but he sighed, rubbed one hand over his thinning top hair and sat back on his bench with a weary slouch to his shoulders. Willens leaned in to whisper some brief suggestion but Oldcastle shook his head.

Tyburn picked up his empty battered tankard and after inspecting it, waved it at the ostler who had emerged from his place of hiding to resume service. The man refilled the mug and Tyburn took a deep gulp, feeling the warm ale settling his abused stomach. He sent the man back for another and once it arrived, kicked a bench out and sat across from Oldcastle, plunking the drink down in front of the older man. Oldcastle ignored the player, but reached out and took a draught.

"That complicates things."

Tyburn nodded in agreement.

Oldcastle looked pointedly at Willens and gave a quick jerk of his head. Willens nodded, stood and walked over to observe the now subdued dice game in the corner.

"You think Alec was carrying some rot for someone?"

"No. It's nonsense. Alec never thought past his next drink or whore."

"He did go to Oxford," Oldcastle observed in a bleak voice. The reputation of the college as a haven of Papists and humanists was well-known. Several years before, Edmund Campion, one of the most renowned scholars at the university, had departed Oxford first for Ireland and then Douai, heralding a rush of like-minded Catholic sympathizers.

Tyburn snorted. "He spent his entire time drinking and gaming. Theatricals were the only other thing that interested him. He's no Papist courier."

"No," agreed Oldcastle. "But somebody desperately wants everyone to think he was."

Tyburn took another drink. "So they do."

"And you know something about what's going on." It wasn't a question.

"Me?" Tyburn queried offhand. "I am a man labouring in ignorance and darkness."

"Of that I have no doubt, but you know something about these events." He gave a sardonic laugh. "I'm not some prating fool, Kit. I've been in this business since Henry's day. I've seen my share of close packings[94] and byzantine plots. I played the court under

_____

[94] Secrets

Mary and watched all those bastard pimps and lords circling around, baiting and scheming like a bunch of bloody Italians."

Tyburn did not reply. He wondered what the weathered player was driving at, for the man never held a conversation without a purpose.

"I'll make you a deal. You squire us out from under Lucy's thumb and free us to move onto Coventry, and I'll square your debts with me. Completely. Not a penny unpaid, free and clear."

Tyburn looked at Oldcastle's guileless stare.

"I don't care how you do it," the man continued. "Swive his wife, butter his bread, tell him your tales of derring-do from Flanders, kiss his lordly arse if need be," he grated forcefully, "but free my troupe." He glared into Tyburn's grey eyes.

Tyburn met Oldcastle's gaze. He nodded once and raised his tankard in response. "I have your word on it?"

Oldcastle stared back at him, and gave his mug a brief tilt. "You do, bastard liar that I am."

"So now what?"

"Now, we get drunk. And laugh about how much you buggered up that poor bastard Gibbs. . . ."

Chapter the Thirteenth

TYBURN'S HEAD ACHED.

His mouth felt thick and foul, coated with a thick, rancid fur that would not dissipate, no matter how much water he sluiced to rinse out the taste. He rubbed one hand over his face and contemplated for a moment gulping down another tankard of sour ale or guzzling the dregs of the fetid canary[95] that Willens had sprung for the previous evening to help chase away the unpleasant tang. *Hair of the dog that bit you*, Tyburn thought. He shuddered and felt his abused stomach heave.

Whether it had been the run-in with Lucy or the pent-up frustration of the last two days that pressed him to it, the previous evening Kit had determined to do his utmost to drink away his problems. He wasn't alone. The remaining members of the troupe had thrown themselves into the evening's bacchanal with unreserved enthusiasm, partially as a belated send-off for Alec and partially out of a morbid sense that they soon wouldn't be able to

---

[95] Fortified wine

afford ale, if their restriction to Stratford remained in effect for any length of time. None of the troupe was sanguine about the chance of having Worcester intervene and, in any case, it would take several weeks for any reply from their patron to arrive once he was informed of the situation.

He winced. His head throbbed with a slow, relentless pulsation, accompanied by the rumble of a heavy wagon passing along the road. Earlier he had dunked his head in the horse trough outside the Bear Inn in the vain hope that a dousing in cold water would ease the pounding in his skull. It was, he thought in retrospect, not an efficacious treatment.

The player threaded his way down the now busy Stratford street. The roadway led west from the long, elegant, arched span of Clopton Bridge frowning over the slow-moving Avon, through the Bar Gates and up into the town proper. Once past the Bear and Swan inns, houses built up in quick succession, many of them elegant with glass windows, bespeaking the commercial success of many of Stratford's merchant class. Middle Row rose like a low timbered hedge of smaller houses, dividing the street into two separate streams connected by small alleyways between the buildings. Tyburn elected to follow the left hand path past Middle Row, along the route that led to the market cross at High Street.

Though it was still early, it was a market day in Stratford and the streets bustled with morning commerce. Makeshift stalls had sprung up on every corner while laden carts and wagons piled high with produce stood along the roadway. Thick bundles of carrots, fat cabbages, lettuces, beans, peapods and other sundries were stacked in baskets and blanketed the rickety tabletops. Women moved with calm purpose through the bustle picking over the offerings. Small children raced among the stalls, chasing one another in an elaborate game of tag. One little boy sat unmoved by the chaos around him, crunching on an apple he had filched from a nearby wagon. A fishmonger was busy prying off the top of a cask filled with fat salted herring shipped in from the coast. A thin coat of white fuzzy mold covered the top layer of fish, the sight and smell of which made Tyburn's stomach roil anew. Ahead of him a stout man and a young lad prodded a small herd of limping cattle towards Rother Market. One beast angled towards one of the tables piled high with vegetables with curious intent but was shooed away by a small girl of no more than five, waving a long elm switch.

The raucous cries of the various hawkers split the air. A strident shout of "Hot codlings!"[96] echoed off the timbered buildings and the stony cobbles. As he drew nearer to Henley Street, ahead he could see the tall timbered façade of the glover's house. The vertical wooden beams gave the house a deceptive tall look, as though it were stretching itself skyward an inch at a time. He could see the glover had set out a narrow table and a leather rack in front of his abode, draped with a selection of fine gloves and other sundry leather goods.

He paused, tugged at by a sudden sense of caution. Sidestepping a robust pair of Puritan matrons who gave him a matched set of reproachful glances, Tyburn angled his way across the street and stopped several buildings shy of his goal. He examined the neighborhood activity. A still figure leaning against the corner of a laneway between two houses a few doors down. Kit smiled slowly, recognizing one of the men from the altercation in the tavern alleyway two nights before. Headache forgotten, he ducked between the houses, moving parallel to where the man loitered. Turning to the right, he clambering over a low split-rail fence, and ducked under a trellis. He passed a vegetable garden and a small shed, clambered over another fence and dropped down behind a cart piled high with firewood. He stole a glance from behind the cart. The watcher was lingering under edge of the overhang of the building, his eyes fixed on the glover's house on the north-eastern side of the street. Tyburn drew his dagger. He

---

[96] Baked apples

preferred his rapier but for this type of close quarters, knife work was best.

Tyburn moved at an unhurried pace behind the man, placing each foot on the ground before rolling his weight forward. The watcher continued his surveillance unabated. Kit moved the last few steps behind the man, the dagger held loose in his long fingers.

He slipped the blade up against the man's unshaven throat. He lifted his chin, startled, but froze as Tyburn hissed in his ear. "You twitch again and I butcher you like a hog."

The watcher subsided. He gave an audible gulp. Tyburn reached up with his free hand and tugged him back into the alleyway away from the sight of the street, unceremoniously pushing him back against the woodpile.

"What do you want?" the loiterer muttered over one shoulder, his fear evident in his voice. He was broad and heavy, yet a full head shorter than the player. His face was crowned with a drunkard's nose that had been broken many times and was covered with a fine tracery of burgundy vessels, perambulating like a river delta across the protuberance. A long, greasy moustache hung like a pair of bats under an eave. He was dressed as a day labourer. Tyburn continued to hold the dagger along the thug's throat, wrinkling his nose at the rank smell. *Probably pissed himself.*

"You are going to answer my queries. All of them, or I leave you here with your throat slit open for the kites to peck." He punctuated his demand with a jab of the blade tip under the man's chin. A bead of blood welled forth and dripped away. After a moment, the man nodded. His moustache bobbed in concordance.

"Why are you watching the glover's house?"

"Cuttle ordered me to keep watch. The glover's on the chain and Cuttle thought he might know where . . ." He hesitated and Tyburn leaned imperceptibly on his blade. ". . . where the Jesuit is hiding."

"Who's Cuttle?"

"You . . . you met 'em. In the lane, t'other evening. You put him down. Never seen that done before." The man gave Tyburn a searching look. "He'll never forgive that 'un. Not a safe man to cross, he is."

"I'll keep that in mind. What do you mean 'on the chain?'"

"He's a courier for those letters the Papists send around."

"How do you know?"

"That priest gave 'em up. We been eyeballing them every time a letter goes up the chain. Collecting the replies."

"Why?"

The man gaped. "Cause we were tol' to."

"Told by who?"

"Cuttle."

"Who told Cuttle?"

"Don't know the man's name. He lives over in Henley, to the northwest of here. Only met him once. He's a real blood[97]."

"So why," Tyburn asked with a harsh tone and tightening of his hold on the blade, "does this blood care about a bunch of damned recusants passing messages? Why doesn't he just whistle up the pursuivants and have the lot of them condemned?"

The man started to shrug but stopped as Tyburn leaned in on the blade.

"I just do what I'm told. Cuttle said to watch the glover's place in case Hall came back--that's the priest," he added in a helpful tone. "And to . . ." He hesitated. Tyburn prodded, once. "To watch for you in case you showed up with the letter."

"What's in the letter?"

The man looked confused. "I dunno. I don't read."

"So what do you want the Jesuit for?"

"S'blood want's him, not me. I dunno why, but he claimed he was mint.[98]"

---

[97] A fast or foppish man
[98] gold

"Mint how?"

"Jus' mint. That's all. That an' the letter."

"Where do I find this priest?"

The man tried to ease his throat away from the blade but Tyburn continued to press it tight against the man's bristled gorge.

"Dunno. He's flown. Maybe at Arden's. "

"Arden's?"

"S'where he lives. Supposed to be a gardener but he's Arden's priest, Edward Arden."

At last, Tyburn thought, *I'm making some progress. I should have threatened to slit throats earlier.*

"And this blood and Cuttle want Arden's letters to this Jesuit?"

The man nodded again.

"So tell me about Arden."

"He's the high sheriff. Owns huge tracts of land in Warwickshire. Prissy bastard so's I hear. He's also a bloody Papist." He added in haste, "Or so Cuttle tells it."

"So where do I find him?"

"Coads, I don't know." He winced as the tip of the blade drew another small droplet of blood in response. "They got a place, an estate, north of here."

"Who killed the player?"

"Not me!" the man exclaimed, his face wan. "I don't know nothing about that. Might 'ave been Cuttle. He wants you done, I know that much."

Tyburn gazed at the man in consideration, contemplating how to deal with him. More complications and a murder wouldn't do, he decided. "I'm tired of killing people, so I'd rather not waste any more of my time on you. Nor do I want to be tripping over you. You need to disappear. Out of the parish."

His victim began to protest volubly. Tyburn shrugged in nonchalance. "Very well, dead then." He raised the blade and the lout shrank back against the wall, babbling in protest. Tyburn stilled him with a look. He lowered his dagger. "I told you, I'm tired of killing people. I could just cut out that meaty tongue of yours and feed it to those crows; that would suit my purpose well enough." With impeccable timing a harsh croak came from the tall elm beyond the glover's house. The man looked at the player and the flat grey eyes looking back left little doubt in his mind that the player was serious.

Tyburn pulled out his purse with his left hand and removed several small copper coins. He held the coins up and then dropped them onto the ground. "You are smoke on the wind or your tongue is worm food. The choice is yours." He stepped back, dagger still in his hand.

The loiterer stared down at the coins. "For how long?" he asked. "Never been further than Warwick before . . ."

"You stay out of Stratford for at least a month. By then, we'll be gone and you won't be dead and buried, which is what will happen if you cross my path again."

The lout rubbed his face with one hand, glanced down at the coins and back at the blade in Tyburn's hand. Watching the player, he nodded a reluctant assent and bent to pick up the coins, cautious eyes drifting up. He pocketed the coins and stood.

"Now bing a waste." Tyburn watched him disappear down the alleyway, slow at first and then faster as he realized he wasn't being followed.

Tyburn pursed his lips in reflection. He wouldn't stay gone for long, Tyburn thought. The man's courage would billow up with every step he took away from the player. At least he wouldn't be watching the glover's house anytime soon. Given Cuttle's apparent nature, Tyburn doubted the watcher would ever report their encounter, so at least he had gained some breathing space.

He sheathed his dagger and started across the street to speak with the glover.

"Master Shakespeare. God be with you on this fine day."

"Ahhh, the player Tyburn. Welcome! I have your goods waiting." The glover sorted through a small pile of leather goods and pulled out a set of small, flat leather bladders with a set of ties threaded through one end. "These should do you proper. I made them from kidskin, very thin, light and fine. The pull-strings you clasp just so." He demonstrated, giving the string a tug, causing the funnel-like end to open.

"They won't leak, will they?" Tyburn was dubious at the new design.

John Shakespeare looked affronted. "These sir, are a vast improvement over the sample you brought me on your previous visit. They will hold their seals well, exceptional, tight and fine," he concluded.

"I don't know," said Tyburn, amused at the man's exasperation. "The last batch, bought from a very reputable leathermaker in London no less, leaked like sieves. It was a sight, blood pouring out in the middle of a morris[99] all over the boards." He shook his head. "I don't know about these pull-ties."

Shakespeare pulled the bladder out of Tyburn's hand and, gesturing for the player to wait a moment, disappeared through the sturdy timber door into his house. Tyburn grinned to himself and glanced around. "You can come out." He called in a low voice.

Will's head popped up from behind the table by the corner. "How did you know I was there?" Tyburn grinned.

John Shakespeare re-emerged, the bladder in his hand now swollen. "Will, aren't you supposed to be bringing out that stack of cheveril sheets?" In response the boy pointed to the table which was covered by a stack of fine, almost white leather. Shakespeare nodded and passed the bladder over to the player. Tyburn weighed the taut pouch in his hand. It gurgled. Filled, it was an inch thick and could easily be palmed or slid under a layer of clothing. He tilted it upside down and regarded the bladder with grudging respect as no liquid seeped from either the seams or the tied end.

---

[99] dance

"If I may," Shakespeare said with brisk efficiency, and took the bladder from him. He pointed the spout away and tugged on one of the strings. The bladder deflated, sending a small stream of water cascading out. "So you can see, no leakage, no spillage and it re-seals tight as a drum. As a drum." He repeated for emphasis, giving the table a quick knock for luck.

Recognizing that his attempt to beat down the agreed price was floundering, Tyburn parted with the handful of coins still owed in exchange for the prop bladders. The simple devices were secreted in a player's costume or, on occasion, smaller ones even slipped into the mouth. Once triggered, they generated a neat cascade of blood, which lent a melodramatic flair to any death scene or stage fight. One could also place a metal backing behind the bladder and use a quick knife stab to slice it open. Oldcastle had told the troupe one night of a traveling performer of his acquaintance who had been drinking heavily prior to his performance. In the key climactic scene, the man whipped out a knife and stabbed himself in the stomach. The bladder worked as it should, spilling a flood of pig's blood across the makeshift stage; however, in his inebriated state, the player had neglected to place the metal shield protecting his own mortal flesh from the blade. He drove the dagger three inches into his own belly and bled to death within an hour. Tyburn shook his head at the thought and slid the bladders into his doublet.

"Master Shakespeare, your boy here," Tyburn indicated Will, who was shuffling with feigned indifference through a pile of dark leathers. "Is he available for hire? We need a guide to escort us to Charlecote. Pay is two pennies for the escort."

John Shakespeare scowled in thought. "I suppose I could spare him for the afternoon. Being as it's a market day I've kept him from his schooling to help but he's fair indifferent about that in any case." He frowned, remembering the number of whippings with which he had tried to push the boy into more regular attendance.

"A chance to earn good wages," Tyburn suggested in a diffident voice. "We may have some more labour for him anon, we're short now with our loss."

The glover nodded. "Will, you fancy earning a penny? Mind you, you need to provide the work for the gentleman or he's free to clout that large head clean off your shoulders and I'll not stop him. Well?"

Will nodded his acquiescence and said "I'll mind my work, Father."

"Good. Would that you minded your chores and your schooling with the same diligence." He gave Tyburn a keen look. "Loose him in time for supper, or he's in your keeping for mealtime."

"Agreed. Fetch your things, boy, and meet me at Clopton Bridge." Tyburn gave the boy the barest of winks; Will nodded his understanding and disappeared behind the Shakespeare abode. Tyburn hoped the boy had the wit to fetch the letter and the silver. With a cheery farewell to the glover, now busy flagging down a well-dressed gentleman inspecting the market tables, the player turned and headed back to the inn where Worcester's Men were organizing for the upcoming performance.

Chapter the Fourteenth

THE TWO DUCKS paddled through the cool, slow moving-current, eyeing the small group of people seated on the stepped stone veranda that bordered the river. A large, flat-bottomed punt tied to a small stone quay made a muted clunking sound as it tugged against its rope and nudged the stones.

A sliver of bread landed with a small ripple in the shallows and both ducks arrowed towards it with determined speed. The male gulped down the sodden crust and, tense at the proximity of the humans, paddled back out to gain some careful distance before turning back to face the shore, watching for more largesse. A pair of regal white swans cruised past, shepherding a procession of seven cygnets. Several cygnets meandered sideways across the water before being herded back into formation by the stern honk of the trailing parent.

Clair sat on the stone-paved veranda, her eyes closed, head tilted back, enjoying the warm sunshine and the gentle breeze rippling across the river. The conversation had flowed past her in a slow murmur, not unlike the drift of the river's current, but with an inward sigh she realized that conversational politeness demanded her consideration and she straightened up, tilted her head forward and opened her eyes. There were eight women on the patio, most of whom Clair at least knew by reputation or through the handful of social engagements she had attended during her brief return home. They were all staid, tedious, and pedestrian to Clair's eyes and they returned her disdain tenfold. Her father's wealth, her widowed status, her clear skin, youth and bright hair: all of these earned her a score of reproachful looks and murmured asides, without any effort on her part.

She sighed. The conversation among the women centered on sewing, children, and the difficulties in finding honest household servants. She doubted if any of them had even read a book (if they were lettered) other than a hymnal or Foxe's Book of Martyrs[100]. *Dear God*, she thought with savage frustration, *I don't think I could stand another instant on this green earth if I'm to be sentenced to this sorry Fate--destined to be a broodmare for some pitiful, chinless wretch with a smattering of noble blood and no saving grace but acres of land.* It was unconscionable yet inexorable.

Still, the conversation, dull though it might be, was better than brooding over her father's intentions, she thought. She had always known her father was ambitious and greedy for land but she had seldom realized the extent of his hunger and his inability to satiate it on local acquisitions. Her blunder, she knew, had been mistaking his solicitous behavior after her husband's death for genuine familial warmth, rather than a deliberate ploy to ensconce

---

[100] Commonly known as Foxe's Book of Martyrs, the book, *"Actes and Monuments of these Latter and Perillous Days, touching Matters of the Church"* was a staple of early Protestantism. Written by John Foxe, an evangelical Protestant, the lavishly illustrated book outlined the persecution of the Protestants by the Catholic Church under Mary. Published in 1563, it was the largest publishing project of its kind in England, making Foxe's book a staple in many homes and virtually all churches. Foxe himself actually served as a tutor in the Lucy household at Charlecote in 1547.

her in a legal wrangle over her husband's lands and her dowry. Wracked with grief, she had, in her foolishness, removed herself back to her father's estate and now, with her inheritance tied up in deBrage's legal tussle with the Carey family, she was well and truly trapped, with no home of her own to return to and no revenues to establish her widowed independence.

And now a forced marriage loomed. It was infuriating. The urge to spit in her father's eye was almost overwhelming but if she was to stand any chance of avoiding her fate, she had to play along until she understood his intentions. She was puzzled over her father's involvement with Leicester. The Earl of Leicester, Robert Dudley was the younger son of the Duke of Northumberland and, despite his father's execution for treason years before[101], the earl flew in far loftier circles than the deBrage family had ever dreamt of inhabiting. The conversation she had overheard made it clear that the Jesuit was a key element in whatever arrangement her father had worked out with Leicester, even if she didn't understand why an unknown Catholic priest would matter.

They had arrived at Charlecote more than two hours earlier on horseback, accompanied by two additional beasts bearing their baggage. They were the earliest set of guests to arrive, due to her father's desire to meet alone with Sir Thomas. They had passed the familiar decorative pillars surmounted with carved stone boars and under the red brick gatehouse's elaborate and arched entranceway to be greeted by several young grooms and one of Sir Thomas's liveried retainers. Without so much as a nod or a gesture of introduction, her father had turned away to greet Lucy and with her brother trailing behind, had left her standing alone on the hard

---

[101] John Dudley, the 1st Duke of Northumberland, was executed for treason by Queen Mary in 1553 for his part in attempting to put his daughter-in-law Lady Jane Grey on the throne. Robert Dudley's grandfather, Edmund Dudley, the 1st Baron Dudley, was also executed in wake of Henry VII's death on what was widely believed to be trumped-up charges from his enemies at court.

cobblestones, blinking in the sun. After several minutes of waiting in the sunshine, Clair took matters into her own hands by accosting one of the servants and requesting to be escorted to Lady Joyce, whom she had met on several occasions.

Lady Joyce was thin and ungainly, with narrow hips that were a dressmakers' despair. However, she was also every bit the opposite of her husband's impoliteness, fussing over the lack of consideration in the greeting of her guest, offering choice food and drink and a warm courtesy that stood in stark contrast to the earlier staid welcome. Dull she might be, Clair thought, but she was impeccably polite. Servants were dispatched with alacrity to delivery the baggage to their guest rooms and Clair had been invited to join the ladies on the river terrace until the great hall was prepared.

Charlecote was bustling with activity. A group of workmen were toiling in the great hall, setting out rows of seating for Worcester's Men's performance. The kitchens and pantries of the manor were an endless stream of aproned cooks and servants carrying trays, meats, bread, fowl, delicate glassware, silvered cups, trenchers and plates. Servants shot to and fro. An old gardener, much stooped from years of labour, fussed over the delicate plants that made up the intricate knot garden bordering the rear of the house, sweeping away stray leaves and seed pods from the cobbles. A yellow-eyed, mud-coloured cat eyed the chaos with nervous eyes, tilting its head owlishly and hissing askance at every person crossing the forecourt before turning away and disappearing through a hedge. A steady procession of carts, riders, and numerous litters borne by liveried servants created bedlam in the forecourt despite one of Sir Thomas's retainers standing in the archway directing the traffic.

In the midst of this bedlam the arrival of the playing troupe went almost unnoticed and unheralded until they let fly with a blast of a trumpet, the dull bass thump of a drum and the rattle of timbrels. At the noise, Clair stood and walked over to where she could view the forecourt, observing the leader of the troupe engaged in a voluble argument with the steward. With much visible hand-waving and gesturing, Oldcastle made it plain that he was not to be swayed until, with a gesture made from equal parts exasperation and annoyance, the steward waved the troupe past the jam of carts towards the side entrance to the Great Hall.

Stifling a laugh, Clair looked across the forecourt until she spotted him, the tall saturnine ex-soldier turned player. He was striding across the cobblestone forecourt, glancing at the main manor house and talking with a young boy and one of the older players. She knew her cheeks were flushed as she watched the man. She was not sure why she had demonstrated such effrontery in pushing her way into Master Bromley's conversation with the player. She had an unaccountable urge to do so, a daring and abrupt flight of fancy that her maid had found quite scandalous. It gave Clair a sense of exhilaration despite the abrupt turn their conversation had taken. In retrospect she could understand the anger that lurked just beneath the surface of the man, a fatal shoal she had laid bare like an outgoing tide. Her casual comments had been unintentionally presumptive and belittling. . She couldn't presume to know the reality of the wars in Flanders and the Low Countries, she thought to herself. Rude and abrasive as the man's response had been, she was filled with a strong sense of sympathy and a wave of regret that she, with casual indifference, had flicked off the scars of something she sensed ran very deep indeed.

She turned away, aware that she was staring. The pink that suffused her cheeks deepened and she turned back to the river to contemplate the seeming endless optimism of the ducks that bobbed and dipped in the slow current.

The quiet of the countryside was broken by squeal of the unlubricated wagon wheels, the incessant sound of warblers darting along the river fringe and the pulsating buzz of cicadas that ebbed and flowed from the tall grass along the roadway. The warm summer breeze stirred the trees along the river, and made the earl's silver, blue and red blazon snap in the wind. Cloud scudded past, regarding the world from Olympian heights.

The task of guiding the troupe to the estate had been a simple one for Will. The road to Charlecote was straightforward, across Clopton Bridge and then bearing away eastwards, paralleling the gentle waters of the Avon until the river looped away beyond the trees like a wandering child. It came meandering back within another half-mile, the cool waters glinting through the woods. The manor lay north but the troupe was forced to follow the worn, rutted road another half-mile before turning to cross the River Dene by way of a narrow moss-encrusted stone bridge that looked as though it had once seen the dusty hobnailed boots of Caesar's legions.

From his perch on the wagon seat beside Much the Elder, Oldcastle surveyed the troupe who walked ahead of the wagon to avoid the particles kicked up from the hard dry rutted surface. He looked at the tall figure of Tyburn and seethed.

The man irritated him. He didn't know why his patron had foisted an untried ex-soldier on the troupe last year when better actors had been available for hire. They could have poached Collins or Willoughby from Hunsdon's Men without too much difficulty, he reflected. Collins was a fool for coin or strumpet and could have been lured easily enough. The man was a neglectful drunkard much of the time off-stage but drunk or sober he would have been an experienced asset for the performers, unlike that gibbet-named bastard, he thought. Tyburn, Oldcastle acknowledged with reluctance, had demonstrated particular acumen for his various roles. The man had a razor-sharp memory and could pick up a character as though he had been dipped in it. Despite his abilities something about the man grated on Oldcastle's nerves. He seemed to treat the troupe as the means to some end, an end that he did not or could not articulate.

It was, he thought, all Worcester's fault. Worcester alternated between the twin poles of benign neglect and eye-crossing meddling where his troupe was concerned, with no real middle ground. Knowing his patron's oft mercurial nature, he guessed that Worcester had been paying back a favor in pushing Tyburn forward the previous year.

Oldcastle frowned at the laughing men preceding the wagon as they drew up the long tree-lined road that led to the Charlecote manor house. The procession moved forward through the arched gatehouse with Motely blasting on his horn while Much the Younger rattled the timbrels in accompaniment with a marked lack of enthusiasm.

"It's a bloody big house." Tyburn surveyed the manor with a practiced eye. The main building beyond the forecourt branched off into several wings, following the traditional E-shape of the manor home, albeit larger than many similar dwellings that were scattered across Warwickshire. Outbuildings, including an extensive stable and a number of barns, were tucked away to the right of the forecourt but the manor house itself made them seem small in stature, although they stretched back beyond the screen of trees. The manor building was constructed of warm red brick and replete with ornate lattices of diamond-shaped window panes facing all sides. The main entrance presented itself as a square faux-tower, topped with several carved standing lions holding fast on the roof, serpentine crossed yellow banners trailing in the breeze. The corners of the house each held a cylindrical turreted tower, giving the stately house a martial appearance at odds with the many glass windows.

"Seen bigger," grunted Allyn as he hefted a chest from the wagon. "Don't make any difference. They'll still make us sleep in the barn."

"If'n 'twere mine, I'd make you sleep in the barn too," commented Mundy with uncharacteristic spite.

"We be stuck in Stratford much longer, we'll all be sleeping in barns," observed Willens. "Now move your arse."

"Been to Charlecote before, Will?" Tyburn looked down at his young guide who assumed an air of studied nonchalance, a look that was ruined by his inability to hide his expansive grin. In truth, Will had more than a passing familiarity with Charlecote's extensive property. He and Richard often haunted the manor's summer orchards, filling their pockets with plundered apples and plums, and roaming through the thick copse of forest that crossed the estate grounds in search of mushrooms.

When Oldcastle finished cajoling his instructions and permissions from the harassed-looking Charlecote steward, the troupe moved towards side entrance of the manor house to survey the Great Hall where the performance was to be held. Will was still gawking at the intricate stonework evident on the manor's corner tower when the clatter of hooves echoed loud from under the archway and a well-appointed horseman plunged into the forecourt at a full gallop.

Tyburn reached over and yanked Will bodily back as the mount, hooves sparking on the stone forecourt, charged through the space the boy had been occupying without slowing. Tyburn sensed the horse's passage and felt the rider's leg impact his shoulder in the instant of pulling the boy out of the way, spinning him about. . The rider reined up at the entrance to the house and, without so much as a glance back at the people he had almost ridden down, tossed the reins to a groom. The dust from the swift passage still floated in the air.

The horse was larger than most, a pale grey courser bred to carry a man encased in the weight of full armor, with a high trimmed saddle that cost more than the troupe earned in a year. It shied away from its rider the instant the man dismounted, seeming to share Tyburn's immediate dislike of its passenger. The man was thick of torso, not fat but stolid, dressed in expensive clothing trimmed with fur and delicate lace despite the warmth of the mid-summer sun. He cast a sidelong look at the gate, giving Tyburn a clearer glimpse of him. The man's round and pouchy face hovered between the wide expensive felted hat and the delicate embroidered coloured ruff like a waning ruddy moon scudding between deep cloud and a distant dark horizon. The man's skin was tight and smooth, flushed and permeated with red and purple , giving him an almost tumescent appearance. His eyes were small and mordacious, and passed over the many people in the forecourt without flicker or pause. His was a face that embodied entitlement and privilege, with a haughty, casual arrogance that Tyburn despised. The player felt the heat of anger coloring his skin and took two steps to follow the man when Willens stepped in front and, holding Tyburn's arms with urgent intensity, pushed him back in the direction of the troupe.

"You want no part of that one, Kit," Willens stated, his voice flat. .

Tyburn took a deep breath and reminded himself to keep his ready temper in check. "Why?" he asked.

"The right bastard riding the dead Spaniard[102] is Richard Topcliffe. He's a respected member of Parliament, a man of the court, well landed in Yorkshire and has the ear of the queen on occasion. He's also one of Leicester's pocket ruffians and is as vicious a dog as was ever kicked. He hunts recusants for sport. He's a priest-killer, a sadistic torturer and a man not fussy about whom he racks."

Tyburn nodded in response, his eyes on the retreating back as it disappeared into the manor.

"How do you know about him?" he asked.

"All the players know Topcliffe," Willens said with a grim tone. "He took a member of Strange's Men two years ago as a recusant. Hung him up on a wall in fetters for a week and then racked him for good measure. He was tossed in the Marshalsea and it was six months before Lord Strange intervened and he was freed. He never trod the boards again, shook all the time like he had the falling sickness[103], so yes, we all know who Topcliffe is, and avoid him like a venomous plague."

---

[102] Dead Spaniard = expression used to describe a grey horse.
[103] Epilepsy

Topcliffe's boots rang on the tile floor of the entrance hall as he strode into the manor house. He paused to give the room a brief survey, noting the expensive plaster friezes that ringed the ceiling of the gallery. The support beams were in turn decorated with intricate carved flowers and leaves that intertwined their way up the beams in a subtle tangle, giving the illusion of a delicate forest topped with small grinning sprites and wood nymphs. A large bold woven wall hanging covered one side wall, displaying a scene that Topcliffe didn't recognize but the upward cast of the eyes and the halo of smug certainty that suffused the persons on the tapestry suggested biblical rather than mythological origins. The flickering glint of silvered and gold thread indicated the expense of the piece. A doorman bowed as Topcliffe handed over his riding cloak and stick.

A second servant gestured. "Sir, Master Lucy awaits you in his study." The servant led the scowling Topcliffe down a wood-paneled hallway, through several turns and into a wide room, bright lit by long glass windows.

"Master Topcliffe, as always, a pleasure to see you again. You are welcome to Charlecote." Sir Thomas Lucy motioned for Topcliffe to sit in one of the several dark cushioned chairs. An older man, looking pallid despite the bright sunshine, was seated in one chair, both hands clasped on his walking stick, next to a tall, lean young man that Topcliffe recognized from court as Albert deBrage.

Topcliffe was curious what the deBrages were doing in a private audience with Lucy. The family was at court but not, he knew, *of* the court. They had some land but no distinction, little noble blood and held no Crown trade licenses or patents that warranted revenue or recognition. Aside from minor scandals and a landowner's position in Warwickshire, they were little more than hangers-on, Topcliffe thought with brusque irritation.

He deigned a brief curt nod to the deBrages aand then addressed himself to Sir Thomas. "My Lord the Earl of Leicester suggested I come. He implied that some matter of grave import was afoot."

"Indeed yes! The gravest." Sir Thomas picked up a tall wine flagon from the sideboard. "Would you care for some Madeira? I have a ship that brings me a case from the Canaries. It is quite passable." Topcliffe nodded in polite acquiescence and took a glass.

"So what grave matter disturbs your midsummer, Sir Thomas?" Topcliffe left unspoken the more important question of why it required him to be disturbed when he was loath to be absent from the queen's summer progress and the lavish festivities at Kenilworth. The court, he knew, was infested with sycophantic opportunists, quick to take advantage of a gentleman's absence. They were adders who would turn and strike the instant he demonstrated any vulnerability or absence, quick to repeat rumor and, in hearsay's absence, to craft it.

Lucy's finger traced the rim of the delicate Venetian wine glass. "A question of treason . . ."

"Profitable treason," interrupted Albert deBrage. His father held up an irritated hand to halt his son's interruption. Lucy gave a wan smile.

"You may be aware of some leading nobility in Warwickshire that are...less than considerate regarding the position to which Lord Leicester has been elevated." Topcliffe nodded, sipping his wine. The maderia was very fine indeed. "These . . . parties posture Protestant sympathies, yet in their fox cunning, they manifestly support the Papists. Indeed they subvert the Crown for the favour of their pope and his pederast cardinals."

Topcliffe nodded agreement. Robert Dudley had been elevated to Lord Leicester only eleven years before. He had been in and out of favour with the queen like the phases of the moon, waxing and waning through the years, most recently due to his secretive supposed marriage to Lady Douglas Sheffield despite his subsequent repudiation of the marriage in the face of the Queen's anger. Interestingly Dudley still recognized the bastard son that was the product of his disavowed union.

The lavish festivities at Kenilworth were part of Leicester's ongoing efforts to sidestep his way back into favour with the queen, who was not well pleased with either marriage or the acknowledged bastard that had resulted from the purported union. The queen, well-versed in presenting a Janus face to her many suitors, alternated between smiling favour and cold indifference, causing Dudley to rain fulsome spectacle upon Elizabeth at the current summer progress. *If the man doesn't go broke first, he might come well out of it*, thought Topcliffe, for Elizabeth always did adore display and lavish flattery. Topcliffe drank a deep draught of the wine, savouring the cool acidic bite of it, impatient for Lucy to come to the point.

"There is one individual in particular that has been a considerable thorn in Lord Leicester's side, a man of considerable holdings in Warwickshire."

"The high sheriff, Edward Arden," interrupted the elder deBrage. His voice was cold, almost emotionless.

Topcliffe snorted in derision. "The man's a prig. Stuff and nonsense. Arden's made no secret of despising Lord Leicester but he's got no power in court. How does he matter?"

"His land holdings in Warwickshire are extensive, as is his influence over the landholders." Lucy paused to sip his wine. "We have reason to believe--"

"He keeps a pet Catholic priest as his gardener." Albert deBrage cut in, tired of the plodding pace of Lucy's explanation. "He's a damned Papist, a recusant and a bloody bastard traitor. As the master goes, so do the servants. His estates are populated with Catholics and Papist dogs."

The silence was pregnant. "You have proof?" Topcliffe asked with a cautious demeanor.

"The priest has been, shall we say, persuaded to cooperate. He has been passing us his master's letters." Lucy paused and the elder deBrage took up the conversation.

"Arden is more than just another proselytizing Catholic noble. The court is full of such shallow turncoats. They are petrified at being exposed and quick to parrot support for the queen but Arden is different. He is in active contact with servants of Rome. He is corresponding with an agent of the pope, a Jesuit, now skulking somewhere in Warwickshire. "

Topcliffe started at the mention of a Jesuit. "One of the pope's footsoldiers? Here?"

"An English priest turned Jesuit, one of that Oxford rabble from Douai." Lucy poured the last of the bottle into his glass and gave the sideboard a contemplative glance. A steward, who had been standing quiet in the doorway hastened forward to exchange the empty bottle for a fresh one. "Why such men turn from their just loyalties to willingly embrace the Devil, I cannot say, yet now we have one of such nature roaming at will in Warwickshire."

"To what end?"

"I can only assume bloody insurrection is his ambition. Despite our exquisite queen's expressions of tolerance for their heresies, or more like because of it, English Papists are growing in numbers. Clemency! Hah! It's a fool's policy. They breed treason like whores breed bastards. Show me a Papist," Lucy said in a stern tone, "and I will show you one with a liar's visage, deformed of countenance and of evil manner. Vipers breed vipers, and we must ferret out this particular nest and expunge it."

Topcliffe felt a quickening sense of excitement. He rather doubted whether a single Catholic priest could serve as the herald of rebellion; however, this was the first time a Jesuit, one of the Soldiers of Christ, had emerged onto English soil. This was no mere hedge-priest but a full-fledged member of the Society of Jesus. This was an opportunity.

"From the intercepted letters," the elder deBrage said in his graveled voice, "there is no overt conspiracy. Arden has not signed any of them so we have no hard proof of his participation. The majority of letters have been from Arden's priest to the Jesuit, although Arden's hand is evident. He has been clever and circumspect in his communication. However, everything we have seen indicates some type of base plot against the Crown."

"Another Ridolfi[104]?

"Possibly. It smacks of assassination. Norfolk being beheaded seems to have at least made the Catholics more circumspect in their treasons."

"Does Walsingham know?" The hatchet-faced principal secretary ran much of Elizabeth's spy network at home and abroad.

"Perhaps. I suspect rumors may have attracted his interest but nothing of authentic substance. We have tried to be vigilant in our dealings with this situation." In short, thought Topcliffe with satisfaction, neither Walsingham nor the queen's primary counselor Burghley had been informed of the Jesuit, allowing the ambitious men in this room to take full credit and ample reward for the apprehension of a secret emissary of the pope and the prevention of an assassination plot against the Crown.

"So what do you need of me?" Topcliffe's voice was harsh. "You have the letters, you have Arden's priest. Tickle him well and you'll have your Jesuit."

The elder deBrage sighed in exasperation. "Yes. So we thought. But the priest doesn't know the Jesuit's location. The letters followed a secret courier chain which we were in the process of unraveling. Unfortunately due to an excess amount of enthusiasm, the chain has been terminally broken and the remaining letter--a letter that I understand implicates Arden's express consent to the conspiracy--has gone astray."

---

[104] The Ridolfi Plot (1571) was a Catholic plot to assassinate Queen Elizabeth and place Mary I, Queen of Scotland, on the throne. The primary conspirators were Robert di Ridolfi, an Italian banker heavily involved in the thwarted 1570 rebellion, King Phillip II of Spain, Mary Queen of Scots and the Duke of Norfolk. The duke was found guilty of treason and executed in 1572.

"Your reputation as a successful pursuivant and hunter of recusants is known. We want you to find this Jesuit and the letter," Lucy continued.

For a moment, in his mind's eye, Topcliffe could see it. Money, wealth, land, reputation: an endless cornucopia of royal favour spread before him. Exclusive patents for trade, entitlements, and estates, perhaps even an earldom.

He gave Lucy a long, considering gaze, then his small eyes slid back to the deBrages. Lucy was an unimaginative and pedantic man, a dog chasing rabbits, one that went where his masters pointed him, but the elder deBrage, for all his low esteem at court, had a reputation for scheming. The younger one was a blade, nothing more, hot-headed and temperamental--but the elder was spoken of with caution. Topcliffe smelled power and position. He understood why Leicester had suggested he ride to Stratford to meet Lucy. The laurels from capturing a Jesuit would be considerable and, Topcliffe suspected, both Leicester and deBrage would benefit from the confiscation of Arden's considerable lands if he could be tied to treason against the Crown. He took a long quaff of his wine.

"I'll need men."

"I have twenty available now, with horses," Lucy responded.

"I'll need gold."

"You'll have it."

Topcliffe nodded and set down his now empty glass. He smiled. "Where do we start?"

"The Earl of Worcester's Men."

Chapter the Fifteenth

THE HALL WAS warm, the air humid with a dense closeness Tyburn associated with the dark cloying lower deck of a channel barque but lacking the sour bilge stench that every ship wore like a thick malodorous coat. He mopped his forehead on his embroidered sleeve and pushed his way politely through the crowded room.

The afternoon performance had gone well. The troupe had arranged for one end of the great hall to be reserved as their stage, with two adjacent side entrances from the long paneled hallway serving as their entry and exit points. The hallway itself was used as the players' tiering area. Unlike at the guild hall in Stratford, no staging was available within Charlecote's great hall; however, this was a common occurrence in most manor house performances. Instead, cushioned chairs and benches had been set up for the higher-ranked guests to be seated upon, often impeding on the stage area itself, requiring the actors to maneuver among the guests. Lesser-ranked guests stood behind the benches, but they had the advantage of easy access to the wine carried in by the servants. Scores of candles and several lanterns helped light the room, although the hall had an extensive set of glass windows that allowed the sunlight to flow through for at least the early part of the performance.

The audience had been receptive, the laughter rising steadily and the catcalls limited to a handful of derisive remarks, most aimed at Motely who had assumed his usual female guise. The exception had been Topcliffe, who had placed himself at the forefront of the audience, on a cushioned chair. He sat with a stoic and caustic expression, as though bored with the theatrics, although Tyburn caught an occasional minute shift in the man's demeanor that suggested a certain watchfulness. He sat with one leg extended with casual insolence into the stage area, making no effort to retract it when the players gamboled past, as though daring any of them to fall prey to the obstruction.

At the conclusion of the performance the players had been banished to their hallway tiering area, as servants began to deftly remove the chairs and benches. Long tables on the perimeter of the room were loaded with savory foodstuffs. A small group of string musicians in one corner of the hall began to play what, to Tyburn's ears, was an excruciatingly banal tune. Oldcastle stood in the doorway, half-irritation and half polite interest on his features as he kept a watchful eye out for the secretary, Bromley, and the remainder of their compensation.

As the guests ebbed and flowed throughout the expansive room, Tyburn watched. The majority of the guests appeared to be Warwickshire landowners, leading merchants with a smattering of wealthier, more powerful nobility scattered throughout. The rich fabrics, jeweled sleeves and bodices glowed and glinted in the light. Laughter rose rich and bubbling from the far corner.

Bromley appeared out of the crowd like a breaching leviathan, sliding his bulk through the crowd with unexpected grace. Spying Tyburn, he gave a sharp gesture for the player to follow him. Oldcastle caught Tyburn's eye and the old player rubbed his fingers together in the unmistakable gesture of payment. Tyburn nodded and pushed off in Bromley's wake.

Clair caught a quick sight of the tall player as he moved through the crowd and watched him be reabsorbed into their number. For some odd reason she found the dark-haired actor strangely compelling. She liked the battered feel of the man. She sensed that under the player's façade lurked a clear and astute intelligence, despite his seeming inability to control his temper in conversation with a lady. He also seemed to exude, she thought, a deep, inexplicable loneliness that seemed at odds with his chosen life and profession.

It was a feeling she could well understand, for the last year in her father's house she had learned a little about emotional exile. She darted a quick glance back where he had vanished into the crowd of guests before moving over to rejoin her hostess by the musicians.

You can always tell rank in a crowded room, Tyburn thought. The leading lights were a locus for lesser men orbiting about them like sycophantic planets bound to the celestial wheel. A small collection of men was gathered about a set of comfortable chairs. Tyburn noted Lucy ensconced in the largest of the set, an ornately carved seat with the remaining chairs clustered about in a loose conversational group.

Behind and beside the chairs was a gaggle of younger men, most fancily dressed hangers-on, including one with elaborate, embroidered silk cuffs edged with pearls. One passing fellow in particular caught Tyburn's eye as he wore a stylish, worn doublet with a short Dutch cape and a long rapier, in the style of the captains of the Flanders companies. He had a short, tight ginger beard with a thin, almost wispy moustache and a slender, consumptive face. The man stepped past Tyburn and the seated group, pausing to take an orangado[105] and a wine goblet from a laden tray carried by a passing servant. With ungloved hands he

---

[105] A popular confection consisting of a Seville orange, cut in half and partially hollowed out and filled with sugar.

picked the full glass off the moving tray without hesitation. His fingers and nails were curiously blotchy and pitted with dark stains that reminded Tyburn of the ominous, livid blotches of plague victims. Kit shivered despite the warmth of the room, remembering the stacks of diseased Dutch dead in Haarlem. The man noticed Tyburn's gaze and gave him a pleasant nod before disappearing into the crowded room.

Tyburn stopped stock-still for a moment, thinking hard. Oranges. By God's bones it was so bloody simple, he couldn't understand why he hadn't thought of it earlier. He shook his head, looking after the man in the Dutch cape, feeling as though a cool wind had swept him over.

Tyburn turned his focus back to the group of seated men. Lucy was expounding on something to an older man whose savage, almost cadaverous features were thrown into sharp contrast by the waning light and the candles. Bromley bent down and spoke to Sir Thomas, who gave a brief nod of acquiescence and some murmured instruction before sending the secretary on his way. Lucy looked up at Tyburn, a restrained smile on his face.

"Well, Captain Tyburn, the Earl of Worcester's Men seem to have provided an excellent diversion for my guests. Please pass my compliments on to Master Oldcastle." Tyburn bowed low in reply. "Captain Tyburn is lately returned from the bold Gilbert's campaigns in Flanders and, given your martial interest, gentlemen, I thought it would

be useful to have him recount his tales."

"If you call turning your backsides to the Dons and scampering away like mice when the first harquebus sounds to be efficacious." The comment came from a younger man, dressed in the fashionable and expensive style that many of the young court bloods had adopted, with high breeches and dark hose worn tight to display the leg. A titter of collective laughter came from the rakish men flanking the younger man's chair.

Tyburn's eyes flicked once to the seated man, giving him a brief assessment before returning to fix on Lucy.

"What would you have me weary your ears with?" he asked Lucy.

"When were you last in Flanders?"

"A little more than a year ago. We departed in some haste, after Mookerheyde[106]. Most of Sir Thomas Morgan's men had already left back in January."

"Ahh, yes. Is it true the Dutch soldiers at Mookerheyde mutinied over a lack of pay and refused to fight?"

"Some," Tyburn admitted. Mutinies over arrears in pay were embarrassingly frequent in the Lowlands. A significant portion of the rebel forces were *condottieri*, volunteer companies of mercenaries. Hard-faced Walloons, stoic Flemish pikemen, scarred German swordsmen, a scattering of French and Italian, and the English and Scottish troops, all seeking their fortunes on a blade's edge. The lack of money had even resulted in some heated debate among the English contingent concerning offering their services to the Spanish.

"Dutch dogs . . . cowards, the lot of them." It was the younger man interjecting once more. Tyburn continued to ignore him.

"And what, do you think, are the prospects that William of Orange will be successful in his revolt against Spain?" asked one portly seated gentleman, a sheen of perspiration glistening on his balding head. Prince William of Orange, or William the Silent as he was known, was one of the leaders of the Dutch rebellion. William had been a reluctant opponent of the Spanish, initially more concerned with the erosion of influence of the Dutch nobility than with Spanish injustices or repression. It wasn't until the Dutch Calvinists began destroying Catholic church statuary, relics and images of saints and suffered the consequent Spanish reprisals that William emerged as a leader of the Dutch rebellion. Why he was

---

[106] The battle of Mookerheyde was fought on April 14th, 1574.

called "William the Silent" Tyburn was unsure, although one German *condottieri* had sworn up and down that William couldn't string a proper sentence together without sounding like he had a mouthful of chestnuts.

Tyburn resisted the urge to snort in derision. "*Nervos belli, pecunium infinitam,* or so Cicero instructs us[107]. I fear the lack of ready coin does more harm than the Spanish *tercios*. Unpaid soldiery is a blight upon the Dutch towns. Such men survive on pillage and plunder, like the Watergeuzen[108]. They hate the Spanish and will fight, but hating and fighting are not enough."

"But they have the advantage of being on the side of God's own justice. The Spanish vermin and their popish lackeys are nothing more than murderers and cowards. Alba[109] seems to do very well when slaughtering unarmed women and children in the Dutch towns but faced with, say, an English Army of equal numbers, how do think they would fare?"

Tyburn paused, mindful of Oldcastle's insistence on giving an inoffensive and diplomatic response. The English forces in the Lowlands were made up of a mixture of cast-off nobility, second sons, fortune seekers, ex-soldiers and pirates. They were poorly equipped, badly trained and difficult to discipline. Despite their many shortcomings, they were brave and had managed to bloody the noses of a number of Spanish *tercios*, but on the whole, the iron-edged, disciplined and well-trained Spanish bands were a more effective and a more numerous fighting force. What the men of

---

[107] "Endless money forms the sinews of war."

[108] Sea Beggars – the name assumed by the Calvinist opposition to the Spanish rule of the Netherlands. They mostly operated as coastal pirates, raiding the Spanish, until they captured the port of Brill in 1572.

[109] Don Fernando Álvarez de Toledo y Pimentel, 3rd Duke of Alba, was a Spanish general and governor of the Netherlands. Notorious for his harsh rule and tenacity in rooting out heresy, and cited for a number of brutal atrocities against civilians in his efforts to bring the Dutch rebellion to heel, he was also widely recognized as a capable general who led the Spanish to a number of notable victories.

Gilbert and Morgan's expedition did have was a powerful hunger for killing the Spanish, which lent a reckless and manic energy to their fights that often made the steel-clad Spaniards pause. On the battlefields of the Netherlands, quarter was rarely asked and even more rarely given.

He was spared answering by another aside from the sharp-faced young man in the dark hose who leaned his chair back with a bored expression on his face. "Asking one of these painted harlequins about war . . . you might as well ask it of my windy arse."

Third time lucky, thought Tyburn. He stepped to one side and hooked the wooden chairleg with his foot and pulled. The heavy chair overbalanced, tilted and Albert gave a startled exclamation as it toppled backwards onto the floor, the heavy impact halting all conversation. Albert cursed, twisting to free himself. He started to swing his legs clear of the chair arm but stopped when the player closed his hand around the hilt of his sword and drew clear a half-inch of razor-edged blade. deBrage realized that should the player decide to draw his weapon, the chances of his being able to free his own sword blade in time to counter any attack were slim. He felt the blood drain from his face, recognizing that he had overreached.

The sudden realization that the actor was responding to his insults caught Albert deBrage by surprise. Players were beneath notice, lower than vagrants, a group of comic fools who pranced for a living and made their bread by pretending to a level they dare not or could not ascend to.

Or so Albert deBrage had thought.

The dark-haired man with the worn sword and the curlicue scar didn't fit into his notion of what a player should be. It had in no way occurred to him that the declamatory fool who had been orating and dancing a crazed jig on the stage a short time before might be a menace, a foe with a ready blade.

"Master Tyburn." Lucy's reedy voice hesitantly broke through the sudden silence that had settled over the group. Tyburn ignored him, his grey eyes intent on Albert deBrage, watching for any indication that the man would draw his blade. Lucy trailed off, recalling the player's astonishing capacity for sudden violence.

Tyburn's face widened into a disconcerting smile.

Confused at Tyburn's sudden change of expression, deBrage grated, "What are you grinning about?"

"Just waiting for your arse's next proclamation on the Low Countries and the Spanish."

The comment brought an abbreviated hiccup of laughter from somewhere in the crowd. Albert slid his legs clear of the chair. Tyburn shifted his weight minutely, one foot slightly ahead of the other. deBrage looked at the dark-haired player standing before him. Painted harlequin or not, the man was clearly a swordsman and, from the well-worn tarnished silver hilt and basket of his sword, apparently a well-versed one.

"Well," the player said low enough that only deBrage and the immediate group could hear him. "Does your arse have any other pronouncements or is it just injudicious wind brought on by too much wine?" The two men stared at one another.

"Enough of this nonsense! Albert, if you cannot be polite, be absent. You are insulting our host with these foolish pratings." William deBrage had been silent until now, watching and listening from his seat at Lucy's right hand. "Go." The voice was mild but the tone absolute.

Tyburn took a careful and measured step back and slid the small expanse of exposed swordblade back into the scabbard. Albert deBrage clambered to his feet, his face a picture of suppressed fury, one hand clenched around the pommel of his sword. He nodded once to his father, considered Tyburn for a long moment and pushed away through the crowded room.

"Your pardon, Master Tyburn. Young men behave foolishly when they are deep in their cups." The older man spoke gruff and matter-of-fact, as though he was well-used to giving indifferent apologies for his son's behavior. "You were telling us about how the Spanish fare against true Englishmen?"

"Indeed my lord, I was, for there is no nobler nor resolute soldier than we English . . ." As Tyburn spoke, his thoughts were filled with, of all things, oranges.

Clair watched her brother, his face mottled with rage as he thrust rudely through the crowd of well-dressed guests and disappeared through the tall double-doors at the entrance to the hall. She smiled to herself. She had been too far away to hear the conversation that had discomfited her brother, but it was clear that her player had infuriated him. Or possibly, she thought, it might have been her father, who had a habit of treating Albert with a dismissive contempt and controlling manner that she knew grated her brother's vicious pride. She smiled, enjoying the moment, knowing it was transitory.

Her player. She shook her head in chagrin, recognizing that she was treading a dangerous path with that line of thought.

She gazed around the room. Seeing the break in the tedious conversation, Clair excused herself and ducked out one of the hallway doors that the players had used for their coming and going. Despite having seen the play before, Clair had enjoyed the performance. It would seem that for this week at least God was willing to grant her the unusual distinction of being able to see two plays. She stepped through the side-door and turned down the wood-paneled hallway. A long ornate tapestry embroidered with flowering plants and twined vines hung on one wall. As she glanced down the hall she recognized her brother speaking with Richard Topcliffe. She grimaced and instead of proceeding down the hallway, she stepped across to the adjoining sitting room, opened the door and entered.

The room was occupied. The quiet conversation halted when Clair opened the door. She took note of the surroundings. Four men were seated at a small round table covered with several flagons and glassware. A pile of coins lay in the centre of the table and a handful of pasteboard cards were scattered about its top, yet, she thought curiously, no one was holding any. One of the young men, with a long narrow face and a tight ginger beard, had been leaning forward as though pleading with one of the other men. Upon her entrance, he sat back and picked up his cards with casual aplomb. "Revie!" he said.

A short, wide, dark-haired woman that Clair recognized as Elizabeth Ferrer stood beside the man, a flickering look of consternation on her face. "Milady Clair, how good to see you," she said.

"Elizabeth, I'm so sorry for barging in. I'm avoiding my brother's drunken ruffian acquaintances." All of the men had now picked up their cards and were now tossing small change into the centre of the table, ignoring the women.

"No apologies are necessary, Clair." The dark-haired woman nodded in sympathy at her. The news of her father's lawsuit against her in-laws had made the rounds of society gossip, Clair thought irritatedly. She hated the idea of people speaking of her affairs. "The gentlemen wanted a quiet game of cards so we shifted into the sitting room. You remember my cousin George . . ."

Clair nodded, recognizing the red nose, square chin and thinning hair of George Ferrer. "And the Throckmortons, with their cousin Master Danby." The ginger-bearded man cocked his head in a brief acknowledgement and then resumed his cards. "Master Danby is staying with us but will soon be moving down to London."

Danby won the hand and shifted each coin to his pile as if it were a hard-fought conquest.

Clair sensed a strange tension in the room. Elizabeth's face was tight and pale.

"I should go." Clair gestured at the door. "My brother and his friends can't long be parted from their wine, so they should no longer be lurking about."

Elizabeth nodded with sympathetic grace and Clair turned to leave, noticing that none of the men so much as deigned to give her a glance. After the door closed behind her, she stopped, puzzled and then shrugged to herself. Her brother and his companions were nowhere in sight.

The hallway was also empty of Worcester's Men. They had quickly and efficiently packed up their costumes and props and retired to the kitchens to filch a free meal from the occasion. They had a distinct advantage over the guests in that they were able to enjoy their food hot rather than tepid after the long journey from oven to serving plate to great hall. Clair turned down the hallway, down a side passage and entered a small empty foyer where the staircase descended from the upper story past the scullery and into the cellar. A dusty cobweb hung in one corner.

"Milady Carey, what an opportune moment to find you."

The voice had a deliberate and practiced smoothness about it yet the nasal sound of it mitigated any potential attraction. She turned to see Richard Topcliffe step out of the shadows of the staircase. Taking an automatic step backwards before stopping herself, she twitched her gown wide of the stair, mindful of catching the material.

Clair made no reply, giving the man an indifferent glance and moving to step past him to return to the hall. Topcliffe strode forward, blocking her passage. Momentarily discomfited, Clair took a half step away from him but one gloved hand shot out and grasped her wrist.

"I do not believe we have been introduced," Topcliffe continued.

"No, sir, we have not and shall not be. You presume much in impeding my passage."

Topcliffe smiled. It reminded her of the same oily, supercilious smile that accompanied the chirurgeon when her husband lay dying, a thin and proprietary smile. She shivered, recalling the man's leering presence. Yes, she thought, here was another of that one's ilk.

"My name is Richard Topcliffe." He executed a cursory bow. "And I presume nothing that is not my right. Have you not spoken with your father and brother?"

She froze.

"They have given me assurances that my suit would not be opposed, but one rarely buys a cow without knowing the quality of the milk. Hence my presumption."

"My father," Clair said in a bitter cold voice, "does not have right of assurance over my property or my hand--a widow's property. And my brother is a rancid worm who should rot in the foulest depths for all eternity." She pulled her hand free and tried to push past him.

She was beautiful, Topcliffe thought, and like all beautiful women she would need a firm hand. Albert had stressed her intransigence and stubbornness but Topcliffe was positive he could emolliate it. It was enough that she was landed and brought with her the widow's endowment of the Carey lands in Buckinghamshire; that she was beautiful as well was gilding on the lily. His eyes roved up and down the length of her, taking in the elegant waist and long neck accentuated by delicate lace. Her attitude, he knew, was one he would exact a measure upon. Indeed, for Topcliffe, resistance was sweeter by far than compliance.

His face red and flushed, button eyes half-lidded, he side-stepped to block her passage again. His hands shot out, pinning her arms to her sides. She tried to kick out, but the long dress and heavy layers impeded her balance and Topcliffe pushed her hard against the wood paneled wall, pressing the length of his body against her to impede any movement.

"Fire. I like that. Wriggle more for me."

Clair tried to move to one side but Topcliffe used his iron strength to push one arm behind her. Intent on freeing his right hand without letting her slip free, he shifted his grip and weight. Both her arms were pinned and she was unable to budge the man. She hissed in horror as his free hand fumbled with her bodice. The practiced brutality with which he carried out his actions terrified her.

"You are a pig!" She twisted and freed her arm, arcing it up hard, clawing for the man's eyes. Topcliffe laughed and caught her by the hand, pushed her back against the wall and slapped her hard across the face. Her eyes swam with pain and she forced it into the back of her mind. *Dear Jesus,* she thought, *spare me this.* His body pressed against her. She shied away, trying in vain to sink through the wooden paneling, shrinking away from the violation. She wondered why no servants had stumbled across her and her assailant, but then came to the chilling realization that even if they did, no one would dare cross Topcliffe.

"Yes," he whispered in her ear. "Your father and brother have pledged you to me, so I need sample the wine . . ."

His hand slid downwards to pull at the fabric of her gown. *No, no, no,* she thought, unable to push him away. She thrashed, raging until his closed fist cracked against the side of her head, sending a flare of red pain through her skull. His hot breath stank on her face as he pushed his lips over hers. His mouth was wet.

She lolled, her strength sliding away. *I will die here, die in my host's hallway, die for a drunken lecher's pleasure.* For an instant she thought she heard her mother's voice echoing in her ears but it was only Topcliffe hissing his intentions and itemizing a relentless and horrific list of violations.

Her mind swam into sudden focus as the groping fingers of her left hand, pinned against her side and the wall, slid over a small hard button protruding from the top seam of her gown. She focused her thoughts, trying to ignore Topcliffe's panting face inches from her own. His voice was droning in her ear, an endless stream of whispered imprecations and invective.

It was a pin. Not an ordinary pin, so often used to hold the heavy folds of sleeves, lace and layers but a long, thin steel shaft that held her rowle[110] in place, threading through the thick strata of material along the back of her waist. She reached for it, feeling it slipping between her two fingers, tantalizingly close. She caught it between her two fingers just as Topcliffe slid his hand up her thighs. She locked her legs tight and at the same time concentrated on drawing the long fastener from the thick folds of material. It slipped from her fingers.

No, she thought anxiously. *Where is it? Where . .* Her fingers caught the edge, and then gripped it hard and tugged. With maddening slowness, the needle slid out. She clenched it tight in her left hand and leaned over to her right, pushing herself hard against the man, willing her arm to slide free. Mistaking her pressure for a response to his ministrations, Topcliffe redoubled his efforts, growing increasingly frustrated with his inability to delve through the material of the gown. He began to pull and tear at her kirtle, slamming the girl's head against the wall.

Dizzy and sick with fear, Clair had enough presence of mind to maintain her grip on the thin shaft. She shifted it in her hand, sliding her arm clear, focusing on her target. She would, she decided in her daze, aim the stiff metal needle direct into his throat. She took a breath, bracing her nerves. She turned her head, trying to measure the distance from her target. She would get one attempt, her only chance.

"I fear I am interrupting."

Topcliffe swung around at the voice.

Christopher Tyburn stood square in the hallway, his grey eyes cold with barely disguised anger. Clair caught a brief glimpse of the player and felt a momentary chill. If death had ever an avatar in the earthly realm, it did so now. Though his face was expressionless the look in his eyes was a promise graven in stone.

---

[110] A rowle, or bumroll, was a padded crescent worn under a gown to make the skirts spring out at the hips.

"God's blood, you prating fool, begone!" Topcliffe shouted at the disturbance, oblivious to the look on the player's face. Clair took advantage of the distraction to pull away, her green eyes wild with fear, hair askew, left hand still gripping the long pin with manic strength. A sudden horror sank through her at the thought that the player might obey Topcliffe's shouted command.

Tyburn gave a performer's practiced obsequious smile. "Alas, I fear I cannot."

Topcliffe gave a long quiver and pushed Clair hard against the wall, his left hand sliding up to her throat. His right hand reached across his body to grasp the hilt of his sword. He turned towards Tyburn. "I'll have you whipped and hung from a gibbet if you don't leave now," he snarled.

"Indeed sir, however, Sir Thomas has sent me to find you on an urgent matter," he lied with smooth grace, "and he would have such a Fate for me also if I failed in my requested task. Otherwise I would not dream of interrupting your . . . conversations."

Eyes glaring, teeth bared, the panting Topcliffe released the grip on his sword and with reluctance pulled his left hand away from Clair's throat. She choked back a breath and watched as Topcliffe pulled his doublet back into place. Clair fingered the long needle, wondering if she dared to rip the thin metal into her assailant's throat. Tyburn caught her eyeing the makeshift weapon in her left hand and gave her a barely perceptible shake of his head before turning his full attention back to Topcliffe. The man's head twitched sideways to look at her standing frozen against the wood paneling of the wall, like a mouse spellbound before a snake.

Topcliffe gave himself a sudden shake, a coursing shudder that rippled through the entirety of his body. It seemed to steady him, and his voice and breathing returned to normalcy. He made an abrupt nod to Tyburn followed by a quick half-bow to Clair, who still gripped the needle white-knuckled in her left hand.

"My lady, I look forward to renewing our conversation at a later occasion." He gave her that unctuous, thin smile and stepped forward. Tyburn stepped obediently to one side, giving Topcliffe right of passage through the hallway, and watched him out of sight.

"Dear Jesus . . ." Clair slumped against the wood panel, feeling hot and light-headed. Her head swam. The cool edge of a glass was pressed to her lips.

"Drink this." The liquid tasted warm and spicy as it slipped down her throat, burning in her stomach, spreading through her with welcome warmth. She coughed at the aftertaste, and Kit pulled the glass away. "Easy," he said. "You're safe. He's gone. For now anyway."

She coughed again, finding her herself steadying. "What is it?"

"A bit of clary[111]. I lifted a sack from the kitchen. There now, how do you feel?"

She looked up into a pair of concerned eyes boring into hers.

"I'm well enough." She shivered. She sat slumped against one wall of the hallway, knees pulled up, her gown arranged to cover her legs. She reached out and tucked the torn remnants of her kirtle out of sight and reached up to straighten her cap. She knew her hair was in utter disarray so she spent a moment carefully tucking the long auburn strands back into place. She looked up. The player was sitting back on his haunches, back leaning against the opposite wall, his scabbarded sword held horizontally across his knees. He was watching her. She flushed.

"I thank you, sir, for your intervention," she began.

Tyburn chuckled. "Saved his miserable life in any case." He nodded at the long needle sitting on the floor beside her. "More the pity you didn't get to spike him, but I'm pleased you didn't."

"Pleased?" she said, confused.

"I do hate watching women hang."

---

[111] Wine mixed with honey and spices

She shivered again, remembering Topcliffe's weight on her. She glanced up, meeting Tyburn's eyes. "You've seen a number of women hanged have you, Master Tyburn?"

"A few," he replied. "A good few. But I digress. I came to offer you an apology."

"For what in God's name do you need to apologize to me?" Clair said, faintly astonished. "Your arrival could have not been more timely."

Tyburn smiled. It was, she thought, a nice smile. "For my actions yesterday. I was abrupt and ungracious to what was a simple question."

She smiled in turn, forgetting Topcliffe for a moment. "Not a simple question to you, I fear, Master Tyburn. On the contrary, I'm the one that owes you an apology for making light of your experiences. I think you were owed more than just a feathered barb. You were owed the respect due to any weighty endeavor, not a chance and jesting query from some passing woman."

"You don't get to carry the weight of my choices. I chose to go to the Lowlands. You owe me no apologies."

He pushed his back against the wall and stood in one fluid motion. He settled his worn rapier on his left hip and stretched out one gloved hand to Clair. "Best be getting back. Topcliffe will figure he was gybed[112] before long. You should be safe enough among the ladies."

"For now," Clair said in a toneless voice. "My father and brother have given him permission to press his suit for my hand."

Tyburn cocked his head in puzzlement. "I'm widowed." She felt her face redden under his gaze.

He looked at her, her auburn hair still disarrayed, one plaited length curling against that long artful neck. Even in disorder

---

[112] A gybe is a falsified passport or forged document.

and stress the woman exuded a powerful sense of calm and direction.

"Then you can say no."

Her laughter was hollow. "A simple solution which isn't that simple for a woman. My father is quite relentless in his machinations and my brother . . Well, you've met my brother."

Tyburn nodded. "The law stands with you. As a widow you own your property and your husband's bequests. If you stand on that refusal I daresay they can't easily force the issue."

She nodded. "True, but at this time I foolishly abide under my father's roof. He has laid suit on my husband's relations, laid claim to the Carey estates. Until that is settled, I am exiled to my father's mercy. Now they have traded me to this Topcliffe in exchange for his help finding some hedge-priest."

Tyburn shot her a look. "Priest?"

"Yes," she said. "Apparently there is some English priest about the land, conniving a scheme of some nature. Topcliffe is the mastiff they have chosen to set upon the poor man, whoever he might be."

Controlling his interest, Kit asked, "And have you heard anything of this matter?"

The look she gave him was half-pity and half-mockery. "Enough to know when you fish, you need to at least bait the hook somewhat, Master Tyburn." At the player's strangled expression she laughed. "I know enough to know that you and your troupe are well-entangled in this affair. Whether it is to a purpose or not, I am unclear. Whether this places us at odds or not, I am also unclear. In short, I know little, listen well and hope that somewhere in this affray I may find a thread I can pull that will lead me out from under my father's thumb and well free of Topcliffe's attentions. And yourself?"

Tyburn laughed then, too, enjoying the quick riposte of the conversation. "I am trapped by debt, obligation, authority, duty and by my own poor sense of honour, when all I truly want to do is tread the boards."

"Soldier to player seems a strange transition," Clair observed as they began to walk down the long corridor back towards the main hall. Two servants bearing empty trenchers passed by, both averting their gaze from the pair. Tyburn took care to maintain a mannered distance from the woman, walking a good arm's length away along the opposite wall. There would be, he thought caustically, enough servant gossip about Topcliffe accosting Clair, without his adding more fuel to the fire.

"Not as much as you would think. We all play roles. Players merely do it with deliberation and forethought, for an hour and for a wage." *Not unlike a whore,* he thought sarcastically.

She looked at him and under the intensity of his gaze felt her face warm. She tucked another stray hair under the confines of her cap. "So, am I presentable enough?"

Tyburn gave her a glance. She had artfully repaired most of the surface damage that Topcliffe's assault had inflicted on her gown. The colour had returned to her face and her hair and jewelry were again arranged. Her bodice was absent some lace on one edge but it was barely noticeable. He tried not to stare. "You are a picture of elegance, Mistress Carey," Tyburn said honestly, "Aegle personified[113]." He stopped himself from saying any more, surprised that he had voiced the thought. Her eyes were luminous hooks and he found himself unable to escape them.

She leaned in for a moment. "For my part," she said in a low, intense voice, "I will say it: Thank you." Her hand gripped his for an instant and and the vibrant energy of it was like a brand on his skin. She turned and rustled through the doorway, her gown swirling in her wake. Tyburn stood and breathed deep, catching the drift of her scent as it hung in the hallway, feeling the metronomic thump in his chest.

---

[113] A Naiad, or a water nymph from Greek mythology. Aegle was the most beautiful of the Naiads, daughter of Zeus and Neaera.

Chapter the Sixteenth

"THAT POXED BASTARD, that barber-monger[114], that God-cursed spawn of a fetid rotting polecat!" Oldcastle was shouting as Tyburn entered the barn. "You know what that cozening piece of tripe told me? Our remittance will be paid in the morning! So now we get the grand enjoyment of dossing in the barn for our hard efforts. Bastard turds!"

Several troupe members had to hide their grins. Oldcastle rarely spent a night sleeping rough if he could help it but the rest of the troupe, aside from Willens, avoided the expensive comfort of the inns. For them, the barn was a typical stop.

"Much! Robbie! You pair of thieving Dioscuri[115] need to fetch me some bedding from the house. Take that poxed bastard Tyburn with you. I'll not sleep in a sty!"

---

[114] Fop
[115] The Hero Twins, Castor & Pollux ,from Greek mythology

Tyburn followed Much and Robbie out of the barn, ignoring Oldcastle's imprecations to fetch his bedding but using the preemptory demand as an excuse to seek some privacy. He walked away from the manor, well past the gatehouse and along the red brick curtain wall until he was invisible to any casual passerby on the laneway or from the buildings. He pulled out a small beeswax candle he had retrieved from one of the hallway sconces after leaving Clair Carey in the great hall. He propped the candle in a convenient decorative niche and slid the letter from the top of his right boot, smoothing the now curved paper. He opened the letter and held it up to his nose. He smiled. A faint fruity smell drifted up.

He set the letter down and pulled out a small tinderbox with a flint. Working quickly and deftly, the player sparked a small scrap of tinder alight and shielding the tentative flame he lit the candle. He put the tinder box away and pulled out the letter, unfolding it and giving the peculiar list of merchandise one last look. Holding the candle in one hand and the letter in the other, he began to wave the letter back and forth over the candle flame.

After several minutes of watchful flickering, careful not to set the paper afire, he stopped, satisfied. "Experience teaches fools . . . More fool am I," he muttered to himself.

Threading out of the slightly charred parchment was dark brownish lettering, written in a thin and precise hand, quite different from the inked list of commodities.

It had been the sight of the sugared oranges served at the performance that had triggered Tyburn's recollection of clandestine inks, and caused the player a deep sense of chagrin once he realized his mistake in chasing after a non-existent cipher. He should have guessed the message was a subterfuge. The best place to hide a message was under another one.

He leaned forward and smelt the paper again. *Oranges. So bloody simple*, he thought. . There were a number of secret inks but the juice of oranges was the ink of choice for someone engaged in something hidden. When the pages were heated, the writing became permanently visible, making it evident if anyone had read your secret correspondence. Hanseatic trading ships brought shipments of oranges up from the Canaries and Spain, so while the fruit was expensive, it was not hard to obtain.

He squinted at the thin handwriting and began to read.

My Dear Friend and Correspondent,

It is with a tempered heart that I acknowledge the veracity of your thoughts and your plans, though it pains me to see such effort is required when it is plain that England must soon capitulate to the inevitable and return to the Holy Church as it is wont and just, thanks be to our Savior.

My fortune and abilities are now cast with you in this endeavor, although I fear it will land upon stony indifference from the Throne unless your arrangement and preparations can be successful. Time is now of the essence, for the Queen is resident for some continuing weeks at Kenilworth and one must strike while the iron is hot.

My faith abides with you and your enterprise. I will do all in my power to bring this Fate to a just fulfillment.

Yours in Christ,
EA

"Edward Arden," Tyburn muttered to himself. "Somehow I don't like the sound of that."

In the sixteen years that Elizabeth had held the throne there had been myriad schemes against her, ranging from the subtle to the ridiculous. The Northern earls Westmorland and Northumberland had launched a half-baked plan in 1569 to depose the queen and supplant her with Mary of Scotland, then living in exile, imprisoned in Tutbury Castle. It had started promisingly enough with the earl's men seizing Durham Cathedral, burning the English Bibles and prayerbooks and holding a strict Catholic Mass before marching out to ravage and loot the countryside in steel-clad brutality. The rebellion unraveled at a swift pace once the Earl of Essex's forces marched north to meet them. The earls abandoned their plans, fled to Scotland and their army fell apart and scattered to the four winds. Westmorland and more than seven hundred followers had their heads parted from their bodies.

More plots followed, a dark and bitter web of tangled intrigue and confusion both imagined and real that fuelled ambition and paranoia in equal measures. Most recently, Norfolk had fallen in with the machinations of the Florentine banker Ridolphi, pulled down by his own aspirations, poor judgment and sheer inability to resist the scheme for an arranged marriage to the Queen of Scots. Norfolk's head was also soon severed but the machinations always seemed to continue.

Mary. Always Mary.

She was a lodestone for conspiracy, thought Tyburn, even if she wasn't involved. There were fanatical Catholics enough to intrigue on her behalf; she didn't need to even hold tinder to light the fire. The harsh reality was that England was beset with enemies both within and abroad. The Spanish ravaged the Lowlands, putting a fearful retribution on the Dutch rebellion. In France, the Huguenots had been slaughtered by the thousands with the Catholic Church sublimely indifferent to the massacre of the heretics.

And now a Jesuit was abroad, in secret correspondence with the high sheriff of Warwickshire. Tyburn shivered. This was a rat-trap if he'd ever seen one. Just having the letter in his possession was tantamount to a death sentence. It was unequivocal evidence of treason.

He weighed the brief, unholy temptation to burn the letter on the spot, then shook his head. They already knew he was involved. The lack of the letter wouldn't prevent them from racking him until he confessed just to end the bone-grating agony.

At least I have a better idea of why they want it. It might just be the only bargaining chip I have to get me out from under this peine forte et dure[116]. He winced at the thought of what it might mean to the boy and his family. He had sent Will back to Stratford after the performance was finished, richer with two pennies pay in his pocket and a spring in his step. The boy had enjoyed his day with the troupe and, Tyburn had to admit, he had represented himself well, helping out with gathering up the props and costumes with a cheerful and energetic enthusiasm.

He shook his head. The boy's father was complicit in some type of Jesuitical plot. Whether he had knowledge of the true nature of the plot or not, his role as a courier of the Catholic correspondence was tantamount to treason against the Crown. At best he might hope to suffer the hangman's noose rather than the grisly castration and the slow drawing and quartering that was the horror of a traitor's execution.

Tucking the letter back into his boot top, Tyburn snuffed the candle and tossed it into the hedge and headed along the gatehouse curtain wall back towards the roadway.

It was memory that warned him.

A faint, jingling rumble echoed off the gatehouse. Tyburn turned and sprinted for the undergrowth before he even was conscious of his decision. When the horsemen thundered down the laneway, the player was twenty feet under the shadow of the trees.

In Holland, on the bitter and damp isle of Walcheren, Tyburn and a small English patrol had been caught like rabbits on the dike roads past Middelburg by a steel-clad contingent of Spanish cavalry. The small English patrol had been slaughtered with the exception of two Scots, old in the ways of war, and one young Englishman, Tyburn, fresh-faced and foolish. The Scots had

---

[116] French for "hard and forceful punishment", or more specifically used when for sentencing someone to pressing or crushing, often when they refused to enter a plea in court. Heavy rocks were placed on the secured victim's chest and torso until they pled or fatally suffocated.

heard the rolling sound of the oncoming horsemen and the jingling trace chains and had pleaded with the lieutenant, the hook-nosed second son of a Yorkshire nobleman, to shift into the muddy embrace of a nearby flooded polder, to let the thick and glutinous Dutch ooze impede the oncoming horsemen. The Yorkshire nobleman's second son ignored the Scots' advice and chose instead to make his stand on the high dike.

The young man from Yorkshire died with a Spanish lance through his mouth, his sword unbloodied, alongside most of his men.

Tyburn remembered the thundering noise of the Spanish charge and the ridiculous ease with which the riders had killed the English troops. A handful of harquebusers managed a shot apiece, but most of the men had been marching unloaded and a harquebus was a devilish slow weapon to load. Blood flowed down the side of the dike and puddled red against the dark mud of the polder. The two Scots had turned and slid down the side of the dike the instant the Spanish horsemen slammed into the thinly held line of pikes. Tyburn, nervous in his first real fight, had gaped at the retreating men open-mouthed until a Spanish horse brushed past him, spinning him around, making his bandolier of apostles[117] rattle against each other like a child's toy, one flying up and the thin copper edge slicing the point of his chin. The man beside him fell, a crimson fountain spraying from a hole the size of a fist torn into his side. A second rider plunged past, close enough that Tyburn could smell the man's breath and see his eyes widen as he couched his lance into another of the English contingent, the lance quivering from the impact.

Tyburn had run. He half stumbled, half slid down the embankment, pushing through the tall salt grass into the muddy

---

[117] Apostles were small cylindrical flasks each holding enough powder charge for a single shot. Commonly they were carried in a bandolier belted across the chest. They were called apostles because they were often carried in quantities of 12.

embrace of the polder. The thick, cold glutinous weight of the mire coated his legs and pulled at his feet but he forced himself to continue forward, away from the screaming mass of dying men on the road, hearing the deep, keening sound of the Spanish cavalry as they killed.

He had joined the two Scots and together they watched in silence as the Spanish riders dismounted. They could scarcely breathe as they watched the troops thread their way along the road, pausing every few paces to stoop and plunder the dead, or to thrust a long lance down into an unseen body. The screams of the wounded seemed to hang in the air, long after the blades had thrust down with finality. The Spanish ignored the three survivors, recognizing the futility of trying to ride into the trap of the polder. Even dismounted, the cavalry in their heavy armor would have become mired within seconds. The two Scots had somehow hung onto their harquebuses. Both men stood, slow-matches fuming the air, ready to shoot any Spaniard who felt venturesome.

The Spanish had taken the English pikes and pushed them deep into the soft edge of the dike road. For a few minutes, the men in the polder were unsure what the Spanish were doing until they stepped away from the first pike, leaving a spherical object impaled on the point. It was the lieutenant's head. His long reddish hair flickered in the breeze. Two Spaniards tossed another back and forth like a ball, laughing. They mounted the remaining ones on the pikes, making a long, macabre fence along the roadway. They were one pike short, so after casting about looking for a possible post, the Spanish cavalryman had called out mockingly and then tossed the last head in the direction of the three mud-smeared survivors standing like scarecrows in the dank field.

Tyburn didn't just remember that day. It was seared into his memory, rising unbidden every time he heard the rapid drumming of hoof beats. He could still relive that first taste of battle, the scent of terror, the sounds of confusion and the ignominy of running. It had been an apt lesson.

From the cusp of the wood Tyburn watched a group of almost twenty armed men ride in file through the Charlecote gatehouse. He moved along the line of trees, keeping them in view. The men dismounted in the courtyard and the leader spoke to the steward. Topcliffe came striding down the path from the manor house and spoke to the leader. Then he waved his hand in the direction of the barn, and with a sinking sensation Tyburn recognized what was happening.

The men, led by Topcliffe striding along in a laggard advance, began to move towards the barn where Worcester's Men were quartered. Tyburn watched as they disappeared from view, splitting into two files to prevent any fugitives from bolting.

He cursed to himself. Lucy and Topcliffe must have intended this all along, he thought. Bring the troupe to the manor where they could be taken with little fuss and out of public view. If it had happened in Stratford, it would have drawn attention and word would have spread. Here, at Charlecote, they could bottle up Worcester's Men for a much more extensive period before they would have to justify it to anyone.

The armed men filed into the barn. Two remained at the gatehouse. Kit glanced around. South beyond the trees was open pasture and the river. North lay Charlecote's extensive deer park and thick forest, kept exclusively for Lucy's hunting. He began to walk towards the manor house, angling away from the barn, towards one of the manor side-doors, keeping his pace natural and unhurried. He felt the crunch of the graveled walkway under his feet and heard a distant shout. Topcliffe must have noticed some of the players were missing. The shouting was louder now.

Tyburn pulled on the cold iron door handle. It was immobile. The door was locked. He cursed and pulled again. Nothing. He glanced over his shoulder. Men were coming from the barn. He pulled again at the door, hammering with his free hand.

With a snap and a click, the latch opened. A thin man dressed in a blue smock pushed the door open and stepped past the player without even giving him a glance. Tyburn stepped through the open door and into the narrow servant's hallway. He turned to the right, moving swiftly along the corridor. Ahead of him was the main entrance hall, still crowded with guests departing from Lucy's celebration. Tyburn turned, pushing past the throng to the corridor that ran alongside the Great Hall. The fastest route for him was the most direct – through the house and out and into the trees before Topcliffe's men closed off the manor house.

Tyburn heard a raised voice. He stole a quick look behind him. Two of Topcliffe's men had accosted the blanket-laden Much and Robbie. Tyburn saw one man pulling on Much's arm and Robbie pushing another back, swearing obscenely. Several curious people moved forward and Tyburn's view of the altercation was blocked.

"Time to go," he muttered to himself. It wouldn't take long before they realized he hadn't been fetching bedding. Once they knew he was absent, the hunt would be on.

He ducked past the servants shifting chairs from the Great Hall and down the hallway past the staircase. Another narrow sidedoor abutted the far wall. The player opened it a crack and peered out. The door opened onto the northern edge of the Charlecote gardens. The river lay off to the left. Across the narrow laneway was a low stone wall, beyond which, a mere hundred feet away, lay a thick wall of greenery. Tyburn pulled the door open and stepped through.

"Where are you going?" At the sound of the voice he froze. Clair was seated on a wooden bench set in the corner of the garden.

Tyburn stared at the woman, detained momentarily by her sudden appearance. "It appears Sir Thomas's courtesy has reached its zenith. They've arrested Worcester's Men."

"And they missed you?"

"Not on purpose."

Clair stood, smoothed the fabric of her dress and slid her right arm around his left. "Why would they be arresting the troupe?"

"I have no idea."

She looked at him, one eyebrow cocked. "For an actor, you lie very poorly. If you have no knowledge of why they want you, why run?" She nodded towards the trees. "You'd best go. Where can I find you?"

"You can't."

Clair rolled her eyes in exasperation. "I just could scream instead. Work with me, master player, and stop trying to bend the world to your will." Tyburn gave a reluctant nod and she continued. "One can clearly tell you've not been married."

"I'll try to stay close to the river trail, depending on how they hunt for me. If not, try the glover's on Henley in Stratford, the boy will know."

"I'll find you." She turned away as he slipped through the stone arch and vanished under the shadows of the trees.

Tyburn finished his meal. The cheese was hard and the bread rough and gritty, shot through with small grains, unlike the fine white manchet that had been served at the celebration the previous day. He had filched the small bag of food from one of the smaller storage barns scattered about the estate property, the midday meal of some day laborer, hung on a hook by the barn door.

He glanced at the sky. It was overcast, with low clouds scudding southeast like a vast fleet under sail, gliding across the face of the wilder dark grey sky. Tyburn pulled his worn cloak tight around himself and shivered in the dim half-light, more at the remembrance of similar mornings in Flanders than from any real chill. He was ensconced in a shadowed hollow, between the line of trees that enclosed the laneway and a low stone wall that ran adjacent to a boggy water meadow bordering the river's edge. He leaned back on his haunches, feeling the rough cast of the stony wall against his back, and listened for hoofbeats. The road was silent and empty.

The water chuckled as it slid along the bank. It had been a rainy spring and the water was flowing high despite mid-summer. He would have to try to ford it. He couldn't waste any more time haunting the river banks.

Tyburn had spent the better part of the previous day slipping in and out of the hedgerows and through dank marshland, working his way north along the banks until searching riders had forced him away from the river. He had angled back to the river during the night, using the pale moonlight as his guide as he threaded through the trees. In the far distance, winking torches had illuminated the bridge, indicating that despite the darkness, guards were standing watch.

Compared to the Spanish in the Lowlands, the amateurs pursuing Tyburn were poor hunters of men. They seldom ventured off the roadways and trails, and avoided the wet and sloppy bottom-lands and dense thickets. When they did depart from the roads to venture into the forest, they thrashed about, frightening Lucy's deer and sending birds skyward in a panic. Most of the pursuivants had been drinking over the course of the day and their shouts grew more raucous as it progressed.

With a new morning would come Lucy's foresters, tenant farmers, boys gathering firewood, poachers and labourers. In daylight, Tyburn knew he would be unlikely to last very long in this vicinity before being spotted by prying eyes.

He sighed and hauled himself upright. After the long night's meander through the forest his back was stiff and his legs ached. He pushed his way through the thick line of shrubbery and slid down the muddy bank to the water's edge. Grabbing a thick handful of foliage and branches in his left hand and drawing his rapier with his right. , he edged out over the riverbank, probing with his sword for the bottom of the flowing river. Satisfied, he stepped back, sat and began to tug at his worn boots.

The faint clop of hoof on stone froze him into immobility. He allowed his body to flatten out on the ground, careful not to make any sudden movement that might draw attention. A single rider was coming down the track, the horse moving at a slow and deliberate pace. Tyburn, leaving his one boot sitting forlorn on the muddy riverbank, shifted to the right, using a fallen ash tree for cover. He moved with care, checking the ground for obstacles or branches that might break or shift. Leaves hung thick and languid over his head as he pushed his way past, careful not to move any of the branches, allowing the shadows to hide his shape. At last he had a clear sightline on the roadway. He froze again.

It was the widow.

Clair Carey was walking a bay mare along the pathway, curbing the animal to a lackadaisical pace. The horse was puzzled by its rider's behavior. It snorted and then with great deliberation bent its head down and ripped a mouthful of tall grass from the verge, giving its rider a wary glance like a small child filching sweets. The woman made no effort to check the animal and force it to move forward, content to let the beast feed.

Without thinking, Tyburn stood. The horse startled at the sudden movement, almost sending Clair out of the saddle. However, she had been riding horses since she was eight, and she recovered, pulling back on the reins and turning the horse to face the muddy spectacle that had arisen from the bushes.

"Oh dear God," she said between bits of laughter. "You look like a wrung rag."

Tyburn realized how ridiculous his appearance must have been. He stood with one foot bare, his legs plastered in mud and fallen leaves. Grass sprang from his collar and the sleeves of his doublet were torn. He wouldn't have been surprised to find a bird's nest tucked into the disarray of his hair. He stood facing her and realized he still had his rapier clutched in one hand. He sheathed it and gave her a quick twitch of a smile and his most elegant and courtly bow.

"My lady Carey. We seem to have developed an inopportune habit of strange meetings."

She smiled and the day seemed palpably brighter.

"I've been casting for you along the river path. According to my brother and Master Topcliffe you will be brought to heel and"-- she paused to push a stray tuft of auburn hair back into place--"how did they put it? Oh yes, 'whipped like a treasonous dog and sent to roast in the sulphurous pits of Hell'." She smiled again. "I'm very glad to have found you. "

Tyburn cocked his head. "Why look for me?"

"Debts, Master Tyburn, debts." She smiled again, this time with a tight humourless look. "My father is a cold-blooded, unscrupulous man who would waylay our Savior himself if a hint of gold was attached to the act, but he taught me well the necessity to repay one's debts. And I have one to you."

"My lady Carey, you owe me nothing."

She shrugged and slid from the saddle. "I would prefer it if you would call me Clair." Tyburn gave her a wary nod. "So do you have a first name? Or is a hanging tree your only identity?"

"Christopher. My friends call me Kit."

"Not Captain?"

"Actually I was only a sergeant. Oldcastle gave me a spontaneous promotion when I joined the troupe."

Clair reached over and pulled a small saddle bag off the horse and. tossed it to him. "Dry clothes and some wine but first, I think we should get off the road. Heaven knows who might come by next."

He nodded, disconcerted by her presence. Her face was grave until the instant she smiled, whereupon it became sunlit and vibrant. She had high cheekbones and eyes that, despite the serious cast of her face, danced with a lively energy.

Tyburn retrieved his sodden boot from its riverbank perch shrugging at her open laughter as he tugged it from the clinging mud of the riverbank, "You seem practiced in conversing with a fugitive."

"Well, you are the only person I've spoken to in two days who wasn't determined to wed me off to someone. That gives you a certain inestimable worth in my eyes."

Tyburn sat on the fallen elm and pulled the boot on with a squelch. He followed Clair across the path and the two moved inland, past the thicker cover of the woods to a gentle tree-covered slope that had a good view of the road in both directions. Tyburn could see past the woods and across open pastureland for a half-mile to the northeast. The fields were flanked by a small, decrepit hay barn that stood alone and forlorn like a lost child. Dark thunderheads were building along the western horizon from where they had been chasing the fleet of clouds, piling up like blankets into thick billows, heavy with moisture. The warm mid-summer air felt bulky and expectant, and the wind eddied and jigged as though with anticipation.

"You'd best get back," Tyburn said, pulling clothes from the bag and nodding skyward. "They'll soon miss you and unless I'm mistaken, the Lord has decided the world needs a good sluicing."

Clair laughed. "My father wouldn't notice or care and my brother would assume I was busying myself in the manor kitchen. The only one who might be attentive would be the steward and I paid him well enough to not notice."

"So why take the chance on helping me?" Tyburn peeled off his torn doublet and dropped it on the already discarded cloak. His hat was decorating the soft bottomland somewhere back in Lucy's woodlot.

She leaned against the horse, stroking the mare's neck. It nickered, ducked its head and tore at the grass. "Master Oldcastle."

"Oldcastle?" His voice was sharper than usual. The name startled him.

Clair nodded and glanced over at him as he tossed aside the remains of his collar and then tugged off his shirt. His back was facing her. She started to turn away but stopped, her gaze arrested by the jagged white lacing of scars along his left side.

"Courtesy of the Spanish, at Haarlem. Got stitched up by a Dutch laundress and a drunk barber-surgeon. She did a neat job of it while he drank gin and made scurrilous jokes." Tyburn was looking back at her over one bare shoulder. Her face reddened and she turned away to gaze at the heavy grey clouds accumulating in the northwest.

Tyburn could feel the warm summer breeze redolent with moisture blowing on his face. He liked the feel of the wind. It had an elemental touch to it, lending him a brief irresistible sense of soaring.

"So what wisdom did Oldcastle impart?"

She smiled, remembering the troupe leaders scowling expression. After Topcliffe had departed, she and her maid had taken food and drink out to the barn for the troupe, along with a hefty sack of wine as a garnish for the guards. "He spoke quite freely of you to Topcliffe and Sir Thomas. He called you a dog, a reprobate and a cur. He told them you had stolen silver off the body of your dead friend and that you knew something about the events of late but precisely what he could not tell."

Tyburn grunted. Oldcastle had done what he said he would do and cast Tyburn to the wolves. There were no surprises there.

"He told them you were skulking off to London and the cover of your patron, intending to spend your ill-gotten gains on 'festering hacks[118] and strong drink.' So, they chased away southeast towards Banbury." Tyburn gave her a sidelong look but she maintained a beatific expression as she gazed to the north.

"Then he called you a great number of rather impolite names and told me that you were a gripper, whatever that might be, and would not be departing until you had what you were looking for."

"He called me a gripper?" Tyburn asked. The slight amused tone in his voice made her turn her gaze on him. He was dressed, now wearing a black doublet with attached sleeves, covered by a dark patterned jerkin. The collar was a falling band rather than a

---

[118] Whores

stylish ruff, giving him a distinctly Puritan air that was at odds with the scarred face and wind-tossed hair. He fastened his sword belt.

"So what is a gripper?" She felt foolish for asking. There was a hollow echoing tremble in the air presaging a distant boom of thunder that rolled in the distance.

"It's from the London rat pits. It's a dog that only kills one rat at a time. Grips them, refuses to let go until the rat's dead, then it discards it and goes for another." He settled his sword on his hip. "They're worst kind of animal to have in a rat pit. They lose a lot of money for their owners when they're grippers rather than fast, indiscriminate killers. Rat pits tend to prize quantity over quality in ratting. It's how many you kill, not how or who."

She looked at him sidelong.

"So, kindly though your actions might be, in aiding a wayward fugitive from justice, again I'll ask--why?" There was a sharper edge to his voice.

She looked at him with an unflustered calm, her eyes level. "Why, you ask? Why indeed." Her voice now also held an edge. "I will not allow myself to be married off by my father and brother to a God-forsaken swine like Topcliffe or any man not of my choosing or taste. I am a respectable widow"--she paused at Tyburn's sardonic grin--"when I'm not traipsing after fugitives in the countryside." He noted the firm set of her lips as she paused. "Topcliffe has been promised my hand and my lands as a reward for aiding them in capturing this Jesuit priest. If he fails or is proven the fool, then I can refuse his suit, by our Lord's grace, and need not fear repercussion." Her lips tightened once more. "If he fails, then my father and brother fail. They do not enrich themselves, they do not rise in esteem at court, they do not receive the patronage of Leicester and I am free of their machinations, as this petty lawsuit against the Careys will collapse without court patronage."

She nodded, almost as though speaking to herself. "I will not allow myself to be used, controlled, or dictated to by their appetites. They may not make their prestige upon my life and my freedoms." Her eyes flashed with a hot, lambent and tangible anger: anger at her father; anger at her brother; anger at the oily machinations of powerful men; anger at Topcliffe's supercilious arrogance and cruel lasciviousness; even anger at the player who stood quiet, leaning against the thick trunk of one of the trees, watching her. Men with their smug expectations, arrogant strength and base desires, men who could not abide a woman to rule her own affairs. *Thank God for a queen,* she thought.

Tyburn watched Clair. She was correct in her summation of her difficulties; however, the crux of the problem for the player was that too many people were aware of his tangential role. Whatever the bones of this conspiracy were, the Jesuit was at the heart of it and any outcome that left the Jesuit free to work his machinations would leave Tyburn dead on a gibbet. He did not voice his thought aloud. Instead he asked, "And you come seeking my assistance?"

She laughed, shaking her head. "Men! You all think the orbs of Heaven revolve around your navels. I fear you don't spring to mind as a heroic knight. Not twenty minutes past you were perching on a sludge bank like a piece of tidal flotsam." The vehemence of her response surprised him, and he unwittingly leaned back a bit, away from her. "No, I came to make certain you escaped their clutches and in your exodus cannot pass them whatever information you possess on this Jesuit. You need to depart and take whatever rattles around in that play-actor's skull of yours with you when you go." She stopped, realizing that her voice was rising. Checking her emotion, she continued. "I have money in the bag as well, though if you are as well-laden with stolen silver as Topcliffe claimed, you don't require it."

"And mayhaps you should mount your prancer, pack up your bile and ride anon." Tyburn felt a hot flush of anger wash across his face at the accusation of thievery. "I've issued no invitation to involve you in this dance, nor do I seek additional company as I have more than enough rats in this pit with me already. That Spanish silver is blood money, tainted coins bought with my friend's life. I'll forward it on to his father if I can winnow out his murderers, but neither Topcliffe nor Oldcastle nor anyone else will lay their hands on it while I live."

She froze at his unexpected vehemence. "This is the money you took off your friend?"

"It's the money they left on Alec's body to rook Worcester's Men into whatever conspiracy is afoot."

She was quiet for a moment, weighing his words. "I think," she began, her voice halting, "that my brother might be the one responsible."

Tyburn turned his head to gaze at her. "Why do you think that?"

"I overheard a conversation between my father and brother and another man named Cuttle. It was apparent that they either killed your friend or had him killed to recover this Jesuit's letter that they lost."

Tyburn closed his eyes, feeling a faint sting on his lids. "They thought it was me." All the guilt he had suppressed for the last two days flooded back through him, cresting in a wave of anger. Alec, though dissolute and wayward and forever libidinous, had never harmed anyone in his life. "Bastards thought it was me. Alec never should have died."

Clair watched him. Despite his time on the stage and his effort to control the emotions that chased across his face, his eyes betrayed the impact of her news. He sat on the grass, plucking a small branch from the ground and snapping it into successively smaller and smaller fragments, flicking them away impatiently like stray thoughts. "This makes things more complicated," he said.

"Complicated." Once again her laughter rang hollow. "You need to leave. Just go, don't chase your vengeance. They won't follow you to London. They need the letter now, before the queen's progress departs Kenilworth. By the time they find you the Jesuit will be gone, and their plans gone with him."

Tyburn looked at her and smiled without humour. "Oldcastle was right, I'm a gripper. I can't."

Clair exploded. "Why not? Anyone else would be in London already! I can give you money to speed your passage!"

He stood and grasped her arm, touching her for the first time since that moment in the Charlecote hallway. "I. Can't." He paused between the words to give them weight, keeping his voice low. "I walked away from people in Flanders once and they died because of it. I left the better part of my soul in that country on account of my actions. I damned myself and swore then that I'd not allow it to happen a second time. I need to know, not for revenge, not for anger and not for justice. There isn't any justice, neither from God nor man. I need to know. I need answers. I cannot let it sit."

"You, sir," she insisted, "are a fool."

"I am a player, and that makes me Fortune's Fool, my role on the Great Chain of Being."

Clair covered his hand with hers. Tyburn felt her warm skin. "I want you to go," she said. "To spare me the success of my father's plots, yes, but also to spare your life. I would rather not have you maimed and killed. You saved me, and now"--she looked straight at him--"I would save you, in repayment of that debt."

He paused, his eyes darting back and forth over hers. He was spared answering by distant movement on the road.

He held up one hand in warning. The mare lifted her head from the grass she was chewing and her ears twitched back and forth. Tyburn put one hand on the horse's muzzle and quieted the animal. A rider was coming into view around the curve of the road beyond the pastureland. Tyburn led the horse behind the screen of trees and tied off the reins to a low branch. Clair studied the distant figure. Tyburn joined her, both of them standing in the shadowy recesses.

"I think that is my brother. But I thought he had gone on to Banbury."

"What's he doing riding around the outskirts of Charlecote by himself?" Tyburn asked. "Looking for me?" The rider was indeed Clair's brother. The ornate rapier was visible.

"Not by himself, and not seeking me either, in God's truth. He isn't riding for sport or enjoyment. That's not his habit."

Tyburn watched the man. "He's heading for the hay barn." Albert deBrage had left the road and cantered across the pasture. Though Kit couldn't see it at this distance, he was sure deBrage had a ready scowl on his face. In their brief meeting he had struck Tyburn as the sort of person to whom life was empty of simple joys, a man filled with a terrible certitude of self and a need for dominance, control and power, personified ambition without a compass. He was a man who embraced his dark gifts of strength and rejected everything else as feckless, someone who fed his own appetites first and last. A second figure emerged from the dark entrance to the barn and gave the rider a quick wave.

"Meeting someone," Tyburn commented to himself. Thunder drummed in the distance. He gave the sky a brief glance. The clouds were piling high. A bright flicker of lightning lit one cloud, the flaring white light making the thunderhead appear to ripple and bubble, like a translucent honeycomb held up to light. "Stay here." He began to skirt along the edge of a gully that led to the pasture, keeping his eye on deBrage as he dismounted and moved into the dark interior of the barn. The crack of a branch stole Kit's attention. Clair was picking her way along the gully's edge, struggling to stay out of the hollow's soft bottom in her heavy dress.

"Where in the bloody hell do you think you're going?" He tried to keep his tone level but the irritation was clear in his voice.

"With you." Her reply was sharp.

"You are damned well not. Stay with the horse."

"Do I look like one of your troupe?"

Tyburn bit back a curt rejoinder and forced a civil one. "You'll never move quick or quiet in that dress. Stay here."

"Fine." She reached around and tugged at one of the stays and began pulling on the neckline to loosen the fabric. Tyburn was puzzled. Then she slid first one arm, then the other, out of the long sleeves, and pulled the apparel over her head. The player stared in astonishment. Clair folded the dress and set it on the grass. She threw him a glare and without pausing slid her farthingale over her hips and down her legs. She stepped out of the untidy pile of fabric and began to undo the laces that held her corset.

"What are you doing?" Tyburn asked in a faint voice.

"If my dress impedes our silent movement and listening to my brother and his companion . . ." She shrugged out of the corset and tossed it unceremoniously on top of the farthingale, breathing a silent sigh of relief. ". . . then my dress needs to go."

Tyburn made no reply, gazing at the auburn-haired woman who stood, glaring at him, arms akimbo, in her embroidered linen shift. The thin shift left little to the imagination and Tyburn felt his breath catch in his throat at the sight of the light fabric clinging to her.

"Well?" The acid tone brought him out of his reverie He nodded once, recognizing the futility of argument and turned to resume the careful trek to the barn.

The short journey took almost ten minutes as Tyburn moved with caution, skirting the edge of the trees and avoiding any open ground. Clair determinedly picked her way behind him, making her presence known on occasion by cursing softly under her breath. Tyburn was relieved about one thing. At least she could move quietly now that she was unencumbered by heavy clothing. That thought seemed to hang in his imagination overlong. He shook his head, pushing the persistent image of the thin shift hugging the contours of Clair's slim body out of his mind. *Damn fool. Keep your mind on the business at hand.* He fought the urge to turn and watch her.

The hay barn was old. A bygone relic of an older tenant farm that had once encompassed the fields north of the estate, the barn had faded timber walls, with a long, high, blackened scorch mark marring one side, testament to a long-dead fire. The high peaked frame was visible in places where the thatch had fallen away in untidy dry piles around the outskirts of the building. The desiccated skin of a fox or a feral dog was pegged to the wide lintel above the front and Tyburn could hear the low drift of voices through the opening. A drop of rain spattered into the dust of the barnyard, a precursor to the threatening storm gathering overhead.

A man stepped into view. It was Clair's brother, wearing the same crooked smile that Tyburn remembered from Charlecote. He was richly dressed, wearing an expensive riding half-cloak which hung from one shoulder. His face was a pale narrow lozenge surmounting a wide, fashionably coloured ruff. Albert stepped back out of immediate view, gesturing as he spoke to an unseen companion. Tyburn couldn't make out his words. A small rustle beside him drew his attention away from the open doorway. Clair lowered herself onto the damp ground beside him.

"Who is he speaking to?" she asked.

"We need to get closer." Tyburn peered around them. The open ground between the trees and the barn offered little cover but once alongside the solid timbered western wall, the barn should shield them from any prying eyes. "Follow me. Quietly."

She rolled her eyes askance at the instructions but did as he asked. Tyburn slid out and moved to the right in a low crouch, angling towards the scorched wall. He reached the barn wall and turned, gesturing for Clair to follow. She crouched and, head down and heart pounding, walked swiftly across the open space. She was startled to realize how terrifying it was to be hunted, to have to stay hidden. Even a simple act like sneaking across an open space made her feel like a mouse about to be stooped upon by some unseen predator. She almost ran headlong into the barn wall because she had been watching her feet. Tyburn reached out a reassuring hand and caught hers. She gave him a relieved squeeze.

Staying low, Tyburn led her along the wall and around the corner. Several open windows, the shutters long since collapsed, were visible at the midpoint along the building. Tyburn dropped lengthwise onto the grass and crawled until he was below the open window, hard up against the barn wall and a long pile of dry fallen thatch from the damaged roof. He gestured for Clair who slid herself along the base of the wall until she, like Tyburn, was stretched out, feeling the itchy sensation of the dusty thatch beside her, listening to the conversation. The sound of her brother's voice sent a deep rippling shiver down her spine.

". . . following the Evesham Road. Let Topcliffe keep chasing shadows. We can't afford to wait for the recovery of the letter."

"So what would you 'ave us do?" The voice spoke with a clipped Southwark cadence. Tyburn smiled to himself. He recognized the sullen voice as belonging to Cuttle, the knife artist from the Stratford alleyway. Poor fellow, he sounded aggrieved.

Albert's voice was butter smooth. He sounded like a man trying to play a role of prestige, attempting to sound magnanimous and commanding but coming across as arrogant and condescending. . "We lack the Jesuit and Arden's letter. If Topcliffe can locate the priest, we still lack the letter tying him by name to Arden. He signed it. To make the name of treason stick, we must have Arden's name writ upon it."

Cuttle grunted in acknowledgement as deBrage continued. "Hall has gone to ground but he is like a dog circling his shit; we'll find him at Kenilworth, not far from his master's beck and call. Tickle him and he'll produce as many letters as we require."

After a pause Cuttle said, in a careful, almost rehearsed tone, "It's your father pays us, not you."

"You put your trust in his machinations? My father schemes and plots and turns but he doesn't have the stones to do what is necessary to make his schemes come to fruition." Albert laughed, a derisive sound. "My father lacks willpower. He doesn't rack Worcester's Men for fear of Worcester's enmity, he bows down to Leicester's demands for irrevocable proof of Arden's treason, he brings in Lucy and Topcliffe and Christ only knows who else. What will be left for us when Arden is quartered as a traitor? He will have given away half of Warwickshire."

Cuttle said nothing in response. Albert continued in a low voice. "His time is passing him. He is not what he once was. Not now. It is my turn, my time. I'll rook Arden for Leicester, buy off that petty fool Topcliffe with Clair's pretty flesh and rake in half of the Arden lands on the back of that damned Jesuit"--his voice rose

210

to a shout--"but first we need to find him, and you purblind fools lost the letter and couldn't find your arses in a shithouse."

There was a tense silence. Cuttle's voice sounded amused to Tyburn's ear when he spoke. "So what's our bait[119]?" There was the sound of someone gulping from a bottle.

"Gold. Women. Power. You wear my livery, carry your blades for me. We get Leicester in our pocket and there is nothing we can't do in Warwickshire. "

There was a long expectant pause.

"Easy enough to say. But yer father pays good coin. So far you've shown us naught but wind."

A brief rustle and the muffled sound of a bag well-laden with coins thumping onto the dirt floor of the barn came to the listeners' ears.

"Crack it, Hawkins." Tyburn could hear the faint shuffle of feet and the brief sound of coins being poured out followed by a low whistle. "Nowat we jus' need the women. Right then, Master deBrage, you've gone and bought our attentions for a time. What now?"

"You and Hawkins ride to Kenilworth. Track down Hall and get him to author some letters that tie Arden to the Jesuit, signed letters--Arden's name by God, nothing less. For that you get another bag of lour. Once we have the letters . . ." Tyburn could sense that familiar thin, supercilious smile on deBrage's face.

Tyburn looked at Clair. She was listening with intensity.

"And then?"

Tyburn felt Clair start beside him. A thin, wan-looking rat with a long naked tail pushed its way out from under the thatch and scrambled past her. The thatch rustled as she shifted her weight. He put out his hand, gesturing in warning. Another drop of rain spat onto his face. He felt it slide wet down his chin.

---

[119] Literally "something to eat"

"Then the Papist heretic bastard dies," deBrage said matter-of-factly. The man sounded inordinately pleased but whether it was at the prospect of acquiring Arden's lands or coaxing him to his death, Tyburn was uncertain. He had seen similar men in the Lowlands, men who had given themselves over to greed or dogma, finding comfort in the absoluteness of their beliefs. Willingly, they walked into the fire and many had found their deaths on Spanish blades. Tyburn had taken other lessons from the war, lessons pragmatic and canonical, that left him both more skeptical and more lost.

Cuttle grunted in response. His footsteps grew louder through the window.

"And yer father?"

There was a long tense pause. "His health of late has been somewhat lacking . ." Albert trailed off and Tyburn heard Cuttle's low chuckle.

"So I hear."

Clair drew a sharp breath.

Tyburn heard the creak of wood and the quiet crunch of a footfall. It was inches away, right beside the wall. He reached over and pulled Clair towards himself, rolling her tight against the barn wall. He covered her mouth with one hand and held his breath. The footstep was close. He paused, cocking his head and listening, then reached out and grasped the edge of the thatch pile. An easy tug and smoothing, and the wide fan of thatch lay over the pair of silent eavesdroppers.

Clair shrank back against Tyburn. He had one eye cocked upwards through the thin thatch cover. A callused hand gripped the windowsill. He could scarce breathe but even under the imminent threat of detection he was profoundly aware of the long, warm body pressed against him. Clair's hair lay soft on his face and her faint citron fragrance teased his nose. For a moment, despite the fear, excitement quickened in his chest, his heart pounding for what felt like the first time in years.

There was a long silence pregnant with expectation.

"What if Hall talks?"

deBrage laughed. It was not an enticing sound. "Hall? He's not going to live long enough to talk. Once you get the letters, send him to go and meet God, since he craves his martyrdom so much. Then we inform Walsingham and Leicester, pass them the evidence on Arden and reap our rewards. If we have the Jesuit, so much the better. If not, well, I'm sure Topcliffe can smoke him out with his usual methods. Rack a few of these Papist bastards and they sing anon. Just like Hall did."

"And the players? I don't like loose ends." To Tyburn, the Southwark knifeman sounded exasperated and tired of these machinations--like someone who just wanted to settle his problems with the simple expedient of a blade between the ribs.

"They're nothing. We wait a few days, maybe have Topcliffe tickle a few for the joy of it, see what spills."

"And Tyburn?"

"He's a clever one. Slipped our nets twice now. If he's a dram of sense, he's well away to London by this time. If he does turn up, kill him and we'll sort it out later."

Clair turned minutely to regard Tyburn. He looked at her and realized he was still covering her mouth with his hand. He gently and apologetically removed it. She breathed out and slipped one hand up to turn his face towards her again. Puzzled, he looked at her. She tilted her face up and kissed him.

Tyburn felt her warm lips on his and the shock of her touch sent a shiver through his body, a coursing gleam like ripples of sunshine on a bubbling river. Clair pulled back and looked into his eyes, storm-grey and for once, utterly open. She was shocked at her own boldness, her own sense of desire, a desire she thought long dead within her. He reached over and slid his rough hand along the back of her neck and pulled her lips to his. As he returned the kiss, his body pressed against her, a rough magic that transcended their thoughts.

For a long moment the two were conscious of nothing else other than the concordant pounding of their pulses. Tyburn heard the trio leaving the barn as though from a great distance, no other sound breaking through the hammering of his heart as they kissed under the thin thatch cover as though the world were new and fresh.

And then it began to rain.

Chapter the Seventeenth

C LAIR STOOD, FRAMED by the open doorway, watching the grey rain pouring from the heavy fleece that buried the sky. She was wrapped in a red patterned horse blanket that left one pale shoulder and arm bare. The light knitted fringe bordering the edge of the blanket met over her torso like the cross on a surcoat. Her damp dress was hung over a paddock railing to dry, just out of reach of the tied-off black mare who rustled and snorted and picked at the dried and dusty hay that lay scattered about the barn floor.

Kit was watching her.

Tyburn sat on the damp floor, his back pressed against a thick wooden support beam, one arm leaning on the heavy leather saddle. He knew it was a mistake to stay at the ruined barn. Any sensible man would have moved on, taken advantage of the rain to slip the guard at the bridges and get back to Stratford. He needed to move. He needed to find the Jesuit. He needed to go to Kenilworth.

But try as he might to bring focus to his thoughts, they kept following his eyes to Clair.

He needed to stay.

She spoke without turning. "Who was she?"

Tyburn didn't reply at first, waiting until she turned her head, allowing him to see her profile, sharp and backlit by the light of the open doorway. Then he asked, "Who was who?"

"The woman. The one in Holland . . . the one you lost."

There was another long silence until Clair turned her head and gave Tyburn a delicate smile. "You aren't that good of a pretender. You carry it well, but the more I look at you the more obvious it is that you've wrapped a ghost about your heart."

His silence was answer enough. Clair leaned against the door frame, the warm wind flicking droplets of rain in through the open door. She pushed her hair out of her eyes and gave him that calm glance that seemed to see right through him. The look pried a reluctant answer from his lips.

"Her name was Annika."

"You loved her." It was not a question.

Tyburn's response was soft, barely heard over the downpour outside and the incessant splashing and dripping that slipped through the remnants of the barn roof. The receding sound of thunder in the distance rose and fell as he tried to find his voice.

"I met her in Haarlem. She spoke no English . . ." He laughed. "And I spoke only gutter Dutch and German, but we managed. She had a four-year-old daughter named Miriam. Her husband had died the year before." He idly twirled a length of straw between thumb and forefinger. "We should have left Haarlem when most of the English troops left, but you know that saying; 'credulous hope supports our life, and always says that tomorrow will be better[120].' We were fools. I was a fool."

He stared out at the falling rain. "They wouldn't take any of the women when they left--no strumpets, doxies, whores, queans, or Magdalenes permitted. Orders from Sir Humphrey Gilbert

---

[120] Tibullus

himself, although he managed to take his personal seamstress along." Tyburn felt a practiced bitter smile cross his face. "So we stayed. Myself, a handful of Englishmen, Scots and some Germans. Stayed through the siege and watched our friends and lovers dying by inches."

He looked up. Clair was listening, her eyes fixed on his. His chest was taut and clenched at the memories. "The Spanish used to lob heads over the walls. Sometimes dead bodies. Some claimed children on occasion. We'd raid their lines at night, during that long dark winter, kill the sentries and steal supplies. Sometimes people would try to slip out of the city but it was a chancy thing." He shook his head. "Not a lot of mercy in a Spanish *tercio*, and we didn't offer much either. The Dutch tendered up a dozen Spaniards for a prisoner exchange once. The Spanish officers came under a truce and Dutch gave over a couple of canvas bags with a dozen heads in them. Then they pulled out a thirteenth one and tossed it to the Spanish officers and told them out of God's mercy they could have a baker's dozen instead."

She just kept watching him, her eyes full of warmth. She could identify with the hopeless sense of futility, being caught up in the wheels of Fortune and thrashing helpless while you witnessed a remorseless shade advancing on your loved ones.

"Annika wanted to run, but I thought . . . I hoped, anyway, that the Spanish would break. They had before. The *tercios* hadn't been paid in more than a year. The deserters who crossed the lines-- mostly Flemish mercenaries--kept telling tales of mutiny in the Spanish ranks but it was just rumor. When spring came what was left of the contingent decided to run, try to pass the lines while the waterways were still frozen. And hope for God's mercy." Tyburn stopped. His eyes burned.

"What happened?" Clair asked in a quiet voice.

"Almost made it. Almost." The player's voice was even. He stroked his beard. "Ran into a Spanish ambush--harquebusiers, I think. It was like Hell erupted, like the End of Days. You could smell the sulphur in the air, writhing like a live thing. The devil was abroad that day walking in the snow. People screaming, children wailing, smoke, blowing snow, no order. Half the group were women and children and everyone ran to protect their own. The confusion was all that saved most. I was hit in the thigh and went down like a stone. Sat up, looked across and Annika was seated on the snowbank opposite, eyes wide open, hair all spread out on the half-melted snow like it was a feathered pillow. She was dead. Harquebus ball stove in the side of her head."

There is nothing like Flanders. That thought echoed through his head, a remorseless mantra of fate. Tyburn looked down at the damp floor remembering the blood like frozen roses in the snow. "Next thing I knew, I was being dragged along by a couple of my men. I was kicking and thrashing, trying to get back to Annika. I couldn't . . . I didn't want to leave her in the snow. I had no idea what happened to Miriam, she was gone.

"I found out later that the Spanish rounded up the prisoners, took them out onto a small lake and forced them through some holes in the ice. They took bets on how long they could stay afloat. Miriam was one of them."

The rain was still flooding down but the barn was silent except for the mare which peed, the sound blending into the downpour outside.

The wind blew a gust of rain under the overhang and in through the open doorway. Clair shivered, clutching the blanket as it fluttered. Tyburn stood up and crossed the open space to her. She leaned into his open arms, craving the touch of him, the smell of his skin, pressing herself hard against him. She reached up and tilted his face towards her, pressing her lips on his. She stood on her toes and whispered in his ear. "By Jesus's mercy, they are safe with God, and you are here. You look too much for meaning when there is none to be had in this mortal world. We must both choose to love and release our pains, to let go of our shades. We've carried them for too long."

She felt his lips on hers, the soft flutter of his tongue sending shivers up her spine. One of her hands gripped the back of his dark hair as his mouth traced the line of her throat, gliding downwards with remorseless intent. She tugged at the damp cloth of his shirt, pulling it over his head, feeling the heated glow of his skin. As she slid her hand along his back, her fingers followed the delicate tracery of raised white scars down his left side. The blanket fell away. His mouth slid over her breasts and she gasped as he teased her nipples with his teeth and tongue. She felt his fingers sliding up the inside of her leg, their touch hot like a brand on her skin.

They slid higher, gliding between her thighs. She writhed beneath them, her breathing heavy, eyes clenched shut as his fingers opened her and slid inside. Tyburn pulled the rough woolen blanket aside and, holding her tightly, lowered both of them to the floor. His mouth worked its intent, slow path back up her body, his breath warm and moist on hers, both of them breathing deep in unison. His skin felt hot as she lay across him, her mouth open on his as she felt him slide into her.

The rustle of the blanket sliding down onto the floor made the horse turn its head. It watched the couple with curiosity for several moments and, realizing no sugared treats or apples were forthcoming, resumed its snuffling quest for stray strands of hay and grass, disdaining the sounds coming from the two people in the barn.

Will was nervous. It had been two days since he had left Worcester's Men at Charlecote and made trek home through the lengthening evening shadows to the tall house on Henley Street, his pay jingling in his pocket with each stride. Will had found the springy lightness of his steps diminishing with each footfall as his earlier worries began to resurface. By the time he neared Stratford, he was convinced that the sour-faced man Cuttle was lurking behind every shadowed bush, shrub and woodpile. He crossed the frowning stone arch of Clopton Bridge at a dead run and flew up Henley Street.

Now, as he helped his father with the noxious job of topping up the tanning vats, Will was worried. The rumor, at least according to the Hornbys' young kitchen maid (a scrawny, pock-marked thirteen-year old who talked in a constant voluble stream to everyone) was that Worcester's Men had been arrested by Sir Thomas Lucy and were to be hanged for thievery. She had confided to Will that the true story was that the players had offended Lucy's sensibilities with their corrupt, depraved and evil performance, and had then lured Lucy's wife into a licentious liaison with their troupe leader. Will shook his head in disbelief.

He piled a selection of thick hides on the bench near the puering vat and thought again about telling his father the truth about the letter. He wasn't afraid of his father's punishments. He had been whipped often and fruitlessly enough by his schoolmasters who were frustrated by his inability to focus on their lessons. Will had proven to be a recalcitrant student, and his attention meandered like the breath of the west wind. Blessed with a superb memory and a vivid imagination, the boy found his schooling to be a mixed blessing. It freed him from the mundane chores of stacking wool and sorting hides, yet failed to ignite his passion or interest as the few bright moments were occluded by the oppressive boredom of the everyday. He had to fight to keep his thoughts from constant straying from whatever text or lesson lay on the table before him, or himself from yawning at the endless sermonizing of the teachers.

He would, Will thought, tell his father if the player didn't return by tomorrow. He toyed with the hope that perhaps the strange parties behind the murders hadn't made a connection between him, Tyburn and the missing letter. He shook his head, angry for allowing himself that comforting illusion. *It was foolishness*, he thought. *They knew who he was and, in time, would make their appearance. No,* Will decided, *my father will need to know and be prepared.* But what he might do, was unclear.

Steeled by his decision, Will straightened up, his back aching from moving the heavy piles of sodden hides. He would wait until tomorrow and then lay the affair in its entirety before his father. *Perhaps Father can find answers where we could not.*

"Will!" His father's peremptory voice cut through his thoughts. "Your mother promised Mary Hiccock a loaf of the good bread, as her daughter's ailing. Run one down to her." The Shakespeare family nominally shared the Sunday pew at church with the Hiccoks, at least on the infrequent occasions his recusant mother was pressured into attending with his father and siblings. As a result, Will was well acquainted with the endless stream of malaise, rumor and illness that seemed to lay low the neighbouring family on a regular basis. The Hiccocks had been absent from the services that day due to the children and the mother being ill. Will cheerfully abandoned the sodden hides and, wiping his hands on his smock, ducked through the open doorway into the narrow kitchen.

The kitchen was hot. A partially plucked chicken sprawled supine across the preparation counter, the pile of white and tawny feathers set to one side to be used for mattress stuffing. A dozen spice cakes were cooling on the sideboard, which Will gravitated towards. Will's mother spotted him and, with unerring instinct, steered the boy away from the confections and over to a full wash basin in order for him to scrape the grime off his hands. She then gave him and his hands a quick inspection, and handed him a pair of muslin-wrapped loaves, ushering him out before he could nab or ingest anything.

Will ducked around the corner of the house and paused, feeling ill at ease on his own street. He glanced up and down the roadway, seeing nothing but the everyday rumbustious bustle of his neighbors and the townsfolk. The sense of ill ease did not diminish. It, like every stranger, was giving him a narrow, gimlet-eyed stare. He took a deep breath and marched out into the street, deftly avoiding the ever-growing feculent dung pile on the corner by the Watleys' house. A fine would be forthcoming, if the bailiff ever deigned to notice. A day labourer, bent almost horizontal under a massive bound stack of branches and thatch, was working his way up the street. A trio of somber, dark-visaged housewives swept by like a murder of crows, ignoring the boy on his errand. Will spied the Hiccock household, a short, wide shamble of a house perched adjacent to the alley to Water Street.

Will walked up to the house and gave the heavy stained door a brisk thump. It opened to reveal the round moonface of the youngest Hiccock. With nary a pause Will handed over the loaves and was well-back up the street before the belated thank-you had even been uttered.

Will was so relieved to be moving back towards the refuge that was home that he almost didn't register the low voice that spoke as he passed.

"You walk like someone with something to hide." The boy jumped and stepped back, startled. The only man near enough to speak to him was the day labourer, bent under his load of wood. Will glanced about, trying to find the origin of the voice.

The labourer straightened with a grunt and Kit Tyburn grinned out at him from under his thick burden. "Open your glims and close your mouth before you catch flies in it."

Will was astonished. He had walked right past the player, given him a careful fear-driven scrutiny and yet had not recognized the man. Now that he was aware of the player's presence, he realized why. Tyburn was dressed as a poor country labourer, his back bent, his gait and stance displaying the careful spavined pace of a man whose life was given over to the bearing of heavy loads for little pay.

The player grunted as he shifted the load. "Meet me at the boundary elms at the leet[121]. Bring the silver with you." He resumed his slow and methodical pace, his sharp amused eyes falling back into the vacant, glassy stare that saw only the immediate tread of his feet. "And by Christ, stop staring."

---

[121] Crossroad or intersection

With an effort, Will tore his gaze off the player and hurried back to the house, resisting the urge to crane his neck about and watch the player's slow progress up the avenue. When he arrived home, he darted upstairs and slipped into the narrow space he and Gilbert shared. Standing on the bed furniture, Will reached upwards and caught the low cross-beam supporting the roof. He pulled himself up about a foot and, locking his legs around the beam, thrust one hand high into the apex where the joinery came together. He felt the smooth polish of the leather bag under his fingertips and traced the hard outlines of the silver within. He let go and landed with a dull thump on the edge of the bed. The high roof joists were perfect for hiding everyday items from Gilbert's persistent fingers and ready curiosity. Will kept his valuables well out of reach of his brother, along with the small collection of poems he had started to compose.

He paused, wary of Gilbert's habit of appearing out of the void. Nothing, he thought with satisfaction. His brother was still preoccupied with the new litter of kittens in the barn. Will tucked the bag into his waistband and slipped down the stairs, listening for the heavy tread of his father or his mother's voice. He stepped out the back and raced across the yard, clambering over the low stone wall that marked the edge of the property. He cut across the Badger family's property, cutting through to join the road which was hidden from view beyond the sheds, shanties and barns. Ahead of him, he could see the tall elms that marked the boundaries of Stratford and the leet, the intersection of the roads to Clopton and Henley.

The crossroads were empty but Will spotted the abandoned pile of branches that the player had been carrying stacked by the low stone wall on the west side of the road. As he moved closer he spied the player sitting against the far side of the wall, chewing on an apple. He clambered over the wall and dropped down beside Tyburn, who had changed out of the filthy labourer's attire and into a clean set of clothes.

All of the pent-up questions Will had been nursing for the past few days flew out at once. "Where have you been? What's going on? We heard Worcester's Men were arrested? How did you escape?"

Tyburn grinned at the sudden torrent of inquiry. "I've been raiding Lucy's orchard." He tossed Will an apple. "They're green but good, not Hesperides[122] but still tasty." The boy took a bite, then wiped juice from his lips with his sleeve.

"Why were you picking apples?" The words were muffled by fruit, but understandable.

"I was hungry."

The boy's exasperated sigh said everything.

"Calm your choleric temperament, Master Shakespeare. I'll give you your answers, but not while seated on a public roadway waiting for more of Lucy's men to trot past." He stood. "I need to head for Kenilworth, and I need the silver."

Will was crestfallen. He had hoped for answers after having lived for several days in uncertainty but all the player wanted was the silver. The boy handed over the purse, a sour look crossing his face. Tyburn almost laughed at the boy's expression.

"Can your father spare you for a time?"

"Yes."

"Then walk with me on the road and I'll spin you a yarn before I send you home."

Will nodded his assent and the two set off north up the road to Clopton. Tyburn gave Will a quick and succinct overview of the events at Charlecote and the subsequent imprisonment of Worcester's Men.

Listening, Will felt an appalling sense of certainty that the Fates were conspiring against him for some unknown reason. He

---

[122] The Garden of Hesperides was the mythical orchard of Hera, at the centre of which grew the Tree of Life. Hercules was tasked with stealing apples from the Garden as one of his twelve labours.

would have hoped that God would recognize the justness of his actions and bring him and his family some measure of salvation. Instead every step he took seemed to be immersing him deeper in trouble. He looked at the tall figure walking along the roadway and wondered again if he had tainted his soul with sin by allying himself with the player. The man was no Catholic.

Tyburn regarded the boy trudging beside him and Will felt a frisson of dread, as though the player could read his thoughts. The man spoke. "I need to get to Kenilworth. We need to find this Jesuit to obtain some leverage to get out from under this press."

"And you think the Jesuit is at Kenilworth?" Will was wary. As much as he wanted to be free of these machinations, he also knew his father was pious enough to shy away from profiting on the bones of a priest, much less a Jesuit sanctified by Rome to help save English souls.

Tyburn shook his head. "The one man who might have an inkling of where to find this Jesuit is at Kenilworth. I need to speak with Edward Arden. He seems to be the crux of these events, although I doubt he is aware of the circumstances. He signed the letter. We might be able to use that to force him to assist us."

"But . . ." Will started to argue but a distant shout drifting across the warm summer air made him stop and turn.

Five horsemen were rounding the far bend in the road, about three hundred yards away. Tyburn swore under his breath. "The trees. Move!" Tyburn barked. The player gestured to the left, indicating the tangled mass of greenery that edged the sheep pasture.

The thick woodland jutted ahead of them like the prow of ship. The forest was a shade of the past, a chaotic maze of oak, beech and silver birch that stretched along the edge of the pastureland for several miles. The stumps and thin, younger trees along the wood's edge gave way to a tall and twisted scramble of brush and heavy thicket, punctuated by the slanting gleam of sunlight thrusting its way through the tight leafy foliage. This was all that remained of the once-vast Forest of Arden. The woods had once dominated the Midlands, its heavy growth, ancient oaks and thick brambles discouraging even the Romans from pushing their relentless roads through the region. It was easier by far for them to skirt the ancient woodland rather than dare the tangle and so it was bypassed by both the Romans' Salt Road and the Fosse Way, leaving this land, the heartland of England, to itself and the dark and often malign spirits that inhabited the shadows beneath the boughs. It had become a place of green refuge, a hidden and forgotten place, a place that kept its anxious secrets from the recesses of time. Notorious for brigands and thieves, the deeper remnants of the forest were believed to be the haunt of changelings and urchins, naiads and foliots, hobgoblins and bullbeggars that bewitched and preyed upon the unwary. Arden was not a place lightly travelled.

The two fugitives ran headlong across the pasture scattering startled sheep from their path. Tyburn threw a quick glance over one shoulder to gauge their pursuers' progress. A puff of grey smoke followed a second later by the hollow pop of a shot told him that at least one of them had a gun he didn't know how to use. They were well out of range.

Tyburn ran towards the shelter of the thick woods, feeling his leg muscles burn from the slight incline, all his earlier misgivings about the shadowy forest forgotten. He cursed himself. There must have been some watcher in Stratford following the boy that he hadn't spotted.

The light under the leaves was diminished but sunlight still slipped through like the teeth of a long comb, dappling the thickets and brush with constant movement as the breeze danced through the upper reaches of the forest. Tyburn plunged along a narrow forest path that seemed to open before his feet, writhing along between the trees and up and down a set of small gullies. He winced as a branch slapped at his eyes.

"This way! Follow me!" The boy was well ahead of him, able to avoid the tangling roots that stippled the ground and the reaching branches above. "This way you purblind fool!" Will's voice cut through the underbrush with such a peremptory command that Tyburn paused and then decided to take the youngster's vehemence and confidence at face value. After all, he reasoned, the lad lived here and so might be expected to know something about these labyrinthine woods. He could hear a vague shouting and a thrashing of brush behind them as their pursuers pushed their way past the light, thin forest edge and into the entangling foliage.

Will moved fast through the forest, humming to himself, pausing at times to ensure that the player, plowing along behind him, was still following. The boy knew this branch of the forest well. It lay close to home and served as a welcome hiding spot for those avoiding chores and schooling. Although he seldom ventured further than a couple of miles through it, and never at night, he was comfortable in the broken wood. He knew the bogs and the low-lying areas on the forest edge where you could stalk frogs and catch grass snakes. He knew the dark recesses of the forest festooned with fairie rings and thick white mushrooms that clustered among the rotted stumps and fallen oaks. He also knew that this patch of forest was just a few miles long and extended like a fat, outstretched finger parallel to the road before giving way to broken copses and open pastureland with fewer safe places for two fugitives to pause.

Once past the pastureland, Will's local knowledge petered out although he knew that the forest, though much diminished from the once-contiguous growth that had covered the regions north of Stratford, was still dense and thick enough to cover much of the march north, at least until they drew closer to Warwick.

Tyburn was edgy. The thrashing sounds behind him had lessened but every few minutes he would hear a series of loud halloos from the pursuers and the far-off sound of angry shouting. Will was at least twenty yards ahead, pausing to wave for the player to hurry but Tyburn was less deft at moving through the heavy undergrowth. The branches seemed to hitch and grasp at his feet and arms. He unfastened his scabbarded rapier and carried it, one-handed, in front of him to avoid snags and push the thin branches away from his face as he trailed after Will. The trail was sloping downhill, now and was masked by the long, feathery leaves of the bracken.

The periodic shouting rose again and Tyburn slowed. He turned his head, listening. The noise had assumed a systematic regularity. Suspiciously regular, he thought. He gave a brief hiss to try to attract Will's attention but the boy had disappeared through the verdant growth. Tyburn could see a shadowy blur moving through the tall trunks ahead of him but little else. He slowed even further, curbing his steps, watching for any loose branches or litter that might crack or break. The shouts behind him continued but the player's energy and attention was focused forward now, along the narrow, fern-covered forest path.

He heard a low rustle ahead, the sound of something large moving. A lithe brown shape bounded out of the thicket; the deer's tail flashed bright and it sprang away. Kit had just begun to relax when the shot crashed out, reverberating hollowly among the tall trunks and echoing skyward. Tyburn dropped to the forest floor and lay still.

"You stupid whoreson! I tol' you it were a deer."

"Fuck you, you bastard. You tol' me to pop 'em."

"I said ter fuckin' kill the man, not some damn deer! You'll get us nipped fer poachin' at this rate." The voices were close. Tyburn heard the clink of a ramrod as the man began the laborious task of reloading his weapon.

"Belike they knowing we're here now," the leader muttered. Tyburn heard the sound of a sword being drawn. The man began to move towards Tyburn, pushing his way through the undergrowth. The player had a clear view down the path and winced as Will's tousled head emerged from the greenery ahead, anxiously looking for the player. A low muttered curse indicated that the gunman was still preoccupied with loading his weapon.

Will took a cautious step out of the foliage. Tyburn began to slide his long blade out of the leather sheath. The boy took another tentative step, peering for any sign of the player. The acrid smell of burned powder hung in the air. Tyburn slid his hands under his chest and began to slide into a low crouch.

"Jesu! Get that prat!" The gunman pointed his ramrod down the path at the boy. The taller man with the blade spun away from the overgrown ruts where Tyburn lay to plunge after the fleeing Will.

Tyburn could hear men cursing and branches breaking. He stood in one clean, economical movement and, rapier in hand, stepped past the thick tree and the brush. The gunman had his back to Tyburn and was preoccupied with loading his weapon. Tyburn slammed the heavy pommel of his rapier into the back of the man's skull without breaking stride. He fell against the trunk of the oak and slid to the ground, his handgun dropping from nerveless fingers. Tyburn stooped and grabbed the weapon, giving it a cursory glance before tossing it far into the brush. It was a heavy, expensive wheellock pistol, not yet loaded as the pan was empty. He tugged the man up for a moment and removed the shoulder belt with its small collection of apostles, draping it over his own shoulder. Tyburn dropped the body into the bracken and hurried off into the forest, following the crashing and shouting emanating from the other searcher.

The shouting came to an abrupt halt. The trees were thinner here as the forest began to diverge and open into mixed woodland and pasture. Tyburn slowed his pace, wary of running into the other pursuer and unsure how far ahead the pursuit had gotten.

A muffled cry and a triumphant yell from the clearing ahead made it evident where the chase had ended. Sword in hand, Tyburn broke into a run.

"Not so cocky now, you little shite. Where's yer friend?" The man held a rapier in his right hand while he dragged Will by the arm over a fallen tree he had hidden behind. The boy cried out from pain and the man laughed.

Kit entered the clearing at a run. The swordsman must have heard the actor's frantic approach, as he shoved the boy hard into the fallen tree and spun away, his blade swinging. Tyburn hit the ground rolling, feeling the weapon cut the air above him. He somersaulted past the man and brought his blade around in a wild, off-balance swing that had no hope of connecting. The swing worked. The man jumped back to avoid the sword, buying Tyburn the time he needed to roll to his feet, turn and face his opponent.

The two men circled each other warily. Tyburn slid into the guard position, his right foot forward, testing the soft forest floor, shuffling in a slow circle away from the fallen log. His left foot was back, toes pointed outward, knees slightly bent as he watched his opponent, gauging his stance and grip. He kept his focus wide, watching the man's burly chest for indications of movement. "You never watch the eyes." Tyburn could hear the voice in his head, the weary, atonal rasp of the Dutchman who had spent hours drilling him in swordplay. "Never the eyes. Eyes play tricks. They catch you looking and you follow that glance--such a little glance--and so! Steel through your gullet. So watch the chest. As it goes, so goes the blade." So the player watched the man's thick chest and tried to gauge his opponent's skill.

The man facing the player was burly, but moved with a light and sure step, his blade held firm and low, ready to parry or thrust should Tyburn grant an opening. Tyburn watched the sunlight dripping through the trees play across the long blade and waited. Patience, he had found, was a rare virtue in a swordfight. It was problematic in battle, but for a duel, a fast, reckless attack against a skilled opponent was a fool's tactic.

The blades moved.

Will, crouching behind the fallen log, saw the attack in a blur. Both men moved with a fluid and deadly grace that was the hallmark of hours upon hours of relentless and systematic training, muscles that burned with the memory of endless repetition. The thick man's blade flickered in a twisting thrust, which Tyburn parried, the steel ringing off the forte of the blade. He flicked the heavy blade back and upward, a quick wrist flip cut to the man's face which was warded off by a gloved hand.

The man countered with a low thrust which Tyburn avoided by the simple expedient of a quick step. A silvered flicker cut the air. The two blades corkscrewed and darted. The clash of the steel seemed muffled by the heavy forest, as though the trees themselves were watching the combat with verdant indifference. The two adversaries drew apart, the heavy man's face set in a deepening scowl under his thick beard as he realized the player was not the easy kill he had thought. The man circled left, trying to position Tyburn with the fallen tree to his back, hoping to trap the play-actor with a sudden rush, pinning him against the log.

Tyburn moved forward, the blade moving in his hand, right foot gliding in a quick shuffle. He thrust low, sliding along his opponent's blade, trying to beat it out of line and end the fight with a tight lunge. The man twisted, bringing his blade back barely in time and the force of the blow reverberated though Kit's weapon and up his arm. He slipped back, halting the aggressive counter-thrust with a quick parry that rang like a bell. Will watched, slack-jawed. The speed of the fight was astonishing. It had never occurred to the boy that the sensible course of action would have been to disappear into the thick greenery. He continued to watch.

"I hope they paid you in advance," Tyburn said in a dry, almost amused voice. The man was strong and well-versed, but Tyburn had noticed he tended to be slow coming off an attack.

"Keep gabbing, you cullion. I'll piss on yer corpse."

"Can't beat a fey play-actor? What kind of ruffians are they hiring these days?" Tyburn mocked him. "Are you Topcliffe's arse-kissing lackey or one of Lucy's clowns?"

The man hawked a thick wad of phlegm at the player and continued to try to circle to the left, the long rapier extended, the tip making slow, relentless orbits just out of reach of Tyburn's steel.

"You think I'm fool enough to get angry and stupid?" the bearded man grated. "I'll do for you anon . . ."

Tyburn feinted left and drove his blade forward in a short, aggressive, oblique thrust at the man's stomach. The bearded man followed the feint, blade well out of line, but skipped backwards instead. The razor point of Tyburn's thirty-four-inch steel just brushed his lower belly, ripping a neat puncture in the man's heavy waistcoat. The player blocked the counter-thrust and back-pedaled fast as the man attacked, fear lending him speed and fury at the near miss. The swords pealed like bells as the man slid his blade back from where it had been halted in mid-thrust, hard against Tyburn's forte, the pressure on the blade vanished as the player slid his line off the edge. Before the man could react to the shift, the steel ripped upwards into his throat.

The razor-edged Spanish steel thrust through the man's neck and was torn out so quick that all Will saw was a burning gleam and a red spray that mottled the lower branches of the oaks.

Tyburn took two quick steps back, rapier still leveled, and watched as the man shook once like someone with the ague. The long sword tip dropped, reluctant at first, but then it fell as though from a frozen hand. Wet rasping met Kit's ears, as blood spurted rhythmically from the throat wound, a slow weakening pulsation like the ripple on a pond fading. The man fell.

Tyburn nodded to himself and gave his sword a quick flick to remove the blood before wiping it on the dead man's clothes, and then sheathed it.

"You well, boy?"

Will didn't move. His hands gripping the edge of the fallen tree were white-knuckled. "Boy?" the player asked again. "Will!" Will looked up in response to his name. "You hurt, boy?" Will shook his head.

"On your feet. We need to be going." Tyburn knelt beside the still-bleeding corpse and rolled it onto its back. He ransacked the pockets and torn waistcoat, retrieving a small purse of coin. Around the body's neck was a small iron amulet, which Tyburn left untouched. *Whatever magical luck that amulet was meant to harness, it obviously failed mightly on this day.*

The boy was quiet. Tyburn gave him a fleeting glance but recognized that the impact of the violence would probably fade fast, once they were away from the corpse. He pulled a folded document from one pocket, opened it and gave it a cursory scan.

"What is it?" The boy's voice was dry and tentative, like a branch cracking.

"A writ. He's one of Topcliffe's men. They must have had someone watching your place who followed you to the road and then went back for them. We'd best be moving. The other ones will be coming fast. They will have heard the shot."

Rising, Tyburn tucked the writ away in one pocket. "Lead on, Will. Best speed, I think."

The boy forced his eyes away from the body to look at the player. He nodded in silence and the two set off quickly through the trees.

Chapter the Eighteenth

THE DOOR LOCK mechanism was heavy and stiff. Clair pulled hard downwards until she heard the dry metallic snap of the latch release. She winced. To her ears, the sound echoed in the corridor like a cannonshot but no inquisitive footsteps or querulous voices came in response, so she took a deep breath and opened the door.

This one-story wing of the manor house was her father's private study, off-limits to all the servants except the steward. Clair recalled visiting the study once, when her father had called her in to discuss his ambitions for her marriage to James Carey, the one time in her life she could recall his desires and control being in concordance with her own.

She glanced around. The room was high ceilinged, large and long, and contained a massive dining table for entertaining and a heavy ornate desk at the far end. An oversized sideboard stood opposite the fireplace, the grate of which was cold and filled with a heap of ashes, indicating the steward had not yet been by to clean.

A wine carafe with several dusty glasses sat on the sideboard. A folded map of Warwickshire was draped over one of the chairs. A long tapestry portraying an idyllic country scene with a woodland hunting party romping through the meadows and trees hung on the wall.

Clair stepped into the room, her footsteps echoing on the polished wooden floor. She was uncertain of just what she expected to find but she knew that if her father had left any tangible evidence of his plans for her or his pursuit of the Jesuit, it would be found in his study and nowhere else. He was, she knew, a secretive man by nature, confiding on rare occasions to her mother, and then only on the lightest of issues.

Her father confused her. She wondered at times whether her father had, hidden somewhere deep under his years of bile, anything approaching a genuine emotion. She shook her head. Little seemed to drive him besides ambition and avarice. Clair herself seemed to matter merely as a trophy or an asset to be bought, sold or traded.

She glanced through the neat stack of correspondence and ledgers piled on the desk. It contained the usual detritus that was part and parcel of managing the deBrage estate. There were lists of produce, tenant allotments, letters from London creditors, an investment proposal from the Muscovy Company, a petition for tax remuneration but nothing related to any Jesuit. She grimaced as she noted a stack of letters from Chancery Lane and the Inns of the Court, recognizing the Careys' legal advisor's name.

She pulled open one of the heavy drawers and rummaged through the various papers, most of which were property assessments and enclosure notices. She slid open a second drawer but it held only a set of neat inkpots, quills and a sander. Frustrated, she slumped back in the heavy chair, her thoughts spinning in frustration.

Her father would never entrust valuable correspondence to anyone and he was loath to trust a locked chest. She knew him well enough to know that the materials would be secreted somewhere he could retrieve them from at need, even if that need was just his own desire to gaze upon them and gloat at the success of his machinations. The desk, she thought, was obvious, the first place any searcher would examine, yet it was for her father the most convenient place for anything he needed. He was painfully rheumatic, so any location that involved reaching or stooping was unlikely.

A distant rattle in the outside hall made her jump. The steward would be by at some point to clean the study. The longer she remained, the greater chance of discovery. She put both hands on the arms of the chair and stood up. The mystery would have to remain a mystery for the time being. She stepped behind the chair and pushed it back to the position it had been in before she had searched the desk. Clair hesitated, then pulled the chair back out and sat down again. Reaching down, she slid her fingers over the intricate carved chair seat facing. One of the carved decorative protrusions moved slightly when her fingers brushed over it. Emboldened, Clair pushed and then twisted it. She felt rather than heard the popping sound of a catch releasing. Hooking her fingers around the bottom edge of the chair, she pulled.

The ornate front face of the chair seat slid forward with a jerk, the wood swollen in the summer heat, revealing a small hidden drawer. The drawer was shallow but wide and contained two neat bundled stacks of letters. Clair glanced around, her nerves jangling. She pulled the first pile of letters out and began to scan them. They appeared to be between the Jesuit priest and his patron. Tyburn had told her that the patron was Edward Arden but no seals, signatures or names appeared on any of the correspondence except for those of Hugh Hall, Arden's supposed priest, who had written several of the communications.

As far as she could tell, most of the correspondence was pertaining to spiritual guidance for the patron and mundane accounting. There were the usual enquiries after each person's health, a summary of a homily, some general musings about how to move forward with advancing the Catholic cause in Warwickshire, and some discussion over card play, but no plots, conspiracies or schemes sprang out from the thin spidery script on the page.

Clair bound up the first packet and pulled out the second one. This collection was much thinner, consisting of only four documents, all close written across multiple pages. She let her eyes rove over the tightly scrawled words. It appeared to be a draft of a joint letter, with edits, cross-outs and changes scrawled across one another, making the text difficult to follow. As she read, a thin line furrowed her brow in concentration. She laughed. She began to understand what the authors were working towards. Small wonder, she thought, her father had had separated these letters. They cut to the heart of the conspiracy.

Footsteps sounded in the hall. Clair placed the two letter stacks back into the chair drawer and slid it shut, making sure she heard the click of the catch engaging. She stood and walked over to the doorway, positioning herself so the door would obscure her when it opened. The latch gave that familiar dry snap. The door swung open and the manor steward entered the room, a small stack of firewood in one arm. Clair waited until he had walked further into the long room, and then stepped around the door and exited unseen.

Kit fed small pieces of dried bark and a handful of spindly twigs into the smoldering flames and blew. They flickered and flared bright as the gunpowder emptied from one of the apostles caught. The flames grew steadier and he placed a couple of larger, thicker branches on the fire. Shadows of the low-hanging branches danced and rippled in the bright glow. Will sat silent against the oak, watching.

The pair had camped under the edge of the woodland, in a small hollow formed between two oaks whose wide branches reached out like an embrace. Tyburn had weighed the dangers of a blaze attracting possible searchers and, tired of a diet of apples, onions and cheese, had decided the need for a cooked meal won out.

"I think this is the longest silence I've ever heard from you, Will." Tyburn broke a long branch and tossed both pieces onto the rising flames.

The boy looked at him. "You killed that man." It wasn't a question.

"I did indeed, God rest his poor soul."

"How can you? I mean . . ."

"How can I live with myself? Am I not conscience-stricken and bereft?"

The boy nodded with a bleak expression.

The player snorted. "I can live with myself just fine, and I've far worse stains on my soul than killing that piece of work. It may have escaped your discerning eye, young Master Shakespeare, but those fine fellows would have killed us, pocketed their gelt and slept well."

The boy grimaced. "But . . ."

"He made his choice. He could have run or stood down but he chose to fight. So I laid him out as hard and fast as I could." He leaned over and pushed a stray coal back into the fire with a stick. "I was a soldier in Flanders. I've seen more dead men than you can imagine. It's not pretty or noble, just harsh, brutal work. Kill them before they kill you or your friends. You can put an honourable luster and shine on it, call it heroic or chivalrous, just to give it a good buffing. It helps make soldiers step up when needed, to think they are just and Godly in their duties, but it's just killing, nothing more, nothing less. It is a duty, a necessity."

Tyburn poked the fire with a stick, sending sparks flitting skyward. "The first man I ever killed was in Brill. He died in a duel--a fair fight--both armed, both sober, both idiots who didn't have any appreciation of what they were stepping into. But always better a live idiot than a dead one. You fight for a reason, for a purpose, with the objective of winning, first and foremost. Once the swords are drawn, fair goes out the nearest window. Fair is winning."

Will nodded, uncertain of how to respond. Kit pulled out a small bag of provisions. Late in the afternoon, after spending much of the day winding their way overland northeast towards Warwick and Kenilworth, Tyburn had sent Will to visit a small farmhouse to purchase some food with a handful of copper pennies. He had come back with a small skin of thick sour ale, some hard bread, cheese and a small, thin chicken which Tyburn had cleaned in a nearby stream, skewered with his dagger and propped up on some rocks to cook over the open flame. Tyburn turned the chicken again, then sprawled on the damp forest floor and stared up at the mournful darkening sky. He could smell the scent of moss and decaying leaves and the tang of woodsmoke, and the sky was clear and sharp, like a sea horizon. They had made good time, despite having to go overland for most of the distance. He estimated another five miles or so to Kenilworth, so with an early start they should be there by mid-morning, barring any problems on the road.

Once in Kenilworth, he would need to locate Arden or Hall. The hard part, he mused, would be eliciting any type of cooperation from either of them. Hall, by all accounts, was supremely bendable, but unlikely to have any idea of where the Jesuit was secreted. If it had been as simple as putting Hall under pressure, deBrage and his cronies would have had the Jesuit in their pocket months ago. Arden, from what little he had been able to determine, was a devoted Catholic and not a man to bend to pressure or threats, in particular when they came from an unknown wayward source like one of Worcester's Men.

"What's that?" Will asked, sitting up.

"You hear something?" "Listen." A faint echoing snapping sound, followed by a hollow succession of pops. The sound drifted in and out of earshot, almost drowned out by the crackle of the fire and the faint hiss of chicken fat dripping on embers.

"Gunfire? Too much for a hunting party," Tyburn muttered. Quietly he got to his feet and stood akimbo, one hand cupped around his ear. The sound was coming from the north, the popping now interspersed with a deeper bellow that Tyburn recognized as the sound of great guns.

"Look!" Will exclaimed, pointing at the low clouds to the far north which were glowing and pulsating with dim reflected light.

Tyburn laughed. "It's the queen."

Will looked puzzled. Tyburn reached over and gave the boy's dark frizzed hair a quick tousle. "It's Kenilworth, lad. The queen's summer progress. Fireworks, artillery. Bloody Leicester must be spending himself a fortune. That's a lot of powder he's blowing off."

The boy stared at the flickering glow reflecting off the clouds with an expression of awe. "That's more money being lit off in an evening than you or I will see in a lifetime," Kit said, laughing, "so enjoy what you can see of it."

He tossed a ragged hunk of bread and the aleskin to Will. "Here. Eat. The chicken will be charred though soon enough." Tyburn took a chunk of bread and piece of cheese for himself and leaned back against the hollow of the tree. Will began to eat, and Tyburn smiled. He watched the guttering light of the fire, flaring and sputtering, and chewed on the tough bread while humming to himself.

In the far distance, the light of the queen's celebration faded away and the stars emerged from behind the thin clouds like distant lanterns on a riverbank.

After their meal, Will dozed off while Kit lay back watching the stars wheeling above. The sky was clear and felt empty and vast. Tyburn always liked the deep recesses of the night. The darkness brought an element of clarity, an almost pristine calming pause to him, like the respite between breaths, a moment suspended between act and motion, unsustainable and irreversible, yet vital. The stars danced in their subtle concordance with the earth below and Tyburn felt himself suspended between, a soul divided, until his eyes closed and sleep took him for its own.

Richard Topcliffe was frustrated.

It had been three days and what had appeared to be a straight-forward endeavor to locate the Jesuit hiding in Warwickshire had turned into a morass that bedeviled the very core of him. He had allowed himself to listen to the honeyed words of deBrage and Lucy who had bedazzled him with the possibility of wealth, land and riches, and then dangled that bitch of a daughter in front of him like a tantalizing fruit, yet he remained unable to locate the bastard Papist scum. Worcester's Men were useless, and Lucy, wary of stirring Worcester's wrath, would not permit him to utilize his usual questioning methods. That bastard player Tyburn was still at large and had, by all accounts, killed at least one of his searchers, although the other member of the party had admitted he did not know who had assaulted him, so it may well have been one of the many vagrants or wanderers that called Arden home.

And worst of all, Topcliffe fumed, he was absent from court at a critical time. He had missed the evening's celebratory revelry and a day's hunting party with the queen. He was determined not to miss the lake-borne pageant Leicester had planned for the morrow. Why was he wasting his time to suit deBrage and Lucy? This Jesuit, prize catch though he might be, could always be scooped up on another date. Topcliffe sensed that deBrage was driving the timing of this event to suit himself, to ensure that the matter was raised and attended to while the court was in residence at Kenilworth. The man and his son were non-entities in London but here, in rural Warwickshire, it would be much harder for their contributions in unmasking a traitor like Arden to be overwhelmed or overlooked by men of higher status.

Leicester seemed content to let them be his proxies in baiting Arden, a man that Leicester despised. Arden had criticized Leicester without restraint in public and had refused to wear Leicester's livery. So why should Topcliffe not pursue Arden directly, while his men scoured the countryside for that bastard player? Arden would know where this Jesuit was lurking, although Topcliffe knew he would have to be circumspect if he was to question the high sheriff.

The Arden family, as one of the oldest in England, enjoyed far-reaching connections—and Topcliffe, despite his patrons, did not.

As an added bonus, he would pass on the latest information on the missing Jesuit to Leicester, something he was sure that Lucy and deBrage were playing very close. When the Jesuit was run to ground by Topcliffe's hounds, he wanted Leicester to know who was responsible and deserved just rewards. Yes, he thought, it was time to take off the gloves and exact a slow vengeance on Arden, on deBrage and, God willing, on that bastard player who had interrupted his courtship of the elegant Clair Carey. He would soon correct that issue soon enough.

"Smitherton!" he shouted. His aide appeared in the doorway.

"My lord?"

"We're riding for Kenilworth but before we leave, speak with that secretary of Lucy's and pick his brains. I want a list of all the known or suspected recusant estates in Warwickshire. That Papist bastard has gone to ground somewhere and I mean to sniff him out."

"Yes my lord! At once."

Topcliffe lifted the rounded Venetian wineglass to his lips, savouring the deep burgundy. A droplet pattered across his white laced cuffs like a splash of blood. A good omen, he thought, smiling at the thought of the Jesuit in his hands, the taut creaking of the ropes and the tension-wracked limbs outstretched and helpless, as all enemies should be. He drained the glass and carelessly dropped it onto the stone flagstones of the floor. *Yes, blood, verily just like blood.*

Chapter the Nineteenth

IN THE EARLY afternoon light the distant stone walls were the warm colour of amber. But to Tyburn they were the color of a good ale, which sounded grand to him as he scraped the flat flat of his dagger against the thin sole of his boot. He was footsore, dusty and his throat felt as dry as the roadway.

The pair of fugitives had been forced to follow a more circuitous route to Kenilworth than Tyburn had anticipated, one that bypassed the busy market town of Warwick and the more travelled roads that fed into it. The danger of running into Topcliffe's or Lucy's men was enough that Tyburn's sense of caution had won out. The alternate route had led them away from the road, slipping through damp green pastures and wet bottomland that had culminated in a thick, fly-infested mere that had caked Tyburn's boots with a heavy layer of foul-smelling muck. Kit wiped the cloying mud from the blade and began to scrape the other boot, grimacing at the odor. He wouldn't have thought that

English mud could compare to the muck of Flanders, but the current crop he was cleaning off matched the worst that the Low Countries had ever presented.

The castle lay north of the roadway. The southern approaches were visible across the open pastureland with the glittering water defenses that guarded three sides of the fortification spreading cool and indifferent behind the outer bastion. The village of Kenilworth lay off to the northeast, like the derelict child of a sprawling, rapine older sire. In the distance rang the high brassy notes of trumpets. Will stood by the side of the road, watching Tyburn with an amused expression as the player cursed Warwickshire, first in English and then, apparently feeling it was inadequate, again in gutter Dutch. Kit wiped the blade clean with a thick handful of long grass and sheathed it.

The road to Kenilworth was busy. Carts laden with produce and kegs of ale and wine trundled past, their ungreased wheels shrieking in torment along the rutted sideroad. Liveried servants darted to and fro on errands and rich-clothed merchants and their retinues carried on a brisk trade without even slowing their horses. Three young women who appeared barely out of childhood were making their way towards the causeway gatehouse, their bodices more absent than present, the lace failing to conceal their dark rouged nipples under the material. Will felt a strange thrill watching them as they moved past, their dresses clinging to the line of their bodies. One of them noticed Will staring and stuck out her tongue. For a brief moment she looked her age.

Tyburn noticed Will's puzzlement. "Queans." The boy looked confused. "Morts, doxies . . . Magdalenes," he explained. "Selling themselves to the men at court. Give you the French pox, like as not." Will looked back at the girls, shocked. "Don't look so horrified, Will, sometimes you have to pick a salad.[123]"

---

[123] To pick a salad = to live as best you can

The pair of travelers passed the far edge of the long bastion wall that guarded the southern approach to the castle. At last Will and Tyburn had a clear view of the fortress. Will's first thought was that he expected to see a giant, thick with matted hair, striding out of the gates and across the causeway, a massive oaken cudgel across one shoulder as he scanned the land for his enemies.

Water bordered the castle on three sides, with the north protected by a wide double-moat. The stone causeway stretched between fortified gatehouse and fortified tower, like a long mailed finger pointing into the southern entry of the battlements. The causeway was decorated with a long succession of silken banners and ribbons that snapped and flapped bright in the afternoon breeze, interspersed at intervals with flat bridgeposts topped by large decorative silvered bowls laden with fruit, cereals and other foodstuffs. Two large gilt cages filled with live birds stood on the first set of bridgeposts, tended by two grooms. On the further castle side of the causeway, the bridgeposts were decorated with sets of musical instruments, lutes and cornets, an offering to Phoebus, the god of music and health. One of the other sets of posts was surrounded by silvered and gold-edged armor and weapons, an offering to Mars.

Kenilworth Castle itself sat on a chalky rise of ground, surrounded on three sides by what was once marsh but had been converted into two large man-made lakes called the Great Lake and the Lesser Lake. The Great Lake guarded the southern and western approaches, while the Lesser Lake held the east fast against siege engines or tunneling. The walls were massive, thick and heavy, quarried from local sandstone which gave the citadel and its surrounding walls a warm and rich amber tone that belied its martial strength. To Tyburn's practiced eye, Kenilworth was a killer. The water defenses channeled attackers to the north, a bastion guarded by the double moat, a heavy outer wall, towers and an open killing ground. Even there, siegeworks would have a difficult time reaching the keep and the castle proper, although with time, heavy guns could breach the defenses.

The queen had granted Kenilworth to Robert Dudley twelve years before and appointed him the Earl of Leicester less than a year later. His father, the Duke of Northumberland, had held the same fortress under Edward, but had lost it when he had tried and failed to place Lady Jane Grey on the throne. He had paid for that bit of duplicity with his head, but Kenilworth remained one of England's great fortresses, to be held by someone the queen trusted. Leicester had built a large decorative gatehouse on the northern approach, which was now the primary entrance to the fortress. The earl had also added a massive residential block overlooking the lake, for the queen on her visits. Despite the decorative gardens, marbled fountains and wide windows of the new wing, Kenilworth remained a mailed fist swathed in lace.

A group of riders in hunting garb accompanied with a yelping pack of dogs trotted past. Will and Tyburn moved off the road to allow the party right of passage. None of the riders gave the two vagabonds even a cursory glance. At the crossroads, Will and Kit veered to the right, heading away from the castle. Tyburn was unsure of where he might find either Arden or his priest, but he doubted Leicester's courtesy extended towards granting residence in the castle during the Summer Progress to a man he disliked. Arden might be in one of the local inns or neighbouring manors. On the walk to the castle, Tyburn and Will had decided that Will would try to ferret out the high sheriff's location. The boy was smart, quick and inventive and could move freely in the village and surroundings without garnering the same level of suspicion that Tyburn would evoke. Tyburn would stay out of sight and allow the effusive glover's son to winnow out some answers.

The boy had been gone two hours when he reappeared, grinning. Tyburn was seated on a bench outside of a crowded ordinary, drinking an ale that had, in his judgment, been pissed out by a previous customer. He pushed the foul swill aside and the two walked around the rear of the ordinary away from any prying ears. The back of the ordinary smelt of stale urine and rotting garbage.

"So boy, what do you know?" he asked Will.

"Edward Arden and his wife will be attending the festivities this evening and on the morrow the pageant being put on by the Men of Coventry." Somewhat crestfallen, he poked at a pebble with his toe. "I don't know where Master Arden is staying; however, I have located Master Hall. He is staying at a small house near St. Mary's Abbey." Will explained that a water pageant was planned for the royal court in the evening, to be held on the Greater Lake. The public would be permitted to observe the spectacle from a distance and Arden, though attending, would be with the court revelers.

Kit gave Will a smile. "Well done, Master Shakespeare." The player rubbed his beard. "I think we will seek Master Hall tonight, after the lake pageant. After we've had our words with him, we will see about contacting the high sheriff tomorrow, when the Men of Coventry parade."

Tyburn sent Will out to find the pair a barn or cattle byre in which to spend the night. Kenilworth thronged with people and the noise and tempo spoke of a town bursting at the seams. Merchants and buyers from Warwick and Coventry, and some from as far away as Birmingham, were trading and selling. Carts laden with produce flowed past in a steady stream from the countryside, most bound for the castle and eating houses. The summer progress had more than three hundred people in the queen's and the court's retinues, not counting servants, attendants, guards, relations, hangers-on, up-and-coming bloods wishing to cut a swath, eligible daughters, money-lenders, maids, whores, petty-thieves, beggars and pickpockets. Even this rancid little penny ordinary was jammed with day labourers and servants. Small wonder the ale was swill, the player thought, this was at least a week into the queen's stay. The decent ale had long since been drunk by the crowds filling Kenilworth's small marketplace.

Tyburn stepped out into the full sun and then turned back under the dim shade provided by the overhang, his head tilted down. Cuttle was sauntering past, seated on a tall bay horse. The player recognized the hard face and glanced up after the rider had passed. Cuttle had not even turned his head. He was accompanied by several other armed men, including one who appeared to be of Leicester's household guard, judging by the livery he was wearing. The Southwark knifeman seemed intent on his destination. He looked to be going in the direction of the now dissolute St. Mary's Abbey, near where Will had indicated Hall had secreted himself.

The player cursed under his breath, pushed past a group of young, beardless, blue-smocked apprentices drinking outside the ordinary and began to follow the small party.

Cuttle seemed to know his destination. He reined up in front of a low house with dark shutters, stained grey walls and thin beams. Leicester's man gave the group a quick nod and turned back down the roadway towards the castle. The other riders stayed outside, seated on a worn bench by the doorway, laughing and passing a leather wineskin back and forth and hooting at a woman pulling laundry off the neighbouring hedge where it had been laid out to dry. Tyburn stood near the corner of the intersection and watched the house. He was certain that Hall was in residence. Recalling the conversation that he and Clair had overheard, he thought he might not have the leisure of waiting until evening to deal with Hall, if Cuttle was true to form. He felt a tug on his leg and glanced down to see a beggar, one side of his face pocked with thick ulcerated sores, extending his arm in an imploring gesture. The man had one hand; the other arm ended in a truncated stump at the elbow.

Tyburn dropped a penny into the man's outstretched hand. "Find a new corner for the next hour and I'll give you another." The man nodded agreement and taking the payment, swung to his feet and hobbled away in the direction of the nearest drink. The player settled himself into the street corner, just out of the line of sight of the riders but where he could still see the door to the house.

After about an hour Cuttle emerged followed by two armed men. He walked over to where the riders who had accompanied him were sitting and waved them up. Cuttle gave the seated men a quick harangue of instructions; two of them stood and disappeared into the building. The remaining men clambered aboard their horses, one of them wavering from side to side in a drunken slouch. Tyburn concentrated on the dirt at his feet as they cantered past, his face hidden.

Kit glanced at the sun. The afternoon was waning. He assumed that this was the house Will had mentioned Hall was residing in. He rubbed his beard in thought. From the conversation he and Clair had overheard at Charlecote, he was guessing that Hall was back under Cuttle's rancid thumb, now working away on a new set of letters that would help deBrage implicate Arden more directly. The move from informer to jackman[124] was not an exceptional one and Cuttle would be a hard man to refuse, given his proclivities.

The player stood and headed back to the ordinary to find Will, his head already spinning around an idea on how to reach the priest before Cuttle could complete his pursuit of new materials.

The rattling and banging pulled Hawkins out of his placid, dozing state like a hook. He glanced around but nothing appeared to be amiss. That pallid piss-pot of a clerk was still bent over and squinting at the stack of papers on the table, his quill scratching away with the interminable pace of a dawdling child, while he mumbled imprecations under his breath. Dandle was seated at one end of the table, idling the time away by flicking through primero hands with a cheap deck of cards he had picked up from a merchant.

The rattle-bang came again. It was outside. Hawkins stood up, rubbing his face, and cracked open the front door. A young boy

---

[124] Forger

was trying in vain to lift up a cask that seemed to have rolled over and bumped against the house front.

"Boy, leave off," Hawkins growled.

The boy glanced up from under a thick shock of dark hair. "Sorry sir, it got away from us."

Hawkins stared at the cask. "What do you got there?"

The boy looked distressed at the inquiry. "Nothing worth asking about, just some supplies for the castle."

"Oh aye," said Hawkins, "so's it's at my door, wouldn't it be belongin ta me." It was not a question.

"No, it's for the castle . . ." The boy's explanation trailed off as Hawkins pushed his door open further and stepped out.

"I'm not seeing no cart, nor anyone who can claim it, excepted you. And you're going to vanish quick before I push your face into the road." Hawkins spat once at the boy's feet and the look of fear made him smile. "Fie, begone!" The boy fled into the street and the man gave the cask a brief push, smiling as he confirmed the sloshing sound he thought he had heard earlier when he cracked open the door. He reached down and hefted the cask and reentered the house, calling out triumphantly to Dandle. "Got us some nappy stuff here." Dandle glanced up, his cards forgotten. He tugged out the stopper with some difficulty and sniffed the contents. "Rare stuff!"

Hawkins tilted the cask and poured a brief measure into an unwashed tankard. He took a gulp and gave a sharp exhale. "Garn, she's a nappy one for certain. Try a spike." He handed the tankard to Dandle who gulped the remainder down in one smooth motion. The older man at the table paused in his endless writing and attracted Hawkins's ire. "Get back to yer scratching, you coxcomb!" he bellowed at the man. The man flinched and resumed his writing. The two men poured themselves a full set of drinks.

Tyburn had resumed his observation post on the corner. The cask of brandy had taken almost all of his remaining coins to purchase so he had chased away the one-armed beggar with a snarl and a kick instead of a penny. Fugitive status would be going hand in hand with vagrancy soon at this rate. He waited and watched, as the shadows lengthened. The sound of raucous laughter and shouting was plain to hear, even over the din of the busy avenue. After an hour, it had died away to an occasional muffled shout.

The player stood and walked across the street, moving with the indifferent pace of a man accustomed to this street, this house. He pulled hard on the door latch and stepped across the threshold to stand in the dusty entranceway. A small narrow front room that seemed to be a tradesman's shop lay to the right, although it was not presently in use. To the left was a sitting room of some type, with a long narrow table stretching the length of it. A worn tapestry hung along one wall, portraying a faded baptismal scene. An untidy pile of paper was stacked on one end of the table and a thin, fastidious looking man with a square, graying beard sat with a quill, inkstand and sander in front of him. His face was bruised and worn.

The large man named Hawkins who had taken the cask from Will was sprawled asleep against one chair, having slipped from the seat to drape across one of the wooden chairs. The second man, a younger, ginger-haired man with a thick, wide face, was trying to pull himself up from where he was seated. One hand still gripped his leather tankard. His face was a cross between puzzlement and anger but his balance was questionable at best. The cask lay on its side, almost empty, testament to the guards drinking prowess. The ginger-haired man reached out for Tyburn, his fist sweeping through the air a good four feet from where the player stood. The swing proved to be too much and the man overbalanced and toppled, pouring himself out onto the floor.

Tyburn winced in mock sympathy and then turned his attentions to the seated man.

"Father Hall, I take it?" the player asked.

The man glanced up, an uncertain look in his eye. "I . . ." He trailed off, unable to articulate a response.

"Gather up your things, Father, we are leaving."

A brief spark seemed to flare in the priest's eyes. "But I'm not done!" he pointed at the papers scattered across the table.

251

"Father," the player explained, "'done' to Cuttle means it's past time to slit your throat and bury you in a dung-heap. If you verily want that done, I'll step up and oblige you later but for now pick up your papers and come with me." The player never raised his voice but the iron of his words sank into the priest's head. Hall set about picking up all the loose leaves of paper scattered about the table, trying to shuffle them in a neat bundle until Tyburn reached out and plucked the sheets away from him.

"Out." Tyburn grabbed the priest by the arm and steered him past the table and around the insensate body of Dandle. The two men emerged onto the street. Hall recoiled as a cart being pulled by two labourers trundled past. The priest, the player realized, was terrified. God knows how long he had been under Cuttle's attentions or what threats the Southwark knifeman and Albert deBrage had been wielding over him but whatever they had been, they had been effective. Hall walked with the stiff, uncertain steps of an invalid, hesitant and cautious, swaying with each stride before halting and eyeing Tyburn with suspicion.

"Good day Master Hall!" The cheery greeting from Will made the man gape.

"Who . . . is . . ." Hall focused his eyes, squinting in the sunlight. "It's young Will, isn't it?"

Will reached out and took one of Hall's arms. "Yessir. But we need to move away from here soonest and then we can talk." The priest glared down at the boy but then gave him a stiff nod of acquiescence and resumed walking. One on either side of him, the two led the priest away from the house, skirting the edge of the roadway before turning and heading away from the main street.

A half hour later, ensconced in a thick-raftered, low-roofed barn a half mile from the village, Tyburn watched as the colour returned to Hall's face and the stiff awkwardness dissipated as the realization that he was no longer under Cuttle's control began to sink in. Tyburn said little but Will kept up a continual stream of light chatter and conversation that seemed to help put the priest at ease. While Will talked on, telling Hall about their journey to

Kenilworth, the player began to sort through the small pile of correspondence he had carried from the house. There were more than a dozen letters; some were drafts with certain passages scored out and re-written in the margins in a different hand. It appeared that Hall had been drafting a set of letters from Arden to the absent Jesuit. *But for whom?* wondered Tyburn.

The priest cleared his throat and the player looked up. Will had stopped talking and was watching Kit. It was evident that the priest had begun to regain his equanimity. His long face had taken on a haughty mien very familiar to Tyburn. It was a crafted combination of affable condescension and disdain that reminded Tyburn of a cat that had shared his quarters in London for a time.

"I must return to Park Hall and will require refreshment before my journey." Hall's tone was abrupt and sharp. "Boy, you will go to the market and fetch me some food and wine."Will started in surprise at the order, and gave Tyburn a puzzled glance, reluctant to obey.

"Now, boy!" said the priest with a snap. Will stood.

Tyburn, sprawled against a corner post, waved Will back down and fixed the sham gardener with an amused look. "He helped fish you out of some chill waters, Master Hall, best not to treat him like a common drudge. We have some things to discuss." The player continued to leaf through the papers. "I see you've been developing some correspondence."

Hall's mouth took on a pursed thin look of disapproval. "Those papers are not your concern," he snapped. "By God's blessing you have sufficed to remove me from that devil's pit and you will be rewarded in Heaven by our Lord and Savior and in this realm by my master, but those papers are the private correspondence of the high sheriff of Warwickshire, Edward Arden."

"Point of fact, they aren't." The player said without raising his head. He held one sheet up to the dusty light filtering through the slats in the window. "Will, what's that say? Can you read it?"

Will leaned over and scanned the page. The player pointed at a passage. "That one."

"*By God's grace a bloody insurrection will ensure and the Babylon harlot shall fall,*" the boy read aloud.

"What about that passage there?" the actor asked, pointing again.

Will continued. "*I shall aid you in all your endeavors, as God wills.*" The boy squinted at the paper in the rippled light. "*Your servant before God, Edward Arden,*" he concluded.

"Really? That's what it says? These chicken tracks he's strewn across the page make it regard astonishingly like treason. Must be his penmanship, after all he is a priest and they can't make true use of their pens." Kit made an obscene gesture with his hand. The barb was wasted on the priest whose face was reddening in anger.

"Those papers do not belong to you!" Hall rejoined in a heated tone. "Return them to me at once!"

Tyburn pulled out the original letter from his doublet and waved it at the priest. "This one doesn't belong to me either but Fate seems to have set it before me anyway. Strange thing isn't it, how Fortune's great wheel turns." Hall was horrified at the sight of the original letter, the packet that he had entrusted to John Shakespeare. "Odd, it doesn't seem to be written in the same hand." Tyburn paused and glanced at Will, widening his eyes and letting his face slacken in amazement. "Will, do you think that Master Hall might have written this stack of florid correspondence that we recovered when we rescued him? Mayhaps it is not Edward Arden's as the papers claim? After all, what's in a signature? Just another's hand at play. You can be as free with ink as I am with the stage, assume any role, gambol in another's treads, it is a faceless mien."

Will shrugged, unsure of what Tyburn was driving at but reluctant to interrupt his performance.

"Set-to on paper is our scene and our byzantine plot. A strange tale of wayward treason, conspiracy and forgery, all in one neat package for you, Will, fit to be played. And Catholic, for a bonus," the player intoned, his voice desert-dry.

Hall was sputtering in anger. "I demand, in God's Holy name, that--"

"You demand nothing." Will heard the flat growl of anger in the player's reply. Kit's voice was biting. "Your inability to manage your affairs with circumspection and discretion has not only tainted yourself and your master but put the lives of myself, this boy and his family in danger, and caused the death of my particular friend."

Tyburn stood and held out the papers. "You've committed treason, as has your master, by corresponding with an agent of the papacy, a Jesuit, whose intent is the promulgation of a faith and a loyalty that is dedicated to the overthrow of the Crown."

Hall crossed himself. The player's face was like a gathering storm.

"Worse still you've gone and betrayed your faith and your master. In the face of adversity, you rolled over on your back like a dog when deBrage and Cuttle came calling, offering up yourself as payment, like some carrion whore of a maid bent over a milking stool. You sold yourself to them for considerably less than thirty pieces of silver." Tyburn flung the heavy purse he had taken from Alec's corpse at the priest. It struck him in the chest and Hall flinched. "Count your blood money, priest."

Will watched, shaken by the player's anger.

"I never betrayed--" The voice was a whisper.

"*Medacem memorem esse oportet,*[125]" Tyburn hissed. "Did you forget that you were willfully forging your master's correspondence to implicate him at Cuttle's orders?" Tyburn tossed the papers onto the dirt floor of the barn. "This is inventive drivel and hardly legible. You led them to Shakespeare and the correspondence chain knowing full well what might ensue. What happened? They were

---

[125] "A liar needs a good memory"

pressing you too hard to find out where the Jesuit was lurking so you decided to push them elsewhere for a time? Thought you could give them what they wanted indirectly and slip away with no one the wiser?"

Hall was shivering despite the warm summer air.

Tyburn stood. He stepped over to where the priest was still sitting. "I'm going to ask you once and once only, so think about what answer you give me because I am not Cuttle and not bound by his master's restrictions nor those of the Church. Where is the Jesuit?"

"I don't know." The words came out as almost a sob.

"How can I find him?"

"I'm not sure," Hall said in a faint voice. "He is secreted with a Catholic family. It must be on an estate or in a manor house of some type, they would be the only ones that could keep his presence secret." The priest was almost fawning in his attempts to answer Tyburn's questions. The player felt a little touch of contemptuous bile in the back of his throat. Hall had crumbled like an overgrown bank in the rain. "Most of the Catholic families have Catholic servants and Catholic tenants, so no one would ever speak of it to others. I know he moves on occasion, from house to house, but in God's name, I know not where or with whom!"

"How does Arden correspond with him?"

"Always by letter, for near two years now. We would deposit the letters with the glover in Stratford or with another man in Deptford. They would pass them to another contact and to a merchant who would carry them onwards."

Tyburn flexed his hand on the pommel of his sword and, mistaking the gesture, Hall continued. "But I know he must be nearby!"

"How so?"

"Once the letter went out and the reply was back within three days. It was so quick, they could only be in Warwickshire." He paused, tongue darting between dry lips like an adder's. "It's said he moves about through disguise and dissimilation, and attends celebrations and holidays seeking converts and believers."

"And the letters--always the same type? Always hidden with orange juice?"

"Yes! Yes! Always on the same type of paper."

"Like this one?" Tyburn asked, holding out the letter from Arden.

"No, that was written on Master Arden's stationery. It comes up from London. The Jesuit's letters were written on a heavier parchment, very well cut."

"What other correspondence does Master Arden receive? Other letters? Other contacts?"

Hall paused, thinking. "He receives letters and petitions from property owners, supplicants, correspondence from London, requests for patronage . . . there are too many, it is a multitude."

"Any of them send him letters written on similar paper to what the Jesuit sends?"

The priest burst out. "I'm not his secretary or his factor! I do not manage his correspondence. I don't know."

Tyburn tapped the hilt of his rapier pointedly. "Think hard." The man shuddered.

"Well, maybe, possibly . . . a few, I can recall." Seeing the teeth in Tyburn's eyes Hall rushed on. "The bishop, but he's not Catholic. There is the Corwold family, the Somervilles, the Platts, the Ferrers . . there are too many to count and these are only the ones I know."

"Which ones are Catholic?"

"Almost all of them! The True Faith survives everywhere across Warwickshire."

Tyburn cursed. The priest was speaking the truth. He knew no solid estimate existed of the number of Catholics who remained practicing followers of the Church in England, a fact that was the font for much of the Crown's deep and abiding concern. After thirty years of constant turmoil, Elizabeth's succession to the throne had been hoped to herald reconciliation but what it had done instead was leaven the vagaries of faith with politics. To be Catholic was to be of questionable loyalty to the Throne, to owe an allegiance to the pope, the Catholic League, and Mary, the would-be queen imprisoned in Tutbury. And all the while Philip of Spain sat watching for opportunity to bring England back to the Faith and secure for himself power and prestige everlasting for crushing the heretics. Of Spanish ambition at least, Tyburn had no doubts.

"Does Arden know where the Jesuit is located? Does he know where he is?"

The priest paled. "I . . ."

"Does he know?"

"Yes." The voice was a whisper. "He knows."

Tyburn turned away, his hand tapping the hilt of his sword as he thought. "Will."

The boy popped up like a spring. "Sir?"

"Any blank sheets in that paper? Can you get a quill?"

The boy shuffled the papers. "Plenty." The boy held up his hands in triumph. "Already have a quill. Master Hall was clutching it in his hands when we brought him from the house."

"And oranges. We'll need some oranges."

"Why?"

The player smiled. It was a grim smile. "You and Master Hall here are going to write me a letter, a very special letter. A letter for our high sheriff. Would you like to learn a new trade, Master Shakespeare? You're about to become a jackman."

Chapter the Twentieth

WILL SHAKESPEARE STEPS floated in the light summer air as he walked along the sunlit roadway following the player. He bobbed about the man like one of his brother Gilbert's small cork boats set adrift on the Avon. The pair were backtracking along the road they had taken the previous day, returning towards the indifferent bulk of Kenilworth Castle, accompanied by an apparent endless flood of townsfolk and visitors going to witness the day's celebrations.

As they walked along the rutted roadway, Will's thoughts kept floating back to the evening before. After sending the priest unceremoniously back to Park Hall, Tyburn and Will had trailed along after the crowds moving along the path and found themselves perched on a damp open space on the shore near the Lesser Lake. From their muddy roost the two had watched the queen's evening water pageant from across the rippling water. The castle had been lit with hundreds of flickering lamps and torches lining the stone causeway, the roadway and the walls. Yellow light danced and glittered in the night air, splashing off the dark bulk of the battlements and casting iridescent flashes across the smooth surface of the lake. A fat summer moon, almost full, hung like a soft white pearl over the trees, laving the lakeside in pale luminescence.

On the lake itself a small island had floated, surmounted by flowering plants and heavy vines and hung with gleaming lanterns. A tall, ethereal woman in long flowing white robes surrounded by garlanded handmaidens stood upon the island. In one hand she held a long silver sword that gleamed in the lamplight. From their vantage point, neither Tyburn nor Will could discern many details but the woman appeared to be singing as she faced the causeway lined with the royal party.

Tyburn had grinned to himself. He knew the tall otherworldly woman was one of Warwick's Men, though the player's name escaped him. Women were barred by law from stage appearances, their roles played instead by young men or beardless youths like Motely. For comedic effect, Warwick's Men were known for using a tall lanky youth who, at times, stood head and shoulders above the shorter main actors. The musical interlude with the Lady of the Lake complete, the woman and her handmaidens had withdrawn behind their sanctuary of foliage, the lamps had been doused and the 'island' softly paddled off to one side.

A bright, flaring rupture had fractured the night and a long series of hollow pops echoed across the lake as fireworks arched up into the ebon sky and burst with a thunderous crackle, sending reflective flares racing across the surface of the water like startled fireflies, shattering and breaking apart into a million iridescent shards before fading into darkness. The crowd had gasped in awe at the comet-like trails of the rockets as they ascended and then either exploded with a crack or faded away into nothing. The causeway and the castle battlement were brightly illuminated by a dozen spinning wheels. The flaring light washed over the nobility watching from the causeway and for an instant Will had thought he could spy a woman bedecked with jewelry and silvered lace seated on a raised platform. He had almost toppled over onto the muddy bank as he strained to catch another glimpse of the queen.

The smoke from the fireworks had drifted thick and lazy across the lake, idling in a curious clinging fashion that Tyburn recognized. Gunsmoke from great guns always seemed to plod its way across the battlefield. The choking stench drifting in the air brought with it a razored memory of bloody, churned mud, screaming horses and ragged lines of steel-clad men shouting "Santiago! Santiago![126]" in a fury as they advanced. It had spun through his thoughts so abruptly Tyburn took a physical step back. His insides were like a closed fist and for the barest of moments he thought he could smell the rotting stench of dying men rather than the fetid muddy shore the lake. He shut his eyes, trying to empty his mind of the memory that seemed more vivid than the slow summer air. He would never be quit of Flanders, he thought.

Will had gasped in excitement, oblivious of Tyburn's sudden change in demeanor. The boy's eyes were locked on the lake, his hand grasping the player's sleeve, as a dark, monstrous shape emerged from the stygian abyss. It was dazzlingly lit by two flaring light fountains revealing an ornate statue of a dolphin that glistened in the torchlight. The statue was attached to a float being pulled by a rope across the lake towards the causeway. Seated atop the dolphin was a man draped in a white cloth toga, clutching a large lyre or harp. As he drew near the causeway he began to play and sing but the sounds drifted away over the water.

Tyburn had felt the light dissipating on his closed lids and the smell of Flanders vanished along with the sounds of the churning battlefield. He had opened his eyes and. glanced around, feeling the sudden chill of sweat on his face. Will had still been watching the lake spectacle, rapt. Tyburn shook his head, and turned away. He had seen enough. His taste for the occasion had eroded in the face of memory. The player slipped through the trees and left Will to enjoy the remaining displays. Several minutes had

---

[126] Santiago, or Saint James, is the patron saint of Spain

passed before Will noticed Kit had departed. He glanced at the lake pageant a final time before darting after his companion.

That night was now cemented in the boy's memory. Will had been fortunate enough as an alderman's son to have seen theatrics and spectacles before at the marketplace in Stratford. Outside of the lone trip to Coventry the previous year with his father, nothing had ever approached the evening's pageant at Kenilworth. *It had been like stepping into a waking dream*, he thought.

And today promised much more of the same. After a restless night in the distant byre, a privilege that Tyburn had parted with another two pennies for, the pair had walked back along the road to Kenilworth in the morning, hoping to be able to obtain a brief audience or appointment with Edward Arden, the high sheriff of Warwickshire.

The throng on the road grew in density and noise as they neared their destination. It was not the fortress itself the crowd was moving towards but the wide grassy fields opposite Leicester's new gatehouse on the northern side of the road. A large spacious hayfield, fresh cut and mown, was blocked off by long ribboned ropes strung from tree to tree, demarking areas reserved for spectators and hawkers. A low raised platform with a large enclosed area surmounted by a light silk canopy was positioned at one end of the field where a dozen grim-faced, armoured men with halberds, their blades glittering in the sunlight, growled at anyone that dared to venture close to the platform. A group of musicians was seated along a long bench adjacent to the platform, testing and tuning their strings in preparation.

A group of small children ran screeching out into the blocked off open space of the field, chased by two exasperated marshals. They captured the hindmost child and dragged him off to one side, whipping him with their canes before turning him, sobbing, back out into the crowd with a hard kick.

Tyburn felt his doublet for the third time, the rustle of the stiff, tight-folded paper reassuring him that the letter was still in place. The ruse he had planned might be effective but if it failed he was not any worse off. *Being hanged for forgery would probably be a blessing in place of being drawn and quartered for treason.*

Kit tried to orient himself. The common area they were standing in was standing off to one side. He would need to find a way to enter the other enclosed area where the court, the special guests and the nobility would be ensconced in order to find Arden. A handful of well-dressed individuals were already moving into the area, trying to position themselves for the best advantage. It was too early for Arden. Kit expected the higher ranked personages to arrive last and their arrival would shift the current occupants to the more tightly packed sidelines. *Just another day in the intricate dance of court favour.* He chuckled to himself.

On the far side of the field a large contingent of men and flags were milling about, along with several dozen men on horseback, including one with an oversized horned helm that threatened to topple from his head with each step of his horse. Through the chaos Tyburn could see servants wearing Leicester's ragged bear and staff trying to impose order on the group but their shouts seemed to be falling on deaf ears and the men milled about in loud raucous disorder until a clean-looking tall man on horseback with an enormous longsword spurred his pale horse forward and shouted at them. The crowd began to withdraw into the cool shade of the trees.

A distant thumping of music heralded the departure of the royal progress from Kenilworth and the crowd streamed into the viewing areas. Tyburn stood near the roped-off entry point straining to see past the guards to try to spot Edward Arden from the brief and scanty description Hall had given him. He looked for the three gold cinquefoils of the Arden badge but was soon lost in the procession of ornate gilt lace ruffs and expensive silks that paraded past. Rich velvet embroidery and ermine trimmings seemed to be the court fashion for the day, despite the summer heat.

Tyburn pushed his way back to where he had left Will pressed up beside a convenient oak with an unobstructed view of the hayfield. The smell of the fresh cut grass hung in the air, green and rich. The royal platform at the end of the field was filling up, although the queen's viewing pavilion was obscured by long silken curtains that hung in shimmering patterned folds. Music drifted over the shouts of the crowd and the smell of roasting meats brought a sharp pang of hunger to the player's stomach. He had not eaten since the previous evening.

A long line of men on horseback carrying lances and flags filed in from the trees, followed by an assortment of men dressed in rough grey sacking, cast off bits of fleece like a herd of badly shorn sheep, and leather leggings, carrying a variety of long staves, blunt spears and wooden shields. They were cheering and shouting, many hoisting wineskins and waving them towards the royal pavilion and the swarm of onlookers. A small group of them beat their staves haphazardly on their shields, lending a cacophonic rhythm to the occasion; these last were the Danes. Will had found out the previous day that the local men of Coventry would be recreating the famous English defeat of the Danes that had occurred on St. Brice's Day[127].

The crowd began to good-naturedly boo and catcall at the contingent, shouting insults and gibes by which the mock Danes pretended to be driven into a frenzy. One man slammed his ribboned spear against his wooden shield calling for a challenger to come forth and do battle. A small boy slipped under the rope, ran up to the man and poked him with a short stick. The man howled in pretend agony and toppled while the crowd cheered the boy until all were hoarse.

---

[127] On St. Brice's Day, 1002 AD, Æthelred, the King of Wessex, ordered all the Danish men in England to be massacred. Realistically, this only impacted about 1/3 of the country, there being altogether too many Danes in the rest of the kingdom to readily defeat. The success of the "battle" was strictly transitory as the Danes re-attacked the following year and again in 1007, 1009 and 1013, eventually leading to England's complete conquest by the Danes under King Canute. Æthelred's nickname was *Æþelræd Unræ*, or Æthelred the Unready, supposedly due to the persistent inept blundering of his counselors.

Another contingent of men, their cheap cloth surcoats emblazoned with the cross of St. George, marched out from under the trees, led by the tall man with the enormous longsword. Dozens of other mounted men followed, bearing long lances with small bright flags dancing on the end. The "Danes" howled their challenges down the field while the "English" army painstakingly was shuffled into position by the marshals.

Both the "English" and the "Danes" milled about at their respective ends of the field while the crowd shouted and jeered for action. One man stumbled out of the English ranks and reeled drunk down the field to charge the Danish line. The Danes gave him an ironic cheer and handed him a full tankard when he arrived at the far end of the field. More horsemen were spilling out on both ends of the field and taking up positions, a fact that Tyburn noted. His attention was on a stocky, thickset man and several retainers moving towards the royal pavilion. The player was positive he had seen a quick glimpse of Arden's badge on one of the retainers but he couldn't be sure. The guards along the barrier between the public viewing area and the more privileged court were cautious and didn't hesitate to crack anyone trying to push forward with the heavy wooden staves they carried.

Tyburn moved along the rope barrier until he neared the entrance. He waved over one of the wardens. The man gave the player a skeptical look but ambled over to listen.

"I've a message to deliver to the high sheriff of Warwickshire, Edward Arden. I will need to pass."

The man's thick brows beetled together at this inopportune request. The warden, the recipient of an endless stream of pleadings from hangers-on, mendicants, merchants, suitors, whores and mistresses, prided himself on resisting their petitions. He gave Tyburn a quick and skeptical survey, noting the once fine but now stained and grubby clothing the player had received from Clair. The man gave a snort. In his assessment Tyburn was yet another downbeat court sycophant, full of fine promises but little of merit. The warden gestured for the player to leave, his contempt for the man's poor garb writ plain on his face. "You and every ragged wastrel in the park. Bugger off."

Kit didn't waste any time arguing with the warden; he took out his last two silver groats and jingled them in his fist. . The warden froze in mid-step and gave the player a querulous glance.

"Just a message. For Arden," Tyburn said. He shook his closed fist a second time, the muffled ringing bait for a hook. One of the nearby guards sniggered but was silenced by the warden's sharp look. The warden took Tyburn by the elbow and led him a few feet away.

He was shorter than Kit, with a flat, thin-lipped face and a hatchet nose that had seen better days. "And what might this 'message' for the sheriff be that I need to let you in ta see 'im? We don't just let in every prat waving a groat."

"Two groats."

"And why'n't I take the message to his lordship and you wait here? Or better yet, why'n't I jus have my boys here filch[128] you into the ground fer being a piss on my day? You think, before God, my duty is turned by a couple of groats . . ." The man's voice trailed off as Tyburn tossed a silver coin in the air with casual aplomb and caught it. It was one of the thick silver Spanish coins from the purse that had been left with Alec's body. It flashed invitingly in the sunlight like a spider web bedazzled with morning dew. The player caught the coin and began to walk it across his fingers with a deft motion, a parlor trick that Alec had taught him when he first joined the troupe.

Tyburn was loath to use the coins. He had been determined to pass the monies onto Alec's family but given his own limited resources, at this point Kit had no choice. In the barn during the previous night he had hammered the coin faces with a heavy stone so the Spanish engraving was now flattened and defaced. It was still

---

[128] To beat

visible to anyone that knew coinage but Tyburn thought it unlikely any of the whores or barmaids the warden would spend the money on would notice or care. Silver had no country.

The warden licked his lips and watched, eyes bulging like a trout's. Tyburn walked the coin across his knuckles one last time and then, flicking it up between his two fingers with a sharp flourish, he passed his hand over it, making the coin vanish.

The warden stared in consternation.

"And it's gone." Tyburn turned away without a glance and began to walk back to the spectator's gallery.

"Wait!" The warden had spoken louder than intended and shuffled after Tyburn, his face turned up to him in a tight rictus of a false smile, his narrow cheeks puffing under their stubble. "Wait," he repeated in a low tone, his thick brows stitching together like a pair of fingers. "If I let you enter, you swear before Almighty God, you will jus' deliver yer message and then bugger off? No getting whittled[129] or acting the ruffler[130]?"

The player nodded in a reassuring fashion. "Just a message, before God and our Savior."

"Very well then," the warden said in a deep, authoritative voice, loud enough to be overheard by the nearby guards, "you may deliver yer message, leaving, of course, a token with us as surety for your good behavior." The guard sniggered again but the warden ignored him and looked at Tyburn with an air of expectation. The player waved his hand near the man's face, making him take a startled step backward. Tyburn grinned to himself and then brought his hand back, manifesting the coin between two fingers. The warden reached out and Tyburn let the coin drop as he stepped past the gate without even looking at him.

As he pushed his way through the court enclosure, Kit was cognizant his appearance was lacking among even the worst

---

[129] Drunk
[130] Thief or a robber

dressed court retainers and servants. He kept his gaze averted and moved carefully through the throng.

He paused and tried to locate the men he had seen wearing the three cinquefoils. The crowd flowed back and forth parallel to the field as audience members shifted to more advantageous viewing points or were ousted by rivals and ranking nobility. Small knots of men of higher rank stood like rocks in mid-stream, rocks clad in rich layered doublets covering bulbous, ruffled sleeves striped with bright silk. They were weighed down with heavy jeweled chains, laughing and talking in loud slurred voices. Tyburn estimated that any one of the men wore the equivalent of at least three years of pay for an actor.

The smell of citrus, perfume and sharp spices hung heavy in the air, helping to mask the acrid scent of body odor. Several women were fanning themselves, feeling the summer heat in their heavy, layered dresses and copious lace, even the few whose bodices were dangerously low. A number of tall stools had been set out for the ladies, a necessity as the heavy gowns did not permit comfortable sitting. Servants in smocks scurried back and forth, threading through the press with practiced ease.

Tyburn espied one of the men he had seen earlier walking along the far side of the enclosure. He sidestepped and squeezed past a group of retainers.

A loud roar from the open field and a staccato rush of hoofbeats marked the beginning of the staged battle. The men of Coventry were shouting and clashing staves on shields as the first small groups of horsemen crashed together at the centre of the field. One horseman reeled out from the melee, either drunk or injured, and toppled bonelessly out of the saddle to disappear in the throng. Horns sounded clear and triumphant as the "English" contingent that had been fruitlessly maneuvering around the far end of the field bellowed a challenge and charged their "Danish" counterparts. A long line of the false Danes filed out and pivoted into a wedge, their blunt-pointed spears making a bristled hedge as they met the charge with raucous bellowing.

Tyburn turned his head at the sudden noise and watched the melee for a moment. The sedate pace of the charge creased his face in an ironic smile. Few of the watchers understood the bowel-loosening terror a massive wedge of charging horse moving at speed could instill in footsoldiers. *It swept towards you with a relentless killing momentum, a murderous intent come to shocking confluence and force. When it withdrew, you stood like a man in a tidal flood, feeling the relentless pull of the dark waters corroding the sand beneath your feet.* The men of Coventry were all noise and drunken bluster, but the audience cheered madly anyway.

The player turned back into the crowd. A server laden with a tray of delicacies blocking his path stepped aside and Tyburn froze in surprise.

Facing him was Albert deBrage. The man's expression was blank but Tyburn saw his mouth move soundlessly as recognition flooded his face. Before the man could react Tyburn lowered one shoulder and charged past, sending deBrage flailing backwards into a group of courtiers. A drink splashed across his chest but the player didn't hesitate and darted through the opening to cut through the crowd. One courtier went down and another spun about, struck across the face by Albert's arm as he fell. The remaining men began to shout and push at deBrage as he climbed to his feet, his face flushed with anger. He shook the men off and scrambled after the player.

Tyburn drove his way through the crowd, unmindful now of moving with care. He needed to get out of the court enclosure with all of its armed guards and retainers before Albert raised a general hue and cry. The roped edge was in sight. The crowd he pushed through squirmed and writhed in his wake like ripples trailing across a pond. A buzz of voices and shouts began to rise behind him as Tyburn came to a quick halt. On the opposite side of the barrier rope was Cuttle and at least one of the other men that Tyburn recognized from the house. They were watching the clashing battle on the field until deBrage hammered through the crowd ten feet to the right; his shouts drew their attention. Cuttle's pebbled eyes slid over and narrowed at the sight of the player.

Tyburn didn't hesitate. He went in the only direction still open to him, out into the open field of battle. He rolled under the rope barrier and out onto the grassy field, ignoring the angry shouts of the marshals behind him. The two mock armies were done maneuvering and had met in a vast and wild scrimmage in the centre of the pasture. Tyburn scrambled to his feet and charged into the melee, sensing his best chance was to lose himself in the chaos and the crowd.

The Men of Coventry had walked the four miles from Coventry the previous afternoon and had spent their night encamped on the damp grass near Kenilworth. Their performance was a part of a larger petition to the Crown on behalf of the town to be permitted to continue their annual re-enactment of the events of St. Brice's Day. The tradition, along with the Coventry Mystery Cycles, had fallen victim to the vehemence and anti-Catholic fervor of the Puritans and Protestant hard-liners. Feast days celebrating the lives of various saints and holidays had been curtailed, and while Coventry was not overtly Catholic, the steady erosion of traditional holidays had abraded many commoners' sensibilities to the point that the town's aldermen had determined to place their petition before the queen herself in the most dramatic and engaging way possible. The men of Coventry had laid aside their tools and trade for a few days and were determined to impress upon the Crown the merits of their re-enactment. Their enthusiasm had been buttressed with copious amounts of ale and small beer, with most of the men spending the night in their encampment drinking away the long hours of darkness rather than sleeping. The result was that Coventry brought boundless enthusiasm and energy to their field of battle, but little restraint.

Tyburn drove through the thick press of men. Most of the Coventry performers were shouting and slamming their makeshift wooden shields together or trading desultory blows with their veney sticks. A man in a thin patterned doublet was bent over, clutching the shoulder of the man next to him and vomiting. Tyburn guessed that maybe one man in four was sober.

A short, stolid man with a bald pate roared a challenge at Tyburn as he pushed his way through the back of the makeshift Danish shield wall. The player had a quick glimpse of the man lunging forward on his left as he shoved his way past the restrictive press of bodies. The player pivoted, letting the blunt, heavy practice stick slide past his stomach. With one hand Kit yanked the man towards him. The man from Coventry flailed for balance and Tyburn twisted the veney stick sideways, turning and extending his hip to send the man sailing into the Danish line. The player sidestepped through the melee, moving in the direction of the horses, where the skirmish line of shouting and hollering shieldmen was thinner.

A horseman spurred past, looking for an English knight to battle. Tyburn dodged past a second horse with its head down, cropping at the grass while its rider waved his makeshift flag with mock intensity. A small group of the English soldiers were pretending to slaughter a laughing group of drunken Danes who refused to stay dead, to the English company's growing frustration. Another horseman spurred past, knocking Tyburn to one knee as he passed. The player caught himself and turned. Two men were threading their way through the throng, shoving aside any Coventry men that strayed into their path. Their eyes were locked on Tyburn.

"Damn," Tyburn said to himself. He straightened, feeling the weighty balance of the veney stick in one hand. The venomous glint of bared steel was in their right hands, held tight alongside their legs. The dense throng of pushing and shoving Coventry men seemed to sense something was amiss and shifted back, reflexively giving them passage. Tyburn felt his pulse pounding in his ears and time seemed to slow as though the arc of the sky were opening and the spheres of heaven freezing in their relentless march, to take in this particular moment.

The first man came fast and low, the dagger slicing upwards in a cut that would have split the player from groin to chin had it landed. Tyburn moved without conscious thought, taking a half-step back and whipping the veney stick around to hammer the man's elbow. Tyburn might have taken a moment to savour the resultant bellow but the second man came at a lunge, the point of the long blade almost catching him in the thigh. The player moved back, blocking a second thrust with the wooden stick. The second man was Hawkins, the intemperate guard from the Kenilworth house. He had the look of a starving man at a long-denied feast.

The puzzled Coventry men around the trio had shifted back to watch the fight, uncertain whether to intervene or just watch. The first man began to edge to the left, circling the beleaguered play-actor. Tyburn kept his eyes on Hawkins. He watched the man's easy stance and the slow, tight circles of the blade as he moved. Everything about the man screamed danger. The first man bellowed and charged in a quick feint. Tyburn twisted to meet his charge. Hawkins darted forward, blade extended, sensing blood.

Or so it seemed.

Tyburn had anticipated the first man's feint, gambling on the fact that the man would not charge home, reacting to it to draw Hawkins in close. Hawkins's long, narrow blade cut nothing but air as the player parried the dagger with the veney stick, pushing it out of line with his body and countering the attack, spinning like a quintain[131] and slamming the end of the heavy wooden stave into the man's temple. Hawkins's eyes rolled back and he slumped to the turf.

The first man, startled at the turn of events, stared at the player for an instant before raising his blade and stepping forward. The man's planned attack was cut short as a pale horse rode into him from behind, sending him sprawling onto the matted and torn

---

[131] Quintain – a training device used for knights consisting of a revolving target dummy on pole with two outstretched arms, one being a target shield, the other a weighted bag of sand.

grass of the field. He started to roll to his feet but stopped motionless. Hanging in front of his eyes was the razored tip of a longsword.

"I'm not fond of people disturbing my battle." The voice was mild and off-hand but the sword stood rock-steady. "If you have business with that man"--a quick nod indicated Tyburn--. "I suggest you take it elsewhere. Or leave him be, which might be a more sensible course, considering how quick he laid out your friend."

The man on the ground licked his lips and then gave a reluctant nod. He sheathed his dagger and climbed to his feet. The man on horseback shifted his blade an inch, pausing it just beside the man's neck. Tyburn admired the man's precision. It took considerable strength to hold a longsword steady but the man on the pale horse seemed unperturbed.

"Take your rotted, fetid coxcomb of a friend and yourself away from my field. Or I may plant you here." This brought an appreciative laugh from the small circle of Coventry men watching. The man nodded, eyes fixed on the yard of sharp steel. He grabbed Hawkins by the legs and proceeded to drag him away across the field towards the rope barriers. Several wardens ran over and helped shift the man's unconscious form from the battlefield.

The man on horseback turned his attentions to Tyburn. He stared down at the player, his eyes keen under a velvet cap. "I'm Cox," he said, "captain of this bloody rabble. So are you Danish or English for today?"

"For this performance, English by God's truth," Tyburn replied.

"Then you are one of fucking mine," said Cox with a slight grin, resting the sword across the pommel of his saddle, "as should be any man who can drop a bastard ruffler like that. I won't ask how or why, as much as it would fascinate me to know. You'd best be on your way, without any further addendums to our performance. The queen is in attendance"--he nodded towards the distant royal enclosure--"or so we hope, and my preference is her favour, by Jesu, not some riotous disturbance of dead men on the field with their eyes a-glaze, at least not unless I'm the one that gets the joy of sending their fucking souls screaming to Hell."

He turned to regard the small circle of observers as though noticing them for the first time. "God's blood! What are you lot staring at? Don't you have some shit-arsed Danes to kill?" With a roar of laughter the men resumed their battle by heading further downfield to where the Danes were now retreating in pretend disarray and pleading for mercy.

The man gave Tyburn a nod and spurred his pale horse back down the field with a shout, the longsword held high.

Kit pushed his way past the stragglers and paused on the far edge of the field. The battle had shifted upfield, closer to the Royal enclosure. Small parties of Coventry men were bustling on and off the field. A small group of wardens was collecting several unconscious bodies, casualties of either battle or bottle. He glanced back through the trees to the Kenilworth Road, heavy with foot traffic. A long, slow litany of Dutch profanity flowed from his lips.

Three figures were visible on the verge of the Kenilworth Road. Tyburn recognized the short, almost bumpy form of Cuttle and the taller, more aquiline shape of Clair's brother. The third figure was short, topped with a familiar mop of dark and curly hair and a high forehead. Tyburn cursed again. He liked to swear in Dutch; it was a guttural language, well suited for profanity.

Tossing the veney stick aside, he pulled his sword belt around and headed along the edge of the thin sloping woodland to meet the trio standing by the road. Albert was expressionless, both hands sitting on Will's shoulders. To one side stood Cuttle, shifting his weight back and forth, one hand fingering the wrapped handle of a long knife dangling from his belt.

Tyburn stopped and, ignoring Cuttle, looked at deBrage.

"Give me the letter."

Tyburn reached into his doublet and tossed Arden's secret letter to the Jesuit onto the ground. The wax seal was broken and the paper torn where Tyburn had spiked it with his sword to retrieve it. Cuttle stooped and picked it up, tapping it on his left hand with a tight expression on his face.

"I assume you've read it," Albert stated. Tyburn did not respond.

"If you've read it, then you know we are engaged in the Crown's business, a business to which you have interfered and obstructed and made a Christ-damned shit-heap of by taking what wasn't yours." Tyburn regarded him still, in silence.

"You are a bitter pill to manage, and cause no end of troubles to everyone around you. Your troupe imprisoned; your friend dead; you, a rogue and a felon, bound for the gallows or the gibbet; your boy here . . . well, we can discuss his fate, provided you behave. Otherwise his blood waters the grass, you understand me, you shit-licking bastard?" Albert tightened his grip on Will's shoulders, his thumbs digging into the sides of the boy's neck. Will stiffened in pain but gave no outcry. Tyburn gave no response. Albert's lips twisted in a momentary grimace of annoyance and he shoved the boy over to Cuttle.

"I asked if you understood me, you cunt."

Tyburn caught the glint of bared steel in the man's hand, a small and deft blade under Will's chin. The boy stiffened at the touch of the cold metal.

The player nodded.

Albert spat on the grass and gave Cuttle a quick gesture. The hand with the short blade dropped away from the boy's throat.

Albert gave Tyburn a thin and humourless smile. "Now walk with me, master player, as we have things to discuss." The two men walked along the roadway, Cuttle trailing behind with Will in tow.

"Come to Kenilworth to see the festivities, have you?" Albert laughed. "We underestimated you. I believed your Oldcastle when he said you fled to London. He's a better liar than I gave him credit for, although," he paused, "I had forgotten, yours is a bastard liar's profession." Tyburn ignored the gibe.

A triumphant cheer arose from the re-enactment as the English captain Cox toppled the Danish leader from his horse and raised the English standard in victory.

"The clothes look familiar. Mine, I'll warrant. Well, we can add theft to your list of treasonous activities." Albert gave the player a sly glance. "Or did you come by them through another chance? Clair, perhaps?" He laughed as Tyburn stiffened for an instant at the mention of her name. "Out whoring, was she? I heard you fished her from Topcliffe's lecherous paws. No matter, my father and I will be baiting her off to him soon enough."

For a moment Tyburn toyed with the idea of just killing the man where he stood.

"We are plain-spoken men, you and I, so let us speak of this blunt. Anyone sensible would have done as Oldcastle said--run for London or the Channel ports, but you stayed. You stayed," he repeated. "You stayed, like some festering, poxed clyster[132] under my skin and I don't think it was just that mort, my sister. I would like to know why. I insist on knowing why." He stopped and looked at Tyburn, his eyes wire-tight. "Or I'll have Cuttle slit the boy's throat and damn the consequences."

deBrage's words had the flat ring of truth. The player lifted his head and replied. "Revenge."

"Revenge? Revenge?" Albert laughed. "Coads! Revenge is the weak pleasure of a little and narrow mind[133]. Revenge for what? For killing your friend, is it? That wretch of a player?" He grinned and leaned forward, his lips almost at Tyburn's ear. His voice was a low-pitched murmur. "You want to know who killed your friend? Is that the crux of this drama, play-actor?" Albert's wide smile vanished and Tyburn looked at the man's hooded eyes. They were, he thought, for the first time showing him who this man was, at the

---

[132] A clyster thread was inserted under the skin as an irritant. It was intended to draw away an infection.

[133] Juvenal, Decimus Iunius Iuvenalis, a Roman poet

core of himself. They were smooth and cold and as empty as a frost-borne night.

Albert leaned in again, and whispered. "I killed him."

Tyburn felt the fury rising and with force of will he pushed it back down.

"I enjoyed it. I walked up and just shoved in the steel. He stood there like a fool, didn't utter a sound, until I . . . twisted it."

Tyburn's face was a mask. He wondered that he didn't burst into flames; the anger within was an inferno, banked by sheer force of will and the knowledge of cold steel on a boy's throat.

Albert was circling the player, a slow and malicious gyre, a yellow predatory gleam in his eyes. "Angry, are you? You want me dead now, do you? Revenge? Well soldier, you can't, no *arcana ultio* for dead players[134], just a rotten hole in a churchyard. You fucking actors are nothing but shit, nothing but a bunch of dogs, fit for a bloody shambles." Albert's dagger slid out with a metallic scrape as he grabbed the doublet's collar and pulled Tyburn close, the narrow tip of the blade pressing against his kidney. Tyburn felt the point tear through the cloth, nicking his skin. He didn't move.

"So now, you shit-faced play-actor, now you are going to play a role for me. And the price will be your little buggering rent-boy's life."

---

[134] Latin, secret revenge

Chapter the Twenty-first

THE ROUND, BEATIFIC faces on the wall hanging were meant to be pious and uplifting, despite the rural hunting scene being depicted. After two hours seated on a hard walnut bench, the saturnine player had developed a measured simmering distaste for the figures hanging across from him. Their virtuous miens gazed out from the fabric with a vacant certitude bordering on the imbecilic. Candlelight playing on the rich, intricate, woven border with its labyrinthine interlocking patterns created the illusion of movement that kept catching his eyes, tired as they were, and pulling him out of the repetitive path of his thoughts.

Tyburn surveyed the narrow hallway for the thousandth time. The narrow oak table with the thick, curving, melon-shaped legs still stood beside the heavy polished door, topped by a decorative inlaid box that looked Flemish to his unschooled eye. A set of wide court cupboards flanked the bench on which he idled, displaying an enviable set of plates and flagons along with a set of tinted crystalline wine goblets that Tyburn recognized as Venetian. The floor was a tight-laid, elaborate geometrical pattern of pale white marble that drew one's eyes down the hallway to the ornate carved entry frame enclosing a thick wooden door that remained closed.

The actor breathed out an exasperated curse and returned to contemplating the dutiful fat hunter on the tapestry.

The door at the far end of the hallway cracked open and a thin, sallow man in livery moved past and entered the far room, brushing by the player with a supreme indifference born of a thousand petitioners. Tyburn cursed again and contemplated setting the bloody tapestry alight with one of the guttering tapers.

He had left Kenilworth that morning berating his own foolishness and arrogance. Bringing the glover's son to Kenilworth had been a foolish and pointless risk. As much as he told himself he had been uncertain of the boy's safety in returning home to Stratford, the reality was he had grown selfishly fond of the boy's endless prattling and fancies. It had helped to exile the sense of loss that had grown in him since Alec's death and from meeting Clair.

Clair. That had been unexpected. When he had left Holland, one part of a limping contingent of escapees from Haarlem, he had fought the urge to look back at the low, receding coastline as the coastal flute bore him across the choppy waters of the Channel. Holland had left him bereft and rudderless, but not broken. Running from Spanish vengeance, with Heaven's looming condemnation above him, England still beckoned. London was dense and noisome, with a bustle and heightened energy that had helped him ignore the sense of gnawing uncertainty and loss that plagued him in the wake of Annika's and Miriam's deaths. Worcester's Men had pulled him in like a ragged discard, unraveling his skein of indifference and lassitude.

He knew that Alec's death was neither purposeless nor random. It was his fault, a vagrant fragment of what he once was, a little piece of his soul being returned to him. The only thing worse than hate was indifference; Alec's death had propelled him out of the indifferent veneer he had used as shield for so long.

And then Clair.

In the bleak aftermath of Holland, Tyburn had thought himself immune from any desire or emotion for another woman. In London it was easy to keep such thoughts at a distance, to treat desire as a commercial transaction in the many stews and brothels that dotted the city. It would have been effortless to lose himself in the fleshpots of Southwark, but in God's truth, the player had no abiding interest, a fact that had probably saved him all manner of poxes. And now Clair had slipped into his world as elemental as a spring wind, and like metal beside a lodestone, she pulled him willingly askew.

It had taken him the better part of the afternoon to find out where Edward Arden was staying while at Kenilworth. The man seemed to own a copious number of holdings in Warwickshire and had a small manor house a few miles from the castle that he was using for the queen's summer progress.

So the player waited.

It was another endless thirty minutes before the slender man wearing the trinity of cinquefoils on his livery returned to the hall. Without a sound he paused at the door and gestured for the player. Tyburn rose, his legs stiff from the long wait, and followed the man through the portal.

The room was large and airy, lit with a dozen thick, white beeswax candles that burned steady and bright. A set of heavy leather-bound volumes teetered on one of the chairs, the faint gleam of gilt lettering on the covers glowing in the candlelight. A large carved oak table with a small neat stack of papers stood four-square in the centre of the room, flanked by several ornate chairs. Amidst the letters on the table sat a glass inkpot shaped like a swan, accompanied by several quills and a sander. Next to this last crouched a small white covered bowl. A glass wine carafe was half-empty on the sideboard. Beside the window a large ornate Bible on a stand stood open, the faint sheen of gold leaf and bright colour thickening the margins of the text like an elegant frame. From its refuge under the table a small spaniel emerged and ambled over, its foreclaws clicking faint on the tiled floor, to give Tyburn's feet a curious and somewhat haughty sniff and an eager tail wag before padding over to settle with a languid sigh on a large flat pillow by the fireplace. A man stood by the open window, gazing out at the slow westerning sunlight and the shadow that was thickening under the trees of the walled garden.

The man turned away from the window and picked up a small waxen disc from the table.

"I am curious; why you have presented this token to me?" His eyes gave Tyburn a careful inspection, noting the frayed clothing and worn boots.

Tyburn offered the man a cautious obeisance. The man was stout, shorter than the player, with dark eyes that hung in his face like a bruise. He wore a heavy velvet-trimmed gown with a silk cap; a thick chain of office hung around his neck. The hair that poked out from under the cap was the colour of straw, leavened with grey. On his right hand he wore several jeweled rings, one of which, fat as a pigeon's egg, glittered scarlet in the candlelight like a glass of burgundy.

"My lord Arden, I come bearing a message."

"You come bearing a message of heresy and treason with this particular token," Arden replied. "A sacramental symbol blessed by the pope himself. '*Agnus Dei, qui tollis peccata mundi, miserere nobis*'[135]." He snorted. "Hmmm, a shame to be drawn and quartered over such a small lamb." He fixed Tyburn with a sharp stare. "Who sent you? What fool thinks I should be lured to treason with such petty artifices? Leicester? Burghley? That cold snake Walsingham?"

"You need look no closer for a Judas than your own household, my lord." Tyburn returned the man's look with a level gaze.

---

[135] Lamb of God, you who take away the sins of the world, have mercy upon us.

Christopher Tyburn had spent considerable time assessing how to play out this particular scene in his own mind, working through the outcomes and possible permutations. Arden was an unknown quantity to him but the man was a known Catholic who, despite that burden, remained a powerful presence in court and in the queen's favour. Where most of the nobility had eschewed and disavowed their old roots in Catholicism, falling over themselves to don the cloak of Puritanism after the rebellion in the North, Arden still embraced his faith. In spite of this, he had maintained his standing and position with the queen, although he was despised by Leicester. He was a man accustomed to the vagaries and spiteful plotting of the court, immured in all of its nuances and political dealings. The player doubted if he could spin a believable enough tale to convince the man to point him to the Jesuit.

Unless Arden thought he had found an ally.

Arden's mouth tightened, the bright candlelight accentuating the deepening lines along his face. "Do I look a man that embraces folly? More bait for your plot?"

"No plot of mine, my lord. This token was left on the corpse of one of Worcester's Men in Stratford-on-Avon. It was meant to implicate him in a conspiracy. They believed him to be a messenger of yours, transiting letters on your behalf."

Arden hesitated an instant. "I know nothing of this. A messenger, you say? I have no connection to Worcester or any of his playing troupe."

"Indeed, my lord. The man was an innocent, murdered to give veracity to letters the conspirators had intercepted through your gardener-priest Master Hall--and desired to make public in such a way that would implicate you in a treasonous plot."

Arden turned. The bruised eyes seemed to sag in his face. "Impossible."

"I regret to be the one to inform you, my lord, but Master Hall has been passing copies of your correspondence. I am not privy to the contents of your letters, so I do not have any knowledge of the extent or details of your exchange," Tyburn paused, "and that is not my charge."

Arden's face was darkening in anger. "You lie. You seek to turn my head, to deceive me with blatant falsehoods. Master Hall is steadfast in his service to me."

"*My fortune and abilities are now cast with you in this endeavor, although I fear it will land upon stony indifference from the Throne...*" Tyburn intoned, quoting the letter he had intercepted.

Arden's face froze as he recognized the words.

"Proof enough? My apologies, my lord, but your most recent missive was meant to be left on the corpse in Stratford, accompanied by a considerable quantity of Spanish silver."

Arden's face was pale granite as he sat. The spaniel lifted its head and its tail thumped against the pillow.

"I write many letters . . . to many correspondents. I cannot be expected to have recall of them all, or to control to whom they may wander."

"Indeed."

"And you claim Master Hall has been suborning my correspondence? Yet you have no proof or evidence? Am I to take the word of a street player on this matter? I don't know whose pet dog you may be, though I can guess. You may return to your master and tell him I failed to take your bait, though the performance was apt."

The player slid a single sheet of folded paper across the table to rest beside Arden's hand. "You may judge this as you will. I think you will recognize the hand at work. I thank you for your time, my lord." Tyburn gave Arden a deep bow and turned away, putting his wide hat back on his head as he moved towards the exit.

The player was mentally cursing as he reached a hand for the cool iron door handle when Arden spoke. "Wait."

Tyburn paused and turned. Arden was looking at him, his eyes thoughtful. He reached out and unfolded the sheet, reading it.

"Where did this come from?"

"It was recovered along with your priest from a house in Kenilworth, where he was held."

"Held by whom?" The player shrugged. "This is a forgery."

"Yes, my lord. Forged by your priest, under threat."

"It is rife with falsehoods and unashamed lies. It claims we seek insurrection . . ."

"Indeed, my lord."

Arden leaned back and slid the sheet through the narrow gap at the top of the fireplace grate. The dry parchment flared as it burned.

"And where is Master Hall now?"

"He should, my lord, be tending your gardens at Park Hall by now, God willing. I removed him and his papers from the house at Kenilworth and sent him on his way."

"And the remaining papers?" Arden's voice trailed off.

"Ashes."

Arden leaned back in his chair, steepled his fingers and gazed at the player for a full minute in absolute silence. Tyburn stood and waited.

"Why, by God's light, have you intervened in my favour?" . Tyburn gave a slight guilty start and with slow deliberation nodded. He slipped one hand under the edge of his collar and removed a tight folded paper. Stepping forward he slid the missive across the table for Arden to examine.

Arden picked up the paper. The sheet had been folded flat and tight, accordioned into a sharp and compact shape that fit under his collar points. Arden slowly picked out the folds and opened the missive. It was blank on both sides. The player gave a quick gesture at the candle and, with practiced familiarity, Arden slid the paper back and forth above the flames. The curve and spiral of letters began to appear on one side of the letter. Arden sat back and began to read.

Tyburn fought down his nerves. The letter had been written in Latin, penned by Will whose tight, scrabbled lettering was mixed with ornate flourishes for added verisimilitude. The boy, the player reflected, had a bureaucrat's penmanship, and a schoolmaster's vocabulary, but even then, it had taken four tries before Tyburn had been satisfied. They had despaired of getting the tight folds creased and worn enough to pass inspection, even after piling flat rock weights upon it, until Will had hit upon the idea of having the milking cow they were sharing the barn with step upon the document. The heavy tread of their unwitting bovine accomplice had not only tightly creased the many folds, but had provided a realistic worn tone to the expensive paper.

Arden finished reading the letter. He dropped it on the desk and leaned forward, lacing his fingers. "Am I to believe the content of this missive? That you are an agent of the Holy See, of William Allen of the English College at Douai?" The dark eyes fluttered like a bird's wing. "I find it . . . unlikely . . . that a street player would be selected for such a critical role."

"My lord, if I may-- we travel the countryside at will, venturing amidst both the high and low without comment or needful glance. We are skilled at dissembling, artful in our speech and despised by the Puritans and Catholics alike as purveyors of corruption and a low art. We are perfect."

Arden nodded. "And yet, you seem to carry with you an element of distaste, master player. I perceive an opaque thread in you that I cannot assess or find comfort in. I do not know clear whom you serve. Players, as you note, are practiced liars and keen dissemblers."

"Who I am, my lord, is the man that should now be lying dead in the cold ground of Stratford. But for the vagaries of the Fates, I am not. . I am not the only party seeking this Jesuit. A certain Topcliffe is hunting him."

Arden snorted. "Yes. I've received several notes from him over the last two days requesting, or rather demanding, of my time. He veils his threats much more poorly than you do, master player, but I yet disaccommodate him, so why should I not disaccommodate you as well?"

"You must decide, my lord, where your trust must lie. There are lives in the balance, not the least of which is our mutual Jesuitical charge."

Arden reached out and lifted the lid off the small bowl on the table. At the faint chink of the porcelain, the dog's head lifted from its pillow. Taking a small scrap of dried meat between his fingers, the high sheriff leaned down and waved the food enticingly. The dog scurried over and waited until Arden said "Take it!" The animal lipped the meat from its master's fingers and carried it back to its pillow.

"Do you believe in God's holy purpose?"

"My lord?"

"God," Arden said in a sanguine tone, "has a purpose, a plan for all of us." Arden gave the player a long and searching look. "Do you believe, by God's truth, that you are fulfilling God's plan?"

Tyburn felt a tight node of anxiety in his chest, though he was unsure why. "I'm not sure what you mean, my lord."

Arden slammed his hand onto the polished wood of the table, making the swan inkpot and the porcelain bowl jump. "Do you believe you are fulfilling God's purpose?" The dog raised a querulous head at the noise and then settled back down to watch.

The player hesitated. Tyburn had not found any resolution in faith since he returned from the Low Countries; it had been rather the opposite. God had felt like a distant and indifferent presence, an empty exercise. The thought of pretending otherwise to a man of faith was vaguely sickening to him. He responded, "I don't presume to know God's plan or purpose, my lord. He has gifted me with trials and vicissitudes, and yet I ended up here, on your doorstep, asking for your assistance. In truth, I have never thought myself worthy of God's designs."

"Yes, yes," said Arden with a frown. "Few of us are worthy of God's purpose. We are His tools, fallible and weak though we might be. Our Faith guides us to our pre-determined fate, and yours has brought you to me, through all the vagaries of Fortune. So we must all, in turn, serve a higher purpose, a nobler purpose, to help bring this nation back into God's grace. England must be Catholic. England *will* be Catholic." He stared at Tyburn, eyes intent. "God has sent you. Who am I to question's God's design?"

Arden picked up the paper and without comment refolded it and handed it back to Kit. "You may yet need this for future performances. Master Tyburn, I think you are a lying deceitful wretch, a sinner at odds with God but I believe you mean no harm, though you have not told me the complete truth. You were hesitant in asserting your faith in God's holy purpose, something a base-born liar and dissembler would not be." He gave the player a dark look. "If you were one of the Devil's spawn, you would have fallen over yourself in honeyed words and protestations of faith, not leavening it with the doubt or hesitation or the failings of a mortal soul. I sense that beneath your faults, you are an honourable man with a higher and Heaven-sent purpose about him. Our Savior has sent you to me and so I send you onwards to help his messenger.

"Grant me your word--your promise on God and our Savior--that you will not permit harm to befall the Jesuit, that you will not remit him to the authority of the Crown, nor trouble his path away from such strictures, and I will tell you where you may find him."

Chapter the Twenty-second

THE COLD BITE of steel was the first indication that things were awry.

Christopher Tyburn had left the small manor house containing Edward Arden and his household with urgency evident in his step and frustration etched onto his countenance. Arden had agreed to share the whereabouts of the Jesuit but at the same time had bound and sworn the player to protect the clandestine priest from harm. Tyburn had agreed to the reluctant bargain, lacking any other avenues of investigation to pursue, with the knowledge that he no longer had the luxury of time.

The Devil is in the details, he thought with savage resentment. He was hemmed in by obligations, duties and promises: to Clair; to Will; and to the dead, both recent and long-buried. His patience had been ground down and worn away to the thinnest of threads, and at the moment with this blade at his throat he fought the desire to give himself over to wrath and blind anger. It was a familiar berserker fury well suited to wartime but dangerous and self-indulgent. It had happened at Walcheren and the results of that night's work still harrowed him. He took a slow breath, forcing himself to reassemble his thoughts and dampen his fury.

The phlegmatic presence of a blade at the throat had a way of clarifying things. Tyburn felt two sets of hands propelling him hard into a narrow alcove between two buildings and the flash of steel rose up in the periphery of his vision like a feeding trout ensconced in a rippling stream.

"Well, what a bullock we've got ourselves? Amazing what wanders the streets, just ripe for plucking."

"Like a maiden's virtue it is." The voice drifted sing-song behind the player.

Kit winced as his head was shoved hard against the stone brickwork of the tavern.

"So do we geld him here or take him inside?"

"Unless you're volunteering to clean up after, we'd best geld him on the street." Tyburn didn't wait for a response, but kicked out his left foot, feeling it brush against one captor as the man deftly sidestepped. The point of the knife pricked the underside of his chin in warning.

"Vigorous, this one is. Right, lads, turn him about."

Tyburn felt two sets of hands grasping him and forcibly turning him so his back was to the wall. He tensed against the grip. The blade at his throat didn't shift.

"What now?" Tyburn, his head being pulled back by a hand on his forehead, could barely make out his knife-wielding assailant.

"Now? Now we slice your throat, or maybe just give you a little something." The player choked as liquid was unexpectedly squirted down his throat from a goatskin. He sputtered on vinegary, syrupy wine. The two men on either side of him laughed uproariously as the liquid guttered from his mouth. The man holding the knife skipped aside with an adroit motion and gave Tyburn a quick open-handed slap on the back.

"I always knew none of Worcester's Men could hold their drink!" Tyburn spat into the dirt of the road as he recognized

Cleve's booming voice. He spat again and glanced sideways, identifying John Lanahan's lean hooked profile and slanted grin. It was Warwick's Men, the playing troupe he had watched performing on the lake at Kenilworth Castle the previous night.

"You poxed bastards," Tyburn muttered.

"Fine words from a fellow we should be gelding right now! Lucky you're not Oldcastle, Kit, we still remember Lincoln." The three laughed again and Lanahan handed Tyburn the heavy wineskin.

With a wary look, Kit took a careful sip and made a face. "Did you piss in it first, Cleve?" He handed the wineskin back.

Cleve laughed. "It's sauced. Dried leaf, from the Americas, with some hemp seed. Bill traded it off some soldiers."

"Trade it back."

One of the leading sharers of Warwick's Men, Cleve wore his affluence in a statement in lace and gilt thread, his patterned doublet adorned with bright cinnamon-brown silk points and lace purls. "What brings you to our digs? You haven't come to your senses and abandoned that worthless turd Oldcastle?"

"No, but at this rate I may have to. The boys are in gaol at Charlecote." The explanation as to why Worcester's Men had been arrested and what Tyburn was doing in Kenilworth took enough time for the wineskin to make multiple rounds of the small group. Kit found the bitter syrupy wine actually tasted better after several passes.

Lanahan puffed out his cheeks in thought. "Topcliffe's a bastard through and through, but I've met Lucy and he's a cautious man. He won't be permitting no racking or questionable methods. Mind you, they may be locked up tighter than virgin quim for the next few months." He eyed Tyburn. "Kit, you might consider crossing the street to work with us. You're sharp on the boards, quick on your feet, and deft with the blades. We could use that. Burbage is building his theatre in Shoreditch and we're first on his list of troupes--might be an opportune time to be shut of that arse-faced bastard Oldcastle. The coin would be good, I promise you."

Tyburn shook his head. "I can't think of that right now. I need to get out from under this or I'll be performing at Tyburn tree, not Shoreditch or the Red Lion. I need to get transport."

"There's a livery near the ordinary, if'n you have coin. You can get yourself a prancer there but don't expect much, they most ain't even fit for the shambles[136]. You need anything else? We can't have morts like Topcliffe and Lucy waylaying troupes wholesale, like we're some wastrels or cursitors[137]. Bad enough with the London aldermen closing us down on every excuse and the Master of Revels[138] lifting every ready coin we have for writs and approvals."

The player thought for a moment and then outlined his requirements to them. Lanahan nodded. "We can help you with that," he noted in a dubious tone, "though you're a fool's cob for trying it." Tyburn couldn't help but nod in agreement.

The horse, a thin piebald, was nervous, shifting its hooves back and forth on the eroded edge of the laneway. Tyburn tugged sharp on the reins and led the reluctant mount back through the rolling shadow of the trees, tying it to a convenient branch well back from the road. Then he threaded his way back to the laneway on foot and slipped through the thick hedgerow that bordered the estate.

The manor house was called Baddesley Clinton. The house consisted of four rectangular wings in a large square. It was moated, with access across a double-arched stone bridge with a wide

---

[136] Butchering yard

[137] Tramps or wandering vagabonds

[138] The Master of the Revels was a Crown-appointed position responsible for managing all court and Crown theatre performances and later for censoring and licensing plays and playing troupes. Sir Thomas Blagrave was the Master of the Revels in 1575, succeeded by the more well-known Edmund Tilney in 1578

wooden drawbridge on the north side. It was built of dressed grey stone and brick, with a gatehouse tower squatting intrusive, robust and imposing across the entrance. The moat, the player estimated, was thirty feet of sour-smelling murk, narrowing to maybe fifteen feet on the south side of the obstacle. Yellow light gleamed in the windows and Tyburn thought he could glimpse the occasional shapes of people moving about beyond the thick paned glass.

A muffled noise drew his attention. The midsummer sun was balanced on the western horizon like a squashed orange on a table. Loose skeletal tendrils of thin light washed across the landscape and through the trees, casting the hedge in deep shadow. He raised his head with caution. Two men were moving up the left side of the laneway, taking care to remain out of the line of sight of the building, moving from one shadow to the next with deliberate care. The sound of laughter rose from an open window of the manor house. Tyburn watched the two conversing in low tones. One turned and hurried away down the laneway, disappearing from sight. The other crossed the laneway and, espying the deep shadow and shallow declivity where Tyburn had hidden himself, began to move towards the player.

Kit cursed to himself. He lay down, flattening out in the shallow hollow and waited. The man's head slid into sight, turned towards the house.

"Hello," said Kit.

The man startled and his head snapped around to meet Tyburn's clenched fist. The player rolled over and yanked the stunned man into the hollow, using the man's weight to swing himself astride the man. The player knelt hard on his chest, knees digging into the intruder's lower ribcage. He quieted the sudden thrashing by placing the needle-sharp point of his dagger over the fellow's right eye.

Tyburn reached down and tugged the dagger from the man's belt. He tossed it to the left and was rewarded with a splash and flurry of startled ducks swimming away. "What are you doing here?"

The man kept his gaze fixed on the dagger point, suspended a half-inch above his eye. "Master Topcliffe ordered us to scout the manor and report back, so he could determine how best to bottle it up."

"How many men?"

"Eighteen, including myself."

"How far away?"

"They're waiting about a half-mile back, near the Warwick Road." Tyburn moved the dagger away from the man's eye and heard a slow sigh of relief. Reversing the dagger he hammered down once with the heavy steel pommel. The man beneath him subsided without a sound.

Topcliffe has either tracked down the Jesuit's hiding place or he's raiding any suspect Catholic estates in an effort to winkle out the priest. Kit's options had narrowed.

Tyburn stood and strode across the bridge. He was out of time. His worn boots crunched in the gravel of the laneway as he crossed over the moat and echoed hollowly as he traversed the drawbridge. Standing under the edge of the gatehouse tower facing a fat oaken door reinforced with iron. He hammered hard on the knocker and waited. A small barred wicket door for viewing visitors and passing small items was inset in the larger oak door. Tyburn heard footsteps and the wicket door slid open. A round, wide face peered out. He appeared startled.

"Who are you?"

"Open the door!" Tyburn said.

"I wha--who are you?"

"Open the door in the name of the high sheriff," the player ordered. "Do it! Now!"

The wicket door snapped shut. Another precious minute ticked past before it slid open a second time. A woman's face peered out through the bars.

"What do you want?" The voice crackled with suspicion.

"Edward Arden sent me. There isn't time for long-winded explanations. I need that priest you have lurking in your scullery and I need him now."

The woman stiffened and her dark brows knitted together. "I don't know what you are talking about." She began to close the wicket.

"Stop." The player imbued his voice with all the conviction he could muster. "You can close that hatch and resume your dinner and in about ten minutes you will have the great joy of receiving Richard Topcliffe and twenty of his pursuivants for your dessert. They will search your home, destroy your belongings, raze your walls and excavate your foundations. They won't stop until they find him and all of you will end up enjoying the comforts of the Tower--right up until your appointment with the headsman's axe or the gallows." Tyburn glared through the grill. She hesitated. An speaker behind her said, "Let him in."

The wicket door snapped closed. A second later Tyburn heard bolts grating. The door swung open and he stepped across the threshold into the gatehouse tunnel. The short passage lit by two bright lanterns opened up beyond into a fairly large square garden courtyard, surrounded by the four wings of the house.

The woman who had opened the doorway to him was short and stolid, with dark hair tied back and a lace cap perched on top. "Now explain who you are this instant or--"

"There isn't time for this nonsense. We have five minutes or less to get clear of this house, or you'll be bottled up behind your own moat." His cold tone brooked no argument. "Where's the priest?"

"You sir, are a rude, ungodly man," she began in a remonstrative tone.

"You're the player from Lucy's celebration, the one who spoke of the Lowlands and the Flanders campaign. What do you want?" The man that spoke stepped into the lamplight. He was younger and shorter than Tyburn, with a thin ginger beard and a face that seemed pale and watery. He wore a poorly starched but expensive ruff that was collapsing around the edges like a sandy embankment in the rain, and an embroidered doublet with separated sleeves. Tyburn glanced at the man's hands.

"We need to leave now, Father, the pleasantries can come later."

The man screwed his face up in convincing puzzlement. "I'm not sure--"

Tyburn interrupted. "You've more ink on you than any clerk and your clothes speak of a rank and level beyond that of a scrivener or factor. You looked wrong at Lucy's but I couldn't evoke why until I spotted your hands again." The man looked askance for an instant. The player grabbed him by the expensive doublet, pulling him towards the door. "We need to move!"

The woman gave a quiet shriek and moved to intervene, stopping when the ginger-bearded man raised a cautionary hand. "It's fine, Elizabeth. We'll go now. Everything is fine."

Tyburn snuffed out the two door lanterns and then pulled on the iron door latch. The door swung open. The gatehouse and the laneway appeared clear in the dim evening light.

"Go. Across the bridge and to the left of the hedgerow, no further. Mistress Ferrer, you need to remove any trace of his presence--clothes, books, letters--anything that looks like it could provide proof of harboring a priest needs to go into the bottom of the moat or straight into the fire. Now go."

The priest turned and mumbled a quick blessing to Elizabeth Ferrer before hastening across the bridge with Tyburn right behind him.

No shouts, no outcry. If Topcliffe was set up around the manor house yet, he was exhibiting an uncharacteristic level of restraint, Tyburn thought. He reached the shallow hollow he had discovered earlier and yanked the priest down hard. The man was shocked to stumble over the body lying in the weeds and grass.

"Dear Lord, blessed Savior, is he . . ."

"Just a little addle-pated, Father, nothing permanent." Tyburn paused, thinking he heard the faint chink of a hoof on stone. "Quiet."

He crawled up to the thick hedgerow and peered out. The sun was now set and although the tops of the highest clouds were still tinged with pink fire, the mortal world was plunging into darkness. The roadway, which curved away to the northeast, was a grey smear against a darker background. As his eyes adjusted to the gloom, Tyburn could make out a brace of monstrous shapes frozen in a group on the roadway, illuminated by the almost invisible glimmer of a closed lantern. Horsemen in the laneway.

Tyburn slid back into the hollow. He reached over and pulled the cloak off the unconscious traveler and, keeping low, slipped over to the edge of the moat. He reached to the waters' edge and scooped out several handfuls of watery mud onto the cloak and then slid back to the hollow. The priest was peering out into the dark like a short-eared owl. Tyburn pulled the man back down and handed him a sloppy handful of black mud. "Here. Coat that doublet, the shirt and your face and hands."

The priest looked at the mud and then looked at the player. Tyburn was sure had there been light enough to see the expression on the man's face that he would have been blanching. Tyburn reached out and snapped off the pale ruff. "Do it," he growled and proceeded to smear the thick black mud over his own face and clothes.

Muffled footsteps sounded in the laneway and the player heard a branch snap off to the right, in the edge of the woods. "Leave off that," he stopped the priest. "Now," he whispered, "you follow direct behind me, keep low, don't speak, don't move fast. We run into anyone, you freeze like a rabbit. You lose me in the dark, you turn to stone, just stop and wait. I'll find you. No calling out, no shouts, no noise. Got it?"

The priest nodded and then whispered back, "Understood."

His stomach scraping the ground, Tyburn eased up the declivity and silently moved to the hedgerow, the Jesuit in tow. He had noticed a thinning spot on the foliage when he had first approached after tying up the horse, about thirty feet further from the laneway. It appeared to be the remnants of an old path now overgrown, used to bypass the long walk around to the lane. The player was uncertain of the location, so he skirted the hedge, one hand trailing along the surface of the foliage on the right, seeking for a break in the tall growth, the other reaching back and grasping the cumbersome muddied cloak to which the Jesuit clung as he followed.

He could hear them now, Topcliffe's men, some moving through the trees to the left and at least two or more by the laneway. He assumed more were moving up from the south through the quiet gardens and in the west, using the small lake and stables that lay behind the estate to cut off anyone leaving the manor house and prevent them from escaping over the fields. Tyburn knew if he could slip through the outer ring of the cordon, he should be well clear by the time Topcliffe finished searching the house.

A low voice called out by the lane. Tyburn continued his blind drift along the hedge. When the foliage thinned, he slowed and reached out. *This must be the opening I spotted earlier.* A lantern flared to life behind him in the laneway, then waved back and forth, bobbing speculatively in the darkness. Tyburn guessed they were looking for the scout he had laid out. The dim yellow light was enough to show him the section of hedge he had thought was an opening was a slight bend away from him, but a darkened passage lay a few feet further on. He tugged on the cloak to encourage the Jesuit to move towards him just as a shout arose from the edge of the laneway.

They had found the unconscious scout.

Tyburn ducked through the gap in the hedge in an instant, towing the priest behind him. Two men were hammering on the gatehouse door, demanding entrance. The man with the lantern began coursing along the area between the hedge and moat, gripping a long sword that gleamed hungry in the evening murk.

The player paused to get his bearings. He could see the curving arc of the roadway off to the right and the heavy sheltering gloom of the trees to the left. Tugging on the cloak he angled away from the road, staying low and moving slow. From experience he knew that in darkness abrupt movement could often be discerned out of the corner of the eye, even when the shape or source of the movement was hidden. He remembered the night raids they had carried out against Spanish supply trains in the Lowlands, and the morbid sense of imminent discovery that overlaid even the sodden cold and the ache of frozen feet. *There is nothing like Flanders.*

The pursuivants at the manor continued to hammer and shout at the door, which suited Tyburn as their noise helped obscure the rustle and stumbling gait of the two fugitives. A voice from the trees to the right brought the player to an abrupt halt. The Jesuit stumbled into Tyburn who pushed him down with undeserved irritation. Someone had found his horse. Kit yanked the Jesuit back to his feet and turned to the right, moving towards the road.

Richard Topcliffe was impatient. He tightened his grip on the reins. This was the fourth manor house they had raided today, all rumored to be Catholic, all filled with the same impudent and mulish persons who refused and refuted his demands. It was outrageous, he thought, that a man of his stature, a man of Parliament, should be subject to the abuse and dissolute insolence of these Papist landowners. *Rights,* he sneered in derision, *Papists bastards have no rights.* He longed for the opportunity, the joy of subjecting these dogs to a long and searching examination, strapped to his tables. They would howl quick enough then. But it mattered not. He had his writ, signed by Lucy and Leicester, granting him the right to seek for the renegade Jesuit. He hoped that the priest was hidden at Baddesley Clinton, for the land was rich and wide, and the moated manor house, though smallish, was sturdy and appealing to the eye. *A house of traitors*, he thought, a justly awarded prize for the Crown that he was certain could be transferred to him as a reward to destroying this popish plot. Find the Jesuit and all his wishes would be granted.

He felt a quick spur of excitement at the thought of putting a Jesuit to the question, one of the pope's own footsoldiers. He would show him a more commanding strength than their pitiful Inquisition or effeminate papacy could bring. He shivered at the thought of leather straps biting into the priest's trembling flesh. Perhaps he would make Clair Carey watch, he thought, let her see his strength and resolve, then service the bitch with a thrashing, show the priest how a true Englishman rules.

"Have they entered yet?" he called to his servant, his tone biting. "Smitherton, you purblind fool, are they in the manor yet?" His horse whinnied in anxiety. Cursing, Topcliffe raised his shuttered lantern and opened it. In the yellow lanternlight, Smitherton's horse stood alone on the roadway, riderless. "Smitherton, you wretched fool, get back here! You shit on your own time not mine!"

Topcliffe's horse jumped as a huge darkened shape rose out of ground at its feet. Topcliffe caught a glimpse of a whirling sodden enveloping darkness that flew upwards into his face. With a horrific screech he clawed at it, reflexively dropping his grip on the reins. Something grabbed at his foot and snarled. He kicked out and found himself pushed back, falling. He heard the lantern clank and he hit the ground thrashing, suffocating under the wet smothering weight of mud-encrusted cloth. He reached up with his hands and flung the sopping cloak away.

Tyburn waited an instant for the man to inhale a single shocked breath and then struck him over the head. Topcliffe lay still.

"God help me but I enjoyed that," Tyburn said to himself, suppressing a grin. The player grasped the reins of the nervous light grey courser and hissed at the priest, still hidden in the drainage ditch, to grab the other horse. The priest made haste to do so, grabbing the reins of the other animal and whispering to it in a soothing tone.

"You sir, are vicious. You have no cause to behave like an animal."

Tyburn gave the priest a caustic glance. "That rancid piece of shit would rack and burn you, given a chance. He's got the smell of death on him and I'd be serving the world a portion of good were I to slit his gizzard this instant. Now get on that horse, we've miles to go." Tyburn pulled Topcliffe's mount closer and, using his unconscious body as a mounting block, swung up into the saddle. He heard Topcliffe moan in response.

The priest stared at the player, his eyes glittery in the lantern light, but he obeyed and the two men spurred off down the dim roadway.

After several minutes of silence the priest spoke. "Though I cannot condone or accept the violence of your actions, I need to thank you for your assistance in helping me escape. I did have a hiding place in the house but am thankful not to have to test its efficacy."

The player was amused. "Doesn't that make you a bit of a hypocrite? Benefiting from the wages of another's sin while avoiding the pain and the punishment?"

"Had I been aware of the violence of your intentions prior to fleeing the Ferrers, I would have put my fate in God's capable hands and remained in hiding. Accidental benefit from another's sin does not, by circumstance, imply the beneficier was sinful as well. Your sins are your own, I'm afraid." He paused. "You may of course confess your sins, no one is beyond redemption."

"Don't preach at me Father, I haven't the patience for it. God and I fell out a long time past." The priest lapsed into silence.

After riding for more than a mile down the country laneway in the night air and listening for the sound of pursuit, Tyburn was satisfied they were well away from Baddesely Clinton and Topcliffe's pursuivants. There was no sound but the lowing of some distant cattle and the nocturnal buzz of summer insects. He scratched at the mud drying on his face, and doublet, scraping a fine shower of dried mud particles onto the roadway.

"I am curious," the priest said, "how a play-actor ended up doing God's work, rescuing wayward priests? But, how rude of me, though I recognize you from your performance at Charlecote, I should properly introduce myself. I am Father Neville Danby. I am from Colchester, in Essex."

Tyburn ignored the attempted pleasantries. "What you should do is ride."

The priest was nonplussed. "Your performance was good, very articulate. You had a nice, chilling venom in your role as Vice, although it was a bit mannered at times."

"Mannered?" Tyburn couldn't stop himself from asking.

"Yes. A bit false at points. Mind you, only during a couple of your speeches. You seemed to be reciting them from rote, rather than the heart."

"Mannered?" Tyburn repeated.

"Indeed! If I may, you might want to consider your body movement as well, maybe more emphasis on your posture? I knew a chap at the university who could command the stage without a word, just by how he held himself."

"Went to Oxford, did you?"

"Indeed! I studied under Edmund Campion both at Oxford and later at Douai. He helped me reconcile myself to returning to England and our great cause. He provided me with an introduction to your master, Edward Arden."

"By chance, did you know Alec Masterson at Oxford?"

"No, I'm afraid not. Who is he?"

"Just a man you killed with one of your letters." The player sensed rather than saw the priest's confusion. "That's a lethal pen you wield, Father Danby. I tallied up at least four dead on it so far, and the night is still young."

"What are you talking about?" Danby said, confused.

"You must aware that your correspondence has reckoned up a good number of killings, Father. You can't plot treasonous workings without spicing it with a little blood. So far almost everyone associated with delivering your correspondence has ended up as worm food."

"I know nothing of any murders," Danby replied sharp-voiced.

The player reined in his horse and motioned for the priest to stop. Tyburn climbed down from the pale grey beast. It seemed calmer in Topcliffe's absence, a sentiment the player shared. He walked over to the priest's horse and pulled the reins towards him. Puzzled the priest released them. "Give me your hands."

"What?" In the dim light, the Jesuit looked puzzled.

"Your hands."

Comprehension flooded the priest's face. He kicked his heels back and his hand fluttered for the reins. Tyburn pulled the reins taut with his left hand and held the horse tight. He reached across his body and drew his rapier with a slow, deliberate scrape. The blade was a thin line of pale silver in the night.

"Your hands," he repeated.

"Why go to the trouble of preserving me from Topcliffe if you are not here to help? Why would you conduct yourself with such infamy--"

Tyburn extended his arm. The prick of the sword was enough to bring the Jesuit's diatribe to an abrupt halt. He extended his hands. The player yanked one Danby's oversleeves off and sliced it lengthwise, twisting the fabric into a makeshift cord. Tyburn bound the man's hands. Taking the reins in his hands, he sheathed his sword and swung himself astride the pale horse.

"Now listen to me," Tyburn said, "You may not have the foreknowledge or the wit to realize that when you dabble in political machinations and secret treason, there are bloody and painful consequences. And in this case the consequences have befallen a number of people that neither deserved nor dealt in such infamies rather than on you and yours. You will ride with me to where I am going. You will not attempt to escape or hinder me in any way, shape or manner or I will kill you. You won't be the first priest I've killed. I'm already well damned and done, so another log thrown onto that particular pyre is inconsequential to me and, in truth, alive or dead you will suit my needs. Now, am I projecting myself enough or is it still too mannered?" Father Danby was silent, his face pale behind the thin beard. . "We're riding to Wilmcote."

"To what end?" Danby's voice was calm.

"You're a much sought commodity, Father, we'll be making a little exchange."

The priest snorted. "Selling me for gold and ducats or thirty coins of silver. I'm curious how you managed to find me."

"The good high sheriff told me where to find you."

The momentary silence was underscored by the clopping hooves on the uneven roadway and the soughing wind through the elms.

"I refuse to believe that Master Arden would stoop to such a betrayal."

"You can rest your indignation, Father, he didn't. I lied to him."

"So you are a liar, a violent miscreant, a betrayer and a murderer of priests."

"I am indeed. What can I say? War changes a man. Still think I'm salvageable in the eyes of God, Father? Quick to cast that stone, aren't you? Best you look to your own conscience. I wasn't exaggerating the number of dead you can lay at your feet due to your damned correspondence." Scorn colored his voice. Danby was silent for a moment.

"When did you kill a priest?" he asked.

"In Flanders. Fighting the minions of his most gracious Catholic Majesty, Phillip of Spain." Having his hands tied evidently did little to quiet the voluble priest.

"This priest you slew was Spanish?"

Tyburn took a deep exasperated breath. "I can tell you the next one I kill will be English."

Danby gave a mild chuckle. "At this point any death you could provide me would be a present, not a threat. I'm well aware of what will happen once I have been handed over to the authorities so please, indulge me."

Tyburn rode in silence for a several minutes. He could feel the man's patient scrutiny. "He was Spanish, a Dominican I believe, named Father Silvio de Ignace Campillo, an Inquisitor." Tyburn drew the last word out slow. "He was.. . . . practicing his trade in a village outside Goes. The Spanish herded about twenty women, children and folks too old to fight into a barn, barricaded the doors and set it afire. When we arrived, he was standing in front, chanting a victorious *te deum* while the children screamed and roasted. We killed the Spanish soldiers and then I killed him."

"And so you are damned."

"For all eternity," the player said, "along with all the rest of the Protestant heretics in the land."

"And your soul is irredeemable, lost to God." It was not a question.

"Well, I didn't attend Oxford, Father. Doesn't that automatically make me damned?" The priest laughed. "I place more faith in reason than the celestial. A church that burns children wholesale has no place in it for me."

The priest was quiet. After a time he spoke. "You should not allow the acts of mankind to separate you from the kingdom of Heaven or drive you to heresy. Faithfulness is the most sacred excellence and endowment of the human mind."

"That was 'Faithfulness and truth are the most sacred excellences and endowments of the human mind', Father. Be careful when corrupting your Cicero."

Danby arched a brow. "A scholarly brigand, no less."

"Product of a humanist Cambridge education but blood drove my schism, not ink. You would be wise to remember that Father."

The pair rode in silence for several minutes, the player leading the Jesuit's horse. "What lies ahead for me in Wilmcote?"Danby asked. Tyburn thought he could detect an undercurrent of anxiety in the Jesuit's query.

Tyburn thought for a moment and then gave the priest a quick and succinct overview of the situation, concluding, "I exchange you for the boy and the writs are dropped."

The priest snorted in derision. "And you think it will end there for you? I thought you were a 'rational' man of the world? That's the assumption of a fool."

Tyburn nodded. "It had best end there for them, but I suspect they won't cooperate."

"And your plan is to march into the lion's den, bare your flesh for the raking and trust that they will allow you to leave with your reward?"

Tyburn gave the man a thin-lipped, grim smile. "Something like that."

"Best allow me to shrive you now," the Jesuit observed. He recalled the actor's name and on impulse crossed himself--Tyburn, the place of execution. He shuddered.

The priest looked at the player ahead of him, riding the whitish horse, the landscape awash and unsettled in the pallid light of the moon. He stiffened as, unbidden, his memory recalled a passage from Revelations: "And when he had opened the fourth seal, I heard the voice of the fourth beast say, Come and see. And I looked, and behold a pale horse: and his name that sat on him was Death, and Hell followed with him. And power was given unto them over the fourth part of the earth, to kill with sword, and with hunger, and with death, and with the beasts of the earth."

It felt like a cold finger had traced a line down his back, peeling through cloth and skin and bone.

And they rode on.

Chapter the Twenty-third

TYBURN RUBBED HIS eyes. They felt tired and grainy. The deBrage manor house lay before him, bathed in the silk lace of a waning moon. Yellow candlelight flickered in the tall windows in the far wing of the house, but the remainder of the building was dim.

It had been a long ride through the dark night. Despite the light of the moon to guide them, they had lost the road three times. Each time it had been the Jesuit who had steered them back on course for Wilmcote. After more than a year in Warwickshire, the priest knew the rutted local roads well. Baddesley Clinton had been his most recent temporary residence. The priest had shifted locations every few months, holding Mass at various secluded manors and farms, attending gatherings and festivals, dinners and parties, and secretly officiating at baptisms and funerals. Warwickshire was dotted with dozens, if not hundreds, of Catholic families and manors, both great and small. He would arrive by night at a pre-arranged manor house, stay for a week or two and the recusants would trickle in, as word spread that a priest was to be found. Most of the tenants he had visited were ardent Catholics , leaving little chance of any the authorities hearing about his visits. His geographic lore had enabled the two fugitives to chart a winding, if slow, course to the deBrage manor house, situated about a mile north of Wilmcote, near the River Alne.

The player had considered finding a thick copse or a cow byre to wait out the day but he had little faith in Albert deBrage's or Cuttle's sense of restraint. deBrage had given him three days to find the Jesuit, but the player had no illusions about how ill things could go for Will during that time. With Topcliffe hunting them, a day spent crouched in hiding felt like a day wasted. *Better things were done swiftly. Arriving quickly might surprise them.*

The player had been watching the house for more than thirty minutes. He had just completed a slow circuit of the grounds, but as far as he could determine, no pursuivants were in sight. Nothing had stirred except a startled fox who had peered with quizzical yellow eyes at the player crouched in its hayfield before loping back into the night to resume its hunt.

It was time, the player decided. He clambered over the rail fence on the border of the hayfield and slid down into the forested hollow. The two stolen horses were tied to a low tree branch and were stripping the foliage within easy reach. Danby was seated with his back against the bole of a tree, looking remarkably sanguine for a man abducted, tied up and force-marched across twelve miles of countryside in the dead of night. The player felt a mild sense of respect for the pasty priest's fortitude.

"Time to go, Father." "I suppose nothing I could say would dissuade you from this folly?"

"At this juncture, almost anything you say would dissuade me, so by preference, please don't." Tyburn reached down and helped the priest to his feet.

"Thank you."

"And don't thank me, Father, it makes me feel . . . culpable." The churring of a nightjar broke the quiet and the player paused for a moment to listen. Tyburn slid his dagger out of its sheath and cut the bindings around the man's wrists. The priest looked up at the player's dark features in surprise. Kit waved one hand to silence the inevitable enquiry and tied the remnants of the rope into two loops. He slid them over the priest's hands and tightened the cord like a noose. He tucked the two wayward ends into the priest's grip. "There. Keep that tight until it's time, then drop the ends and loose your hands." He pulled a small stiletto blade from one of the saddlebags and slid it into Danby's right boot.

"You might as well keep it," the priest observed. "I will not participate in violence."

"You may find it handy at some point." Tyburn slid his own sword out, gave it a quick inspection and re-sheathed it, adjusting the belt clasps. He removed a dagger from his right belt and replaced it with another shorter, more ornate one, tucking the original in the back of his doublet.

The priest watched the player with a calm look. "This is foolishness."

"Normally I play Vice, but playing Tom Bedlam might do me well for a change," Tyburn replied. "Come on." He led the priest and the horses across the field and down the road towards the manor house. Once close enough to suit, he tied both horses to a fence post and positioned the priest out of sight of the entranceway.

"You'll not run." It was not a question. Danby nodded in reply. The player walked up the stone-paved path to the heavy, iron-bound doorway,. paused before the entrance and muttered the actor's prayer to himself. "Stage set and God Bless." He took the cold chill of the knobby wrought iron door knocker firmly in hand and hammered it down several times. The player waited.

The house was still silent but the empty quiescence he had sensed earlier seemed to have sloughed off. The dark building felt tense and watchful; the faint moonlight on the glass stared outward in reproach and wary observation. He hammered the knocker a second time. The hatch snapped open with a sharp dry click.

"What the fuck do you want?"

Tyburn didn't respond, just stepped backwards so he was visible in the moonlight.

"Wait." The hatch closed. Several minutes trickled past and the door latch snapped. The door swung open and yellow light flooded out. Occluding the light was Cuttle, his short bulk grim and purposeful in the doorway. "Well, well, the play-actor returns. Where's the priest, you capering shit?"

"Where's your master? I don't deal with antics[139]."

"Maybe I just gut you slow and then you tell me where the priest is at?"

"If you're going to keep this dance up all night, I can come back another time. Fetch your master."

"By all means, let him in." Albert deBrage stepped up into the doorway. "You had best have fulfilled your side of the bargain, play-actor."

Tyburn gave Albert a look of scathing contempt. "I said fetch your master, not this lackey."

Albert's expression tightened. "I will slit your cullion throat."

"You aren't the man in charge. Your father is. I deal with him, not with you. Your promises are worthless. You fetch him, and the boy, so I know he is intact and alive. Then I fetch the priest and we make our exchange." Albert's mouth twitched but he forced a nod. The door closed and Tyburn backed away.

Tyburn retreated to the horses, untied them and rode over to where the priest was secreted. He helped Father Danby onto the horse and returned to the front entrance of the manor house. The sky to the east was still dark with no promise of morning yet visible.

The door opened and Cuttle came out. "Here we go," Tyburn muttered to the priest.

"You do have a plan?" Faint trepidation tinted Danby's voice..

---

[139] Clowns

Tyburn responded with a shrug. "We'll trust God to see us through."

"Didn't you tell me that you were damned in the eyes of God?"

"This should be a fair indicator of how well I sit in his graces." Tyburn spurred his horse forward, leading the priest's animal.

Cuttle stopped about twenty feet away. One hand rested on a sword hilt. He spat. "You and the priest go inside. You go down the hall to the right, into the study. Servants are locked up in the west wing, so no trouble."

Or witnesses. "No. We do this outside."

"Coads. We can do it outside, but you don't do it like we say, the boy gets his gizzard split."

Tyburn nodded. "Very well, show me the boy first."

Cuttle canted his head as if in consideration and nodded. "Hawkins, show him the git." The doorway darkened again as Will was shoved bodily into the side of the doorframe. His face was bruised and swollen, but he seemed intact and from the sidelong glare he threw at Hawkins, his spirits seemed unbroken. Tyburn kept his expression impassive.

"Take him in. I'll follow." Tyburn dismounted and led the horses over to a metal ring set in the low wall and tied them off. Danby swung his leg over and slid to the ground. Tyburn drew the finely decorated dagger and, grasping the priest with his left hand, moved the man forward to follow Cuttle down the stone path to the manor house door.

The entranceway opened up into a wide foyer. The left-hand side was taken up by a carved staircase that rose upwards into the gloom of the second floor. The player wasn't sure, but thought he could heard the faint sound of someone on the stair shifting their weight. *That makes at least four.* . They proceeded down the hallway to the right, opening up into the great hall beyond the staircase. At the end of the hall an open door led to the west wing of the house. Cuttle passed through the doorway without pausing and turned to the left. Tyburn stopped in the entrance. "Push the door open as far as it goes,"he told the priest. Danby shoved the heavy oak door back with his bound hands. The door swung partway and stopped; something behind it was blocking it.

"Have your man move out where I can see him," Tyburn said. Albert gestured and a man with thin reddish hair and a slight build moved out of the recesses and into the candlelight. Tyburn gave Danby a nudge and the priest shoved the door until it touched the wall. The player nodded to himself and stepped into the room. The man with the reddish hair took a half-step forward and Tyburn raised his blade to Danby's throat.

"He's worth a great deal less to you if he's dead."

"Atkin, move away." Albert's voice was thick with amused contempt. Tyburn watched the man named Atkin. He was slight, with a narrow hawk face beneath a flat felt hat, but his eyes were cold and steady as he watched the player and the Jesuit step warily into the room. *This might get very bad, very fast.*

The room was high-ceilinged and long, dominated by a robust fireplace at the midpoint of the wall along the left. The light of the fire flung itself about the room in a haphazard rhythm. A long fine wooden table lay down the center of the room with a dozen chairs positioned around it. A silver candleholder holding six lit tapers stood at the centre of the table. Along the far wall in the shadows Tyburn could see a large ornate desk laden with papers and ledgers , but his attention was drawn by the man seated near the fire, attended by Albert deBrage. The white hair and cadaverous face of Clair's father, Sir William deBrage, was immediately recognizable. Cuttle stood several feet to the right, one hand holding Will by the neck, the other on the blade at his belt. Hawkins hung off to the left while Atkin drifted lazily to the right, just in the periphery of Tyburn's vision.

"You wanted to see me, Master Tyburn?" Sir William's voice was sharp and impatient.

"I like to deal with kings, not footmen," Tyburn responded. "It makes negotiations smoother."

"You presume there is something to negotiate, yet there is nothing of the kind. You are calling upon us rather presumptuously, but at my son's invitation so I will indulge this foolishness."

"I was led to believe you were seeking a particular item of value."

The man snorted. "Even dung is worth coin to the cart-man so in that case, yes, a unique and particular item, well-sought but difficult to obtain."

Tyburn nudged Danby and lifted the dagger blade up to prick the priest under the chin. The priest raised his head and sucked in his breath at the touch of the point and then subsided, a puzzled expression flitting over his face. .

"I happen to have access to that item," Tyburn replied.

Albert deBrage smiled a thin and impatient smile. The man peered at Tyburn through the candlelight. "This is the priest?"

"Meet Father Neville Danby, of the *Societas Iesu*, late of the English College of Douai and Essex. Don't get him started talking or you won't get him to shut up."

The elder deBrage's laugh sounded like rusted metal scraped on stone. Albert stepped forward to grab Danby's arm but Tyburn pulled the priest a half-step back. One of Atkin's hands slid behind his back.

"Not your property--yet," Tyburn said with a harsh tone.

"I like you, play-actor." Sir William appraised him from beneath arched brows, as if he were at a horse fair, then laughed dryly. "You have a practical streak in you. I keep forgetting you were a soldier." He gestured at Will. "I could just kill the boy, then kill you. Why shouldn't I have Albert wrap up all the loose ends at once?"

"A dead priest isn't as compelling in court as a live one. Letters," Tyburn said, "can be subject to dispute, signatures can be forged." The player gave Cuttle an ironic glance. "Think about how much more rewarding bringing a live Jesuit to your patron would be, rather than a corpse?"

The silver-haired man nodded in agreement. "True. Leicester would have a more difficult time reneging, and he will be pleased to draw out the trial and humiliation as much as possible. For that privilege, he would pay much."

"Arden."

William deBrage's head snapped around as though jerked by a fishing line. "Clever play-actor, putting all the pieces together. The Earl of Leicester hates our good sheriff. They live in a relationship of mutual concordant despisement. Leicester has titles, privileges, the queen's ear and, some say, her heart, yet Arden mocks and derides him. Arden is a Catholic, pope-loving, preening bastard who also happens to be one of the richest landholders in England."

"Condemn him as a traitor and those lands revert to the Crown."

"Precisely."

"Leicester gets his enemy condemned as a traitor, the Crown gets a Jesuit to rack, Topcliffe gets a new mistress and the lands reverted to the throne are disposed of as appropriate rewards to the men who uncovered the conspiracy. Let me guess--you and Lucy?"

"Rather more us than Lucy. Leicester will take some, the Crown will keep some and a lesser portion will be appointed to our properties, but it will more than triple our current holdings. A good return for a minor investment in blood"--he laughed, a mirthless, hollow sound--"particularly when the blood is someone else's."

deBrage the elder traced the carving on the arm of his chair with a knobby finger. "Land, Master Tyburn, is wealth. It is power. It is *control*. How do you think these lords built their fiefdoms? They acquired and controlled land, stole it or took it by force of arms. The Church was once a supremacy in this realm. It could topple kings, but Henry, ah Henry . . . he broke it. He broke it not by writ or by setting himself as head of the Church, but by dissolving the monasteries, seizing the land and property for the Crown. He took their power, their livelihood, their taxes and their tenants. He maintained his own rule by elevating supporters and laying waste to his enemies. He stripped them of their lands and titles and awarded them to his loyal servants. Our queen does the same. Has she not elevated that Burghley[140] creature to a role high above his natural stature?"

That knobby finger joined with the others on his hand, tightening in a white-knuckled grip on the chair arm. "I know what they say at court about us. They mock my family and my son as unfit for advancement, as not of the proper blood or familial connections, as low-born weavers of plots and entanglements, yet we have served the Crown for years. When that bloody bitch-cur Mary was on the throne we kept faith with England's Church. We supported Elizabeth when she came to the Crown, we helped burn the faithless Papists who would have toppled her, stood by her with monies and arms and men when the North rose and she ignored us. She rebuked my son for killing that spavined court bastard that insulted us and now--now we have one of her favorites kissing our arse for the opportunity to lay low his enemy and raise up his esteem." He steepled his fingers. "At our moment of triumph, the end of more than a year of planning, all our ends are pulled askew by a landless bastard player."

He turned and glared at Albert, his eyes hot with anger. "All because you cannot follow the simplest of tasks, to follow the courier chain back to the Jesuit and reclaim the letter with Arden's signature. I wonder at times if the court rumors of your ruinous stupidity are not true, for the evidence is laid before me." Albert's face was flaring red in the firelight. Rage danced under his expression but his eyes, Tyburn noticed, were fixated on his father.

Sir William held his thin hands out to catch the warmth of the fire. "Forgive me, the bones of an old man require rather more warmth than most. So you see, Master Tyburn, everyone receives rewards." There was a thump as he tossed a leather purse onto the

---

[140] William Cecil, 1st Baron Burghley served as Secretary of State and chief advisor of Queen Elizabeth I. He was appointed Lord High Treasurer in 1572.

long trestle table. Tyburn glanced at it. "You've captured a Jesuit priest, play-actor! You've helped prevent a conspiracy to attack the throne. You deserve to be amply rewarded. You may take the boy. The writs against you will be withdrawn. The coin in that purse is more than adequate recompense for your troubles."

Tyburn ignored the purse. As soon as he released the Jesuit, he and the boy were dead, deBrage's proclamations of surety notwithstanding.

A metallic snap-click behind him made the player stiffen but out of the corner of his eye, he could see Atkin's head turn to the left and his eyes narrow. It wasn't fear; Atkin was one of those men that lived in a place well beyond fear. It was caution and a chill assessment that made the man's thin face twitch.

"This nonsense has gone on long enough." Clair's quiet voice came out of the open doorway. The ornate wheellock pistol she held with two hands was pointed at Albert. "You two, move over there." She held the long weapon rock-steady and nodded towards the table. Hawkins and Atkins both sidestepped over to it.

"Clair. What do you think you are doing? This is business for men." Her father's voice was cutting. "Put that weapon down and remove yourself. You have no place here."

"I'm a widow, Father, and no longer answerable to you." She smiled with bitter emphasis. "I am not one of your hounds to be ordered about."

"What about whipped?" Albert sneered. "I will have you scourged, you bitch."

"Anything else to say, dear brother?" The round muzzle canted upwards to aim at Albert's eyes and he settled back at the sight of it.

Clair stepped forwards until she stood beside Tyburn. Without looking she asked "How are you, master player?"

"You need to leave, my lady."

"I saw your arrival from the stairs," she said, still not looking at him. "You looked like a man swept in upon a tide."

"You need to leave now, Clair."

"No. I told you, I'm not answerable to you or any other man. My father saw fit to involve my life in his plots, so now he need suffer my interference. Take the boy and the priest and go."

Atkin began to drift to the left. His right hand, just visible below his long sleeve, cupped the butt of a stiletto.

"Let me have the gun, Clair," said Tyburn. She shook her head but when he grasped it by the barrel with his left hand, she let go. The pistol had a familiar heft to it. Tyburn had carried a similar weapon through the Low Countries. Wheellocks were simultaneously elegant in design and complex in their mechanics. Unlike matchlocks, they needed no burning cord to ignite their powder charge, relying instead on a sophisticated spring mechanism and an iron pyrite striker mounted on the end of a metal lever called a dog. Clair had the dog cocked and ready to fire. A gentle squeeze of the trigger would release the wheel spring, spinning against the dog and igniting the powder charge in the pan.

For a moment Tyburn leveled the gun at Atkin until the latter stepped well back. The player rotated the dog forward, uncocking the weapon. He smiled and tucked the gun butt-first into the front of his open doublet, taking care to keep the barrel elevated. In Flanders, he had seen untamped pistol balls and powder charges roll out of the barrel of the pistol as soon as the person carrying them let the barrel dip. He doubted if Clair knew of the trick of wrapping the balls in cloth or leather wadding to prevent slippage.

"Now where were we?" he asked in an even tone.

Clair's head whipped around, her eyes shocked. "What are you doing? You can't--"

"Quiet." Tyburn's voice was the same as it had been in the hallway when Topcliffe had accosted her. The look on his face was implacable, hard like a woodcut. Clair stared at the man, stricken. She took a half-step away, her stomach clenching. Her breath was fast and shallow. Her pulse hammered in her ears.

"We need to conclude this business, gentlemen." Tyburn's voice sounded distant and harsh. Clair felt a hot flood of anger course through her, bringing a flush to her face. The player did not meet her eyes.

Albert deBrage gestured to Cuttle. "Give him the boy." Cuttle gave Will a shove that sent him sprawling in front of the fireplace.

"What makes you think I want that addled little git?" Will froze on his knees. Albert stared at the player, uncomprehending.

"If not the boy, what do you want from us, Master Tyburn?" Sir William deBrage was watching the player, a look of fierce concentration on his face.

"Not some glover's son. Or even that cold bitch. In Flanders, I was a soldier. We killed the godless Spaniards. We killed Flemish traitors. We killed the Dutch when they cheated us. We took what we needed and damned all but our own company. We had respect, we had acclaim and honour. No one fucked with us and lived." He paused to look at each face in the room, and then continued. "Now I'm a piece-meal player, a rag-tag, a wastrel you called me. I dance a jig on the boards for half-pennies and breadcrumbs. I'm answerable to a fat, bloated fool who dangles a handful of groats in front of me and makes me caper for it. I'm tired of it."

Sir William nodded.

"I want what you have--money, power, land. I want the respect due me. I'm not some low-born bastard player, I'm a gentleman and this," he gestured, "is my opportunity to have the Great Wheel raise me back to my proper station."

Albert rolled his eyes in derision. "Your proper station is licking out the privy."

"Quiet." The elder deBrage pushed himself out of his chair and stepped forward, his gaze pointed and fixed on the player. "What are you proposing?"

"A partnership," Tyburn replied. "Not an equal one--it is your plan, long set in motion, but I've brought you the key to its success, and that equates to a share. Not a purse of coins, a partnership. God's bones, but you need a dependable right hand for acting with precision and intelligence. That's well beyond Cuttle or Hawkins here, or your antic son, for that matter."

"Damn you, sir. Damn you." Clair's voice was steady, though her face was mottled.

Sir William looked thoughtful.

"You cannot be--" Albert seethed. His father waved him to silence with one absent hand.

"It may be worth consideration," Sir William said. "But I am uncertain whether you bring anything or merit of real value." He glanced up and Tyburn felt the weight of the man's gaze with palpable intensity. "What can you do for us that we do not already have in hand, Master Tyburn?"

The player's gaze locked with de Brage's and then shifted sidelong to the glover's son kneeling on the flagstones.

"Give him to me."

deBrage followed Tyburn's look and nodded. "I think I begin to see. Furnish him the boy."

The player kicked the Jesuit behind the knees and forced him down into a kneeling position on the floor. Hawkins pulled Will to his feet and bodily pushed him across to sprawl on the floor beside the priest. Danby tried to give Will a reassuring smile but the stiff rictus on his face did nothing to alleviate the fear Will felt growing inside of him.

Tyburn took a deep breath. "You two, step back." He pointed at Atkin and Hawkins. They moved away. He reached down and pulled Will to his feet. The boy was shaking his head. "No, please, no!"

"Quiet, boy."

"You cannot do this, before God you cannot . . . in the name of Our Saviour . . ." Tyburn gave the priest a booted kick in the ribs that cut off his speech. Clair watched in mounting confusion. Will tried to pull away but the player held his arm in an iron grip. "Don't make this harder than it needs to be, boy," he grated, hauling the boy back. As Will opened his mouth to shout, Tyburn's left hand covered it.

The player leaned his head down and muttered in the boy's ear. "I did tell you no one ever shows their true face to the world. Your turn on stage. Goodbye, Will." The boy tried to pull away with frantic movements but the player wasted no time. He leaned back in a half-turn, lifting the boy until his feet were off the ground. His right hand crossed in front and the decorative blade slid into the boy's chest. Will thrashed for an instant, a muffled cry coming from his mouth as Tyburn held him fast, wriggling in spastic and frantic motion like a fish on a line. The only sound in the room was the crackle of the fire and Clair's sobbing. Red blood began to seep from under the hand covering the boy's mouth. The player lowered the boy to the floor in a slow and deliberate motion. Dark blood began to pool around the small body, gleaming in the firelight. Tyburn glanced down at his red-laced left hand and turned back to pull the Jesuit back to his feet.

Tyburn felt his head snap back as Clair hit him full across the jaw. He shook his head and pushed the woman away as she scrabbled for the wheellock. She stumbled backwards and Atkin grabbed her by the arms, his face expressionless but his eyes gleaming. The player rubbed his jaw and gave Clair a look that seemed to promise retribution. Atkin's hands were tight on her elbows and his thin body pressed against her. His beard rasped against her neck.

"You murderous bastard." Clair's voice broke more with each syllable..

"I'm already well-damned. Another body or two along Fate's path won't make much difference now." Tyburn did not so much as turn his head. He was watching Sir William, who at the instant the player had slid the blade home, had a slight, twisted half-smile on his face, a passing momentary gleam of triumph. The player slid a foot under Will's limp body and rolled the boy under the lip of the long table. Danby began a mumbled prayer.

"Are we in concordance?"

Sir William smiled, an expression not reflected in his eyes. "You do have that air of usefulness about you. I think we can come to an agreement that will greatly enrich your state."

"Your word on it."

"My word and oath, Master Tyburn. But I would have you hand back that weapon." deBrage resumed his seat and looked at the actor with expectant eyes. Without any perceptible hesitation, Tyburn pulled the wheellock from his belt, checked to make sure it was not cocked, and handed it butt-first to the elder deBrage. Sir William hefted the gun, giving the player a long look, and then handed it to Albert.

"Your agreement won't help you." Clair's voice was ragged but determined. Atkin, still gripping her around the waist with his left arm, reached across to cover her mouth. Clair twisted in his grasp until Albert waved him to desist.

"Poor Clair," he said in a caustic tone. "Your player has deserted you for better company, and soon we'll see you off to Topcliffe's Yorkshire estate. A few months with his company should teach you to temper that mouth. He has better uses for it."

"I burned the letters."

The air froze.

Sir William's head snapped around.

"I burned them. All of them. Both packets."

The elder deBrage bent down and without a word began to scrabble at the front base facing of his ornate chair. He tugged out the drawer hidden behind the carved face. It was empty. A harsh sound mourned deep in his chest; he sank in his seat. His voice was low. "You wouldn't."

"I did."

"She burned them?" Albert's voice held an odd note. Sir William ignored him.

Clair laughed. Sir William was clutching his chair arms, his fingers once again white on the dark wood. He was struggling to speak. "Why would you do such a thing? You have destroyed your family, Clair, laid ruin to your inheritance."

"My inheritance? My bequest from you is nothing but pain and enduring humiliation. You lay suit on my in-laws and husband's property and you farm me out to Topcliffe as a whore as my inheritance. I do not accept that fate. You entangle me in your connivances, so I exercise my right to decline with the sole weapon at my disposal-- since my allies desert me." She shot the player a look.

Albert repeated his question. "She burned them?" Tyburn watched Albert's face, his face taut and white in the firelight. Clair and Sir William continued to ignore him, their faces intent on each other. Albert's knuckles whitened in tension. Cuttle was shifting his weight, his hand around the weapon at his belt.

"You know what was in your Jesuit letters, Master Tyburn? What you place your avaricious hopes upon?" Her eyes beneath the tangled mess of auburn hair were angry. Atkin tightened his grip around her waist and held her immobile. "Nothing. No conspiracy to overturn the Crown, no secretive correspondence to assassinate the queen." She laughed again, the sound bitter and hot. "It was a draft of a letter to the Crown, calling for tolerance and permission to service the Catholic souls of England. No papal army, no uprising, no murderous Spanish plot--just a measured, polite and very prayerful entreaty for the queen to cease oppression of the Faith in return for a pledge of loyalty to England and the Crown."

She turned her head to glare at her father again. "That's why you had to separate the letters into two packets. A boring, pedestrian petition for Catholic worship is not near as overt or threatening as a Spanish and papal conspiracy against the Crown, so you removed all the letters that were open to interpretation to use as evidence to implicate Arden, and hid the rest."

Clair's father slumped in his chair, his face sagged. "Do you know what you've done? You've ruined us, girl. Destroyed your family's fortune. You've flung us into the muck. Leicester won't settle for the priest, he wanted to destroy Arden and Arden's power in Warwickshire and in court. Those letters were his weapons and our ladder to fortune, property and high office--and you've flung us into the muck." His voice was ragged.

"We still have the Jesuit," Albert said. "Leicester will . . ."

Sir William laughed, the contempt in his voice almost palpable. "You don't listen, do you boy? You never listen. Your ears and your head are clogged with shit. It's over. We have the Jesuit, but Leicester won't share that credit. Without the letters implicating Arden, we can't link Arden to the Jesuit and the conspiracy. We made promises, assurances! Leicester isn't a forgiving man. Without the letters he can't condemn Arden or his properties. It means we get nothing." He coughed and for the first time that night looked his age. "Two years of planning, all that work, all that . . . killing. Gone, gone because of a daughter's selfish displeasure and son's venal stupidity." He fluttered his hands like a man afflicted with palsy. "Like sand through my fingers."

Albert's face was shadowed and drawn in the firelight. "We are too far along to let this go. We forge some letters, rack the priest, create the evidence."

"No, it's over." Sir William sounded tired.

"Have your stones withered with age? We don't just let some missing scraps of parchment keep us from our fortune." Albert spat the words in venomous rage.

"There is no longer any point."

"It's not over, we still have the Jesuit. He's worth a small fortune in the right hands."

"Once we hand him to Leicester, we don't control that reward."

"We don't give him to Leicester," Albert continued doggedly.

"We can't afford Leicester for an enemy. Topcliffe and Lucy are Leicester's men and they won't cross him. Once we lost the proof of Arden's complicity, we lost any control we had over Leicester. He's spent a fortune on the queen's progress. He will be looking to recoup, not to share. For vengeance, he would grant us a portion of someone else's fortune, for this . . . for this he will just take. It is over." Sir William sounded tired but spoke with finality.

"It is not over." Albert tugged the wheellock pistol from his belt, cocked the dog forward into position and fired into the side of his father's head.

Chapter the Twenty-fourth

THE HEAVY BALL punched through deBrage's skull, sending a wet red splash of bone and brain matter into the fire. The force of the shot sent the man sprawling sideways against the heavy arm of his tall wooden chair and then reeling back again. In the enclosed space of the long room, the thunderclap of the pistol felt like a punch to the chest. The body twitched and, as Clair watched in horror, half toppled, half slid in an ungainly pile out of the ornate seat. The upper portion of Sir William's head was misshapen and gaping though the torn and lacerated scalp. Blood, black in the flickering light of the fire, ran like smoke across the flagstones. The fire sizzled and spat as the blood and brain matter thrown into the flames smoldered.

"It is not over." Albert said, his voice clipped and precise, powder smoke wreathed about him like a matching shadow.

Clair's intake of breath said more than any scream or cry. It had the staccato rhythm of wind-blown rain. Tyburn could taste bile in the back of his throat. He watched Albert deBrage. The man's eyes were pinpoints, tiny beads of light glittering in the firelight, empty and unreadable.

The silence was broken by Albert's laugh. "I should have rid myself of that irritant a long time ago. Too often he curbed my steps." His gaze darted up to his sister. "Why so shocked, Clair? You've hated him for years."

Clair looked shaken. She raised her head and looked at her brother. "I never hated him, I hated what I've seen him become: a manipulative, secretive and venal old man obsessed with his land and his standing. You . . ." She said in a tired, passionless voice, "You I just despise as vicious."

Her brother laughed. "Careful, I may not even bother giving you to Topcliffe. You can be partial payment to Atkin here. He looks like he would enjoy your company, and Atkin has so few enjoyments." The thin man holding Clair gave a slight smile that looked out of place on his hatchet face. One hand slid up from around her waist to cup her breast through the thin material of her gown, his long, pale fingers spreading. She flinched.

Tyburn slid his left hand under the back of his doublet, his fingers closing surreptitiously around the dagger. He glanced to his right, assessing the distance to the pair.

"Now, on to more pressing matters," Albert said. "Time to slit the player's throat."

"No partnership?" said Tyburn in mock disappointment.

Albert chuckled. "My father was never a play-goer, he failed to appreciate the depth of your craft. I, on the other hand, have seen enough plays to know when you are performing. You came for the fortune tied to that priest and thought you could sway my father with that nonsense. It might have worked; he was gullible enough but I can see through that tapestry. Under that player's exterior, you are just a man consumed with anger. You came for your vengeance, as I knew you would, as I myself would." He paused. "And possibly you came for her. You do seem like the sort of romantic, half-chivalrous fool who would walk through fire for a cause or a woman." He smiled. "Don't worry, Atkin and Cuttle will assuage her. I fear Master Topcliffe will be a recipient of damaged goods, but he has never struck me as the type to differentiate." He tossed the spent wheellock onto the table with a clatter. "Kill him," he ordered Cuttle.

Tyburn threw the ornate dagger in his right hand at Cuttle's face, and gave the still-kneeling priest a hard shove forward so he sprawled into Hawkins's and deBrage's feet. He pivoted to the right. The second dagger flashed in his left hand, its long blade searing upward and across as he took two quick steps and lunged with clockwork precision over Clair's left shoulder.

Clair saw the movement and had no time to react except with an instinctual shudder. The glinting steel caught her long tresses before it slammed into Atkin's exposed neck. Tyburn released the dagger and skipped backwards, his right hand drawing his sword. Clair felt Atkin's nerveless hands fall away and the touch of hot biting pain as the exposed edge of the dagger sliced against the top of her gown and into her flesh as the man fell. Atkin's fall canted Clair over sideways as the dagger, tangled in her hair, pulled them down in a macabre tandem onto the floor. Atkin was choking on blood. She winced and felt through the snarl of her tresses until she found the pommel of the weapon. Pushing down on the wriggling Atkin with her left hand, she grasped the pommel with her right and pulled hard. The dagger slid free and Clair fell away. Her left side was drenched in blood. She could smell the coppery scent in the air. Atkin's hand scrabbled at her arm but she rolled to the side and kicked at the man. His breath misting the air with blood, Atkin subsided onto the floor, his fingers still drumming useless against the wood parquet.

She turned and saw Tyburn moving backwards, blade up, with Hawkins and Cuttle advancing. The two men came in a rapid advance, sidestepping Danby and trying to close the short distance. From an instinct born of dozens of street fights and back-alley tussles, Cuttle knew they had to close on Tyburn and press him, not to give him the time or space to bring his rapier skills into play.

Tyburn's left heel cracked hard against a chair, and he slipped as he stepped backwards. He staggered and parried a quick thrust from Cuttle. Hawkins, better schooled in sword-fighting than Cuttle, timed his attack a beat behind Cuttle's, hoping to catch the player's arm or chest. Tyburn, lacking an off-hand weapon for defense, resorted to a quick slap of his gloved hand to push the thrust out of line.

Hawkins drew his dagger with his left hand and gave a sudden terrified shout as something wrapped around his left leg. He looked down in time to see the dead glover's son wrapping his arms around his leg, shouting. The boy's mouth was wide and bloody, his face twisted in a grimace of fear and anger. Hawkins felt a moment of genuine terror, like a cold scream echoing in his head, at the sight of the spectral dead child trying to pull one of his tormentors into an abyssal hellmouth. He paused for a fleeting moment in panic and lifted his sword intending to plunge it downward into the boy's exposed back. A pair of hands reached around his arm and yanked it back.

It was the priest.

Danby sat up after the two men plunged past just in time to see Will roll over under the table. The boy paused to spit out the small stage blood bladder that Tyburn had palmed into his mouth when he held him and then reached out with frantic hands to catch Hawkin's leg. Danby saw the man stagger off-balance and then look down, turning the blade towards the young boy. The priest hauled himself up and threw his thin frame across the space, grasping at the man's arms. Hawkins bellowed in anger, but off-balance from the boy entangling his legs he staggered sideways, knocking the slouched corpse of Sir William deBrage from its heavy chair. Will, all bravado gone, released Hawkins's leg and scrambled away under the table.

Hawkins, roaring with rage, shoved Danby off. He kicked the fallen priest hard in the face and the man sank to the flagstones in front of the fire.

"Enough!" said Albert deBrage, "That one we need alive. Kill the boy, he seems more your size to deal with. I'll scourge that damned play-actor." Albert drew his silvered rapier and long dagger and strode past the sprawled priest.

Cuttle's uncompromising attacks afforded Tyburn no respite. He had been pushed back to the far end of the room, bottled up by the long table. Tyburn blocked another quick thrust and felt the blade razor past his chest, ripping a long but shallow cut through his doublet and the skin underneath. He countered in a fury and with a quick lunge forced his attacker back a pace. Looking to his side, he saw deBrage advancing in his direction. Tyburn cursed under his breath. He was going be trapped in the corner by the far door if he didn't move.

He countered Cuttle's thrust, pushing forward and forcing the two blades upwards. He kicked out a booted foot and caught Cuttle just above the knee. The man cursed and stepped back but the player ignored the opening and taking advantage of the momentary respite, took two quick steps and rolled across the wide dining table, sending a set of decorative glassware crashing to the floor and brass candle holders flying.

This area of the room was much wider, Tyburn noted with satisfaction. It would give him the space he needed to start controlling this fight, rather than being trapped in the constricted area between the table and the wall and ending up pinned to the wall like a butterfly on a board. He bent and picked up the brass polished candleholder in his left hand, feeling the weight and the heft of it. It wasn't a *main gauche*[141] but might suffice.

Cuttle came around the end of the table with a look of impatient fury suffusing his face. His earlier success with his reckless lunging sword attacks had given him confidence and he

---

[141] Literally "left-hand" in French. The main gauche was a defensive parrying weapon, usually a dagger with a slightly wider guard although the use of other off-hand weapons such as a buckler, a sword-breaker or even a cape were also well-known.

moved without hesitation or pause. Tyburn shifted his stance and parried Cuttle's low attack with his rapier, circling over his opponent's heavier blade and pushing it out and down. Cuttle attacked with knife-fighter's speed but the player was quicker. Tyburn stepped in with his left foot and whipped the heavy candleholder up and across like a man driving in a builder's spike. The solid base caught the short Southwark knife artist across the face, smashing his nose. Cuttle reeled back just as deBrage's blade flicked past Tyburn's throat. The player backpedaled and regained his balance, flipping the rapier up to deflect the off-hand dagger deBrage drove at his torso.

deBrage rocked back and forth on the balls of his feet in a gentle and unhurried rhythm, his left foot forward, and began to circle to the right, his ornate blade held low in a broad ward. The dagger was in his gloved left hand, held mid-height. As he circled, he was back-lit by the red glow of the fire.

Tyburn could feel the blood from the cut he had received running down his side. It must have been deeper than he thought. He gripped his rapier tighter and hefted the heavy candlestick holder, giving it a light twirl. He forced a smile. *Nothing was more disconcerting than a smiling enemy holding steel.*

deBrage smiled back. The player moved in with a quick thrust high and inside, intent on ripping deBrage's grin from his face. The parry was quick and the counter vicious. The dagger deflected Tyburn's rapier outside and deBrage's long blade slithered in with lethal intent. Tyburn batted it aside with the candlestick and narrowly escaped a quick back-cut at his hand. The two continued to circle.

Hawkins pitched a chair to one side as he closed on his prey. The glover's son had rolled under the long table but was impeded by a heavy set of ornate chairs. Before Will was able to squeeze past the chairs and the table leg, a hand seized his ankle and, with a tremendous pull and a clatter of wood, yanked him back.

"Hold still, you fucking capon!" Hawkins muttered, as he fumbled for his dagger with his right hand while pressing the wriggling Will onto the floor. Hawkins felt a red hot pain lance through his foot. Shocked, he glanced down to see a thin stiletto protruding from the midpoint of his booted foot. In desperation, Danby had stabbed the blade that Tyburn had given him into the man's foot. Hawkins bellowed and released the boy. He tried to turn towards the sprawled priest but the thin blade had penetrated deep, pinning his foot to the dark wooden floor. Hawkins bent over to grasp the handle of the weapon.

It was the last bad decision he would ever make.

Clair rose from the floor in the uncertain light, the knife that Tyburn had killed Atkin with firm in her right hand. Her face and side were sheeted in scarlet and firelight. She looked like Tisiphone[142], her visage a tangled and calescent Fury. She raised the blade and plunged it downwards, driving it deep into Hawkins's upper back.

Hawkins arched in surprise and twisted sideways, the look on his face a hybrid of horror and amazement. His free hand scrabbled to reach the blade and his mouth gaped. The knife tore free and her hands rose and fell a second and third time in succession. Hawkins's shocked expression slackened as he slumped to the floor. Clair's determined anger vanished as the impact of her action began to sink in. She released her grip on the weapon and it clattered to the red-rimmed floor. By reflex she wiped her hands on her blood-soaked gown. Will sat up and slid across the floor away from the corpse, careful not to touch it. He reached out and grasped her hand, shivering. Clair looked at the boy's pale drawn face, his eyes fixed on the body, took a deep breath and looked around.

The player and her brother were circling, blades out, intent on their chilling dance. As she watched her brother lunged, twisting his rapier. The steel blades scraped and rang as Tyburn parried the

---

[142] One of the Furies from Greek mythology, Tisiphone is known as the avenger of murder. Her name means 'voice of revenge.' In the Aeneid she is described as 'clothed in a blood-wet dress'.

blow. Cuttle was on his hands and knees at the far end of the table, shaking his head and trying to stand. He looked up and caught Clair's gaze. His dark eyes moved from Clair to Hawkins's body on the floor, then at Atkin's still corpse, then. back at Clair without expression. With deliberate slowness, Cuttle clambered up, picked up his sword and staggered towards the doorway. He leaned on the jamb to catch his breath, and without a backward glance abandoned his employer.

Albert deBrage was enjoying himself. From the instant he had pulled the trigger an almost giddying sense of relief and triumph soared through him. His. It was all his now. The man whose shadow had darkened all aspects of his life was gone and with it the endless crushing control the man had imposed on him. Years of bitter, acrid restraint and suppression ended with the gentle pressure of a finger. He laughed and darted his sword in a quick testing cut. The play-actor was a good swordsman but deBrage knew he was better; he could sense it when their blades met, in the hesitation the player exhibited in countering. The steel always knew. He would kill this man, watch him die choking on his own blood. He would stare into Tyburn's eyes as his life faded, smiling all the while.

The fight had turned the player away from the door, so he was unable to see Cuttle's departure. All Tyburn had was an itching awareness that he needed to finish this fight fast, before the odds shifted too far in deBrage's favour. He had seen Clair strike down Hawkins out of the corner of his eye but the cold reality was that he was all that stood between the others and slaughter. deBrage would kill them all, including his own sister. Tyburn could see it in the red glint in the man's hooded eyes. He had seen it in the eyes of men in Flanders, drunk on the heady scent of death, men beyond any moral bounds. Even the monetary gain to be had from the priest would not stay his hand. Tyburn watched his opponent as he moved. One foot followed the other in a flowing and elemental movement, graceful and deadly, as inexorable as the tide. The player doubted he would catch this man in an error; he was too well-schooled as a swordsman.

The two blades flashed and met in a persistent jangle of metal. deBrage caught Tyburn's long blade on his off-hand dagger and the point of his rapier drove in. Tyburn sidestepped the thrust and drove the heavy candlestick downward and away against the blade, pushing it offline. deBrage slid the weapon back and disengaged. Tyburn felt the first stirring of an idea.

deBrage flipped his blade upwards, slicing at Tyburn's eyes and Kit took the cut on the forte of his sword, his elbow bent to absorb the impact. Albert's dagger came in from the right, driving at his arm. The player tried to retreat but the edge seared across his upper arm. The player skipped back two quick steps and cursed, feeling the blood flowing down his arm. *Time*, he thought, *was getting short.*

Tyburn watched the man. In the wavering fire light, sword instinct ruled. The long quavering shadows made it difficult to discern movement. Every nerve felt wire-tense, stretched taut and afire. deBrage was patient, waiting for Tyburn's wound to weaken him, for the blood to flow down his arm and impede the grip on his rapier. *God curse a patient swordsman*, Tyburn thought. Impatient in everything else in life, deBrage had learned it only in swordplay.

Give him what he wants. Tyburn heard it like a clear voice in his head. He moved. The attack was sudden. One second the player was hovering in a defensive posture, the next the blade was searing in, corkscrewing in over deBrage's weapon.

deBrage all but shouted in exultation at the move, parrying the attack with his dagger and driving his own sword at the player's exposed side.

Tyburn slammed the candlestick base in his left hand downwards with impossible speed, driving the rapier down hard. The weapon's tip caught the wooden flooring, penetrating a fingerwidth, but enough that the heavy falling candlestick forced the length of the rapier downwards. The steel flexed impossibly and then with a sharp vibrant crack, the blade broke.

deBrage didn't hesitate. He released the broken blade and slammed his bent elbow hard into Tyburn's stomach.

Tyburn spun left to get clear as the dagger slid past. His opponent rolled across the open floor to his right and reached his free hand under the edge of the table, grabbing the ornate dagger Tyburn had thrown into Cuttle's face at the beginning of the fight. The player rolled back to his feet and lunged with the rapier. *Too slow*, Tyburn thought in frantic alarm.

Albert stepped aside as the blade drove past. deBrage's leg lashed out and cut the player's feet from under him. Tyburn crashed down. The off-hand dagger slammed into the edge of Tyburn's doublet, severing the stitching along the side, pinning the loose material to the floor. Tyburn heard the sound of cloth ripping as he tried to rise only to have deBrage's knee slam into the side of his head.

Light flared in his eyes and the player slumped back. He tried to rise a second time but a heavy weight was pressing down on his chest. He forced his eyes to focus and in the red lambent gleam of the firelight could see Albert deBrage's smiling face inches away. The man was kneeling on his chest, one foot holding down Tyburn's right arm, knee on the player's chest. Tyburn could feel the hard line of deBrage's main-gauche dagger against his ribs, pinning his torn doublet to the floor. He sensed the trickle of blood down his side where the weapon had sliced the flesh over his ribcage.

Albert could taste salt sweat and the tang of blood in his mouth. He was panting. In the distance he could hear his sister crying and the priest Danby urging the boy and Clair to run but he ignored them, intent upon his prey. He slapped the player across the face.

"Focus, focus, play-actor. Focus on me." He murmured, "I plan to savour every moment of this. My regret is that you won't see me slit my sister's throat before yours." He paused to shrug slightly. "Sometimes one just can't help these things." Tyburn tried to move his arm, but a wave of dizziness washed over him. He could feel the pommel of his rapier under his fingers. He tried to close his hand around it.

deBrage lifted the dagger he had recovered from under the table and smiled again. "This is the enjoyable part."

Staring intently into Tyburn's eyes, Albert slammed the blade into the player's chest. Tyburn's eyes went wide for an instant and then focused on deBrage. The two men locked eyes for an instant and holding deBrage's gaze, Tyburn forced his head up high enough to whisper one soft word into the space between them.

"Prop."

Albert froze and felt, in that brief moment, the wrongness of the blade in his hands, the lack of resistance, of any indication of penetration. Tyburn saw the realization flood into the man's eyes as the player's fingers closed on the pommel of the rapier. Tyburn shoved the dark-clad man backwards hard and whipped the rapier into line.

The worn blade slid without any resistance through the side of Albert's neck and ten inches out the other side. Tyburn twisted the blade.

He felt rather than saw the spray of arterial blood from the man's torn throat. He stared into Albert's eyes, looking for a growing recognition or realization of what awaited him. The anger and hatred flared and dropped into emptiness, a void that reflected the shadow and red light of the room until Albert toppled without a sound to the wooden floor.

Tyburn slumped back, his head swimming. From a great distance he heard Clair's voice asking, "Is he dead?"

Tyburn opened his eyes to see her, her face and hair plastered with blood down one side, kneeling beside her brother.

"Better be," Tyburn said to himself. He sat up, shrugging off the torn doublet that was still pinned to the floor by deBrage's dagger. He hauled himself up and fell into one of the chairs. His hand was trembling. He closed it into a fist and held it hard against his stomach until it subsided.

There is nothing like Flanders.

Tyburn looked up. The room had a strange carmine glow to it, like sunset burning beneath deep cloud as the firelight reflected off the puddle of blood where William deBrage's body sprawled. He should, he reflected, be as stunned and horrified as everyone else by the carnage but he found himself oddly comforted by the sight. He had been on enough battlefields that it was a familiar sort of horror, one leavened, he recognized, by a certain feeling of elation that rose in the aftermath of a fight, something experienced by survivors.

The fear and stale, acid taste of guilt and horror would come after.

Will scuttled out from underneath the table. The boy glanced once at deBrage's torn throat and looked away with swift speed. He coughed and then wiped his wet eyes with his torn sleeve. When he raised his pale face, his expression was tight but controlled. The boy looked at the player with a frank, appraising stare.

"You look a mess," the boy observed. Tyburn laughed.

"Where's Cuttle?"

"Fled." The terse reply came from Danby who paused in his wide circuit of the table to secure and lock the door to the room. "By Christ's holy light, player, you do leave a shambles in your wake." He gazed at the player's injuries with a jaundiced eye. "You should heal well enough, provided you avoid strong drink and have a barber-surgeon bleed you for your humours."

Tyburn shook his head. He had a soldier's fear of surgeons, having watched too many men die from minor wounds that festered and blackened. He would find a good mid-wife who knew how to sew and had a ready supply of poultices.

"Nice to see you alive, Master Shakespeare," Tyburn said to Will.

Will smiled for an instant and took a quick glance around. He wiped his mouth and made a face. "Will I ever be rid of that taste? What was that swill?"

"Chicken blood and vinegar. Got it from the same place I nabbed the prop dagger--Warwick's Men. Ran into Cleve and some fellows at Kenilworth, they were happy enough to pass it on loan. It seemed the best way to get them off-balance long enough to get you out and safe, Will. I didn't expect it to end up in this mayhem." Tyburn didn't look at the boy as he spoke, his eyes watching Clair with open concern. He fingered the wound on his side, grimacing at the red on his fingertips, hissing at the sharp pain.

Clair turned her head. Her eyes were wet. Tyburn met her gaze. "I'm sorry, Clair."

Clair wiped her hands on her gown, and moved away from her fallen brother. She knelt in front of Tyburn's chair, her face level with his. She took his head in both hands, leaned in and he felt the touch of her lips on his. He could taste salt tears and blood. When the kiss ended she whispered in his ear: "My brother has been dead to me for a long time."

Tyburn nodded and traced her cheek with his fingertips. He was unsure what else to say in response. Saying more seemed like a waste of breath, yet saying nothing seemed equally callous.

"You are skilled at weaving tales, Master Tyburn. How does one explain a dead knight, slain son and butchered servants? Or do we all flee into the night like so many rufflers?" Danby gestured at the red ruin that was the study.

Tyburn shifted his weight, giving an involuntary start at the pain in his side. "Did you hear something, Will? A mouse squeaking, mayhaps? Pity that traitorous Catholic priest escaped in the confusion of the fighting, isn't it?" Will smiled and Clair looked from the player to the priest in quick succession. "Bastard probably stole one of the horses I left outside tied to a tree. He'd better take the bay. Christ alone knows where in Warwickshire he disappeared to, although"--Tyburn intoned almost as if saying Mass--"it would be very wise if he were to make for the channel ports as fast as his mount can bear him. Topcliffe and Lucy are still hunting, and as much as I enjoy watching a drawing-and-quartering, that priest wasn't a bad fellow, when he wasn't talking."

Danby smiled. *"Gloria Patri et filii et spiritui sancto. Sicut erat in principio et nunc et simper et in saecula saeculorum. Amen."*

"My point made for me. Papist bastard is never quiet. Longest night ride of my life." Tyburn looked at Clair who, for the first time evinced a ghost of a smile. "The boy and I will ride to Stratford, and lay low for a few days with his father. Clair, you go to the servant's wing, unlock the doors and spin them the terrifying true story of how Hawkins, Cuttle and our unpleasant friend there confronted and attempted to rob your father. You and your brother interrupted their ill-conceived thievery. Your father was murdered and your brother, stalwart fellow, bested them, but fell from his grievous wounds. Cuttle fled, so let's reward him with a surfeit of blame."

"What of Topcliffe and Master Lucy?" Clair ventured.

"I think we leash those dogs with a few choice letters--to Arden for one. And I have another I can send to. Absent a priest to rack or deBrages's involvement, I can't see them continuing this farce." Tyburn stood, paused to steady himself and bent forward. Shifting so he blocked Clair's view, he retrieved his sword from where it lay embedded in Albert's throat. He looked down at Clair's brother for a long moment before he turned away. Will handed him the remnants of his torn doublet and Tyburn used it to wipe the Spanish steel clean before re-sheathing it, and then. The player picked up the ornate prop dagger with a rueful smile. "If I don't return this, Cleve will gut me."

"Wait." Clair's voice was low.

Tyburn turned. She leaned in close. "I know you well enough, Christopher, to know you carry your guilt close and careful. This was not a situation of your making. My father died at the hands he shaped and set to purpose. My brother . . deserved his fate, it was the road he chose and a life he sought."

Tyburn shook his head. "I've killed too many, too often, and I've done more to set these events in motion than you realize."

"You've never killed with frivolity or absent need. If you had that stain on your character, I would have nothing to do with you." The intensity of her gaze almost hurt. "And I want to have to do with you. More than anything."

Tyburn's expression tightened. The player nodded. "Best you get those servants out, they probably heard the shot. Come to Stratford in three days and meet us at the glover's."

Chapter the Twenty-fifth

THE GREY-TINGED DAWN was reluctant, as the player and the boy threaded the pale horse past the stone fence bordering the crossroad. Will could see the dark bulk of his father's storage barn looming ahead, silhouetted against the lightening sky in the east. Birdsong heralded the dawn. A cock crowed in the far distance and the distant rumble of a cart through along a cobbled roadway presaged the town's awakening.

Tyburn ached. Although he had dressed his wounds at the deBrage manor house, they had continued to bleed and seep until they dried stickily against his torn shirt, tugging with every movement. He reined in, gesturing for the boy to dismount. Will swung his leg over the pommel and dropped to the ground. With a painful grimace Tyburn slid out of the saddle. He turned the horse towards the Clopton Road, tied the reins to the pommel, and slapped the animal hard on the rump to send it galloping away into the early morning darkness.

"Now Topcliffe can't hang us as priggers.[143] Come on, let's find your father."

They clambered over the stone wall and headed past the low barn towards the house, casting wary looks at the barn door which gaped open like a bare-knuckler's toothless mouth. The pair threaded their way through the extensive vegetable garden maintained by Will's mother. The remainder of the yard was dominated by the drying racks hung with leathers at various stages of preparation and John Shakespeare's puering vat, dug into the ground and covered with a wooden lid. The yard smelled of earth, greenery and urine, the ammoniate odor cutting through the lighter scent of garden herbs.

The crunch of a footfall behind them was the only warning.

Tyburn turned his head at the sound but felt a tremendous shock on his head and right shoulder that drove him face down into the damp grass. Light flared behind his eyes and his head was swimming and dizzy. The ground tilted and then steadied. He tried to lift himself up, forcing his body to respond until something drove into his kidney with agonizing force. He rolled over, retching and gasping in pain.

The grey sky was tinged with pink, ripples running from the east, feathering the clouds with colour and arching towards the apex of the sky. Dark against it, Tyburn recognized the wide stout bulk of Cuttle.

"Tell me again how I'm nothing but an antic?" The foot swung and the player made a vain attempt to roll away. He felt the sharp cutting pain of a rib cracking. As Kit tried to draw his rapier, Cuttle laughed and leaned down, plucking the weapon from Tyburn's nerveless fingers. He threw it aside and bent to pull the player upright, his short, iron fingers locking around the front of the player's torn shirt.

---

[143] Horse thieves

"Nothin' else to say, play-actor? No clever remark? Told you we weren't finished." Tyburn reached up with both hands and clamped down on Cuttle's grip, holding him tight, and rolled, throwing all his weight sideways.

Caught by surprise and off-balance Cuttle toppled and the two men tumbled into the drying racks. Sodden hides toppled as a wooden rack caught Cuttle in the back. The thin timber snapped under the impact. Tyburn drew back his fist and struck the man twice but Cuttle just blinked and responded with a knee into Tyburn's ribs. Red pain shot through the player and darkness loomed like a cloud.

The Southwark knifeman lifted the player up and heaved him across the open space between the racks and the puering vat. Tyburn tried to focus, a blur obscuring his vision. The shorter man spat, drew his knife and advanced. Cuttle stood over the supine player's body. Tyburn hooked his foot around Cuttle's right leg and kicked out with his left, slamming the heel of his boot into the man's right knee. The leg gave a sickening pop and Tyburn heard Cuttle's strangled yelp. The man threw himself forward onto the player, the knife point burying itself in the turf. Tyburn flung one arm across and locked Cuttle's right arm as he pulled it back and stabbed down a second time. The Southwark man leaned down with his weight, edging the blade down with inexorable force.

A wooden stave cracked down onto Cuttle's head, making him jerk his body to one side. Cuttle slammed hard into the lip of the puering vat, sending the thin cover sliding half off, sagging into the foul liquid within it. The player pushed his opponent backwards, keeping the knife hand extended and locked in his grip as both men sprawled beside the fetid container. Tyburn spun and threw his weight across, locking his legs over Cuttle's torso, keeping Cuttle's knife hand tight in his grip.

The wooden edge of the full puering vat was inches away and Tyburn grunted, using the strength of his legs, locked around Cuttle's upper chest and knife arm, to force the man's head over the low wooden rim of the vat. Cuttle's hair was in the dark, foamy brine now and the player continued to push relentlessly, all of his strength focused on the sole purpose of forcing Cuttle back, his head hanging over the edge of the cracking wooden rim. Cuttle's face slid under the surface.

Tyburn pressed down with all his strength, angling Cuttle's head downward into the vat. The muscles of his legs burned. Cuttle's free arm clawed at the player. His hand tore at the grass and dirt leaving long gouges in the thin turf. Cuttle's feet drummed on the grass. Tyburn held the knife hand tight in his grip, leaning over hard to force the man's head further under the surface. Tyburn could feel the cold foul mixture coating his legs and flowing into his boots.

Cuttle bucked and heaved in frenzied motion. The dank, putrid liquid was foaming above the man's face and Cuttle's free arm flailed more and more until the bubbling slowed and then stopped. The arm drooped and slumped and Tyburn felt the iron tightness of the man's muscles relax. The grip on the knife hilt released. He waited for another minute, the reek filling his nostrils and lungs like a dense cloud until, with a sudden expulsion of breath, he released Cuttle's arm.

Tyburn extricated his legs from Cuttle's now still form and drew them up. His hands were shaking. He looked around. Will stood, open-mouthed and shocked. Beside him, John Shakespeare stood, holding in one hand the long wooden stirring pole he had struck Cuttle with. Gasping for breath, Tyburn nodded his thanks. He reached over and rolled the now lifeless body into the puering vat. It sank into the shallow depths, bobbing like a half-submerged log just below the surface.

"We've a story to spin you, master glover," the player said, each breath punctuated with a stab of pain from his ribs.

The man looked at the puering vat and nodded. "So you have, master player, so you have."

342

The three riders trotted at a brisk pace along the road, moving like men with purpose in mind. They had ridden south along the Warwick Road and followed it as it coursed along the placid Avon riverside past the town, towards the reaching spire of the Holy Trinity Church.

At the churchyard the horsemen reined in, staying under the shadowed edge of the lime trees that lined the road. One of them, dressed in somber clothes topped by a long ascetic's face and a trim dark beard, dismounted, dropped his reins and strode up the stone church steps without a backwards look. The second man, his faced scarred and mottled by the ravages of smallpox, spat into the dirt in a gesture of resigned exasperation, handed over his reins to the third man and followed. The scarred man hastened to the doors and tugged them open, his superior's impatience quite sufficient impetus without any spoken order. The thin man passed into the interior

Pausing to remove his expensive felt hat he looked briefly at the narthex. Holy Trinity was not a large edifice by any sense of the imagination; it was, however, a substantial stone structure for a small market town like Stratford, a testament to the burgeoning wealth of the region and the growing trade in wool and hops. The small parish church rose about him, the stone supporting pillars running the length of the nave curving into delicate arches above which long glass windows interspersed with stone climbed higher to the stained wooden ceiling. The light slanted brilliantly across the interior of the church, leaving one half awash with sunshine and the other in shadow. As in many parish churches across England, the stained glass that once had graced the tall narrow windows had been shattered and replaced with clear panes, and the decorative stone carvings and frescos that had decorated the nave had been hammered off or hidden under a thick coat of lime-wash. Only a handful of stained glass windows remained intact, at the eastern and western ends of the nave.

The man regarded his surroundings with a critical and careful eye, reviewing the world around him like a factor peevishly checking his books. His eyes locked on a figure seated at the far end of the nave, close to the chancel. He nodded to his compatriot who strode down the aisle, one hand on the sword at his side, pausing at the transept to survey the entire expanse of the building. He waved and moved over to lean against the arching stone supports abutting the nave, watching the seated man and the handful of other occupants in the church.

Francis Walsingham walked down the aisle, his booted feet echoing off the stone and slid into the pew in front of Christopher Tyburn, who was leaning back contemplating the plain whitewashed expanse of the chancel. The wooden rood screen for the altar had been removed and burned when the building had been purged of its Catholic roots. The marks where the wood met stone were still visible where the chancel met the transept.

"Your report was notable in its brevity." Walsingham's voice was, as always, devoid of any warmth or inflection but the player thought he could detect the barest hint of irritation.

"I thought you appreciated brevity."

"I appreciate answers. Your letter raises more questions than it resolves. Why did you wait until now to write?"

"You tend to discourage the reporting of rumors and falsehoods."

"I give you leeway, master player, and you give me results. That is the nature of our arrangement. It is my role to discriminate actions with policy, not yours. You should have reported the presence of a Jesuit as soon as you became aware of his existence."

Tyburn made an airy gesture of acquiescence. "You have intelligencers that report rumor and supposition as fact, forge supporting documents for their tales and feed you deceit on a daily basis about their expenses, and you find fault with my report?"

"Sins of omission, Master Tyburn, are mortal ones in our business. Lying is merely venal. I have higher expectations of you. Now, what light can you shed on this murder of Sir William and his son?"

"Apparently several of his men decided to augment their pay with theft. Sir William and his son interfered, to their detriment."

Walsingham sniffed, the equivalent of a derisive snort in another man. His thin lips turned down in a slight frown. "That will do for the official records. And the reality?"

"Sir William and his son conspired to trap Edward Arden in an imaginary Jesuitical conspiracy against the queen. Albert deBrage murdered his father when it appeared evidence of the conspiracy--a set of correspondence between Arden and the Jesuit--had been destroyed."

Walsingham was silent for a moment. "If Arden and the Jesuit were truly in correspondence, the contact remains treasonous; it is still conspiracy against the Crown, and so hardly imaginary." The note of asperity in Walsingham's voice was evident. "Who killed Albert deBrage?" The question was met with silence. Walsingham sniffed a second time, his thin frown deepening in disapproval at his agent. "Well, he was of slight use to anyone, although I am certain Leicester will be displeased." The faint purr of satisfaction in Walsingham's voice gave lie to any expression of sympathy. "The Jesuit?"

"In the wind."

The passionless frown deepened an infinitesimal amount. "That is most unsatisfactory." Tyburn shrugged in response. "And the others?"

"Arden was likely complicit with the Jesuit, but the proof is ash."

Walsingham paused. Tyburn could almost hear the wheels turning in the man's head. "Edward Arden is problematic. His Catholicism taints the court and the Privy Council, but he still holds the queen's affection. I expect he will hang himself with time. What were they conspiring about, if not against the queen?"

"They were writing a letter for Her Majesty, humbly requesting a policy of toleration for Catholics and an end to recusancy." The player dropped a letter embossed with a red blot of sealing wax on the seat beside Walsingham.

Walsingham gazed down at the envelope with an expression of open distaste. He picked it up, noting it was addressed to the queen. He cracked the seal and scanned the contents.

"Articulate, persuasive and honest. Poor fools." He folded the letter and gestured at the scarred man, who quickly crossed the transept. "Burn it." The man nodded and moved over to the altar, lighting the letter with a taper from the alcove. The burning letter fell fluttering to the stone floor. The wax seal puddled and congealed on the stone, leaving a flat irregular blotch amidst the ash and charred scraps.

Tyburn stirred in his seat. Walsingham turned to look at him. "What would you have me do, master player? Support toleration? Pass along this letter composed by our enemies? The queen has already wasted ten years supporting and advocating tolerance and the consequence was treason by the northern earls and an attempt to usurp her throne. England is beset by enemies, both abroad and within. Half the nobility either openly or covertly supports Catholicism, recusancy is a growing plague, the Jesuits and the Catholic League send agents to our shores to foment rebellion, the court is rife with individuals filled with petty ambition and avarice seeking to leverage Mary for the throne . . . and do not make me speak of France. You know as well as I do the blood spilled there and in the Low Countries. I witnessed the atrocities of Paris firsthand." Walsingham's face had darkened in anger at the memory of the Huguenot massacre that had rocked Paris and drenched the city streets in blood and pain a mere three years before, when he had served as ambassador. His tone gave no evidence of the deep anger the memory had stirred. After a moment he continued.

"We are beset and Phillip of Spain has no end of gold and silver and anger and *tercios* upon which to draw to fuel his ambition. This letter might be reasonable, articulate and bound by God's own will, and still I will burn it without hesitation or regret. I am English and bound, as you are bound, to fight England's enemies, in whatever form they take. Be thankful, Master Tyburn, you had the grace and flexibility to be able to make your choice. I have none. My options for redemption are far more limited."

Tyburn's grey eyes locked with Walsingham's hard brown ones. The player nodded, accepting the implicit rebuke.

"Be that as it may, you did well to squash this foolishness. These greedy fools with their machinations do more damage to our ability to intercede and capture these agents of the papacy than they know, although I fear Topcliffe is not well disposed to your actions. I requested Leicester to order the release of Worcester's Men several days ago, along with compensation for their damages from both Master Topcliffe and our good sheriff Lucy. The writs against you are well quashed. Is there anything else of note?"

Tyburn dropped a pair of cheveril gloves on the bench. Walsingham glanced down. "The glover?"

"The boy was of great assistance in this endeavor."

"The boy's father is a Catholic, in league with the forces of the Antichrist, and given your willingness to intercede on his behalf, up to his neck in treason."

"He saved my life."

"You expect that to weigh in his favour?" Walsingham's sarcasm was evident. Tyburn held his gaze. Walsingham picked up the gloves. He examined the tight, intricate circular stitch pattern. "I suppose workmanship like this should be rewarded." He looked at the player with a basilisk gaze. "He may no longer hold the office of alderman. He is to drop all connection to Arden and Arden's priest, conveying no more messages or summons. He is to speak to no one regarding these events or circumstances. So long as he holds to those conditions he will be, shall I say, ignored."

Tyburn nodded. Walsingham must be more pleased than he sounded. The player didn't delude himself to think Walsingham wouldn't have pressed any opportunity to manipulate the situation for his own benefit but he was certain the spymaster would lose no sleep over the failure of Leicester's scheme. He knew his chief was engaged in a delicate and intricate balancing act between Leicester and Burghley as counselors to the queen.

"There is the small matter of my back pay." Walsingham's lips gave a slight twitch. Raising one hand, he gestured with his fingertips at the pock-faced guard. The man fished a small bag out of his doublet and tossed it to the player. Tyburn caught it handily, hearing and feeling the chink and weight of the coins within.

"And money for Alec's family."

Walsingham's face froze in a moment of effrontery and then, catching sight of the tight expression on Tyburn's face, he nodded. "It will be sent to his father in London." Tyburn nodded his thanks.

"And I won't ask for the return of the Spanish silver--which you failed to advise me of," Walsingham noted in a caustic tone as he rose. The player shook his head in bemusement. Not much escaped Walsingham's nets. Tyburn followed him out of the church, crossing from the shadowed area into the sunshine, his footsteps dogged by Walsingham's guard.

The bright sunlight in the churchyard was dazzling after the recesses of the church, but Tyburn could see three figures waiting under the trees near the entrance to the graveyard. The smallest of the three waved his arm as though Tyburn might fail to see them. Walsingham turned towards his mount without a backward glance at the play-actor. His guard gave Tyburn a quick, insouciant salute and followed the principal secretary back to the horses.

Tyburn walked across the churchyard, his booted feet kicking up a small plume of dust. "Everything is fine, Will. There are some conditions for your father." Tyburn looked at John Shakespeare who was standing to one side, shifting from foot to foot, trepidatious. "But nothing that cannot be dealt with.".

He turned from the pair to the woman who stood holding the reins of her horse. Clair smiled at him and the day seemed palpably brighter.

"It is nice to see you on your feet." When Clair had arrived in Stratford the previous day, the player had still been abed, his ribs wrapped tight in a cloth poultice.

Cuttle's body had been discreetly removed from the puering vat by several of John Shakespeare's acquaintances, loaded on a cart under cover of darkness and trundled away for a hidden burial in a sandpit. The player hadn't participated in that last act of subterfuge, merely watched from a chair on the edge of the garden, wincing every time he shifted his weight.

Tyburn took Clair's hand. She leaned in and gave him a long kiss. "And now?"

Tyburn grinned ruefully. "Now I'd best find Oldcastle and the boys, before he hires a replacement or has me picked up for debt."

"That's not what I was referring to and you well know it."

"Worcester's Men are bound for Coventry, Leicester, Nottingham and back down through Cambridge to London. At least another month on the hoof."

"And you need to go." It was not a question.

"And I need to go."

Clair leaned in and kissed him again. "But not at this particular moment."

Tyburn slid his arms around her waist and pulled her close. "No, not at this particular moment." She laughed and Will, who was watching them, shook his head in mock disgust.

Hollow hoofbeats sounded as several riders galloped up the tree-lined path from the road into the churchyard. Tyburn released Clair and turned to face the sound.

Framed by the two trees that gated the churchyard entrance, Richard Topcliffe reined in his horse. The look upon his round face as his small eyes lit on Clair and Tyburn could only be described as one of unholy relish.

"You! You play-acting bastard! You spavined dog . ." His gaze turned to Clair. "And that dried up deBrage cunt, both of them in one fell swoop. God be praised." He gestured at the two men accompanying him. "You two take the girl. I'll arrest the play-actor."

Topcliffe swung off his horse and strode across the open expanse of the dusty churchyard, drawing his sword. His face was bright red, his eyes fixed, bright and pointed and his mouth muttered a long stream of invective as he walked towards them. Clair stepped back in alarm but Tyburn smiled and waited.

"That is not advisable." The quiet voice cut across the open air of the churchyard. Topcliffe ignored the interruption.

"Master Topcliffe, look and listen when I speak to you." Topcliffe's red face turned in exasperated rage towards the source of the voice, his expletives coming to a stuttering halt as he recognized the dark-visaged man sitting on his horse.

"Walsingham." Topcliffe was taken aback at the presence of the Crown's principal secretary in a rural churchyard. "Sir, I . ."

"Ignore Master Tyburn and his acquaintances, including Worcester's Men. If I hear that you have disrupted their activities in any way, you shall answer for it. To me."

"Do you know what he has done? He stole that Jesuit away! He assaulted me! He's a yellow dog--a traitorous, conspiring Papist bastard!"

"I assure you, he is not a Papist," Walsingham replied dryly. Topcliffe's knuckles were white on the pommel of his sword. His two men watched with wary expressions.

"You may draw on him, if you wish. I will tell you now it will be the last piece of rash folly you experience in your life. He is not so much dog as he is wolf." Walsingham gave a barely perceptible, very thin-lipped upturn of one corner of his mouth. "In particular, he is my wolf. If you allow these troubles to persist, I may take him off his leash." Tyburn allowed his slight smile to widen into a grin and dropped his hand onto his rapier.

Topcliffe's face was twitching in rage but he dared not cross Walsingham. The principal secretary wielded a sharp influence at court and within the Privy Council that he applied with the precision of a needle. His face darkening towards purple, Topcliffe grated, "You may keep your dog, but that slut comes with us."

"Mistress Carey may go where she wishes. However, at this time, due to her service to the Crown, she is also under my protection."

Tyburn watched fascinated as Topcliffe's emotions chased their way across his face until the man shuddered, as he had at Charlecote, forcing himself back into a shambling semblance of civilized behavior.

"The lord treasurer will hear of this outrage, sir," he said to Walsingham as he remounted his horse.

"I look forward to his comments," said Walsingham. Topcliffe swung himself into the saddle, spurred his horse with savage anger and rode away without another word.

Walsingham looked amused as he watched Topcliffe depart. "Master Tyburn."

"Sir?"

"I expect you to rejoin your company shortly. Please give Master Oldcastle my best regards." Walsingham turned his graveyard face towards Clair. "My lady Carey, my sincerest condolences for the loss of your father. If Master Topcliffe troubles you again, please do not hesitate to call upon me." He nodded to his two bodyguards and the three rode out of the churchyard at a brisk pace.

Tyburn watched his chief disappear down the roadway. Will came and stood beside him,. watching Tyburn with a keen sidelong look until the player turned.

"Something on your mind, Will?"

"You're leaving?"

"I'm a player in Worcester's Men. We'll be finishing the tour and returning to London."

"My father says I have to go back to school." His voice was rueful.

Tyburn laughed. "When you finish your schooling, you come to London to join our ranks, not before." Tyburn fumbled in his doublet and pulled out the rough leather purse that had been found with Alec. He removed four silver Spanish coins and handed

351

them down to the boy. "For when you take the London road. You've earned them. These should keep you until you find a place on the boards."

Will nodded, unable to speak. His father called him and he started to turn away, but stopped and lunged over to give the player a hug. Tyburn winced from the pain in his ribs but smiled nonetheless. Will slid the coins deep into a pocket, then rejoined his father for the walk back to town. Tyburn watched the two as they passed through the gate road and turned out of sight.

Clair twined her arm around his waist, and the pair began to walk down the tree-lined church roadway back towards town, leading her horse behind them.

"Where can I find you?" the player asked Clair.

"I will be staying with my uncle--my mother's family--in Colchester for a time, at least until my father's estate is settled. They are nice people, very placid and God-fearing. I think they would find my having relations with a wayward stage actor very shocking, even for a widow."

"Is that your way of telling me not to come to Colchester?"

"No, that is my way of telling you I can come to London. I will come to London. Where can I find you?"

"Either the Bull at Bishopsgate or the Boar's Head without Aldgate. Leave a message or a letter at either and I should hear of it." Tyburn stopped. On the right in the distance the long cool stretch of the Avon curved with stately grace towards Clopton Bridge. The road swung left, arcing towards the town. Tyburn could see, where the bridge road entered the town proper near the Bear Tavern, a small group of men gathered around a laden horse cart. A small pennant fluttered bright silver, blue and red from a pole atop the cart. The player recognized the colors and the solid, wide bulk of Oldcastle berating the Muches as they loaded the cart. Worcester's Men.

The breeze brought the fresh scent of the river through the air, brushing aside the town's smell of smoke, cooking and unwashed humanity. Sunlight dappled across the rippling water and green meadowland. Christopher Tyburn turned and slid his arms around Clair. "Time for me to go."

"Yes." Clair made no move to release him. He bent his head and kissed her softly.

An insistent bellow in the distance pulled him away from her lips. "Tyburn, you spavined bastard whoreson! You poxed dog! Move your arse, you cove, we've a road to be on."

The player released her and started to turn away. She grabbed his neck with both hands and pulled him back, turning her head to one side. She shouted "By God's bones, you can wait, you cozening wretch of a man."

Worcester's Men rewarded her with a burst of laughter and a jeering cheer at Oldcastle. Tyburn laughed and kissed her again, a long and lingering kiss that had to last until London.

-fini-

Author's Note

S TUDENTS OF THE Elizabethan era will recognize that I have preempted the entry of the English Jesuits by several years as the first of what would become a steady stream of Jesuit priests did not arrive until 1580.

The first was the much-storied Edmund Campion, late of Oxford and once one of England's leading scholars. Campion was captured in 1581. Imprisoned in the Tower for four months, Campion was questioned, racked three times and forced to engage in four public disputations of his ideas at which, even his detractors admitted, he comported himself well.

In the end Campion and the many Jesuits that eventually followed him were doomed. Despite purportedly having been forbidden to *"deal in any respects with matters of state or policy of this realm,"* the reality was that no letter, testament, claim or order could alter the fact that promoting or preaching a return to the Catholic Church and giving credence to papal supremacy required recognition of an authority beyond that of the Crown and the queen. At the end of the day, the need to eliminate the Jesuits became a profoundly political question, tied directly to treason and sedition.

Campion was sentenced to *"be drawn through the open city of London upon hurdles to the place of execution, and there be hanged and let down alive, and your privy parts cut off, and your entrails taken out and burnt in your sight; then your head to be cut off and your bodies divided into four parts, to be disposed of at Her Majesty's pleasure. And God have mercy on your souls."* He died at Tyburn on December 1st, 1581.

For more reading on the subject, I highly recommend *God's Secret Agents* by Alice Hogge, a superlative account of the religious and political cat-and-mouse war between the Elizabethan Crown and the agents of the Holy See.

Again, those familiar with their Elizabethan history will readily recognize the historical provenance of various characters peppered throughout this tale, including the Shakespeares, Sir Thomas Lucy, Edward Arden, Leicester, Walsingham and many others. These are fictionalized interpretations, barely a shade of the real historical figures that once graced the era and who now live on only in historical records and the often dry imaginations of writers. In particular, I have throughly transduced the memory of Hugh Hall, who did serve as Edward Arden's priest (and purported gardener) and eventually was arrested alongside Arden in 1583 and suffered for that fact in the Tower.

As for the rest, Worcester's Men are, alas, fictional in all but their company's name--with the exception of Edward Alleyn, who became an Elizabethan actor of note but in another preemption of reality, did not join Worcester's Men until 1583.

Christopher Tyburn, his lady and the deBrages are all entirely fictional although the dubious role of play-actors dabbling in espionage and intelligence surfaces time and time again in historical studies of the era, most notably with the playwright Christopher Marlowe and his oft-examined death in a Deptford tavern, in company with several of Walsingham's known agents.

Not fictional was Richard Topcliffe, whose blood-soaked career as a priest-hunter made his name synonymous with torture, to the point "to be topcliffed" became a known Elizabethan reference. . His proclivity for rape is also well-documented. Topcliffe died in bed at the ripe age of 72.

As for Tyburn, his clandestine war with Spain and the Catholic League is only just beginning. . . .

Dean Hamilton
Toronto, Ontario, Canada

www.tyburntree.blogspot.com
Twitter: @Tyburn__Tree

Suggested Reading

Elizabeth's London: Everyday Life in Elizabethan London, Liza Picard. Weidenfeld & Nicolson, 2003

Elizabeth's Spymaster: Francis Walsingham and the Secret War that Saved England, Robert Hutchinson. Weidenfeld & Nicolson, 2006

God's Secret Agents: Queen Elizabeth's Forbidden Priests and the Hatching of the Gunpowder Plot, Alice Hogge. . HarperCollins Books, 2005

Her Majesty's Spymaster: Elizabeth I, Sir Francis Walsingham and the Birth of Modern Espionage, Stephen Budiansky. Viking Penguin, 2005

Rogues, Vagabonds & Sturdy Beggars, Arthur F. Kinney, Editor. University of Massachusetts Press, 1990

Shakespeare: The Biography, Peter Ackroyd. Chatto & Windus, 2005

Shakespeare's England: Life in Elizabethan & Jacobean Times, R.E. Pritchard, Editor. Sutton Publishing, 1999

Soul of the Age: A Biography of the Mind of William Shakespeare, Jonathan Bate. Random House, 2009

The Elizabethan Underworld, Gāmini Salgādo. Sutton Publishing, 2005

Treason in Tudor England: Politics & Paranoia, Lacey Baldwin Smith. Pimlico, 2006

Will in the World: How Shakespeare Became Shakespeare, Stephen Greenblatt. W.M Norton & Co. 2004

On The Web

British History Online
www.british-history.ac.uk/

Folger Shakespeare Library
www.folger.edu/index.cfm

Gunpowder Plot Society
www.gunpowder-plot.org/index.asp

Life in Elizabethan England: A Compodium of Common Knowledge, by
Maggie Secara. **www.elizabethan.org**

Luminarium: Anthology of English Literature
www.luminarium.org/

Modern History Sourcebook: William Harrison (1534-1593): Description Of
Elizabethan England, 1577 (from Holinshed's Chronicles)
www.fordham.edu/halsall/mod/1577harrison-england.asp

Records of Early English Drama
www.reed.utoronto.ca/index.html#r_and_r

Renaissance: The Elizabethan World
www.elizabethan.org/

Shakespeare Resource Centre
www.bardweb.net/globe.html

Enjoy this special sneak preview of

Thieves Castle

Coming in 2019

Chapter the First

THE MAN'S FEET slid in the muck as crossed the open space of the laneway, the darkness yawning moist and thick around him. He leaned against the corner post panting, his breath harsh in the silence of the street. An unsheathed dagger glinted in one hand. The man glanced around, eyes straining at the darkness.

Ivy Lane stank. The smell was a mix of urine, dung and the foul rancid stench of offal drifting down from the butcher's yards north of Newgate Street.

Then man pushed himself away from the corner and turned hastily down the lane. The night was heavy and the darkness near complete, lit only by a handful of window candles and the dim yellow light of a small lamp hung outside one dark doorway. Although the lane was cobbled, the stones were greasy with the accrual of filth and the endless tread of daytime commerce. The man paused, hearing the faint echo of feet behind him, the sound uncertain.

He cursed to himself and began to move down Ivy Lane with as much speed as the darkness and the uncertain footing allowed. He held the dagger at length in front of him, as though to hold the night at a distance. The sounds seemed closer.

He glanced around. The laneway was narrow, a typical London thoroughfare, overhung with jetties that exiled the sky into a narrow strip and made the already oppressive darkness of the night into a stygian gloom. A flare of torchlight sent a set of shadows racing away as someone passed the corner he had vacated. The light sent the man scurrying away, no longer mindful of the slippery footing. He caught a faint gleam of a bare blade in the glowing light of the torch.

"Find 'em lads, winnow him out." The faint voice sounded amused.

The man cursed again and ran down the street, one hand outstretched, bumping along the irregular walls of the laneway. Another flicker of light in the distance ahead of him, coming from Paternoster Row and the distant bulk of St. Pauls.

"Coads." The man muttered and pressed himself into the wall, shaking. The men were getting closer.

"Stay still." The voice was soft but firm. A dim yellow light emerged from the doorway to his right, carried by a young woman. Her hair was short and dark. She stepped out and hung the lantern on a sign bracket above the narrow doorway. She pointed at the darkened alcove to the left of the door, almost hidden by the thick cornerbeam of the house. "Go there."

The man wiped his face and nodded, sliding into the welcome darkness of the alcove like a lover's embrace. He listened as the sound of footsteps grew more distinct. He could see the red flicker of the torch against the wall as they drew near, the shadows dancing back and forth with drunken abandon. He shrank back, feeling the rough timber frame digging into his spine. He listened.

"Bit late for punk[144] trade, isn't it."

"Codso, you lot out looking for sheep?" the girl said in a tired voice. "what's this rag and tag?"

---

[144] Prostitution

"You seen a man? A blood?"

She laughed. "Likes of them in Ivy at this time of night? Not tonight. Any of your ruffler's in coin?"

"Piss off cunt, we're busy."

"Fuck you, you buggering cockless bastards, go find yourselves some rent-boy's arse." The torchlight flickered and began to move away. The man hidden in the alcove let out a long sustained breath of relief as the footsteps faded away. The girl continued to berate the party's retreating backs until they disappeared.

"You can come out."

The man emerged cautiously, his eyes flinching as he scanned the length of the street.

"That lot's gone." The girl said. She canted her head at the man and surveyed him up and down with a practiced eye. "What'd they want you for?"

"No idea love. They came at us when we left the tavern." The man shuddered at the recollection. He had stood mute and stunned as he watched his two friends beaten into the mud and only when the steel had gleamed red did his drink-befuddled reflexes send him careening away as fast as his legs could carry him. He felt his throat choking with bile.

"Here" The dark-haired girl handed him a wineskin. He tilted it back and gulped a mouthful of thin, acrid wine. As he wiped his mouth, he looked at the girl again in the lantern light. Her hair was short and dark, barely past her ears. She wore a long dress with the bodice bare and loose, the swell of her breasts clearly evident. The stays on the dress were untied, allowing the top to flare open, giving the man a tantalizing glimpse of a lean length of untrammeled flesh. The girl tilted her torso back and the tip of one nipple slid out from underneath the thin fabric.

"Why don't you stay with me for a time, until your hunters wear themselves out?" The man felt one hand brush along the front of his breeches, pressing against the hardening length of his member. His breath caught. His eyes closed as her grip tightened.

"That may be the wisest choice…" the man breathed. Her hand slid around his waist and she slowly turned him, her dark eyes locked on his, her mouth open like a wet promise. He slid his hand down between her thighs and the thin material left little to the imagination. Maybe it was due to the terror of being hunted through the nighttime paths of London but the girl's touch made his pulse hammer and his desire quicken. She smiled, a brazen smile of anticipation and lust.

It felt like a thump and a sharp tightness against his right side. He stopped in puzzlement. The girl continued to look at him and gave a slight half-smile as hot pain coursed through him.

"I.., what..?" The girl continued to smile. He felt her brace herself for an instant and then push her right hand against the handle of the long poniard that protruded from his side. He staggered, one hand grasping at the girl. He felt his numbing fingers trail over the hardening nipple of her breast but his lust was overtaken by overwhelming weakness that made the dark alley swim. A sick feeling of horror flooded through him and he reached for her. She laughed and easily deflected his hand, tugging on the handle of the dagger, steering him lurchingly away from her. "You…" his words were incomplete, lost in a red wave of searing pain that seemed to swallow his thoughts.

"Over here, come with me." She crooned in an encouraging voice, one guiding hand on his back and one on the dagger handle, as though driving some farm animal to market. He took a staggered step and then the girl grasped the dagger handle tightly and twisted it with harsh strength. The man felt a tugging sensation and his insides turned to liquid, as though he drunk a skinful of hot spiced wine in one swallow. He could feel the cold length of the steel perforating his flesh, ripping into his bowels and belly. His breath roared in his ears and his eyes filled with tears. The lantern wavered and blurred.

He was on the ground, mouth tasting of blood, fingers grasping at the thin layer of muck that coated the cobbles. The torchlight flared again and he stared upwards at the girl's intent face. She wore a pleased expression like she had made some fresh discovery.

"Want me to finish him?" One of his hunters stood beside the girl, holding the torch and looking down at him with a bemused expression.

"No, I want to watch him go. You would spoil my fun Bent." She smiled. Bent's eyes flickered at the girl with a measured look and then back at the dying man stretched across the muddy stones of Ivy Lane.

Bent nodded in careful acquiescence. "Can't have that." Bent reached down and ripped the blade free and the man felt a calescent, diffuse sensation spreading through his body, as though he had pissed himself. His blood was dark as night in the glow of the torch. He watched it puddle across the greasy cobbles. "Leave this on him when he's done." He handed her a small object. She nodded absently and lowered herself over the supine man's groin, settling herself upon him, eyes fixed on his face, knees on the wet cobbles, unmindful of either dung or bloody rivulets, her expression almost rapt in the flickering torchlight, watching his eyes as the man cried in pain and fear and bled to death in the dank confines of Ivy Lane.

www.ingramcontent.com/pod-product-compliance
Lightning Source LLC
Chambersburg PA
CBHW021215260626
47172CB00002B/432